Sunday by Sunday III

A Work of Fiction

Grounded in the Revised Common Lectionary, Year B

Cristy Fossum

Create in Me Enterprises

Published by
Create in Me Enterprises, LLC
1215 Beaufort St.
Columbia, South Carolina 29201-1401

Cover Art and Design by David Hedges, Studio D

Printed in the United States of America
Library of Congress CIP data applied for.

ISBN: 978-0-9820207-7-7

Praise for CRISTY FOSSUM and *Sunday by Sunday III*

"For anyone who has ever sat with a child in church, or been a child in church; for anyone who has wondered how to bring religion down from the stained glass and up off the pages of scripture; for anyone who has walked in the valley of shadows, and anyone who has seen stars shining in the darkness; for anyone who wants their faith to find a foothold in the everyday, the ordinary – this book is for you.

"Fossum's writing is sharp, sassy, sensitive and prophetic, and it proves that God really is in the details and really does move in mysterious ways – and has a great sense of humor. Fossum's stories bring us to our knees and back up again with new energy to let our own little light shine." ~Ina Hughs, *Knoxville News Sentinel*, Author, *A Prayer for Children*

"Fossum has invented a new genre: part journal, part fictional narrative, part spiritual discipline, part theological and biblical interpretation. I am really impressed…" ~Carl F. W. Ficken, Ph. D., American Literature, Emeritus Faculty, Lutheran Theological Southern Seminary

About the *Sunday by Sunday* series

In this 3-book series, the fictional journals of Rose Harris lead readers through three years of ordinary living in a most extraordinary way. With disarming humor and a faith strong enough to doubt, Rose engages fully with four generations of family, for better and for worse. She stands by the colorful characters at St. Timothy, her community of faith, through all circumstances—the comical, the uplifting, the regrettable. Rose is an equal opportunity friend, opening her heart to people regardless of creed, culture, sexual orientation, or age. She befriends teens in trouble, spouses left alone by divorce or death, resident aliens, non-believers, and prisoners. In *Sunday by Sunday III*, this young at heart octogenarian, surprised by romance, decides whether or not to marry again, seven years after the death of her beloved husband Charlie. To spend a year with Rose is to laugh and cry and share human experience understood to be lived in, with, and for a gracious God.

FOREWORD

Yes, God's Word does have something to do with our everyday lives. You will be reminded of this regularly as you accompany the congregation of St. Timothy on their journey toward understanding what it means to be a community of Christian disciples. You may find yourself asking with the members of St. Timothy, "How do we live with that disconnect between how we want God to be and how God really is?" In these pages, you are sure to find a community whose journey is one of "discipleship in fits and starts." Faith is surprisingly evident even in the characters' doubts as they are challenged with the trials of suffering that come their way as a result of death, addiction and difficult pasts that never cease to rise to the surface.

We are introduced to the congregation by one Rose Harris, a winsome octogenarian whose musings are sometimes pious, other times sassy, but always authentic. Rose claims that "despite our best efforts, examples of imperfection in communal life abound" and yet admits the wonder and joy of a congregation that "on any given Lord's Day includes quite a variety of saints/sinners and a potpourri of reasons for being there." Just when you think Rose is the quintessentially sanctimonious church lady, she challenges traditional theological claims and opens herself to the changing world around her. The younger set may say that Rose is "hip." Combine that with her empathy, insightfulness, candor and independence, and you've got one intriguing protagonist.

I am especially grateful for two of Rose's tendencies. She has a knack for pointing out the sublime that is embedded in the mundane experiences of life (and unabashedly credits the Holy Spirit for providing such recognition). Second, Rose is exemplary of one who "prays without ceasing." Out of moments of action and reflection comes a sudden need to speak to the divine. And so she does. Interspersed in her weekly musings are tender and direct prayers to a God who, she trusts, is listening. Rose appropriates other elements of the liturgy (e.g., engagement with scripture, hymns, confession) into the liturgy of her own life. We can learn from Rose.

Of course, behind Rose Harris is the ecclesially savvy author, Cristy Fossum. Fossum is a lay person in the church who impressively does her biblical exegetical work and then does the homiletical work of translating the text's trajectory of meaning for the immediate context. The result is a narrative that insists that God and the Shippensforgians you are about to meet are working together. With the development of sensitive relationships, regular cameos of wit, and a picture perfect representation of how spiritual convictions are never picture perfect, Fossum adeptly presents the possibilities when scripture, individual and family life situations, congregational life and world events converge.

This final novel in the series of three that arises from the appointed texts for Sunday morning worship is an invaluable conversation partner for congregations that follow the Revised Common Lectionary. Here, life's salient theological questions are contextualized in a way that invites any reader to enter the conversation. Because the story is especially attuned to the rhythms of the every Sunday preacher who has the challenge (and, of course, opportunity) to help church members understand the connection between their lives and God's Word, this will be a helpful addition to the preacher's library.

Delve into the lives of these characters and their joys and challenges as Christian disciples. Doing so is sure to cause you to move beyond their lives to your own as you explore the ways God's Word transforms *your* thoughts, *your* moments of living, *your* journeys of discipleship. You will be blessed as you join Rose in "finding the divine most readily in the details of life."

SHAUNA K. HANNAN
Assistant Professor of Homiletics
Lutheran Theological Southern Seminary
Columbia, South Carolina

For my daughters, Elizabeth and Georgia,
with joy and gratitude for sharing faith along the way so far,
and now, for watching you and helping you nurture
your own children in Christian community

"We are a worshipping people who gather weekly for comfort, sustenance, and good news in houses built of stone and wood. We are people of font and table. We sing and are sent in a rhythm that has become normative and healing for millions. …Paying attention to its old truths, the liturgy reveals the myriad epiphanies occurring in God's created order, just outside our back doors."

~from *Marry a Pregnant Virgin* by The Rev. Frank G. Honeycutt

Sunday by Sunday III

First Sunday in Advent

Isaiah 64:1-9
Psalm 80:1-7, 17-19
1 Corinthians 1:3-9
Mark 13:24-37

Julia Crawford's aunt dropped dead in church this morning, during the sermon! I didn't see it happen; I was way over on the opposite side, intent on our brand new pastor's earnest proclamation of the Word: "Beware, keep alert; for you do not know when the time will come," was the appointed lesson, for heaven's sake.

The Coopers were sitting right behind them, and Marian said that the aunt sat up very straight for a second, almost like she was going to stand up, and then slumped over in Julia's lap. Julia "flung her away," Marian said, and she flopped back the other way onto the pew. Then things began to happen.

Everyone's attention was jerked to the whispered hubbub that was forming. People whipped out phones and called 911. Pam Turner, nurse, hurried to the scene. My neck hairs prickled with tension. This was real. John reached over and squeezed my hand.

"Oh, dear. What's happening?" Pastor Charlene Bryant interrupted herself, moving down from the pulpit toward Julia, followed by Pastor Morris Bryant, co-pastor and spouse. They huddled and murmured with those nearby as the rest of us stared. Pr. Charlene said a prayer invoking God's presence and care. Soon, we heard distant sirens.

Sherry, Danny Bennett's new wife, began to cry softly. He put his arm around her and leaned into her to comfort her in his earnest Down's Syndrome way. "Sh-sh-sh, Sh-sh-Sherry, it's okay. G-G-God's right here, remember? We're in ch-ch-urch, it's G-G-God's house, remember?" But she cried harder, and Danny's mother ushered them out.

Next, Marian said, Pam told Julia there was no pulse and offered to start CPR. "No, no, no, Pam. Read her necklace," Julia said, and Pam fished out a medical alert medal and read it and said, "Okay, we'll just wait," and rearranged the aunt on the pew.

Madge Humphries, always determined to be devout, tapped me on the shoulder and whispered, "Shouldn't we say the 23rd Psalm or something, Rose?" I shook her off with my head.

"I can't take this; let's go," I heard Helen Brewster say to Jack, and they stood up and started sliding through the pew toward the door, but then Jack stopped and said, "I think we should stay." Helen made a face and nodded, and they sat back down to keep vigil with the rest of us.

By this time the sirens arrived and abruptly went dead with one last whoop. In a minute the door on that side opened, and two EMTs in dark blue jump suits—a huge man and a tiny woman—appeared with George Hapless, who had gone out to meet them. They rolled their gurney and equipment to Julia's pew, and people jostled around to let them in. Pam spoke quietly to them as they looked at the aunt—she was 97, Marian said—and got some equipment out. The woman EMT worked with the aunt, and the large guy perched on the back of the pew with a clipboard and asked in a voice that seemed too loud for the situation, "Is there next of kin here?"

"Right here," Julia said, standing up and handing him some papers. "We're all ready, everything's in order." Julia's business-like manner seemed a little harsh, even given that the two didn't get along very well, as seen in little Sunday morning skirmishes. Like that time the aunt said, loudly enough for all to hear, "I refuse to wet myself. The only reason I'm wearing a diaper is because you made me. Now take me to the bathroom this instant, young lady."

"Okay, hang on to these," the EMT said, giving the papers back to Julia and writing something down. More time passed, and he asked his partner, "Got anything?" Apparently she responded in the negative.

He turned to Julia. "Sorry, m'am. She's gone."

Pr. Morris moved in and spoke to Julia. She nodded, and into our shocked silence, he spoke the words of the Commendation for the Dying over the aunt. "From all sin, from all evil, from all suffering, good Lord, deliver...what's her name?" he whispered to Julia, then said, "deliver Dorothy..." and completed the brief ritual.

We watched as the EMTs picked Dorothy up, the big guy holding under her arms, the woman under her knees, and laid her on the gurney. They covered her with a sheet, strapped her in three places, and rolled the gurney out the door. Julia followed.

Oh, how tight my chest muscles were, I suddenly realized! There was a rustling in the pews and we let out a small collective "whew." All eyes were on our new pastors. They looked at each other in astonishment and walked back to the front, quietly conferring, and then Pr. Charlene turned to us and said, "In light of this unexpected turn of events, we'll simply end the service with communion. Brothers and sisters, this has been a startling illustration of that which is unexpected breaking into daily life. As we deal with what has happened, and mourn Dorothy's death, I invite us all to consider what the

2

advent of God into our lives means. In the midst of hustling and bustling, let us also find time for quiet reflection on that question."

Then we celebrated Eucharist in its most essential form, receiving the body and blood from these spiritual leaders for the first time. The benediction was pronounced and we went on our way, speaking in reverent tones outside the building for a few minutes.

And now, after staring at death—and after life going on as planned—I'm trying to take Pr. Charlene's suggestion and reflect upon what turned out to be a busy day, filled with people. I'm not complaining. I had a very special time with Lloyd and Theodore and the pastors at Advent Lessons and Carols this afternoon at the cathedral in the city. I have to admit a little heart tug at missing the Sauers, since we usually went to this service together. After all, Marcus was my pastor and a close spiritual brother for 13+ years, and Carolyn a dear friend, too. But best to stay in the present. Lloyd drove his old Cadillac into the city, with plenty of room for Theodore upfront and the Bryants and me in the back seat.

"So, pastors, welcome to St. Timothy," he quipped as he started the engine, and we all had to laugh, despite the soberness of the morning. "I know I shouldn't say this, but you really knocked 'em dead."

"You certainly shouldn't have, Lloyd," Theodore admonished amidst our groans.

"Especially because the rest of us were thinking it—and it's too corny," Pr. Charlene said with a grin.

"I hope this was not a typical Sunday," Pr. Morris said, and we debriefed the unlikely situation quite thoroughly until he changed the subject. "Now, Lloyd, how long have you been organist at St. Timothy?"

"Since shortly after David invented the harp," he deadpanned. "Actually, about 17 years."

"And Theodore, you've come more recently, right?"

"Right. I arrived in this quaint little burg last February, to be exact."

"Straight from a musical career on the stage," I noted.

"Wow, we have quite the dynamic musical duo," Pr. Charlene commented.

"And," Theodore continued, "I feel it is my bounden Christian duty to forewarn you that I am nephew to the venerable Louella Rutledge. I wouldn't want you to be in the awkward position of utilizing me as an outlet for your frustrations over the dear old girl and then discover our kinship."

"Really? We already admire Louella for her social activism. I don't find her frustrating at all, do you Morris?" He shook his head and Theodore and Lloyd said in unison, "Just wait," and the three of us laughed. People like

Louella, with a strong heart for justice and a fearlessness in the face of powers and principalities, often do not have a warm, cuddly component; she certainly doesn't.

The Bryants wanted to learn more about me, so I gave them the basics: retired English teacher; widow of Charlie Harris for six years now; two children, Virginia (married to Barry) and Stephen (divorced); one grandchild, Stephanie Rose (Virginia's), professor of women's studies and mother of my great-grandchild, Mack.

"Inveterate churchwoman, highly versed in liturgy, theology, and Bible," Lloyd added.

"And patroness of lost causes such as the Chicago Cubs," Theodore teased.

I didn't say anything about John; they'll figure that out, since we sit together on Sunday mornings. Or maybe not, since I can't figure it out myself. Anyway, what a delightful afternoon with those folks.

And Cousin Josephine is still visiting from Mississippi after coming for Stephanie Rose's wedding. Unwedding, I should say, since the marriage didn't go through. Oh, that granddaughter of mine! I've cherished her independence since her first toddler "I-do-it-myself!" days. But then there's the variation on that theme—bull-headed, opinionated, outspoken, a tad self-righteous at times. Despite all advice to the contrary, she was determined to marry Ethan, Mack's daddy, and then called it off at the altar. Never a dull moment with Stephanie. Anyway, Cousin Josephine is still here.

And then against my better judgment, I let John worm his way into Sunday supper. "I've cooked up a big batch of Sloppy Joe and need some help eating it," he had cajoled after the service, and before I could decline, Josephine said how she loves Sloppy Joe, and so he brought it over. And to be perfectly honest, I realized I'd missed him over the last ten days since our falling out at the wedding. And I don't apologize for that. Finding out that he has a son from an illicit affair decades ago is not a small matter for me.

I'm still thinking about Thanksgiving, too, just three days ago. Virginia usually hosts, but she deserved to rest after her mother-of-the-bride duties, so I had the small crowd at my house. I put Stephen at the head of the table opposite me. Virginia and Barry were on one side with Mack in the high chair between them. On the other side were Cousin Josephine and my neighbors, Jim and Anita Ferguson. They brought some "tofurkey," a soy meat surprisingly tasty and turkey-like. Jim and Anita are vegetarian, off-the-grid environmentalists, lovely neighbors, avowed atheists, especially Jim. We have some interesting back and forths. They're expecting a baby in

April. Mixed race, the little one will be, with Jim white and Anita black (more like burnt auburn, actually).

Dinner conversation was lively. Anita opened up the wedding fiasco. "Virginia, I don't mean to be rude, but I'm so curious: what was it like having your daughter call off the wedding right in the middle of everything?"

Caught with her mouth full, Virginia gazed into space and chewed, a picture of self-composed sophistication, as usual. I must say, even if she is my own daughter, she is aging in a most beautiful way. We waited quietly for her response, which began with a small smile and shake of her honey blonde, casually styled hair.

"Steph drives us crazy marching to her own beat, but I was proud of her this time; she did the right thing. And then..." she took Barry's hand, and he picked up the narrative.

"And then this wise woman," he said, gesturing toward Josephine, "suggested that Virginia and I step forward and renew our marriage vows, so all was not lost."

"Barry and Virginia were separated because of an affair he had years ago," Josephine explained to Jim and Anita, her words slurred by antidepressants and southern drawl. "But we could all see the love between 'em, so I reckoned that would be the right thing for 'em to do."

"Okay, right," Barry chimed in, moving the conversation quickly on as Jim and Anita exchanged surprised glances. Virginia, Stephen and I rolled our eyes at each other, used to my cousin's ways. They didn't nickname her Cousin Weirdifine for nothing.

"And then we had a great party," Barry went on, "And now, Steph and Ethan are lying in the sun in Aruba, and we have this little rug rat," he concluded, going noggin to noggin with Mack, up to his elbows in mashed potatoes and squealing happily at his grandpa.

"What? They went on their honeymoon?" Jim exclaimed.

"Remarkable, isn't it?" I agreed. "A couple has a baby, throws a wedding a year later, doesn't get married after all, and then goes on their honeymoon. But, as Stephanie said to me when she kissed me goodbye, 'I know you probably think this is a little crazy, Grandma, but we've already paid and can't change the arrangements, and we're still friends, so...'" Perfectly practical, it's true, but such a 21st century contrast to my wedding day in 1945. Few of us even went on honeymoons. And thinking about that makes me miss Charlie as much as ever.

Which takes me back to John. I sure don't know about us. Marriage at our age? Seems outlandish, and yet, why in the world not, if that will make our lives better? (Besides, as The Bard says, "Love is merely a madness" anyway.) The pros and cons are quite obvious. John's obsession with the whole world of technology and my indifference to it can be a source of tension. (Although, I liked the computer classes he got us into at the library last year. And I have to admit that I'm very glad he set up all my bills for automatic withdrawal.) We argue way more than Charlie and I ever did—and yet, he makes me laugh a lot. And I'm trying not to let his endless use of clichés irritate me so much. Then there's me being so tall and him being so short, but that's how it was with Charlie and me, too, and we managed fine for nearly 50 years.

What bothers me the most right now is what seems to be shaping up as John's promiscuous background. After nearly a year of fairly intense romance, I've just learned that he has a son from an affair with a married woman decades ago. To be fair, he didn't know about it either, until recently, but even so... He's mentioned other affairs, too. For a never-married, conscientious objector, career international aid worker for the Mennonite church, he really got around to the women.

So, I just don't know about John and me. Sometimes he seems like a stranger, almost; and yet, not having him in my life would leave a lonely void. Sigh. We had a moment of closeness during worship this morning remembering Florence Lawrence, my dearest friend, his dearest sister. She died on the first Sunday of Advent a year ago—wow, like Julia's aunt Dorothy. If she could, Florence would say with sarcastic sparkle, "At least I had the decency not to die during worship." *God, you know how I miss that woman!*

Anyway, her brother left a few minutes ago after a fabulous game of Scrabble (I laid 'xebec' on a triple word!), and Josephine "went to bed with the chickens," as John put it. This is a perfect quiet time for me. If I could only find my Advent wreath, I'd light the first candle and gaze into the flame for insight about John. Other matters would float in, too. I'd pray for my beloveds, especially for Miguel Lopez in a jail cell downtown accused of murder, and for Mercedes Scheumann who is fast losing her brain, and for St. Timothy and our pastors, and for our bishops and our conflict-torn Church, and for world peace that seems utterly impossible—and for Aunt Dorothy and Julia, of course, and Florence, too. I'd vow to slow down and find time to reflect and simply to be. I'd vow to look for divine activity in the unexpected. I'd vow to try and be the clay and let God be the potter; be the sheep, God the shepherd; be the plant, God the gardener.

But where is that confounded wreath? I always keep it on the top shelf in the hall closet, and it's simply not there. Not being able to find it is throwing me into a woe-is-me mood. Life suddenly seems disordered and unmanageable; I feel highly inept and too old to remember anything. I'm stressing out Cute Baby, too; she's clawing at my trousers and meowing. So, get over it, Rose! Grab a candle, light it, and move on, you silly old thing.

<u>Second Sunday of Advent</u>

Isaiah 40:1-11
Psalm 85:1-2, 8-13
2 Peter 3:8-15a
Mark 1:1-8

"Tell me about church this morning, Rose; tell me everything. I miss being there so much," Mindy said during the long, cold walk we took this afternoon. John and I had gone down to the county jail to visit Miguel. The faithful Mindy Lucas was standing by her man, as usual.

"Miguel, you're always in our thoughts and prayers," I greeted him with a hug. I should probably have said <u>my</u> thoughts and prayers because many at St. Timothy have no idea what to think about him. They've come to know and love Mindy but were just getting acquainted with Miguel when the murder happened and he got arrested. He's thoroughly Roman Catholic in the Mexican tradition and worshiped mostly at Our Lady but would come with Mindy whenever he had Sunday mornings off from the restaurant. Anyway, when John and Miguel got engrossed in a theological discussion this afternoon—in Spanish—Mindy excused the two of us to get some fresh air.

"The relaxed visiting hours and the atmosphere at the jail amaze me," I commented as we left the building.

"I know; seems way more 'Mayberry' than 'Law and Order,' doesn't it? But c'mon, Rose; tell me about the service this morning and what's happening and stuff. Oh, like how are the new pastors doing? You must have filled them in on Miguel. Pastor Morris has already come to see him."

"They remembered you from the call committee, of course, and asked about you, knowing we were friends, so, yes, I told them about Miguel. Let's see—well, the first thing I should say is how hard I'm trying not to compare the Bryants to Pr. Sauer."

"I'm sure. He was not only your pastor but a BFF. Carolyn, too, huh?"

"Oh, yes. Now this is only their second Sunday, but I think they're doing fine. Of course, last week, an elderly lady died during worship; had you heard that?"

"Yeah, he mentioned that. What a way to start!"

"Really. I believe they're both solid preachers. Morris really spoke to my heart in his sermon today. 'Comfort, comfort ye my people' is a command,' he started out; I'd never thought of it quite that way. And it rang true to me when he said that we come together in the Body of Christ to remind each other that, despite appearances, God is present and powerful. He has a strong delivery style. Here was his basic closing," and I imitated his cadence and inflection: "These valleys that we now walk <u>shall</u> be lifted up; every mountain that seems impossible to climb <u>shall</u> be made low. Buck up, people; you have been baptized with the Holy Spirit, sin is forgiven, Christ is coming soon!"

Mindy was underwhelmed. "Yeah. I believe that, somehow, but I wish it weren't so pie in the sky. It's kind of like we know we have the winning lottery ticket but we can't find a ride to the Speedway to cash it in."

She has a fresh way of putting old truths. How many times I've thanked God to have this young woman in my life! She can come across as a little zany. I suppose her appearance has something to do with that perception. Her hair's pretty poofy and can vary in color from reddish orange to orangeish burgundy. She's a medium tall string bean of a figure. Her thick-lensed glasses and the way she squints through them when concentrating add to the Mindy look. But she's no dummy. My St. Lord (Stephanie's exclamatory phrase at age 5), she's the first one in her family even to graduate from high school, and now, she is certified as a radiology technologist.

"Did anything funny happen in church?" she asked, a usual question for her. I chuckled right away.

"Oh, Mercedes Scheumann is usually good for a laugh these days, and this morning…"

"Rose, that's mean! She has dementia."

"Yes, she does, and that's hard; we're all concerned and quite involved— but we still have to laugh sometimes. Here's what happened: She was heading to the altar to take communion for the third time when 6-year-old Maddie Bowers took her hand and led her back to a pew saying, 'You've had enough, old woman.'"

Mindy smiled. "Who's Maddie Bowers? She sounds like a character."

"She's that, alright. She's captured our hearts. Her teenaged brother Bryan started bringing her shortly after their mother died of cancer back in the fall. Why, that little girl walked in like she owned the place! I can picture Maddie on Broadway as Little Orphan Annie; she seems like she's lived a hard-knock life and has no fear. And everybody knows she's six because a couple weeks ago she announced in church that it was her birthday and we should sing 'Happy Birthday'—which we joyfully did."

"That's hilarious. I want to know Maddie. I'm planning to start back next Sunday. I've hated to miss worship, but after working all week and every other Saturday, I've spent every minute I could with Miguel."

By this time, we'd walked all the way out to Mom's Kitchen and stopped in for a yummy, steaming hot chocolate. As we settled into a booth and wiggled out of our coats, I asked how Miguel's case was coming along.

"It's already been five weeks and not much has happened," she frowned. "You know—paperwork and red tape and a week lost because a judge had an ingrown toenail or something. Thanks to Uncle Marvin, he's got the best defense lawyer around, at least."

"My, that's very kind of Uncle Marvin [an intriguing older man whom I've met a few times]. What about the Officer Schmidt angle?"

"Well, you know Hector, one of the guys from the house, saw Erik Schmidt with Esteban [the murder victim] around 11 o'clock that night. Erik has an alibi, but I know he had something to do with it. What a poor excuse for an officer of the law. He's why people call policemen pigs. And he's had it in for Miguel ever since he first came to town and stood up to Erik's bigotry. Ugh, I can't believe I went out with that loser once in high school."

"At least he's been relieved of duty."

"Right, but that makes him even more determined to get Miguel. The prosecutor acts like she's still going to pursue the death penalty, but Miguel's lawyer doesn't think that'll happen, what with the self-defense part and people lining up to testify to Miguel's good character. But if a jury thinks of him as just one more 'dirty spic,' it could be bad.

"And here's what's really crazy, Rose: I still don't know for sure what happened that night. I don't even know if Miguel actually killed Esteban. He's all mysterious about it and won't give a straight answer." Her magnified eyes held pain. She took her glasses off and rubbed her eyes, then changed the subject.

"What's this about you going to Russia?"

"Yes, I am! Stephen's big surprise. The whole thing is wild, but Stephen's enthusiasm is contagious. I worry about managing, at my age, but I'm sure I'll be fine with him by my side. We fly from Chicago to Hamburg to St. Petersburg on Jan. 4th. We'll get in on their holiday season because the Russian Orthodox Church celebrates Christmas later than we do, so that will be interesting." I asked about her work.

"I'm still loving it. All the aspects come so naturally to me. In my wildest imagination—"she hesitated and leaned in, pledging me to secrecy—"I think about going to medical school. It's probably impossible, but I guess a girl can dream. And, how are you and John doing these days? I know you didn't have a very good time at the wedding."

"That's true. John is, essentially, a fine person, but..."

"You're still bent out of shape over his illegitimate son in India, aren't you? He found out about that on Facebook, right?"

"I hate to admit it, but you're right. Mindy, you know how strong my standards about sexual behavior are. A child out of wedlock, adultery—yes, that troubles me. Do you think I'm overreacting?"

"Yeah, probably. I mean, that was 30 years ago, right? And how old is John?"

"Eighty-six."

She laughed. "I'd say you might as well let that go. Live in the present, Rose, and if he's okay now..." She looked up from stirring her cocoa. "Is he okay now?"

My turn to laugh. "I suppose he's okay. He's very affectionate, despite his age," I said, probably blushing, "but, another worry I have is that even though there's always going to be some distance between any two people, I'm uncomfortable with our distance sometimes. We miscommunicate a lot; I hate that."

"You look like you have fun together."

"We do, we have a lot of fun. And we share our faith at a deep level; obviously, that's important to me. But we also argue more than I wish we did."

"Over what?"

"Different things. We got in a fight the other day over him texting and driving. I got all judgmental and lectured him about people getting killed because somebody just had to LOL behind the wheel. He was petulant and defensive."

"And probably won't stop doing it, but I'm with you on that one. I think you were right. And good arguments don't hurt anything."

"Well, I don't know about John. The way will become clear, I expect. To tell you the truth, I'm looking forward to being apart for ten days while Stephen and I are gone."

"Yeah, that's probably good. By the way, I caught up with your crazy granddaughter the other night. Have you talked with her since they got back from their—well, we can't say honeymoon, can we? Sunnymoon maybe, or how about unnymoon? Anyway, she said it was miserable. They missed Mack, and she and Ethan were both sick with food poisoning or something. So much for that fiasco," Mindy sighed. "I'm so glad Stephanie didn't go through with it. A tad awkward, yes, but I'm not sure if I could have held my tongue if Pastor Gail had told people to speak now or forever hold their peace. I mean, there I was, Steph's maid of honor, standing up right next to her in front of God and everybody and thinking, 'This ain't never gonna' work.'"

I laughed, completely sympathetic. "I'm so glad you and Stephanie are friends."

"Me, too, and we are because of you. I'm so glad <u>we're</u> friends, Rose Harris. Who knew that an old church lady would ever be one of my best friends? You've really helped me go deep, Rose."

That about choked me up. "The feeling is mutual. You are an inspiration to me in so many ways, Mindy Lucas."

We held a tender look briefly, and then slid out and put on our wraps and walked back to the jail, mostly lost in our own thoughts. When my feet began to hurt and I started huffing and puffing a bit, I was wondering how much longer I'll be able to walk this far. We bid Miguel and Mindy goodbye, and John dropped me off with a sweet, lingering kiss. Cousin Josephine had a hot bowl of soup ready, and after that we sat at the piano and sang favorite hymns. Merciful heavens, life is good.

Throughout this writing, I've paused to gaze into the flickering flames of two Advent candles (that I'm using until I find that doggone wreath). I wonder who attended Dorothy's graveside service in Ohio on Wednesday. At least Julia, I hope. I smiled at the delightful evening Sarah Floyd and I had last night at the high school Christmas program. Now, an image from this morning is coming clear: Jacob Turner, Pam's son, lighting the first two candles of the Advent wreath in the wintry grayness of the chancel. His face seemed almost on fire. For that kid to light a candle in the darkness really means something. *Thank you, gracious God, that he's back with us.* Ah, but that's a story for another day.

Third Sunday of Advent

Isaiah 61:1-4, 8-11
Psalm 126 or Luke 1:46b-55
1 Thessalonians 5:16-24
John 1:6-8, 19-28

I luxuriated in the extra silence this morning during worship. We might have squirmed in our seats if the pastors hadn't told us there would be these moments. So as Lloyd's lovely prelude faded away, I closed my eyes, breathed a deep sigh, and relaxed into the pew. John was on my right and Josephine on my left and Mindy next to her, and the whole congregation seemed ready to be together in the stillness and calm and know that God is God.

"Please stand and face the cross for the confession of sins," Pr. Charlene broke in, standing at the entrance to the nave. This innovation, too, had been announced and explained. A little uncertain, we stood and turned toward the back in varying degrees. After we confessed and heard the words of forgiveness, Lloyd broke forth with the bright melody of "Rejoice, Rejoice, Believers, and Let your Lights Appear." The gleaming, gold cross on its pole was hoisted high into the air and moved slowly down the aisle towards the altar. I kept my eyes on the cross, turning as it passed. The choir and pastors fell in behind. Sidney Wright, congregational curmudgeon, didn't turn around at all, way out of his comfort zone, I think. By contrast, Malcolm Stafford, Esquire, bowed to the cross as it passed by him. Malcolm, a spiritual brother for me after many years at St. Timothy together, is always ready for more liturgical activity.

Rhonda Bartholomew, big with child (#6), presented the children's sermon. She and the kids who scamper forward have been setting up the manger scene Sunday by Sunday. Two weeks ago, they placed a cow, a cat, and a turtle dove in the stable with its empty manger. Last week, the shepherds and sheep. Today, the angels.

"You each have a message to proclaim, little angels," she told them.

"What is it?" Maddie Bowers asked.

"That's what I was going to ask you. What is the message, kids?"

"God loves everybody, probably," one of Rhonda's boys offered.

"Doesn't everybody already know that?" a little girl asked.

"No," Maddie said flatly. "But does that mean we're s'posed to walk around saying to everybody, 'God loves you,' 'God loves you,' 'God loves you'?" she pressed, wrinkling her nose at the idea.

Little Amber Smith shyly raised her hand, and Rhonda nodded at her. "You can just do nice things and give 'em pretty stuff." Aw-w-w.

During the adult sermon, Pr. Morris got a little laugh, portraying John the Baptist as "the Doberman Pinscher preacher who guards the manger lest we take it too lightly." He asserted that "the writers of the Gospels urge us to detour to the Jordan and drown our sinful selves in the waters of repentance before proceeding to Bethlehem to worship the babe. For if we don't heed the Baptizer's message, we may not recognize who the baby really is. We may leave the manger feeling warm and fuzzy but unchanged."

I didn't care for that last line; I would have been quite content with warm and fuzzy. But during the sermon, movement caught my eye and I looked over to see Rita Smith weeping a little and Louie putting his arm around her. Oh, how those two beautiful people struggle. I thought of their first time at St. Timothy a few years back. They came to Sunday School, and I remember the scene like it happened this morning...

Susie Wakefield was teaching. She welcomed Louie and Rita and invited them to tell a little about themselves.

"Ain't much to tell, really. We moved up from Kentuckiana, live right over yonder on 12th Avenue and thought we might as well drop in and meet our neighbors," Louie joked, and we laughed politely. Rita smiled, and the class moved on. We were studying C. S. Lewis's <u>Surprised by Joy</u>. Several people shared relevant anecdotes, and when someone mentioned the biblical admonition to "rejoice always," Rita spoke.

"I want to tell you why we came."

Louie looked at her. "Babe...?" he questioned, but she kept talking.

"We lost our only child, a little baby boy." Louie was watching her intently, nervously. So were the rest of us. She looked at the floor as she spoke.

"The baby drowned in the bathtub because I was drunk."

Oh, dear God. I had read the short item in the paper a while back. Rita Smith. 12th street. Infant drowning.

"Louie works second shift at the forge, and when he got home he found the baby. I had passed out on the bed."

Now, we were really nervous. This was a lot more than we bargained for in Sunday School. Plus, it was time to go to worship. Classes had been dismissed; we could hear them in the hallway.

"Three days after it happened, I got up early and drove out to the lake and..."

Louie broke in. "I heard her shut the truck door, and I knowed what she was gonna' try and do. I pulled on my clothes and banged on the neighbor's door and borrowed his truck. When I got to the lake, I seen her go under. We don't neither one swim, but I got her, I pulled her out."

"We sat on the ground holding each other for a long time and Louie was crying and saying, 'JesusJesusJesusJesus.' All I wanted to do was die. I still do."

Oh, this was excruciating. Somebody slipped out the door.

"Over the next few weeks, I kept trying to pray but didn't know how, so I just kept saying 'Jesus' over and over, like Louie. I've always loved Jesus as a precious little baby and a very kind man," she looked up from the floor and into our faces, "but now I need him to be more. I need to be forgiven— but..." and she broke down completely. Susie knelt on the floor in front of them and put her arms around them and the rest of us awkwardly shuffled out of the room to go and worship...

but we've had plenty of chances to hug them and pray for them and help them since then, the biggest one being to help them build a house with Habitat. They are truly part of St. Timothy now, contributing so much. By the time we passed the peace this morning, they were okay and looked over at me and smiled and waved. They <u>were</u> the sermon. "The Lord has done great things for us, and we rejoiced."

The anthem was out of this world—good old J. S. Bach, "Prepare Thyself, Zion." Mindy leaned across Josephine to whisper, "I don't even know what the heck Zion means or where it is, but that was so beautiful!" I think it was the cello accompaniment that got her. Beautiful, indeed; enough to make one weep for no apparent reason. The choir was up to the task; what an improvement since Theodore's arrival.

Our caroling group at Rutledge Home this afternoon didn't sound nearly as good but served its purpose. I didn't carol last year because of Florence dying, but found pretty much the usual group: token youth Stuart Brown, this year with a girlfriend; Danny and Sherry Bennett and his father, Eugene; Louella Rutledge, whose father (Theodore's grandfather) started the place; pudgy, pious little Madge Humphries with her bleached hair and false (?) eyelashes; and the pastors. Oh, and Lois Rizenhouer, who is at Rutledge about every day, since George checked in.

As usual, we walked the halls singing, stopping in the rooms of members and friends, and had 100% participation! Sam Benshaw, 99-year old poet, walked, along with Steve Hagendorf, my former principal, who has Alzheimer's, and Mitch (don't even know his last name) on his walker. George Rizenhouer with Lois pushing and a giggling Pauline Shuster rolled along in their wheelchairs. Mary Thurgood was staying in bed all day, but as we started to leave her room Danny said, "W-w-wait a minute! I s-s-see some wheels on that bed," and looked at us until we rolled her down the hall, too, with a big smile on her face. Quite a parade and then a joyful party, except for Pauline stuffing down cookies until an attendant stopped her and she rolled herself out in a huff. She's a difficult resident, now in her 40s, with developmental delay, mental illness, and diabetes. The delightful Sam rendered his Christmas haiku for this year:

Why not stay awake?
The party will soon begin.
Jesus wants us there.

On the family front—Virginia and I have had good times together this week. She took me shopping one day for my Christmas gift from her and Barry, a warm ensemble for Russia: tall, flat-heeled black leather boots, a long, black, wool cape, and matching hat, scarf and gloves in a brilliant blue-green. At my height, I feel like an Amazon Hessian in that outfit. It's all very comfortable and gives me confidence that I'll be able to withstand the cold and walk a lot.

Then on Friday she and Stephanie and Mack came over—Mindy, too. We cut out and baked gingerbread and sugar cookies and decorated them. Steph dabbed the baby's high chair tray with vari-colored frostings, and he soon decorated himself. Good heavens at that child's vocabulary! He can say hi and bye (in that sweet little velvet voice), muh (milk and mother), cah (car), cah (cat), da-ma (Grandma and Great-grandma—same name for Virginia and me). "Be careful, Steph. He's way too smart," Mindy warned. He delights in Cute Baby. Despite her curiosity, she scampers and hides whenever he gets near. That cat of mine gave us a good laugh when we were singing carols together as we baked. She meowed in distress and clawed at our trousers to get us to stop and the next thing we hear is her tromping up and down the piano keyboard. Too funny!

And then last night Virginia hosted a party. A huge crowd, from her real estate world and Barry's lawyer world, the arts community, the non-profit arena, and church folks. She had decorated with mostly white, including several reindeer, works of art, which she arranged throughout the entry hall, living room, and dining room. Gorgeous. Food and drink were equally creative, from the chafing dishes to the punch bowls to the elegant dessert platters. I think she and Barry went all out, not only to celebrate the season but to celebrate their marital reconciliation. Given my minimalist tendencies and concerns for the poor, the extravagance gave me pause, but then I noticed the basket on the credenza in the entry hall. Guests could buy bricks for $10 each to build the new Catholic school in the inner city.

"Gin, I think we've got enough here to build a wing!" Barry reported, happily counting the money at the kitchen table as we cleaned up. I had seen a check for $500 and put in $100 myself, and the very wealthy and very generous Louella was there, along with society's upper crust, so to speak.

"Birds of a feather flock together, and when they're rich birds, you can kill a bunch of 'em with one party," John cracked. Uh, right.

"Sure wish Steverino could have come," Barry said at one point, and we all shared that sentiment, but he's staying in Chicago until Christmas, enjoying his downtown apartment and the decorations and holiday events. He's also updating his resume so he can start a serious job search when we get back from Russia. He and I talked earlier this evening with him lying flat on the floor to relieve back pain. I advised him to get that checked out before we leave. Don't want an aching back to spoil the trip. He said he would if it persists. I know he's still blue over his break-up with Penelope. Last Christmas, they were very much of a couple, but that seems to be over.

Good heavens, God, romance in the Harris family is soap opera-ish these days. Help each and all of us to be keenly aware of your presence. Help us to be guided by your love and avail ourselves of your wisdom so that our relationships are strong and healthy and in line with your good purpose. We are grateful, as always, for the Body of Christ and our brothers and sisters in the faith, to be together in injury and healing, sorrow and joy. Thank you for the Christ, come as a baby, hope of all the earth, dear desire of every nation, joy of every longing heart. Amen.

<u>Fourth Sunday in Advent</u>

2 Samuel 7:1-11, 16
Psalm 89:1-4, 19-26
Romans 16:25-27
Luke 1:26-38

Here I sit tonight, lighting the fourth candle. I still haven't found my Advent wreath, but these four different candles arranged in a circle on my coffee table work. The room is dark and striking the match and touching the puff of flame to each wick seems bold and defiant—especially after a difficult conversation with Jim and Anita yesterday. Things started pleasantly enough.

"Hello, dear neighbor bearing gifts. Enter!" Jim greeted with his toothy grin, ushering me in from the softly falling snow to deliver a tin of Christmas cookies.

"Rose!" the radiant, pregnant Anita exclaimed, coming up behind him and giving me a big hug. "Come sit by the tree and have a cup of hot cider with us, okay?"

Anita seemed to be on an even keel in her struggles with depression or whatever, exactly, her problem is. "Pathological compassion," Jim describes it. I remember him saying once that he'd "like to strangle John Donne because every single time the damn bell tolls, Anita thinks it's tolling for her." Meds and a therapist are pretty important.

We talked about the baby coming in April. Old-fashioned and older—Anita will be 40 when the baby's born—they're not finding out gender. She was excited about the first real snow outside which led to a bunch of snowed-in stories. And Jim told about Santa Claus walking into a bar and ordering a double whiskey. True. I told about Mack pushing a little toy shopping cart so fast that he's practically parallel to the floor but not quite walking alone. Late afternoon stretched into evening. A tray of cheese and crackers and pickles appeared, and Anita lit a fat, green candle which smelled stronger than the live evergreen in our midst. All very pleasant. And then as we stared into the candlelight, Anita asked, "Do you think we could get our baby baptized at your church?"

I was so taken aback I didn't know what to say.

"She's not kidding," Jim smiled, enjoying my confusion.

"Jim's against it, of course…"

"Being an atheist and all," he quipped.

"...and I'm not for sure myself. I'm working on identifying what I truly believe as opposed to what my grandparents and parents believed and handed on to me. You know, Rose, God just isn't very real to me in a world with so much suffering. But in the midst of all that, I have fond memories of church from when I was a kid. I guess I want my child to have the grounding and exposure that I did."

"Yeah, so when the kid grows up, it'll know exactly what it's rejecting," Jim teased. "Go ahead and say what you're thinking, Rose," he encouraged when I was still silent.

"I'm not sure what I'm thinking, to tell the truth. Of course, the pastors are the ones you'd talk with, not me. But Anita, tell me again—why do you want to have the baby baptized?"

She thought for a moment, then said, "The idea of gathering together weekly to think and talk about life and moral behavior and all that appeals to me, plus I like music. Mostly, it's that I want this little person who is being entrusted to us to develop into a happy, healthy individual. I want his or her life to be special, not random day-after-day without meaning or purpose."

Why was I getting so agitated over this? I would have thought that the prospect of these dear neighbors associating with the church would please me immensely. Instead, I was thinking, "You don't get it. You're talking about living a moral life, not about a God who loves you so much that he died for you." I didn't want to judge, and I certainly didn't want to put Anita off from bringing the baby into the church, yet her understanding of being Christian seemed—superficial. I yearned to reveal to these non-believing friends my deepest convictions about the scandal and wonder of God coming among us, as a fellow human being.

But alas, I couldn't find the words. Instead, I said, lamely, "Well, goodness, have you ever thought about the Unitarian Church? That might be more in line with what you're wanting, and I think they have a dedication service for babies. My friend Sarah is Unitarian; I could put you in touch with each other."

"Good God, Rose, I'm astounded that a devout Christian church lady like yourself would throw a soul over to the Unitarians!"

"Are you serious, Jim, or are you playing devil's advocate or something?" I asked, tiring of his sarcasm and sorely disappointed in my inability to express what was burning in my heart.

"Half and half," he admitted, "but I really am surprised you don't go for the baptism idea."

"Do you two know what's required of parents who have their children baptized?"

"I sure hope we don't have to teach 'em there is a God," Jim cracked.

"Oh, hush, Jim. Basically," Anita responded, "you promise to take them to worship and teach them things like the Lord's Prayer and the Ten Commandments, right?"

I sat there blinking and thinking. Again, I would dearly love them to have the baby baptized into St. Timothy to be loved and nurtured—but what would it be worth if they don't believe that a loving God is the power of the universe? And that Jesus, incomprehensibly and mysteriously, is God in human flesh. I leaned forward and blurted out, "It's about very God of very God." Now, where in the world had that come from? Their faces went blank, understandably, since I didn't even know what I meant. Something deep and mysterious and true—and inexpressible.

Well. Even Jim didn't have a quick comeback for that utterance—and just then the doorbell rang, releasing us from this difficult conversation for that day. It was Josephine. The Fergusons and I bid each other a hasty goodnight, and I stepped out into the cold with my cousin.

"Rose, I have to go home now," Josephine said breathlessly, as we walked through thick falling snow which was starting to blow a bit. "My neighbor Doris called and she's all hopeless."

"Doris? I thought you two didn't get along very well."

"She gets mad at me, sometimes, but she called and said she's feeling all sad and hopeless."

"And you can give her hope?"

"Maybe. I have a lot of it."

I had to smile.

"Well, what's the problem? Why is she hopeless?" I asked as we blew into the house.

"She has the breast cancer, like me. Hers is back, really bad."

"Oh, no, what a shame; that's hard, too bad," I said, trying to take in this sudden change of plans. "But goodness, Josephine, can't you at least stay for Christmas? It's only a few days away. And we'd talked about you house-sitting for me while I'm in Russia. You won't be doing that?"

"I think Doris needs me for Christmas. I'm leaving right now and driving straight through."

"Oh, heavens, not tonight! The roads might get really nasty and everything would be closed and…"

"I'm right sure I can drive out of this. I heard on the radio it's not even snowing in Muncie."

Ten minutes later she was backing out of the driveway on her way through the white and drifting snow. I prayed, *God, thank you for your presence and watchfulness over Josephine, your unique servant. Please escort this crazy woman all the way to Mississippi. Amen.*

So here I am alone with special time to reflect on this Lord's Day. Rhonda and the munchkins added Mary and Joseph and the donkey to the crèche this morning. "Children, why was Mary so special?" she started out.

"Because she had a little lamb," Amber Smith said, and then embarrassed, corrected herself. "I mean a little baby; it was Jesus."

"Right. God chose Mary for that very special job. Sometimes we call her 'the first disciple' because she was the first one to know about God sending Jesus to earth to show everybody how God's love works. And besides being his mother, she was a witness. That means she told everyone about Jesus and how special he was. God expects each one of us to be like Mary and do that, too. How can we do that? How can we be witnesses, kids?"

"Love one another," someone said, sounding bored.

"That's the same thing we said last week," Maddie noted suspiciously.

"Yes, we did, and it's still right, but let's go a little further. Raise your hands if you like to hear stories." Pretty much every hand went up including one little tyke who took his thumb out of his mouth, stuck his hand up, and then put the thumb back in. God love 'em, they're cute.

"That's the thing; everybody loves stories," Rhonda said. "So telling people the stories you know about Jesus is a great way to witness."

"I would tell people, 'Jesus makes me happy,'" Nick Brewster put in. Quite a testimony from a 4-year-old whose dad was killed in Iraq last year.

"You got it, little mister!" Rhonda pronounced. "Everybody go and do likewise," and back they ran, hopped, walked, and toddled.

Pastor Charlene preached about witnessing, too—being Christ bearers in the world—putting the task in rather graphic terms. "During this worship service, while we partake of our Lord's body and blood, 1,600 children around the world will die from the effects of severe poverty. But doesn't our God promise that the hungry will be filled with good things? 'How can this be?' we may want to ask, like Mary did. And then again like Mary, let us say, in doubt and in wonder, 'Here am I, the servant of the Lord; let it be with me according to your word.' God's work, people; our hands."

"Amen. Straight shooter, isn't she? Doesn't pull any punches," John quietly commented as she sat down.

At coffee hour, Virginia asked where Cousin Josephine was.

"Gone home," I said and explained the details.

"She always out-performs my expectations," Virginia observed. "She's such an odd duck and so clueless about what's going on in the world that no one pays her much attention. And then in her mousey, quiet way, she reaches out and touches people."

"She holds fast to what is good, that's what she does," John observed.

I called the odd duck a little while ago, happy to hear that she is safely home (but it scares me half to death to think that she drove the whole way by herself, nonstop, apparently at about 80 mph). Then I checked my email—several links about all things Russian from Stephen, an E-vite to a wedding (tacky), a few electronic Christmas cards, and new pictures of Mack from Steph.

And now I think on the many blessings of this day and light these candles, boldly and defiantly, in a dark world that seems to believe less and less in anything beyond itself. I still regret being unable to articulate the mysteries of the faith to Jim and Anita—and yet absolutely confident that the mysteries are true. I love this—believing in the unlikely, the impossible, God come to earth in a baby, peace on earth, good will to all. I believe it. Can't help it.

Christmas Eve

Isaiah 9:2-7
Psalm 96
Titus 2:11-14
Luke 2:1-14

Honestly, I believe every heart was focused as soon as Pastor Ruskin started proclaiming the gospel lesson in his strong, faithful voice: "In those days a decree went out from Caesar Augustus…" People who might not even have thought of God since last Christmas Eve were surely touched again by Luke's simple story of God come to earth to dwell among us. I heard that it was the Bryants' idea for Pr. Ruskin to deliver the gospel. They are obviously tuned in to his situation—how his dementia progressed rapidly during the months he served us as interim pastor, but how he is nevertheless still capable of reading the Scriptures eloquently, even though he doesn't appear to understand what he's read. What a great surprise. This holy night was filled with them!

Pr. Morris sprang a big one on us. He started out his sermon with something like, "The essential truth of the Jesus story upon which we focus on this night of nights is deeply rooted in the history of our Hebrew ancestors." Then he referred to "ancient scriptural parallels between the births and childhoods of Samuel, King David (whom Samuel anointed), John the Baptizer, and Jesus." And then he said—hm, I can't remember what he was saying when he shuffled the next page of his sermon to the top of the stack, stared at it a minute, and then seemed to realize that his message held no magic. He strode down the center aisle, stopping at the pew where the Fraziers were sitting, and saying, "May I borrow your baby?" The child must be about six months old, and after a bit of a double take, the surprised parents handed it over.

He held the baby up and turned in a circle and asked, "If the Christmas story is about God becoming incarnate in a human being, what can this baby tell us about God and us?"

"G-G-God is sweet and b-beautiful," Danny yelled out. "And gentle and kind," Sherry added, with her little giggle. We can always count on Danny and Sherry.

When the babe came close to where the Brewster clan was seated, little Brucie Brewster observed loudly, "Him looks like him got stars in him eyes."

Pr. M. continued walking, the contented baby cradled in his arms. Cynthia Stafford's low, velvety voice broke into the silence. "The baby's helplessness reminds me that we are dependent on God—and that God takes care of us."

John had to laugh out loud when they came to our pew and the little one smiled right into his face. "The baby is one of us," he announced for all to hear. "It's going to live in the same world and know the same joys and troubles we do."

"Babies are about the future, about hoping things will get better," someone chimed in.

Pr. Morris nodded. "The sweet and tender truths we see in this or any baby invite us to keep coming back for the rest of the story," he said, handing the child back to the parents. "Next Sunday would be a good time," he concluded, sweeping the congregation with a "hint, hint" smile. Pr. Charlene was smiling, too. Morris has not appeared to be too long on spontaneity, so I suspect this impromptu sermon with living object lesson and audience participation was quite a stretch. A good one.

We had our own prototype baby in our pew, little Mr. Mack. He did quite well through the lengthy service, early on happily clapping along with the children's exuberant singing of the calypso tune "He Came Down—that we may have peace—love—joy." Later in the service, he fell asleep, as if on cue, during the Polish carol "Infant Holy, Infant Lowly." His precious cherub face, which resembles me and my people, was "free from sorrow," as the carol says. Stephanie knelt for communion with him fast asleep in her arms, and Pr. Charlene gently touched him and blest him with the words, "Christ the Child was born for you!"

And yet another child, Maddie Bowers, surprised me during the passing of the peace with, "The peace of the Lord be with you, Rose."

"And with you, Maddie. How did you know my name?"

"I hear things," she replied. Oh, how this little girl touches me!

A sad surprise was the whiff of liquor on Pat O'Schaughnessy's breath when he turned to pass the peace. He's been sober for a couple years, so this was the smell of heartache. The truth is, candlelight and poinsettias and precious children and everybody dressed in their best is quite nice but not the whole story. Kneeling for Eucharist and waiting to be served, I found my eyes traveling slowly from one face to another, many of them unfamiliar, wondering what troubles and pain they brought to the altar.

In the narthex before the service, I literally ran into Deedee Brewster/Leppard, war widow, bumbling in with her four youngsters. "We come from chaos," she quipped and kept talking while Grandpa Jack and

Grandma Helen Brewster took the baby out of her arms and herded the children to their pew. "Theresa and Brucie have pink eye, at least it's not the viral kind, and Johnny threw a tantrum right when it was time to leave, and Nick couldn't find his coat, I wrapped him in a blanket. And," she pulled me to her, tearing up, "and, we've lost a loved one and it's the holidays," she whispered into my ear. I hugged her hard, and she quickly wiped her tears away. "You know, Rose, I think this Christmas without Chad is even harder than last year. And those damnable wars grind on," she lamented. But, she closed her eyes and took a deep breath and her face began to relax. "Oh, dear, let me get in here for some R & R," and she rushed in to take her place, calling over her shoulder, "And I hope your Christmas is very happy." Yes, my young sister, go and worship and let the wonders hush your worries. *And, dear Lord, I pray that those who need it the most found a little hope to take with them when they left the service tonight.*

When we returned to our seats after communion, I wanted to make up after the argument John and I had over where to have Christmas dinner and who to invite. My preference was to have a couple people at his house. His guest list included the whole world, practically, at my house. In observance of our good compromise, I put my arm through his and leaned against him. We massaged hands, and I closed my eyes and tingled. Lines from a sonnet by E. B. Browning, learned long ago, came to me: "Let the world's sharpness like a clasping knife/Shut in upon itself and do no harm/In this close hand of Love, now soft and warm..." His Christmas gift to me was a poem, a computer-generated, artistically-appointed rendering of Updike's "Elderly Sex." "Life's buried treasure's buried deeper still..." I read it and flush. And more literature, from me to him. I penned and framed a quotation from JFK that I came across recently, perfectly suited for John: "War will exist until that distant day when the conscientious objector enjoys the same reputation and prestige as the warrior does today."

The music was splendid and seemed to fade into the background even as it transported me to a rich, dark place where fluid, fluorescent images of seeds in the ground, babies in the womb, passionate acts of love in the night drifted through my brain. And then after the peaceful candlelighting and "Silent Night," the world was ablaze, and I think we could have passed for the heavenly hosts proclaiming, "Joy to the world, the Lord is come!" Trumpets blared and drums thundered and earnest voices belted out the news. I couldn't help but think of Jim, missing out on all of this in his lonely (my term, not his) certainty that there is no Lord, no God. Pure projection on my part, I suppose. If he were here, he'd likely get a headache instead of a heart thrill. Nevertheless, I pray, with joy and confidence *that all hearts will one day prepare room for the wonders of your love, gracious God, and let sin and sorrow grow no more! Amen.*

Other surprises of the evening—Ethan joined us at Virginia and Barry's for our family dinner before the service. And I surprised myself by declining to fret over the presence of Stephanie's "baby daddy" as Steph and Mindy sometimes call him; I don't like that flippant title. John was included, too. Virginia had asked if he was to be invited. I said yes, partly because I wanted him to be there and partly because not inviting him would send a message I'm not ready to send.

At the beginning of the meal, Stephen raised his glass and toasted. "Gin, we've been around your table for the past twenty years for Christmas Eve dinner. Members of the family have come and gone [Charlie gone by death and Stephen's Denise gone by divorce, Ethan come by parenthood and Mack by birth and John by—friendship] and your lovely, warm home serves as a constant place of love and peace." We happily clinked our glasses to that, especially because a few months ago, it seemed that this very home might be broken asunder.

Yes, indeed, gracious God, many thanks on this holiest of nights for your presence through all of our changes. The same love incarnate through the Christ child lives in each of us, to sustain and embellish our life together. Glory to you in the highest. Amen.

During dinner, Barry said, "I'm sort of surprised to hear myself say this, but I wish Cousin Josephine were here. What's she doing for Christmas, Rose?"

"Just talked to her a little while ago. She's going to services tonight with her neighbor, Doris. Then tomorrow, she's helping Doris cook dinner. Doris is a gourmet vegetarian and the entrée is—what did she tell me?—I had to look up a word in the dictionary—I know—Spinach and Tofu Stuffed Eggplant Roulades."

"Yum!" said Stephanie and "Yuk!" said Ethan, at exactly the same time, making us laugh.

We exchanged gifts, which have become less and less as we all possess more and more. And now, I'm very ready to "nestle all snug in my bed," so I'll end these reflections with the biggest surprise of all.

After the service, I was delighted to hear Mindy's voice in the hectic merriment. "Rose! Rose!" and here she came twisting and turning down the crowded aisle followed by her entourage of Regina/mom, Cindy/sister, and, of all people, Uncle Marvin. When she was almost to me she tripped and fell into my arms laughing. She made the rounds, hugging John and everybody else and taking Mack who was reaching for her out of Ethan's arms while I greeted her people. As usual, handsome Uncle Marvin kissed my hand in the continental manner.

"You will never, ever guess what!" Mindy exclaimed, looking up at me, twisting her head in circles so Mack couldn't grab her glasses.

"Something about Miguel?" I said, hoping.

"No, but he's doing okay. He's so peaceful, that guy, so 'Mi vida es en Cristo.' Folks from Our Lady held mass for him and a few others this afternoon. But, no—it's about this guy right here; tell her Uncle Marvin."

"It is my pleasure to inform you, Rose, that I will be in St. Petersburg for the Christmas season."

"Florida?" I asked.

"Russia," he smiled. "Melinda had told me of your plans several weeks ago, and so I made arrangements. I often spend January in that splendid city. I would be most honored if you and your son would allow me to join you for some festivities, perhaps show you around a bit."

I looked at Stephen, who extended his hand and introduced himself to Marvin. I looked at Mindy, whose eyes were dancing. I looked at John, who was scowling—to beat the band, one might say.

<u>Christmas Day</u>

Isaiah 62:6-12
Psalm 97
Titus 3:4-7
Luke 2:8-20

Shepherd's Pie for Christmas dinner. What a unique surprise from John. I thought he might not even show up, after the Uncle-Marvin-going-to-Russia bombshell from last night. I didn't sleep well, troubled by the whole thing and worried that today would be stressful. Had this crazy dream—John and Marvin were both in it—dancing, classical ballet—naked—but no genitals. That is absolutely all I remember. I don't know what it meant. Probably something about power, that they were having too much power over me or something—so my psyche emasculated them, I guess. Anyway, it calmed my soul.

John did show up (fully clothed), but definitely tense, throwing around clichés like a drunken sailor (ha!). Everything was "pretty as a picture" or "slow as molasses in January" until I had a headache as big as Texas. He'd been excited about cooking dinner ever since our compromise plan to host Mercedes Scheumann and Sidney Wright at my house.

"I'll bring the main course, and you can do the trimmings," he'd said, eyes sparkling.

"How can I trim without knowing what I'm trimming?" I had to ask.

"Have a fruit salad of some kind and cake for dessert. That'll do 'er."

Sidney wanted to bring something, so I assigned him dessert. Thank heaven Mercedes didn't offer because her cooking has been a disaster since her dementia's taken hold. Getting cinnamon and red pepper mixed up, for example. I still didn't know what the main course was when John arrived around noon to put it together in my kitchen. I tried to be cheerful, but he shut me down with, "It's a bridge too far for us to have a civil conversation right now. You're barking up the wrong tree." So I left him to his task and busied myself with other matters, trying not to compare him to Charlie. When our guests arrived, he put his dish under the broiler to brown. We seated ourselves at the dining room table and sipped cranberry punch for a few minutes until he placed his creation in the middle of the table.

"Shepherd's Pie?" I guessed.

"Yup. Seemed appropriate to the occasion," he muttered.

Mercedes said she loved—hesitation—"those, uh, things you peel and cook and pound and hit until they're soft like that right there."

"Mashed potatoes," Sidney supplied, and she nodded.

"Very thoughtful, John," I said, and meant it. "Reminds me of words of Martin Luther I read this morning, about God overthrowing the lofty by coming as a baby in a lowly manger to poor shepherds."

"Topsy-turvy," Mercedes said, bending under the table to retrieve her napkin. Had she grasped enough to make an apt, theological comment—or was she simply describing her world?

"Yup, it's as plain as the nose on your face that Jesus came to overthrow the rich and powerful," John testified as he served up ample portions of the perfectly browned pie.

"Watch out there, John. You're making Jesus out like a communist," Sidney said, taking a bite. "But, God a'mighty this is good! It's mutton 'stead a beef, isn't it? That's how we used to make it; we called it Cowboy Pie where I come from."

"Sidney," John continued earnestly, "in over fifty years with the Mennonite Service Committee in countries all over the globe from here to Timbuktu [not a cliché—actual], I've seen more human misery than you can shake a stick at, and it's all been at the hands of the wealthy, mean as bulldogs and operating by hook or by crook. And God is not mocked. Time after time, I saw…"

Mercedes started humming "Away in a Manger." I don't know if the conversation was making her nervous or what, but the more animated John got, talking about liberation theology and people's movements, the louder she hummed. Finally, it was so loud John stopped talking, and she sang the whole first verse.

After a moment Sidney said, "That was real pretty, Mercedes," and then "John, you're startin' to sound like a communist again, but I sure would like another piece of that Cowboy Pie, if I might. Why, I believe it's the best I've ever had."

John served him and hunkered down over his plate, looking defeated. I glanced over at him and felt a little pity, and then focused on Sidney, who was oblivious as he dug into his pie. He's often a grump at church, fussing at people over not taking care of the property and complaining about changes in worship. But look at him with Mercedes, driving her around to doctor appointments and wherever, helping her with her insurance papers. He lives modestly, and I've heard he's a huge financial giver. Sidney may not be on the cutting edge of social change, but he is a good guy to have around.

After dinner, Mercedes and I cleared the table, and I cleaned up the kitchen which didn't take long as there were no leftovers. Shepherd's Pie devoured, citrus salad gone, a half Louisiana Crumb Cake that Sidney brought from the store scrumptious to the last crumb. While I loaded the few dishes into the dishwasher and wiped the counter, Mercedes gazed at the Icon of the Nativity I had propped up on the salt and pepper shakers on the kitchen table. It's a weird picture to the uninitiated, but she seemed to take it at its word, smiling and nodding her head.

I was wondering how we would pass the afternoon, but John had the Scrabble board ready on the dining room table. Dubious that Sidney could spell many words, frankly, or that Mercedes would remember any, I was pleasantly surprised at the fun we had! John facilitated beautifully; leniency ruled, with free giving or exchanging of letters and no worry whether words were valid. Mercedes drew on her decades of watching Jeopardy! and we all cheered when she laid down alextrebec. Sidney drew on his guitar knowledge, with little words like koa and big words like trussrod. Of course, Cute Baby wanted to play, and I had to keep throwing her off the table. John cheered up, and I laughed and relaxed, but felt my stomach muscles tighten when Mercedes and Sidney left.

We stood side by side at the front door watching them drive away. They were out of sight and we still stood there, frozen. "What's going on Rose?" John finally said, staring straight ahead. "I don't know," I said, in utter candor. He put his arm around my waist, and we walked into the den and sank down on the davenport.

After more silence, we both started talking at the same time and immediately stopped. I took a deep breath and plunged in. "John, I don't know what in the world is going on with Marvin. I'm stunned that he's going to St. Petersburg. I hardly know him."

"Didn't you go around with him in Chicago last fall?"

"We had that coincidental meeting on the train and went to the Art Museum and had lunch together, yes. But, that's the last time I saw him."

"Who is he, anyway?"

"He's Mindy's uncle. Well, no, not her uncle, actually, I think he's her husband's, well, no, not her husband's, they never married, but Larry's uncle. Larry is Darien's father. Darien is Mindy's son who was killed in the car accident years ago; you remember that, right?"

He nodded. "What's Marvin's last name?"

"Huh. I don't know. I don't think I've ever heard it."

"Where does he live? What does he do? How old is he?"

"Here in Shippensforge, I guess; no, probably not; I don't know where he lives. He's in some kind of import-export business. I have no idea how old he is; in his seventies, I guess." We sat there thinking for a minute.

Then John turned toward me and said, "That's all beside the point anyway," and he took my hands in his. "Here's my bottom line, Rose. I want you to be my wife, I've made that clear. We're like two peas in a pod in so many ways. This last year together has been one of the happiest of [his Blackberry blared and he switched it off and kept talking] my life. We don't know how many more years we'll be blessed with. Let the past be the past and marry me. I need an answer. I'll give you until you get back from Russia, and I'll be praying everyday that Marvin won't be trying to steal you away from me." He held my face in his hands, oh! so tenderly, and we looked at each other deeply and kissed firmly. "That's my bottom line, Rose Harris, from the bottom of my heart."

I listened to him get his dishes and zip up his coat and close the front door and thought what a good and valiant little man he is. To think that I am precious in his sight! A dull ache of loneliness brought tears to my eyes, and I jumped up, to avoid wallowing, and did what I had planned to do: call the Sauers. Brittany answered.

"Oh, hi, Mrs. Harris. Merry Christmas to you, too."

"I hope you've had a nice day. How is everyone?"

"We're pretty good. I had to have my appendix out a couple weeks ago, but I'm okay. Mom and dad are outside. I'll get them," she said before I could tell her not to bother them, I could call back. I felt close to them as soon I heard their voices, even though they're a couple hours away.

"Rose!" came the lovely, lively sound of Carolyn. "How fabulous to hear from you! You'll never guess what Marcus and I were doing—decorating the front porch, isn't that wild? We had the greens and ribbons and lights, and then Brittany's appendix ruptured and there was surgery, and everything's been nuts. So, after my parents left a little while ago, I said, 'I feel like decorating the front porch.' Marcus said, 'Why not? We have twelve days of Christmas to go.' It's really pleasant here, kind of warm and very foggy, and get this—through the mist we can see our neighbors un-decorating, isn't that a hoot?"

Carolyn and I hit the high points, and then Pastor and I visited. He said to be sure and see St. Issac, reminding me that they traveled to Russia a few years back. I didn't mention John or Marvin. I'll ponder these things in my heart. It will all work out. And I need to get with Mindy and find out more about this Uncle Marvin character.

Guard me sleeping and guide me waking, dear God, that even in my old age, my life will reflect your simple, incomprehensible love. In the baby and then man of Jesus, we see as clearly as can be seen *the power and scope of how much you love your creation. Thank you for the fabulous people who I count as my own. May they be aware of your presence and know that you are all they need. Thank you in advance for helping me discern whether or not to marry John, your faithful servant. I know you will provide the wisdom for me to understand my own heart and the strength to live out my decision. Amen.*

"O come, let us adore him!"

First Sunday of Christmas

Isaiah 61:10—62:3
Psalm 148
Galatians 4:4-7
Luke 2:22-40

A cardinal couple flits among the snowflakes as I sit at my kitchen table writing. Birds and snow alike are praising the Lord; that's what I see. Cute Baby's praising, too, perched on the sill, watching intently. And I join the dance, still inspired by worship this morning. My expectations were low, this being the Sunday after Christmas, but we had another occasion to celebrate—the Bryants were officially installed as our pastors.

The crowd was larger than it would have been otherwise, and Lloyd and Theodore treated us with a Vivaldi prelude and festive Christmas hymns. A delightful children's anthem, too; Theodore has such a way with the little ones. In sweet and pure unison, the youngsters swayed and swished—as did some of us—to the tune of "Bring a Torch, O Jeanette Isabella" with happy, fresh words:

> Love has come and never will leave us!
> Love is life everlasting and free.
> Love is Jesus within and among us.
> Love is the peace our hearts are seeking.
> Love! Love! Love is the gift of Christmas.
> Love! Love! Praise to you God on high!

And we sang the beautiful and serene Nunc Dimittis, the faithful old Simeon's sending forth song, following Eucharist. Serene if you don't read the next few verses, that is, where he tells Mary that a sword will pierce her soul. Our guest preacher observed, "This is a bitter foretelling, for this wise man understood the depth of God's love, born in this child, and knew that such love does not go unopposed." Inez Rodriguez from the bishop's office preached and installed the Bryants. She worked with us quite effectively with conflict resolution last year. She and I chatted at the reception, shoulder to shoulder, selecting sweet treats. Naturally, there was more fruit cake than cookies on this Sunday after.

"I'm enjoying being here for a happy event rather than dealing with conflict. And how do you feel the congregation is doing? And please, tell me your name again."

"Rose Harris. People seem unified around our new pastors, but even before they came, I think we were back on the track to being healthy and normal."

"Oh, that sounds good," she said, biting into a snowball cookie, powdered sugar sifting down the front of her black clerical shirt. "I wish more congregations were healthy and normal."

"How are things at headquarters? How's the bishop doing?" I inquired.

She shook her head a little. "We're all exhausted; these are contentious times," she said, brushing the powdered sugar off her chest.

I nodded in sympathy. "I do keep you all, and the Church, in my prayers."

"Much appreciated. Treasure this congregation, Rose," and she patted my shoulder and turned to greet the next person.

I turned, too, and was face-to-face with Jacob Turner. We talked basketball. He's captain of the SCHS team, and we're considered contenders for the state title.

"I'm glad you're playing, Jacob."

He nodded and swallowed, his Adam's apple bobbing. "It's hard."

"I know. And I'm so glad you're back here with us."

"Me, too, Mrs. Harris."

"Hang in there."

"I will."

Few words but loaded because of Jacob's anguished struggle over the death of a friend in a frivolous, freak accident last May. For crying out loud, he was just pushing the girl in a shopping cart in a parking lot, just horsing around, nothing that should have killed anyone—but it happened.

A couple months ago I asked him how he was doing. "I wish I could die," he'd said. He quit worshiping for awhile. Jacob has been a charming witness to the faith since he was a kid; now, he inspires me more than ever, even as my heart hurts for him.

Next, I joined John who was talking with Madge Humphries.

"No, no, that's not what she said."

"I heard it with my own ears, John. She said that Christ is of no value to us if we try to do right and go to church. I don't get that."

Ah, the Galatians passage. Poor Madge, with her skipping-around concentration span and works righteousness theology. I settled in to enjoy the interchange.

John started to speak, paused, looked at me as if to say, "Where does one even begin?" and made his pitch. "Paul's point in those verses, Madge, is that we know God's grace by having faith in Jesus, not by trying to keep the law. It's an either-or situation, that's what the preacher was trying to say. And if we think that attending church and doing good things is going to..."

"I just don't see anything wrong with going to church," she retorted, "and trying to do what's right. I mean, look at everybody here," she said, gesturing around the reception hall. "Are we all doing something wrong? And, I'm not bragging, but I think I make God happy by all the good things I do."

John's eyebrows went up in surrender, but he ended with, "It's not about you, Madge; it's about God. Keep thinking it over." He took my elbow and steered me away, saying quietly, "She's probably harmless."

We moved across the room to congratulate our now official pastors, the Revs. Morris and Charlene Bryant. A few people stopped me or yelled out to tell me to have a good time in Russia. I was mentioned by Anna Louise Burnside in her "Around Town" column in the Evening Gazette yesterday: "Spotted walking around town – Rose Harris in her black cape and Hessian boots getting in shape for her trip to St. Petersburg, Russia, with son, Stephen. Have fun, folks!"

Charlene hugs, Morris shakes hands, which is perfectly fine. I do wish he'd get new glasses, though. His are the kind that automatically adjust to light, inside or out, and are always shaded a little, so he always looks a little shady, to me. As several of us have commented, they look enough alike to be brother and sister. Roundish faces with full cheeks. Similar dark brown haircuts, his longish and hers short. Same ample but not overweight body build and both on the short side with him a couple inches taller. I've decided to call them by their first names, since they've invited us to; simplifies matters. Wishing them well, I also thanked them for their innovations in worship.

"Facing the cross at the beginning of the service is so much better than having our backs to it. And I really cherish the moments of silence."

"Wow, somebody likes change—for a change," Morris cracked, nudging Charlene.

"Uh-oh. Have you gotten some flack?" John asked.

"You might say that," Morris said.

"Oh, it's not been too bad," Charlene picked up. "People need time to adjust."

I hope there's not too much negativity. A remark by Marsha recently gave me pause, something about how "trimming a few minutes off their sermons would be an improvement." Completely inappropriate for a church secretary to say. Why, she's not even there on Sunday mornings, just repeating something she's heard. Marsha has never exhibited the highest professionalism—or Christian behavior (in Rose's humble opinion).

"Well, Rose, have a great time in St. Petersburg," Morris went on. "I envy you. Bring us a little icon, okay?"

"Of course, my pleasure. I'll see you in a couple weeks."

"When do you leave?" Charlene asked.

"I'm taking the train to Chicago on Saturday to Stephen's. We take off from O'Hare a week from today, 2pm."

"Exciting!" she said, eyes sparkling for me.

That's for sure. A little unsettling, too, for an 81-year-old. Will I be able to handle it okay, with all my aches and pains? John's helpful. "You'll be fine," he says. "Take it one step at a time." Good advice, which I am trying to follow literally and figuratively. Yesterday I shopped for little tissue packs and sample sizes of mouthwash, etc. Stephen's cautioned me not to over pack. "We're going to St. Petersburg, not northern Siberia. The city's almost twice the size of Chicago." A side note: I met Claudia Townshend in the drug store. I just love Claudia and still miss seeing her and Michael and the girls every week. But our Church just wasn't moving fast enough for them, and she says their family is much happier in their "more liberal" denomination. She's excited for me about the trip, and I'm excited that she's going to organize a luncheon with Deedee Brewster and Carolyn Sauer and me like we had last February.

After church, John and I had a nice quiet lunch. Oh, and when he went to put the Sunday paper in recycling, he spotted my Advent wreath on the shelf above the dryer, under a plastic bag of old Christmas cards! Yup, I remember that moment.

I had to shoo John out a little while ago to make way for Mindy. She'll be here soon to tell me more about… aha, there she is...

Later

The question remains: Who is Marvin Whittaker? At least I know his last name now. Mindy couldn't tell me too much:

- brother of Larry's maternal grandmother
- rich and generous—always helping out family—put Larry through college—helped Larry's mother with a down payment on a house when she divorced
- has treated Mindy like one of the family ever since she and Larry had Darien— came to Darien's memorial service, that's where I first met him—came to Mindy's graduation—is paying for Miguel's defense lawyer

- world traveler, never in one place for long

"But Mindy, why would he plan a trip to Russia because I'll be there? The whole thing is outlandish."

"Yeah, I don't know. One thing about it, he gets on a plane around the world like it's a drive into town. Another thing, he takes a liking to people, like he has to me. Uncle Marvin's a truly nice guy. Even filthy rich, he's not too big for anybody. So I guess he really likes you. I don't think there's anything to worry about, Rose. All he said to me was that he thought it would be fun. He thinks you're all cultured and everything, and he sure is."

"Where does he live?"

"All over. I know he has houses in Florida and Chicago and Seattle. Spends a lot of time in New York City. When he comes to Shippensforge, he stays with Larry's mom."

"He told me he's in the import export business. Do you know anything about that?"

"Nope. You know more than I do by knowing that much. Basically, he's Larry's mysterious, rich uncle—great uncle, actually. Everybody in the family loves him."

This is just plain strange.

<u>Second Sunday of Christmas</u>

Jeremiah 31:7-14
Psalm 147:12-20
Ephesians 1:3-14
John 1:[1-9] 10-18

Speeding through space over the vast, dark ocean, this vessel that seemed huge on the ground is now a speck in the sky. I am overwhelmed by the vastness of the creation. Shakespeare had it right, calling stars "the blessed candles of the night." They twinkle light years away, and I slip comfortably into my tiny insignificance. Grace seems ever more real because I know how precious I am to this magnificent God.

This journey with Stephen, coming up so suddenly, is filled with all kinds of grace. January seems a month to survive, and an unusual vacation certainly helps. This is also perfect timing for getting some distance from John. And then there's the promise of a special closeness for Stephen and me. Since yesterday morning when he met me in the train station (Chicago covered with "snow like wool") we've been nicely in sync.

"I'm in a great place, Mom," he tells me. "You know that Hebrew word 'tov' you told me about one time, how everything is exactly the way it's supposed to be? That's how my life feels right now—lined up with God. I am totally content, even with the unknowns, and looking forward to whatever lies ahead." How good to hear such.

We've talked about the Marvin Whittaker situation. Stephen thinks it's mighty odd, too, but advises a positive approach. He asked how John's doing with it.

"Oboy. Thursday night he was at my house and Marvin called. John and I were already prickly—or at least I was. I hadn't slept well the night before and was what-iffing myself to pieces over the trip: What if I get a back attack on the plane? What if I can't find a bathroom? What if I can't sleep? And so forth. John suggested a game of Scrabble to help me relax. Oh, Stephen, I went into a silly, little rage. 'No! For heavens sake, John, you can't Scrabble your way through life. Sometimes you just have to cope!' I spewed at him. And then the phone rang, and I hear, 'Hello, lovely Rose. Marvin here. Please tell, dear lady, the name of your hotel so that we can reconnoiter.'"

"My St. Lord," Stephen laughed.

"It's funny now," I agreed, "but it sure wasn't then. I couldn't remember the name of the hotel but told him that it's right across from Dostoyevsky's grave, and he knew it. He's meeting us in the lobby at 10 o'clock Tuesday morning. He warned us not to sleep tomorrow before nightfall no matter how tired we are, just like the guidebook says."

"So was John mad over the phone call?"

"I spoke in a hush and told him it was Virginia," I admitted sheepishly. "Oh, and then on Friday morning, a dozen red roses were delivered with a note from Marvin, 'With best wishes for a safe and pleasant trip across the pond and on to St. Pete. See you there!' What a silly thing to do when I'm leaving town. I took them over to Anita and Jim."

"How did he sign the note?"

"'Fondly.'"

"Oboy."

"I know."

"Who ever knew you'd be in such popular demand in your 80s?" Stephen grinned.

Indeed.

We've been in the air about 5 hours, and I'm faring quite well. Lovely conversation, tasty meal, enjoyable movie, then a little nap. I was shocked awake by the words, "Get your hands off me, Father. I'm not dead." What in the world? Completely disoriented, it took me a minute to figure out that those unsettling words were spoken by the fellow sitting on the other side of Stephen. He'd said them 37 years ago to a Roman Catholic chaplain administering Last Rites to him on a battlefield in Vietnam. Even in that circumstance, he wanted no part of religion.

He said to Stephen, "Church-going Christians like yourself always surprise me. You're obviously highly intelligent and appear to be quite open-minded. If I may ask, what compels you to commit to a religion with implausible beliefs that despises anyone who is different?"

"Actually, that description doesn't fit my religion or my church," Stephen replied easily, and they began to talk in earnest. Their voices receded into the background as I thought of a scene during Holy Communion Stephanie recently described. She was kneeling with Mack standing next to her. As the pastor approached with the bread, Mack took his pacifier out of his mouth and laid it on the altar railing and looked up expectantly to receive what everyone else was getting. "Receive the kingdom as a little child," Jesus bids us. Mack's attitude was simply, "That looks good, I want it." Utterly trusting, unquestioning, ready to receive the good and free gift.

I'll try to let Mack be my role model of faithfulness, but—since God has given us minds that doubt and reason—I can't possibly be that way all the time. To be sure, I'm not unsympathetic to those who feel the way Stephen's non-believing friend does about faith and the Church. Organized religion, through the centuries and now, has plenty to turn people away. (If only we believers could recognize that Christ is our head, always working to fulfill the divine purpose—despite human efforts to the contrary. If we could live out this humble understanding, we would have a more expectant, patient, forgiving spirit than commonly exists in most communities of faith, I daresay.)

Keeping faith can be awfully hard even for diehards like me. I've learned from experience, however, that when doubts freeze my mind and soul, God eventually thaws them. God is in charge of all my back and forths. Lately, fretting about faith has given way to delighting in it. Especially real is God's love fully incarnated in Jesus. Seriously, knowing Jesus through the Bible and feeling the peace of his presence by the power of the Holy Spirit fills me with gratitude and peace. And now, I'm reminded of another church scene, Mercedes rocking in the pew repeating over and over, "Praise God, praise God," as though that is her only purpose for being. Another unwitting example symbolizing a life of faith lived to glorify the God of the cosmos.

Now, I'm thinking about all my people left behind. Not worried about Virginia and Barry. She sold a house last week, despite the economy, plus, they're on a second honeymoon cruise. Virginia says they're resting up for her taking over the Social Ministry Team at St. Tim's. "Barry's going to be my assistant, but don't tell him," she says with a wink. *A thousand thanks again, God, for their reconciliation and that Virginia is blessed to know her need of you.*

Stephanie Rose is getting ready for the new semester and working on a spring symposium: "The Politics of Kitchen Design in the 20th Century." Some of those titles crack me up, intriguing as they are. I am so proud of that wacky girl, Associate Professor of Women's Studies at 33 years old. And a sister of the soul for me, amazingly religious as well as spiritual for one of her generation. She talks the talk and walks the walk, as they say, at her inner city church, Transfiguration. Wonderful mother to Mack, and now, guardian to Angelica, troubled, beloved granddaughter of my dear, departed Florence Lawrence—which makes her John's great niece.

I well know the challenge of Angelica, since she lived with me for a brief, tumultuous time last year. Stephanie's household is a better match for her. All of this would surprise and please Florence—especially Angelica's soul-searching decision to get baptized at 16 years old. Now, she's enrolled in a cyber high school and speeding through the coursework, Steph says, "finally putting her brilliant intellect to good use." *Loving God, may Angelica continue to be aware of your graceful presence. And thanks, as always, for my precious Stephanie Rose and the adventures she provides to spice life up.*

Miguel's situation is always on my mind. John and I spent some time with him last week. John thinks Miguel is protecting one of his compadres. "Tell me, Rose; do you believe that boy could ever plunge a butcher knife into another human heart? No way."

"He's always seemed God-fearing—in the best sense of the word," I agreed. "And we've seen him be really courageous against injustice on several occasions. But, I don't know, John; in that overcrowded house and with all the drinking that went on…"

"I'll never believe it. He's taking the rap for somebody." John's probably right, but <u>why</u>, when his own life is at stake? *We pray for your protection for Miguel and strength for Mindy though this ordeal. How good that they are your children and know it.*

Sidney and Charlene are taking my turns on the schedule for Mercedes. She's had some incidents of wandering/disorientation, in fact, was found standing right in the middle of Washington Street. Yikes. We'd hoped walking would be safe for her since car and bike are no longer options. But she can't stand in the middle of the street! Charlene's holding a meeting soon with all who are helping. Great idea. *Mercedes has been your faithful servant for so many years, dear Lord. Help us to serve her now. Please inspire us with wisdom and strengthen us to respond lovingly to her growing needs.*

Josephine in Mississippi is still helping her neighbor have hope, working side by side with hospice folks and Doris's family. "She loves it when I read her Bible stories. I'll just keep doing it until she dies." *Many thanks, Creator God, for Josephine with her simple faith. Bless this time that she and Doris have together.*

Ah, here they come with hot towels again. Nice touch. Before they get to our row, I'll go to the bathroom, then sink back into my fairly comfortable seat with the luxury of the hot towel on my tired, dry skin. And then try to sleep the rest of the way.

I praise you and thank you, great and powerful God, for my privileged life. Move me more and more to be generous towards those less privileged. Sustain me through the physical challenges that lie ahead, and help Stephen and me be aware of you through the highs and any lows that may come. And this John-Marvin thing—is this maybe a good problem? They are both fine men, I believe. Calm my heart and soul, focus me on your purposes, one of which is that I delight in life. Most of all, accept my grateful joy for Jesus, your son, my Lord, because you are fully in him and he in you. Amen.

Genesis 1:1-5
Psalm 29
Acts 19:1-7
Mark 1:4-11

I love St. Petersburg! Onion domes, canals, broad streets—"Venice of the North." Our hotel is across the street from Alex Nevsky Lavra (monastery) where we walk past the graves of great Russians including Dostoyevsky, Tchaikovsky, Rimsky-Korsakov. And then we step into the church and hear a choir singing heavenly harmonies written by those buried outside. I still can hardly believe the wonder of it all, that I'm actually here.

As promised, Marvin met us in the hotel lobby on Tuesday morning and has been a gallant host all week. That first day, he took us on a luncheon cruise down the Neva River on a private yacht. First time I've ever been on a bona fide yacht. He must be a billionaire, I thought, as we floated past the imposing Hermitage, winter palace of the czars, pale green with cream and gold trim, huge statues lining the roof.

Then, at midnight, he escorted us to orthodox Christmas Eve worship. In the ornate church, Stephen and I were transported by the a cappella voices filling the high space with heart-shattering holiness. There were processions with incense and Bible encased in gold, icons kissed and honored, unseen priestly activities in the holiest space behind a special wall plastered with icons. This is called the iconostasis, Marvin explained. Worshipers stand, there are no pews, only a few chairs for the elderly or infirm. Considering our jet lag—and my age—Marvin insisted we sit and cued us when to stand at moments of high reverence. He was attentive to worship but—what?—uninvolved. In but not of. Afterwards, there was a festive breakfast—breads, cheeses, hard boiled eggs, dried fruit, sweets. The folks were friendly with Marvin, spoke Russian with him and welcomed us warmly. It was almost 4am when we got back to our hotel. Marvin continues to kiss my hand upon greeting and parting. Merciful heavens. Stephen and I slept into the afternoon and felt great, bodies adjusted, except for his nagging backache.

We also have Katya, our guide, who got us a driver, Vadim. Looking at Katya is almost like looking in a mirror! Tall and solid, short gray hair, no makeup, basic clothes, nothing fancy. Probably a decade or two younger than I, though. Highly cultured and very knowledgeable. In fact, she and Marvin have a little rivalry going, I sense.

He joined us for our tour of the Hermitage. This former palace is a museum now, room after magnificent room of carved woodwork, crystal chandeliers, and parquet floors, all filled with masterpieces. Rembrandt's "Return of the Prodigal Son" captivated us, especially with Katya's detailed information about its creation.

There was a funny moment when a tourist asked the attendant if the paintings were originals. Our little group laughed together, and then Marvin put his arm around my shoulder and said, "You, Rose Harris, are most certainly an original." Katya rolled her eyes at me and moved ahead. It was a bit silly—but I also felt very special, I must admit. Though not tingly, like with John.

She and Vadim argue a lot about which route to take, how to drive in the wild traffic, what year in Russian history something happened. Stephen and I listen from the backseat, Russian invective flying between them. We were concerned, at first, but soon realized their arguments are "sound and fury signifying nothing." Quite entertaining, actually.

While I puzzle over Marvin's attentiveness, Stephen has begun speaking of Penelope. They've had no contact since breaking up right after Easter last year, but he thinks he still loves her. He's not sure how to approach her, though, because she's devoted to being a parish pastor. Is there a place for him in her life, he wonders. Could he function as a pastor's spouse? And does he have what it takes to be married again? We've had many a backseat heart-to-heart talks about our love lives.

He teases me about having two boyfriends. Yeah. Pretty crazy. One day there were flowers for me at the front desk. From Marvin, I figured, but no. "Have a great time, Rose. Then come home to me, so we can be one, I hope. I'm taking good care of Cute Baby. All my love, John" I miss him terribly, at times—tenderness and affection, theological discussion, Scrabble and popcorn. Over a late afternoon meal at an elegant restaurant (Stephen staying at the hotel nursing his back), I told Marvin about John, that I'm seriously considering a proposal of marriage. "The short gentleman I met at Melinda's church on Christmas Eve?" he frowned. "Good heavens. Please be judicious in this matter, Rose." Stephen thought that was hilarious. A little snooty, to me.

Stephen's back is killing him. Katya's gotten him to a chiropractor a couple times which has helped. With pills and rest he's managing, but I hate it for him. As he laments, "I didn't come halfway around the world to rest."

We took in Prince Yusupoff's Palace where Rasputin was killed. No wonder there was a revolution, I keep thinking. The extravagance of the aristocracy and royalty in days gone by is appalling—and fascinating.

Winter palaces and summer palaces with theaters, libraries, ballrooms, dozens of guestrooms, formal gardens, all extravagantly and exotically furnished. In contrast—Peter the Great's cabin, the first residence, built in 1703. Peter was 6' 8" but his bed only 5' long because he slept sitting up due to respiratory ailments. Marvin joked he could envision me striding across the frozen wilderness on Peter's arm as he planned the great city, our black capes streaming in the wind. Stephen and I stifled giggles at his extravagant flattery.

Today (Sunday), he came with his shiny black car and driver and took us over several drawbridges to a Protestant church with familiar liturgy—and pews! During the homily, he put his arm around my shoulder and translated in my ear: "Jesus Christ is the locus of divinity... Jesus Christ connects heaven and earth... The revelation of God's glory in Jesus is for the whole world, starting with Israel... Jesus' divinity is revealed in history but also transcends history... 'Beloved' son does not simply mean feeling or affection; 'beloved' means 'chosen' for the divine purpose..." Amen to all that.

We dropped Stephen at the hotel to rest, then shared a lunch of borscht, cottage cheese, and crusty bread at a neighborhood restaurant. "I hope our friendship can grow," Marvin said taking my hand. "You are a delightful companion. Please consider joining me in the Caribbean in February." Yikes. Now, I had to ask: "Have you ever been married?" No, because he has too much respect for women and for the institution of marriage. He could never honor the commitment. I asked him about his import-export business and was he working in St. Pete? "Always working," he said evasively. Then we spent a splendid hour in Dostoyevsky's apartments, sacred territory for a teacher of literature, discussing the great writer's works. I asked Marvin if The Brothers Karamazov affected him at a spiritual level. "Purely intellectual, Rose—politics, social history, religious thought. Please remember, spirituality is an intellectual exercise for me." How can that even be?

When I got back, Stephen wanted to ride the subway and find a restaurant someone had told him about. I was so glad he felt like doing and going. The subway is deep and the escalator steep, intimidating to look up as we rise. People seem unfriendly, but maybe it's the same as U.S. cities—mind your own business. There is open drinking of alcohol on streets and trains. A man was wearing a T-shirt with the message, "Vodka is proof that God loves us and wants us to be happy." Stephen dismissed that with a little shake of his head—not so funny to a recovering alcoholic. Marvin helped him find an AA meeting here, and he's planning to go tomorrow night. People are mostly fashionably dressed, contrasted with beggars and street people, plenty of them, including gypsies. The food was well worth the ride, but then alas, Stephen had very little appetite.

This account covers such a small fraction of what we've done, a fabulous whirlwind, and three more days scheduled with untold delights before departure.

Thank you again, God, for the gift of this marvelous trip. And thank you, as always, for Stephen. He is my son, my beloved, with him I am well pleased— if I may share that sentiment with you. And he is your precious child—and knows that and lives that. Praise to you for both of our sons. Amen.

Wednesday

I'm sad to be leaving tomorrow, but I can't keep up this pace. Katya insisted we go to Peterhof, "the Russian Versailles." I argued I'd seen enough opulent excess, but she ignored me. She was right. Even with the extensive gardens dormant and fountains shut down, this estate on the shore of the Baltic Sea is a treasure of history, artistry, and natural beauty, enhanced today by a gently falling snow. My cape and boots from Virginia have been perfect for the weather. Then back to hotel to pack and rest.

But, hear this—on the way back Vadim stopped at a traffic light on Nevsky Prospect, and Marvin walked across the street right in front of us with two other men, in serious conversation. There was a distinct impression in this startling glimpse that Marvin was not pleased. The other two men looked nervous. Is he a Mafioso, for heavens sake?

"Ah, your boyfriend," Katya said dryly. "Not my business, Rose, but leave that one alone."

"No, marry this rich guy. Leave the John alone," grinned Vadim.

Stephen and I had a good laugh; obviously they'd been listening to our back-seat conversations! We bid them a fond and grateful farewell in front of the hotel. "We are friends, now," Katya said. "You have made a good start on St. Petersburg; come again and I will show you more." Not likely for me, but Stephen might.

Thursday, on the plane, over the ocean

Home again, home again. Just took off. Before heading for the airport, we took one last walk through the monastery grounds. I told the two angel statues who guard Tchaikovsky's grave to guard him well. His creative genius and tortured soul seem to personify Russian history.

There was a "goth" girl on our first flight, dressed all in black, who reminded me of Angelica which reminded me of her grandmother Florence

Lawrence. I wished so much I could talk with Florence about John (Should I marry your brother?) and Marvin—and suddenly I realized exactly what she'd say: "Snap out of it, Rose! You don't need either one of the old fools." And there was my answer. I told this to Stephen during our layover in Hamburg. He smiled and nodded like he'd been patiently waiting for me to discover the truth.

"I've decided, too," he said. "When we get back, I'm calling Penelope as soon as I can to check out getting married. I feel perfect peace about it." As do I, for him and for me—suddenly unburdened. Now, I'll try for sleep, perchance to dream pleasant dreams about this enchanting adventure.

Thank you so much, gracious God, for the blessing and the privilege of this trip. For feeding body and soul with good things, for Stephen, for Marvin, for Katya and Vadim. This time has shined like a star in a world that often seems dark and a darkness that we often take too seriously. Also, please guide me in finding kind words to tell John my decision. Amen.

Second Sunday after Epiphany

1 Samuel 3:1-10, [11-20]
Psalm 139:1-6, 13-18
1 Corinthians 6:12-20
John 1:43-51

Shippensforge is colder today than St. Petersburg, and we have wintry driving conditions, so Virginia stopped by for me this morning. Her hug told me she was glad to see me despite her first words of greeting after 17 days: "Oh, Mother, your blacks don't match—at all! Go ahead and change, we have time." I snorted and headed for the car.

Mindy had fishtailed to church, too. She squeezed my arm and whispered, "Where's John?" as we sat down together. "I'll tell you later," I said, enjoying the quiet, special ambience of the sparse crowd.

Maddie and Bryan Bowers had also made it, and the little girl waved her hand during the announcements to get Charlene to call on her. "This is Mr. Samsonetti, my teacher," she announced to us all. "I asked him to come and see our church and hear us kids sing, and, um—here he is," she ended, extending her arms toward him like Ed Sullivan introducing an act. Charlene chuckled with the rest of us, despite Maddie's serious demeanor, and welcomed Mr. Samsonetti kindly. She does everything kindly. "And now, the reading of God's holy Word. Let us be attentive," she moved us along. I settled back with a big sigh of contentment. I was home.

Morris chose the epistle lesson as his text, and one packed sentence from his sermon expressed well the wallop Paul gave the Corinthians: "Jesus gave himself for us; when we do the same—when we, as baptized children of God, let him dominate us, in big things and small, understanding that we are not our own anymore—our lives will be as rich and joyful as they possibly can be, on this earth and beyond."

How true I have found that to be in my long years. That's how I was raised, too, with my mother as the best model I've ever known of allowing Jesus to dominate one's life.

"She's talking to Jesus again," Dewayne would say, and I heard both amusement and unease in his kid brother voice. Once I witnessed one of her talks with Jesus. I was going downstairs and heard Mother's voice. Her bedroom door was open wide enough that I could look up through the posts and see her on the bench of her dressing table in front of the big round mirror. She was looking up at the picture of Jesus she had hanging on the wall—Sallman's Head, like so many people had in those days—and talking her heart out.

"Tell me what you want me to do, Jesus. If you want me to put Clarence out, I will. I feel like that would kill me," her voice trembled, "but if it's what would be best for all of us, I know you will grant the strength."

Apparently, Jesus never told her to do that because she never did. But she did give Dad an ultimatum; that I know from a journal entry of hers dated Dec. 19, 1941: "Jesus, I've told Clarence that if he doesn't try that new organization called Alcoholics Anonymous we will have to separate. He's killing himself and hurting the rest of us, you know that. You know me inside and out, God. You know my every move. You know what I'm thinking before I do. To try and escape you would be folly—and why would I? You are the former of my bones, the giver of my breath. I can only wonder at your greatness, dear God, never comprehending it, only standing in awe in the certain knowledge that I am yours and you are mine."

Helen Brinkley's strong spirit is with me still. She was not perfect. She had what we now call codependent tendencies, possibly even some obsessive compulsive disorder. On a day-to-day basis, she was picky and called up a feeling from us that we couldn't quite meet her standards. But loving and good she was. Much like the members of St. Timothy.

Malcolm Stafford is heavy on my mind. When I think of Malcolm I think: devout churchman, generous, kind, caring, wise. But Virginia told me after worship that he and Cynthia have split because he's involved with another woman (in Chicago) and has been for years. I keep thinking I'll never be shocked again, after everything I've heard and seen, and then something like this happens. Oh, Malcolm! Why didn't you let Christ dominate your life? I mean totally. What good is all your bowing to the cross and your huge collection of icons now? I am so disappointed, disillusioned, sad and mad.

At least my romantic escapades are over, forever, I vow. On Friday, we landed at O'Hare around 9am, and I was jittery all day thinking about breaking up with John. Stephen and I gave meandering, intermittent consideration to "ways to leave my lover." He was a calming influence, although, at the train station for me to catch the 6:40 evening train home, he tried to crack, "Mom, why don't you just write him a Dear..." I cut him off with a glum, "Don't even say it." But for all my stress, the break up went quite well.

John met me at the train. We shared a quick kiss and then made small talk as we drove. By the time he carried my luggage in, it was nearly midnight; we agreed he would come back on Saturday afternoon. I still didn't have any words planned when he arrived because my mind had gone so crazy thinking about the situation. I hadn't been awake long, either, sleeping away my jet lag. I could tell he was tense, too.

"Sure have missed you, Rose," with a hug, "and here's what I was thinking—instead of jumping right into serious conversation, how about you give me your memory stick, and I'll download your pictures, and you can tell me all about your trip."

Oh, dear God. The expensive digital camera he'd given me. Where was it? Still in my suitcase? I had tried to turn it down, told him I wasn't much of a picture taker, but he insisted I take it. Stephen doesn't take pictures either, but we tried. We got the camera out once, but something didn't work right, and we didn't know what to do, and I stuck it back in a pocket of my suitcase and meant to try again. I was going to see if Marvin or somebody could help us, maybe check the batteries or whatever, and then I forgot all about it. Oh, dear heavens.

"You didn't use it, did you?"

I shook my head, hating the tension stirring in me. His square jaw jutted out a little and accusation and hurt spread across his face. We stared at each other for a second, locked in surprise, and then I said, "I'll get your camera," and hurried to my bedroom. Anger sparked in me, too—at his persistent efforts to make me be like him—but my agitation quickly gave way to amusement at how thoroughly ludicrous our situation was. Being me, I got the giggles but had them under control by the time I walked back to the den. I was now at peace with saying and hearing whatever was necessary to end us.

He was looking out the window into the cold, barren backyard. "Would've never worked for us," he said, without turning around. "I can't compete with Charlie's ghost."

What? Where was that coming from? I haven't called him Charlie by mistake for several months, I'm sure. And I don't think I've ever compared the two of them out loud in his presence. I also try not to bring up memories of Charlie too often—but when you've spent most of your life with a person...

"I'm really surprised at that, John. I was married to Charlie for 50 years—but that doesn't mean my feelings for you aren't genuine. You've been a very special friend—more than a friend—" I choked up. "But it seems we both know that..."

He nodded, looking me in the eye for a sad moment. "All good things must come to an end, I guess."

What else to say? He took the camera and stood on tiptoes to kiss my cheek. And then we walked awkwardly to the front door, where all was now perfunctory. I thanked him for his friendship, said he was a fine person and I felt blessed to know him. "Same back to you, Rose Harris. You're a great lady, good as they come." Neither one of us said anything about a future relationship.

How bizarre—serious consideration of entering into a life totally shared and then presto! no relationship at all. My main emotion was relief, to tell the truth. I stared into space for a few minutes and then called Stephen.

"Wow, Mom; that wasn't so bad after all, huh? But I know you'll miss him; you two had some great times. It helps that you both know it's the right thing—so congratulations, I guess. And you can congratulate me, too," he moved quickly on. "I called Penelope this morning. I meant only to broach the subject of getting together, you know, but blurted out as soon as she answered the phone, 'Penelope, this is Stephen. If you still want to get married, I'm ready,' and she yelled okay!"

"That's my boy, direct and honest. We both found shortcuts around angst-laden, heart-to-heart discussion, didn't we?"

"Exactly. Denise and I had enough of those to last forever. Penelope and I don't need them."

They know each other. Stephen and Penelope know each other's hearts. Like Charlie and I did. After that marathon the night we met of telling our stories, we knew each other. And the simple acts of living and loving—imperfectly, clumsily, at times—were filled with grace sufficient to the day. *What a gift, dear God, and thank you for it!* A gift that John and I have not been given. *C'est la vie*, I can hear him saying.

How spiritual I feel on this Lord's Day! Good heavens, I sound like Madge. Be that as it may, I feel tuned in to the truth of the good life, which I most certainly have, and deeply grateful for precious people and places and resolutions to problems. I'm grateful for the children's choir this morning, too. Rhythm instruments were the crux of the matter, "noisy gongs and clanging cymbals" testifying through a peppy little ditty that we disciples are to "come and see" and then "go and be." Maddie seemed the lead singer, but all of the cherubs were pretty sharp. Applause exploded out of us sit-still-and-be-quiet Christians. Couldn't help it. "Let the people clap their hands!" That's in the Bible somewhere, isn't it? Yes, Lord, how very good to be home.

<u>Third Sunday after Epiphany</u>

Jonah 3:1-5, 10
Psalm 62:5-12
1 Corinthians 7:29-31
Mark 1:14-20

"Raise your hand if you would have liked to have marched through Osama Bin Laden's camp to warn him that he would soon be demolished," Charlene began her sermon this morning. "Jonah's task was very much like that," and she told his brief story, remarking that the fish swallowing him is probably the most plausible part. "But here's the gist of the story for us, folks: Are we willing to let God be God? Jonah wasn't."

"I am," Madge quietly volunteered behind us. Virginia, Mindy and I shared sideways smiles at her persistent piousness. (Not that I don't like Madge. We've had some special times together, and I've discovered a likeable woman way down under her holiness persona.)

Mindy had a different response to letting God be God. "I'm afraid I'm like Jonah; I don't want my God loving that creep Erik Schmidt for example." Marsha, church secretary, is the one I would put in that unlovable spot right now. Her gossiping and divulging confidences are cause for dismissal, as far as I'm concerned, never mind all the clerical mistakes. She caused problems for Pastor Sauer; now, she's doing the same for the Bryants. So, I need to pray for Marsha and then let God be God.

Another phrase, an old one, hit me in a new way—"Jesus calls us; oe'r the tumult of our life's wild, restless sea..." That old hymn zeroed me right into Angelica. I was so glad to see her yesterday. As Florence's grandchild—and John's great-niece—she'll always be precious to me. She came to the party Stephen and I threw to show and tell about our trip. She and Stephanie Rose and Mack arrived early to make borscht in my kitchen. I hadn't seen the child since Steph's (un)wedding. My point is that Angelica's "wild, restless sea" seems to be calming. For example, she'd spent time with both her mother and her father over the holidays. "Actually, I was surprised by fun. It was, like, redemptive at times," she told Stephanie and me.

She caught me staring at her while she was grating beets and said playfully, "What are you lookin' at, Grandma? Haven't you ever seen a girl in jeans and a sweatshirt before?"

"And sneakers instead of lace-up Victorian boots," I observed. "I guess your goth period is over?"

"Like totally, yeah," she said, then added, "A lot's over, really; a lot of hard stuff."

"You got that right," Stephanie agreed, squeezing her around the shoulders, an oh-so-proud guardian and friend.

"Your grandmother would be so happy to see you growing like this," I said, picturing Florence nodding her silvery head and smiling broadly.

"I know. I talk to Grandma Lawrence sometimes; I guess that's weird and I don't know if she like actually hears me, but I like to."

Not weird to me. I talked to Charlie for years after he died.

"I apologize to her and she forgives me for all the stupid, hurtful stuff I did. And Rose, I'm sorry for all the stupidity I did under your roof, too—smoking pot and trashing your beautiful guestroom and being a surly little goth brat. Gosh, I was a mess!"

Sitting in the high chair, Mack stopped eating banana chunks long enough to applaud her dramatic statement. Heavens, that boy keeps us laughing.

"You've got your priorities straight now," Stephanie put in, "since you're walking with God."

"Walking with God? That sounds too religious; I'm just trying to make it from one day to the next."

"Yeah, but don't you think you're trying to—you know—line up your life with God's ways?"

Ang considered as she grated. "That sounds good. Okay, yeah, I guess I'm trying to like line up my life with God's ways, sure. But the best part of this faith stuff is that I don't worry so much about being bad." She kept thinking, and we kept listening.

"I know what's new, what's different," she said brightly after a minute. "I've like totally, finally gotten it that I can't be as good as I want to be—and that I don't have to, for God to love me. I knew the words before, but now it's like in my bones." *Thank you, God, for this Good News. Thank you, Jesus, for calling to her over the tumultuous waters, for she was listening, always listening, even at her lowest, most miserable points of juvenile delinquency and dysfunction.*

She updated us on her parents. Father—"I'm still pretty wary around William" but she likes his wife and kids a lot. Her mother—"Sarah's Sarah, but I've stopped hating her. Now, I more like pity her." From hate to pity. Is that progress?

My English teacher chum Sarah Floyd arrived next. I invited her because 1) she's a pleasant addition to any gathering, 2) Angelica knows her from the short time she was enrolled at the high school, and 3) she has a Russian connection, going there every summer to teach English. "Sarah's becoming your new Florence, isn't she, Mother?" Virginia observed the other day. That's true, I guess. We hit it off immediately when we started teaching together twenty years ago, but now, yes, she's stepping into that best friend space. She gave hugs and then worked with her Russian crème cake, garnishing it with almonds and candied cherries. Oh, my goodness, there are no words to describe adequately its delicate, unique taste—although John would find the words—"good enough to make a dog break its chain," he would say—several times. I do miss him but not his clichés.

"How's Jacob?" Angelica inquired.

"Doing pretty well, considering. He asked about you a while back," I said, bringing a sweet flush to her face.

"Wait a minute; now, who's Jacob again?" Stephanie needed to know.

"He had that freak accident pushing a girl around in a shopping cart."

"Oh, yeah. A Mexican girl, right? She died, didn't she?"

I nodded sadly. "Her family was here harvesting crops, migrant workers. They took her back home, to die in Mexico," I sighed. "The kids were so foolish but so innocent, having a little frolic on a gorgeous spring day." How many times have we thought and said that? "The boy's carrying around a tremendous burden of guilt, naturally, but I think he's moving along. He pulled out of church for awhile, but now he's plugged back in."

"Wait a minute!" Stephanie said again. "Is it Jacob <u>Turner</u>, the basketball star from Shippensforge? Ethan's all the time talking about him. He's breaking all kinds of state records. I didn't know he went to St. Tim's."

"Sure you did; he's Pam's son."

"Pam and Greg Turner?"

"Yes, but they're divorced."

"That's right, I forgot. I hated that; I always thought they were the neatest family. I'm seeing a 7-year-old in my head, but Jacob's in high school, huh? Wow, he's carrying quite a load for a teenager."

"Yeah, but he'll be okay; he's a really strong person," Angelica stated.

"I agree with you, Angelica," Sarah said. "Jacob's not afraid to let his soul show; tragedy will strengthen him. You can tell he's still having it tough, though. He's burying himself in basketball and studies, which is actually a pretty positive response. Now, how about you, young lady? What's this I hear about cyber school?"

"It's like really cool, Ms. Floyd, perfect for me. It's student-paced; I can work as long and hard as I want to."

"She's almost finished a semester this month," Stephanie bragged. I suspected the girl was brilliant—Florence always said so—but she has disguised her intelligence well, especially while under the influence of drugs and the runaway life.

Then Sarah said, "Okay, Rose; let's have the lowdown on your love life."

"Uncle John's going back to California, I saw it on Facebook," Ang reported.

That threw me for a second, hit me in the tender void where he used to be, but apparently he can just move across the country without a twinge. That's projecting on my part; maybe he's twinging. We are no longer privy to each other's feelings.

"But how about charmin' Marvin?" Stephanie inquired sassily, bringing me back.

"Ha! That's a good name for him. He sent the flowers on the dining room table, the second bouquet since we got back. He wants me to spend February with him in Bermuda," I said, a little embarrassed. "I've told him no, but he persists."

"Rose!" Sarah yelled. "Have you looked out the window lately at the dirty mounds of snow—and a blizzard due next week. Why not go? Your passport's in order and..."

"I'm just not!" I said, surprising myself a little with my firmness, even while envisioning his photo of the lovely house surrounded by lush green plants and bright flowers. "Please come, Rose," he'd encouraged. "It's paradise and you deserve paradise. I have a good library. You could be the queen, sitting on the balcony in the ocean breeze..." I don't do queen very well; not my style. Plus, I still hardly know him. And yet, I found myself suddenly wistful at the memory of his gallantry and attention in Russia...

The doorbell rang and Anita, Jim, Mindy and the Bryants were on the front step together. I'd seen my pastors in the grocery store Friday and invited them. Good chance to get better acquainted. Plus, Jim and Anita could get to know them a little bit, too, in case they want to pursue baptism for their baby. Crazy idea to me, but—let God be God.

Oh, it was a happy party! Virginia and Barry had baked this wonderful crusty bread, and Stephen and Penelope—yes, Penelope came—brought some items from a Russian grocery in Chicago. We spread out all over the house to eat, I in the den with Mindy and the Bryants.

Mindy reported on Miguel's case. "Progress is so slow I hardly even ask anymore," she frowned. She guesses lawyers are preparing their cases, but no trial date has been set.

Then Morris asked, "Rose, now tell me—who is John?"

"Don't worry about it; he's gone," Mindy joked, but I explained the situation and told what a fine fellow he was. And I told them about

Stephen's engagement, too. When we crowded around the dining room table for "show and tell," Penelope exuberantly announced a June wedding followed by a trip to the Holy Land. Congratulations all around and they were both beaming. Happiness seems a reasonable expectation. I have to confess, though, that when Stephen reached his decision on the trip, I was so excited for him that I pretty much forgot what a challenge Penelope is. Stephen's always said that one of the reasons he and Denise divorced was because she was too controlling, but Penelope is far more dominating, from what I see. She's too much. Why, I think she talked more than Stephen and I put together about our trip! She had read all the booklets and heard Stephen's accounts and away she went. "This was where..." and "Stephen's favorite was..." and "The Orthodox services there are like..." Too much.

Nonetheless, the questions from the crowd were many and our adventures were well-shared. They teased us that we couldn't prove we were even there, though, since we had no photos of ourselves. We smiled and shrugged, not mentioning John's camera.

Farewells matched the fun of the afternoon. I heard Morris tell Jim he enjoyed their discussion—theological, I wonder? Sarah invited Angelica to come and spend a weekend with her and go to a basketball game. Mindy asked me to do the "St. Pete travelogue" at the jail for Miguel, which I'm looking forward to doing. Mack screamed disconsolately at having to leave. "He's not good with transitions," his mother apologized, and Grandma Gin carrying him to the car helped a little. Meanwhile, my wonderful son-in-law was cleaning up the whole place.

Stephen and Penelope hugged me at the front door, setting out for Chicago. I had noticed him wince a couple times throughout the afternoon and asked about his back. "He has an appointment with his internist on Tuesday. And no more chiropractors on my watch!" Penelope declared. He joked, "What she said—except maybe about the chiropractor; we'll see about that," and they walked down the sidewalk arguing over it. *God be with them.*

So that was yesterday. Now some quiet time to stare into space and meditate and play piano for awhile. Then Masterpiece Theater and good old peanut butter popcorn. Cute Baby sure loves the stuff; comes a-runnin' when she hears me get out the Whirly Pop. Is that normal, for cats to eat popcorn? Not that Cute Baby's normal.

Thank you, Lord, for this rich, full life of mine. I join my prayer with the psalmist—For you alone my soul waits in silence, oh God. You alone are my rock and my salvation, my fortress; I shall never be shaken. Amen.

<u>Fourth Sunday after Epiphany</u>

Deuteronomy 18:15-20
Psalm 111
1 Corinthians 8:1-13
Mark 1:21-28

The Bryants have been with us ten weeks now, and changes are everywhere. They've had training classes for acolytes, crucifers, ushers, altar guild, lectors, and communion assistants, so worship is looking very sharp these days. They've made a point of including people like Danny as worship leaders. He carried the cross in this morning, ever so careful and reverent. Madge Humphries and Pat O'Schaughnessy assisted with communion for the first time. This was extra meaningful to me because of a conversation in the hallway I overheard last week when I was working in the church library.

"Pastor Charlene, I'm worried over something I heard. Can I talk to you about it?"

"Certainly, Madge. What's the problem?"

"This may be wrong, but I heard that Pat O'Schaughnessy is going to be a communion assistant."

A short silence as, I presumed, they looked at each other, Madge thinking the problem had been stated, Charlene waiting to hear it.

"So, I was wondering if that's true—" Madge faltered on, "and if it is, it seems to me that's wrong, with his drinking problem and he doesn't even have a job, I don't think, does he?"

Another pause and I wished I could see Charlene's face. I think she didn't know what to say—so Madge kept talking, as she is wont to do. "Pastor Charlene, I know a lot more about the Bible than Pat, I'm sure. Plus, Holy Communion is about sharing God's love and, please don't think I'm bragging, but I really love the people in this church."

"Well, Madge, would you serve as a communion assistant, too? Can you come to training tomorrow night?"

"Oh, absolutely. Oh, yes, I really want to. I'll be there, Pastor!"

Boy, Charlene's good.

So here we all were this morning. Pat filled my tiny cup with wine, his hands shaking. I noticed Madge's hands were shaking, too. *Thank you, Holy Spirit and humble spirit of Jesus for being here through all of our human high jinks.*

Mindy and I enjoyed chatting with Rita and Louie during coffee hour. Rita thought the sermon was great. "It was like Morris painted a picture of Jesus being all in charge and confident without being high and mighty."

"Yeah, and when Jesus exercised…"

"Ex<u>or</u>cised, Louie," Rita corrected.

"…yeah, ex<u>or</u>cised that devil it was like Jesus was hollerin', 'Hey, people, this is how the world's really supposed to work.' Makes me feel like I have this target to try and hit every day, instead of shootin' in the dark."

I treasure Louie and Rita's lived-out faith. To be honest, I'd found the sermon rather dry and hadn't gotten much out of it, so three cheers for community! People like Louie and Rita remind me that life in the Spirit is more about day-to-day energy than spectacular happenings.

We chatted with the pastors, too. "We were just hearing compliments on your sermon," Mindy told Morris.

"Really? From the living or the dead?—by which I mean sleeping."

"Stop joking, Morris. You're not kidding anyone with your false modesty. Graciously accept a compliment," Charlene urged.

"She's on to me, as usual. Thank you kindly," he said, bowing to us.

Charlene asked, "Did someone like the part about Jesus breaking into people's reality like the star of "This Old House" charging into your workshop telling you how to re-arrange your tools and, while you're at it, give them to the poor?" I chuckled remembering that pretty good illustration.

"Well, it's true," Mindy said. "We don't like our lives being messed with, especially when we've got them the way we want them."

"Exactly. Opposition is often the response to truth," Morris observed.

Everybody was talking about basketball, the Smithys still undefeated for the season, and congratulating Jacob. He had 27 points, five 3-pointers, on Friday night. I go to games with Sarah, and this was the most thrilling so far. Most of the congregation and half the town are there to cheer them on, very high energy. But instead of the smile he used to flash on the court so readily, Jacob plays seriously with clenched jaw. That's the best he can do right now—and that's good enough.

I may see his mother when I go out to Rutledge Home this afternoon. Being supervisor of nursing there is clearly a ministry for Pam, one of my favorite younger friends. And speaking of the younger set, Claudia Townshend, Carolyn Sauer, and Deedee Leppard/Brewster and I had our second annual luncheon on Thursday. They call me "Matriarch" and "Mother Superior" in tribute to my long years, and how I appreciate their attitudes and perspectives to help me not go too far over the old fogey line.

Just getting our food ordered was a little crazy. Claudia, radical peace-with-justice activist and dedicated vegetarian like Stephanie Rose, had a weird and overwhelming desire for red meat. We encouraged her to go ahead and eat that Philly-style cheesesteak and not worry about it, but she was very unsettled and started quoting statistics about how many rainforests are lost providing grain-fed beef to obese Americans, yakkity-yakkity-yak... Carolyn cut her off with, "Oh, for crying out loud, Claudia, how about if we all eat vegetarian—and you stop whining?" So, portabellas and eggplant filled the table. Quick highlights about each of us:

- Claudia – Daughter Rachael is "unfortunately exhibiting all the symptoms of the common teenager" so she and Michael are trying to be "elastic" in both staying close and giving space. Somehow inclusive language came up—usually does with Claudia—and she mentioned a translation of the psalms that eliminates male pronouns when referring to God. "Maybe," she declared earnestly, "my children can mature in faith without being imprinted with God as an old man with a white beard!"

- Deedee – Grief still defines her, sixteen months after Chad's death in Iraq. Naturally so, and even so, for she shows beauty and grace and humanity in her mourning. As for the children, Johnny is still her biggest worry, filled with anger difficult for a 6-year-old to understand or handle. His Grandpa Bruce had the idea of enrolling him in martial arts which has been good. They're all getting counseling through the VA. Nick is her little "stalwart." He and Brucie play "Daddy," taking turns being Chad, and the other day 3-year-old Brucie said to Theresa, the littlest, "Hi, little girl. I'm your daddy and I'm never going to forget you." Oh, my. Breaks and mends the heart in one blow.

- Carolyn – Daughter Brittany drove up with her so she could visit her teenager friends. "How's Marcus doing at his new congregation after—what?—nine months?" Deedee asked for all of us. Carolyn said there are the usual characters. "We have a Sidney Wright and a Louella Rutledge and sort of a Rose Harris," she smiled at me, then sighed. "It's good, everything's okay; it's hard work being a pastor, and tricky to measure success or effectiveness or whatever you want to call it." Pause, like she was deciding whether to share something or not. Not. She closed the subject with, "But we're good." Pretty half-hearted assessment. I hope Pastor's not experiencing major problems and also that marriage struggles are not hard again.

58

- I unloaded about John, encouraged by their caring attitude—empathetic yet light-hearted. It turned out to be a healthy purging, including the moments of sadness and loneliness. Nothing like girlfriends to get one talking! I had fun responding to their questions about Stephanie Rose's aborted wedding, Stephen's engagement, and the Russian trip.

My, 'twas great. I remember fondly and treasure the times when all four of us were together in worship and ministry Sunday by Sunday. But life changes and staying in touch like this compensates. Who knows what changes our third annual luncheon will bring, but I look forward to it.

Thank you, Loving God, for this little group of open, honest sisters. Thank you for your presence with each of us—Deedee, Carolyn, Claudia, and me—as we walk the journey of faith with all of its steep grades, potholes, and hazardous conditions. Amen.

Later – Sunday night call with Stephen

"What's new?" I started out.

"Not much," came the expected reply.

"How's Penelope?" I inquired, to signal that his caring mother is here if he needs to call off his engagement. (Pull in your thorns, Rose.)

"Great. Mom, I know she comes across as pushy, but believe me, we've got that under control. I've been in an unhealthy relationship, and I can tell this is healthy, this is it."

"Okay, Stephen. It's reassuring to hear you say that. In a spirit of full disclosure, I need to say—as you already know—I find Penelope difficult. But I see her beauty, too, and I will love her for your sake. You don't need to have any concerns about problems between us."

"Yeah, I know. I love that about you, Mom, how you insist on seeing the best in people. Things will work out fine. Penelope will relax more as she gets to know you and Gin and everybody. It'll be fine."

His main doctor has referred him to a urologist to check out the kidney system and an orthopedist to check out vertebrae alignment and bone condition. Appointments set for this week. He's managing okay with over-the-counter meds. "Don't worry, Mom," he said. I'm not worried. I just want him to figure out the problem and get rid of the pain. And on top of the backache getting worse, he's got flu, poor boy. But Stephen's in great shape. With the enthusiasm of a kid he said, at one point, "I'll tell you what Mom, I'm looking forward to the rest of my life in a way that I never expected." Music to a mother's ears. *Thank you, God.*

Fifth Sunday after Epiphany

Isaiah 40:21-31
Psalm 147:1-11, 20c
1 Corinthians 9:16-23
Mark 1:29-39

"Get a good night's sleep and a hearty breakfast and put on your running shoes before you start the Gospel of Mark," Pastor Phillips used to say. Immediately! At once! As soon as! Now! Jesus is in perpetual motion, proclaiming and enacting the mighty works of God, virtually breathing out divine forgiveness and healing to the whole world.

"The whole world including us," the preacher emphasized this morning. "Remember, Jesus' revelation of God's nature is surely for us as much as for those he actually looked at and spoke to and touched."

"Yeah. Cool," Mindy murmured.

Life began quietly for me last week, neither event nor people in my day after Sunday morning worship. Nothing/no one on Monday either. Charlene had mentioned meeting about Mercedes on Monday, but I knew I was in need of time for body and soul to catch up with each other and spent the day in personal retreat, praying, reading, journaling.

Oh, how refreshing, dear God. Your Spirit renewed my strength, and I enjoyed a rare night of sound sleeping. I awoke like Jesus after his time in the wilderness, ready to say, "Let us go on."

But activity kicked in dramatically Tuesday morning, starting with the convening of the "Mercedes team"—Charlene, Sidney Wright, Malcolm Stafford, and I. And Mercedes, of course. Malcolm's presence was necessary, since he's been her lawyer for decades, but awkward due to his and Cynthia's divorce situation. I consider him to be a friend; we've had many a good theological talk at retreats and so forth, but we've not conversed since the break-up became public. Awkward and strange, but we managed.

Well, I'm building up to a surprise here. We assessed Mercedes's current condition and medical prognosis, the main input on that being from Sidney who hears every word her doctors say. Dementia associated with Parkinson's disease is the official diagnosis, no surprise. Then Malcolm summarized her financial situation and reported that a search had found no heirs and her money would last less than two years in a nursing home. At appropriate intervals, Charlene would ask Mercedes if she understood. "Some of it," she would say. "Do you want to stay in your house?" she was asked at one point. "Or die," she nodded, matter of factly. We agreed that the optimum solution is to have a live-in person who would work for room and board and a small stipend. We closed with prayer, acutely aware that finding such a person would not be easy. And then last night, Josephine called. Her neighbor Doris has died, and she announced, "Rose, I'm coming back to Shippensforge. I have a feeling I'm needed there." Go-o-od Shepherd (another of Steph's early expletives).

I didn't mention Mercedes to Josephine, but was excited to tell Charlene this morning about the possibility. We both think this might work. In Josephine fashion, she will be here soon.

Then I went to Lydia Circle that evening, after grocery shopping. Zounds! Those bags get heavier all the time, and I was tired but also eager to be with my circle sisters after missing January's meeting. And then confound it, they made me mad. Anna Louise Burnside started it during refreshments. Oh, this woman tries my patience with her cluelessness!

"Marsha's cancer has come back, you know. I worry for her; she's already overworked—church secretary is a huge job—and," Anna Louise's voice and eyebrows turned gossipy, "she's not finding our new pastors too easy to work with."

Then it was like demons entered the crowd.

"Why does Pastor Charlene raise her hand in the air to cue us on responses? We know when to come in, for heaven's sakes."

"Well, at least she's got some spontaneity; that husband of hers is too stiff and formal."

"Well, I don't like all those collection boxes in the hallway. The building's a mess..."

"Do you all realize that there hasn't been a single potluck dinner since they came?"

My dander was rising with each criticism. I didn't want to be preachy or patronizing, but I'd had enough and interjected firmly, "We have called these people to be our spiritual leaders, and we have promised to love, respect, and support them." An uneasy hush prevailed as we ate our dessert, Madge muttering, "We were just having some fun." Fun?! Madge knows better than that.

God, please grant me true humility in this matter, and guide me with your wisdom. Save me from self-righteousness. Help me forgive and love them, for they seem not to know what they are doing. Encourage Charlene and Morris in their loving efforts and help us all act in charity toward one another, the better to serve you. In Jesus' name, Amen.

As soon as I finished lunch on Wednesday, I headed downtown to the jail.

"How are you doing, Miguel?"

"With the Father's blessing, I am okay, Miss (Meese) Rose," he said, making the sign of the cross. Miguel may be the most religious person I know. I can imagine him kneeling in the village church beside his mother, crossing himself with chubby 3-year-old hands, earnestly helping her live through desperate poverty in Mexico, his father already dead from trying to cross the border. In our ordinary Indiana town, I have seen this young man stand courageously for justice, always with love.

"And how are you doing, Miss Rose?" with his kind sonrio (smile).

How I wanted to ask him about the murder. "How was it that night? Did you really do it? Tell me the deepest secrets of this horrible happening." But—he guided us in other directions. He showed me a letter from John in California, heavy with encouragement and cheer, and my eyes stung. He asked me, whenever I pray for him and "Meendy," also to thank God for Uncle Marvin's generosity and for Pastor Morris, faithfully visiting each week—and for Erik Schmidt. "Love your enemies and pray for those who persecute you…"

I had brought my artifacts from Russia, and each one fascinated him. He told me he prays with the icon of the Theotokos—Mary and Child—I brought back for him. He was fascinated by the splendor of St. Issac's, too, and asked many questions about our worship experiences. As has become our playful custom, we reversed languages upon parting. "La paz del Señor esté con usted," I said, grasping his hand. "And also with you," he responded with that smile.

Miguel's fervent piety, invoking Father, Son, Holy Spirit, and "Virgen Maria" at every step, is not my style, exactly, but sometimes I do it, too, when I'm with him. Do I have multiple personalities when sharing faith with others? I'm one way with one person and another way with the next, depending on each one's place on the faith spectrum. I wouldn't, for example, talk with most folks at St. Timothy as piously as I do with Miguel. With Anita and Jim, in contrast, I use God/Jesus language judiciously (except when "very God of very God" pops out of my crazy mouth!). Right after my time with Miguel, I had time with them.

Immediately upon turning into the driveway, as the garage door started up, I saw Anita tromping through the snow carrying Cute Baby. I hurried through the kitchen door and met them at the front. Kitty cat had gotten into their garage again. Anita poured the gray fluff into my arms, and we cuddled for a moment—Cute Baby and I—and then she hopped down and trotted off.

What will I ever do without this cat? She's my age, in human years, and won't go on forever.

Anita and I had a cup of tea. She was all blue because of a Shanghai high-rise fire killing 53, her pathological compassion in full swing. I got her talking about the baby, and she cheered up a little. Then Jim came over. He was impatient with her "funk." The three of us got into a half-hearted, quasi-spiritual conversation. I was glad when they finally left.

I rushed to the food pantry on Thursday morning, having overslept, and worked from 9 to 1. Whew, busy! And sad. And cheery. And difficult. All of the above. Jerry Evans came in for food; he's been laid off for nearly a year. Jerry and I aren't that well acquainted—I know Mary Jane a lot better—but he recognized me from church, I'm sure. He instinctively ducked his head when he first saw me, then reared up and complained loudly about a government that couldn't provide work for its people, forcing them to take handouts.

"Son," a gentleman about my age said, as he received his bags, "I used to give this place twenty-five dollars every month, and look at me. I'm on the other side now, that's how it is. But we're both gonna' make it. I can feel it in my bones! You hang in there; you've got nothing to be ashamed of." Jerry said nothing more—except thank you.

Then on Friday Virginia, Barry, Sarah, and I went out to supper together before the basketball game. Two overtimes, and the Smithys pulled it out. For the winning point, Jacob made an astonishing pass that a teammate jumped high to catch and dunk in one motion, right as the buzzer sounded. "Don't forget to take your blood pressure pill before you come to these games," someone joked. The next two are out of town.

I appeared at Mercedes's door on Saturday to cook. First, we went grocery shopping and then made a batch of chicken salad, big pot of vegetable soup, one of her favorite concoctions with carrots and celery and walnuts and pineapple in orange gelatin, and a recipe of oatmealers. She can do the work okay, just needs someone around to make sure burners get turned off and freshly prepared food gets put in the refrigerator and not the wastebasket. Mercedes alone in that house is a time bomb. Sure do hope the Josephine idea works out.

So—I am exhausted after the week that was. But, along with the rest of the crowd this morning, I was reconstituted and strengthened for service, and, once again, we have something to offer a weary world. And what is the compensation for all this service? Joy. *Thank you, thank you, thank you, God, Jesus, Holy Spirit. Thank you.*

<u>Sixth Sunday after the Epiphany</u>

2 Kings 5:1-14
Psalm 30
1 Corinthians 9:24-27
Mark 1:40-45

Stephen has pancreatic cancer.

Transfiguration of Our Lord

2 Kings 2:1-12
Psalm 50:1-6
2 Corinthians 4:3-6
Mark 9:2-9

5am

There is no hope. *Oh, my God is it true? Are we to believe the doctors? Please God NO! pleasepleasepleasepleaseplease Don't let this be. Take this from us. Not Stephen. Not now. Please God no. I beg of you no.*

Penelope doesn't believe the prognosis. They will fight. There are plenty of people in stage IV pancreatic cancer who live for years. Not very many, actually. I have Internet, too. I want to believe he can survive. I'll join the fight. I won't stop hoping. But...

I don't know what to believe. My brain and heart are under siege. I can barely breathe, much less think. I can barely write. *Oh God no please no! What am I to believe? About the cancer. About you God. I thought my faith was strong, but now all I have is confusion and despair and pain. I want answers—but not the answer that Stephen is... Oh God, not that answer.*

5pm

We gathered at Virginia and Barry's for our noon meal. Nobody ate much and poor little Mack fussed and shrieked most of the afternoon, probably molars cutting through. Today is unseasonably warm, and we sat on their deck in the winter sun, going over and over Stephen's situation.

"So what's a healthy life style worth?" Barry observed bitterly. "Like Frank Hammond. Exactly like Frank. Out of nowhere, no warning signs until it's too late."

"Remember how I told him how trim he looked at Christmas dinner," Virginia mused, "and how he didn't eat much and we thought he was dieting? That was probably the cancer."

"I've thought of a million little things like that," I nodded. "His backaches in Russia..."

The baby fretted in his sleep in Stephanie's arms. "I talked to him yesterday afternoon," she said, "and he sounded..." She couldn't finish the sentence, and we all sniffled quietly until she could speak again. "He sounded so sick and weak. My gosh, we just found out, and his voice has already changed from normal to sick."

"We've got to see him!" Virginia burst out. "I feel like Penelope is keeping us away, moving him to her place way south of Chicago; we don't even know where he is. She's not even one of us, and she's got him. Mother, we've got to do something! What can we…"

Barry cut in. "Calm down, Gin. They're as good as married, remember. She's his caretaker, and from what I've heard, she's been consulting and taking him to appointments pretty much 24/7."

"Right. Barry's absolutely right—Penelope is his helpmate; she's the one, no matter how challenging we may find her, and we need to respect that and trust Stephen's judgment, and that he's in charge," I encouraged my family—and myself. Entrusting my own son—can I even say it?—who ~~is~~ may be dying to a woman I barely know is a terrible thing.

"That's just it! He can't be in control; he's too sick," Virginia persisted. "But—but—oh, hell, I know you're right, Mother, about Penelope." She sank back into the cushions of her chair, holding her face in her hands. "This is just going to be awful."

"We'll see him soon, one way or the other," I vowed. "They may be going to Johns Hopkins next week, and she's in touch with Mayo Clinic, too; her cousin is a nurse there."

They call me almost everyday. Sometimes Stephen is too tired to talk, and Penelope fills me in. His CA 19-9—that's a "tumor marker" measuring some substance produced by cancer—is 48,000 when it should be no higher than 45. I hear of "Whipple surgery" and "Gemzar treatments" and, worst of all, "TNM" for Tumor – Node – Metastasis. Oh, dear God, he has them all. "Aggressive and highly resistant to standard treatments…" Everything comes through a haze of disbelief. *Please God please a miracle. Let this be a crazy nightmare, and we wake up and…not Stephen, please God, not my son.*

We went to church together this morning, too, except for Barry, of course. Stephen's on the prayer list, and there was lots of concern because everybody knows and loves Stephen. He's been at St. Timothy almost every Sunday of his life until moving to Chicago summer before last, serving on council, teaching Sunday School, working shoulder to shoulder with everybody. *Your servant, God. Please save him.*

Your Word was well-preached, Lord God. I heard it, I understood it—we're moving from the brightness of the Transfiguration on the mountain into the Lenten journey, Jesus on the road to Jerusalem, to the crucifixion, to the resurrection. But it was just talk. What has that to do with Stephen? I can make the connection in the abstract, but not in the concrete, not right now. All I can think or feel or say is NO. Oh dear God.

They lined up to hug us: Rita and Louie with his big old bear hug (Stephen was Rita's AA sponsor), Danny ("R-R-Rose, I don't want S-S-Stephen to die!"), Madge, Sidney, Theodore and Lloyd, Paul Wakefield, young Jacob and mother Pam, the pastors, Maddie Bowers with a tight child's hug, Deedee and her crew. Sarah calls often and took me out to dinner last week; she's a great comfort. And talking with the Sauers the other night was good for my soul. Mindy hovers sweetly. I've been avoiding my neighbors; as far as I know, they haven't heard about Stephen. No need to upset Anita, and I have no desire to hear Jim's atheistic thoughts on this subject.

But maybe all this sympathy and concern will turn out not to matter because Stephen will get better and...I can't write anymore. Here comes Cute Baby. She'll climb up my chest and lick away my tears. *But I've never had tears like these, God.* I haven't cried all that much, actually; that would be admitting defeat. I exist in a state of shock, waking up in worry, waiting for the next phone call with huge hopes that there will be good news.

I must write a little bit more—about Stephen—about how he's doing with all this—about what a good man he is—about his faith. He's in shock, too, at the suddenness and severity—"takes my breath away." He wants to live life fully, no matter how much or little of it he may have left, but doesn't feel well enough or have enough energy to do much. "I don't have good feelings about this, Mom; I can't conjure up the determination and hope that Penelope has," my ever honest and open son told me. "But—and this is kind of weird—I have no fear at all, not even a little, at least not yet." And he went on to say that he...I can't write anymore. Cute Baby, come along.

Ash Wednesday

Isaiah 58:1-12
Psalm 51:1-17
2 Corinthians 5:20b—6:10
Matthew 6:1-6, 16-21

"I am so not in the mood for Lent, Grandma," Stephanie's sad voice said on the phone this morning.

"Me either," I sighed back, and decided at that moment to stay home tonight. My heart feels too heavy to drag over to the church. I need no ashes rubbed on my forehead to remind me that we are dust and to dust we will return. That's what I told Virginia when she called and offered to stop by for me. Barry started talking to her in the background, and she said, "Barry says you need to go." I began to fend that off when she said, "He says he'll go if you will." I couldn't stand up against my favorite agnostic offering to worship with me. I'm sure it was a better option than sitting home alone—and going felt like working with God in mysterious ways.

But it was tough. And I didn't go up for ashes. Virginia nudged me and whispered, "Are you going up for ashes?" Bleary-eyed and dull, I shook my head, a hurting mother's stubborn protest.

The pastors both preached, in dialogue. "Psalm 51 is the big gun for when we're up against our own sinfulness," Morris started out, and Charlene reminded us that, traditionally, David is thought to have written this psalm after the prophet Nathan confronted him with God's anger over his adultery with Bathsheba and murder of her husband Uriah. They reflected that the psalm is not only for individuals but is also beautifully appropriated as a communal prayer in our liturgy, and we sang a lovely new setting of "Create in me a clean heart, O God..."

They didn't dwell on adultery, but I think maybe Barry did. He stayed in the pew, hunched and staring, while we went up for communion. Not that he would have partaken anyway. That's my hunch, that he was confronting his own sinfulness, but I'll say this: If Barry ever does believe in divine forgiveness, he will not take it for granted. And then I noticed Malcolm at the far end of a pew on the other side. He was kneeling low and didn't commune. I guess he's going through a hard time, too, with his sinfulness—and I wish I could help—but I don't know how—he would be the one to initiate—and now, with Stephen, it's hard to think about other people's troubles. *Dear God, may Malcolm be aware of your presence and be strengthened by it. Cynthia, too. Amen.*

When we entered the building tonight and smelled the soup supper and then again when fasting was mentioned in the lessons I tried to remember if I'd eaten today. I'm trying to have some tea and cinnamon toast and a banana now, but it has little flavor. How can I enjoy food when Stephen can't? Am I trying to lose weight myself, in a show of sympathy? He's lost eight pounds in the last eight days, for a total of 35 since early November. *Oh my son! God my son! Do you see this?*

We'll see Stephen this weekend; they're driving over. They went through the one-day clinic at Johns Hopkins yesterday. "No encouragement there," I hated to hear him say when we talked a little while ago. They're (he and Penelope) at odds about participating in a clinical trial. His take is that it will only—*Oh, God, I don't even want to write this down*—prolong "things," with virtually no chance of reversing anything or even relieving symptoms. Her take is, well, what mine would be, I think.

She got on the phone and said, in desperate tones, "Mama Rose, he won't even try! He has everything to lose, and he won't even try…won't consider that God's hand might be in the medicines and therapies…"

Stephen got back on and went outside to talk. "She's irrational, not even in the ballpark yet, Mom. They looked at every diagnostic piece and talked to me for over an hour; we're just not going to get what we want on this. She wants to consult on integrative medicine and go to Mexico and—I'm just not up for…" His voice broke, and my heart, again. Oh, and they got married last week. And Penelope's taken a leave of absence from her church.

Oh, God, help! I don't know how to do this. I don't know if I can.

I went nuts checking my email every five minutes this morning, listlessly wandering around the house, unable to think or focus. In this crazy little corner of my brain, I kept thinking there might be an email from a clinic or a doctor or Penelope announcing that the cancer is miraculously gone. No. There was a kind message from John. Angelica had told him about Stephen, and he offered to come, if he could be of help. I wrote back thanks, but no. Marvin heard from Mindy and called with encouraging words, offering "whatever kind of assistance is needed for the splendid chap."

Charlie is the only man who could help. *Charlie! Have you heard about Stephen? Do you know? Oh, what are we to do, Charlie? If only you were here to share this terrible burden with me. It's so painfully cock-eyed, Charlie. I shout to God, "Here I am; take me!" You know that I'm ready to go, but Stephen is in his prime with exciting plans for… These words and thoughts sicken me with their pointlessness… Charlie, I can't get a grip.*

Jim's found out; he heard about Stephen from a mutual acquaintance. He knocked at the front door yesterday.

"I heard about Stephen, Rose. How bad is it?"

"Looks pretty bad, I'm afraid." I started tearing up.

"May I come in?" he asked gently, and I moved to make room for him, feeling bad for not inviting him in right away. He followed me into the den taking his jacket off, and we sat down.

"Do you mind telling me details—or would you rather not?"

Everything poured out, and he understood it all—his mother died of pancreatic cancer not long before he moved to Shippensforge last year. Her case was very similar to Stephen's.

"Jim, I'm surprised you never told me about your mother."

"And I'm surprised you didn't tell me about Stephen," holding my gaze. "I'm not a monster just because I don't believe in God, Rose."

"And I'm not a monster just because I do."

"I was afraid you'd use my atheism against me, maybe try to pray my mother to heaven or something."

"I was afraid you'd use my faith against me, taunting me with God's powerlessness and so forth."

"I would never."

"Neither would I."

He nodded. "I'm sorry."

"Me too."

"Will you come over and have some supper with us? We've got a pot of soup on the stove and a loaf of bread in the oven."

My taste buds came back to life for the cheerful meal in their warm kitchen. Blesséd relief; I could breathe normally again, at least for a bit.

"How long now until the little one makes its debut?"

"About seven weeks," Anita said. "The time's going fast, in a way, but seven more weeks seems like forever, too. We're ready, though, aren't we, Daddy?" she smiled at Jim.

"You betcha, Mommie Dearest. Just say the word, and I'll start the water to boiling," he joked, squeezing the back of her neck. They're having a midwife come to the house for delivery.

And then the thought came to me: I wonder if Stephen will still be here when the baby arrives. I didn't want to leave this clean, well-lighted place on that note, so I helped with the dishes, and we had fun in the process, Anita staying at the table with her feet up. But the time came to go back out into the cold and dark. Jim walked me home and said as I opened my front door, "I do believe in love, Rose, and I hope you know we love you. We'll do whatever we can to help you get through." He hugged me with his strong arms, and it felt so much like Stephen that I really lost it. But he just calmly held me until I could speak and was ready to go in. *Oh, Charlie, I wish you could have known this character, Jim. I have to laugh, just thinking about how you two would do with each other! You'd both have met your match, so to speak.* I still didn't sleep much that night, but there was a little more light shining through my darkness.

Remember, Charlie, how I said I was ready to go? So is Stephen. "Now is the time of salvation, Mom," he said to me the other day, punching now the way Pastor Sauer used to do. I'm smiling a little as I write, because what kind of thing is that for a son to say to his mother? He and Penelope had been reading the lessons together and talking, that's where it had come from.

"I have this keen sense every once in a while," he went on, "of what's coming next, after this life—and it's good, so good. That's all I know, no specifics, and it's the same goodness that we have here, in flashes and little victories, you know?"

"Yes, Stephen, I do know," I answered, torn asunder within by beliefs vs. feelings. Oh, Charlie, I'm a mess.

I've let the "real world" go since our nightmare started. Thank heaven Josephine got here, staying with me a couple nights and now with Mercedes. I haven't had the presence of mind even to go over there—and fie! I forgot to go to the food pantry this morning—but Josephine has called a few times. They're switching to the early service, she said, because Mercedes is nocturnal these days. So, their Sunday routine is worship, eat a big breakfast, and go to bed. Charlene thinks the arrangement is working out well so far. What a God-send, Cousin Weirdifine.

Miguel! Huge development. The story was just on the front page of the paper. Hector Alvarez, Miguel's friend who saw Officer Erik Schmidt with the murder victim shortly before the killing, was found dead in a burned-out car. He was a key witness for Miguel's defense, so this sounded to me like really bad news, but Mindy thinks otherwise.

"Erik is behind Hector's death, I'm sure of it; the man is evil, evil like I've never seen this close up. Hector died because he had the guts to tell the truth. It's horrible, but somehow, I really think it's going to help Miguel." *Please, God, redeem this situation.*

Sometimes I can't write at all and sometimes, like tonight, I can't stop. Writing seems the only place I can say everything, get it all out, garbled and disconnected as it may be. The Bryants came to visit one day. I'm surprised at how easily and quickly we've become "shepherd and sheep." They are already dear to me and the feeling is mutual, I can tell. I talked to them about Stephen's death. I <u>hate</u> doing that when I want to be talking about his prognosis, his chances, his treatments. I probably wouldn't even be mentioning death but for him. I'm following his lead.

Oh, dear God, we're living in dust, breathing it, choking on it. You say, "Come unto me." You say, "Call on me in the day of trouble; I will deliver you, and you shall glorify me." Well, here I am, Lord, here I totally am. Create in me a clean heart, O God, and renew a right spirit within me. Cast me not away from your presence, and take not your Holy Spirit from me. Restore unto me the joy of your salvation and renew a right spirit within me. Please God. Amen.

First Sunday in Lent

Genesis 9:8-17
Psalm 25:1-10
1 Peter 3:18-22
Mark 1:9-15

We had Stephen yesterday and today—and it looks like we'll be having him a lot more. The weekend was not as bad as I thought it might be, but, in another way, worse. He looks and seems more like himself than we expected—thin but not dramatically gaunt—and still not in too much pain. Virginia had staged a wedding celebration for lunch on Saturday. That gave me a jolt; their marriage had hardly registered with me. I'm glad she did though, for I think this meal was the only celebration they had. She did it up classy—roast pork loin with exquisite sides, sparkling grape juice, wedding-type cake. Stephen ate very little of anything. Penelope smiled radiantly, at times. After dinner, though, she looked really haggard, her round face framed by salt and pepper hair in a bowl cut, more salt than pepper now. She hasn't lost those 30 pounds she needs to either, since we saw her last Easter, maybe even gained a little.

"Well, let's talk," Stephen said soberly at the end of the meal. Wrestling with Penelope to keep control of the conversation, he told us that there is a lemon-sized tumor in/on the "tail" (back part) of his pancreas and smaller tumors in his liver and lungs. There are cancer cells throughout his lymph system as well. *Oh God I just can barely breathe when I hear all this.* He's started on a chemotherapy drug called Gemzar which will probably shrink the tumors some. Bad side effects so far—but they might level off.

"How about the pain factor, Uncle Stephen?" Ache all over, all the time. Back pain getting worse. Manageable with meds.

"Stephen, are you sure you've gotten enough opinions? It's hard for me to accept that no treatment will help," his sister said.

"Exactly right, Virginia. If he would only try these clinical trials..." Penelope began, but Stephen took over. Thirteen specialists in the last month. Thorough consultation at a premier institution. Total consensus. Deterioration as predicted. He shut down discussion with, "I'm done with that part. I'm just done with it."

Penelope insisted quietly that all avenues have not been exhausted, and that there have been cases as difficult as Stephen's that have turned around. She rubbed his back and appealed to us, "Please help me try and persuade him to..." Stephen's hand hit the table and he shouted, "Stop!" We all jumped; it was awful. Poor Penelope got up and went outside through the patio doors, out of view. After a minute, Stephen followed her.

"More wedding cake, anyone?" Barry said into the tense silence and started clearing the table. *God be with us. God please please be with us. I know you are. Help me sense your presence.*

I want Penelope to be right and Stephen wrong, and yet her hopefulness can be irritating. She invokes "God's steadfast love and abundant mercy," etc., so much it gets quite tiresome. Honestly, sometimes the woman seems like a faith robot. Poor creature, she has been dealt a cruel blow. Even in my anguish, I can understand that hers is greater. I must not let her bother me so much. *God, listen here! You must help me with Penelope. Emergency!*

After worship this morning we had lunch at my house. I had put together a double batch of Sunshine Chicken—Stephen actually ate a small serving which gave me unreasonable satisfaction. "It's that appetite stimulant; I'm so glad we found those," Penelope exulted. After we ate, Virginia and Stephanie took her to the health food store to look for essiac tea and mushroom extract ("kinky cures," Virginia calls them) while Grandpa Barry and Mack napped.

Though the day was chilly, gray and damp, the moments with just me and my son became a bright treasure in my den. We put our arms around each other and I started out, "I wish…" and he said, "I know…" and before I could start crying, he asked, "Do you remember when your Aunt Bea was nearing the end with breast cancer? She said to Uncle Bill that her last days were a gift they'd been given, and he snapped, 'Then don't open it!' and she said, 'Oh, yes, we will open it, William, and enjoy the hell out of them the best we can.'"

"And they did," I smiled. That story, that time, is legendary in our family.

"Remember the show?" Stephen laughed.

"Like it was yesterday…"

"Your Aunt Beatrice has called a command performance talent show of all descendants at her house on Saturday afternoon," Mother told me over the phone. "Can you come?"

"What in the world? Of course," I said, without even checking the calendar.

Like several other families, Charlie and the kids and I drove the goodly distance on a gorgeous, sunny day. We filled their huge living room and overflowed into the dining room and entry hall with people peering in through the large arched doorways. Aunt Bea sat enthroned in her armchair looking wasted and weak, but dressed up with rouge on her cheeks, and reveled in one act after another from four generations.

Grandma Barnett started off, drawing on her elocution lessons of long years hence to recite "The Charge of the Light Brigade." Not knowing this fussy, unhappy woman had any passion in her, we watched in wonder as she bellowed, "Cannon to right of them, cannon to left of them, cannon in front of them, volley'd and thunder'd ..." Lord Tennyson would surely have been pleased. Everyone grasped the significance—that we were beholding a grieving mother giving a gift to her dying daughter.

Uncle Bill also astounded us with a Clem Kadiddlehopper-type skit from Red Skelton. We could hardly catch a breath for laughing, more at the wildness of seeing our dignified uncle doing this than at the humor itself. Aunt Bea struggled up from her chair to set in motion a standing ovation. I, too, went with comedy for the occasion, playing the roles of both Kate and Petruchio in a scene from "The Taming of the Shrew," Aunt Bea's favorite Shakespeare play.

There was great screeching and squawking of instruments, from Stephen's clarinet to a 5-year-old's beginning violin. Also, accomplished renditions by Mother at the piano and a string trio made up of Aunt Bea's grandchildren. There were tap and ballet dancers, too, and one little great niece recited the state capitols including the newest, Juneau and Honolulu.

By this time, Aunt Bea had to go back to bed. During the lovely catered supper, each sibling and their offspring were summoned into her room so she could say goodbye. When we went in with Mother, Aunt Bea had something special to say to each one of us. She told Charlie she wished there'd been enough space for him to show his talent—roller skating. She thanked me for being a wonderful niece and told me how proud she was that I was helping to keep Shakespeare alive, "a worthy endeavor." "Honor your mother and father and have fun in life," she said to Virginia and Stephen. And then we left and let her and Mother be alone. "Helen, you're more than a sister, you know..." I heard as I closed the door. 'Twas a grand day, full, rich, complete, and she died the next week...

"Help me open the gift, Mom," Stephen was saying. "I hate this, I don't understand it, but I know I'm dying, from the inside out, and there's nothing I can do about it..." he broke off.

I gripped his hand.

"...so help me enjoy the hell out of what time we have left, okay?" he whispered.

I nodded, pulling him to me, cheek to cheek. *Oh, God, this is too cruel. This is my boy!*

"It just seems too wrong, Stephen...too soon, too hard, too..."

"I know..."

"I don't think I can do this."

"You don't think you can do it?" he said, forcing me to laugh through our tears. I grabbed tissue for both of us, and we sank down on the davenport and sniffled and wiped.

"We'll get through it together, Mom," he sighed, and then blew me away. "Here's what I want to do: come home. Is that okay?"

"Here? In this house?" My heart leapt with joy.

"Penelope, too—of course," I added instantaneously, remembering the whole picture.

"Of course," he smiled.

"Of course," I said again, dumbly.

"We can do it—because of what we both believe: God will guide us, and Jesus will be right here."

Yes, to all that, I thought, but asked, "Have you and Penelope talked about this?"

"Not yet. I wanted to clear it with you first." He sighed. "Boy, she's not doing well. Total denial and, naturally, her control-taking is in full swing. I can't blame her, really; this is a raw deal for her—but something's got to give. She's so determined to keep me alive when what I need is for her to help me die."

"You've got to tell her that, son."

"I was thinking maybe you could."

"Tell her that? Nope. You."

"You," he teased.

"I didn't marry her," I said, and then asked when he thought they would come.

"In a few days." Yikes.

And then the others returned, and baby and Grandpa woke up, and we had popcorn and apples before he and Penelope headed back to Chicago. Again, I was thrilled when Stephen ate a handful of popcorn. How twisted things are.

"When will we see you again, little brother?" Virginia demanded more than inquired in the farewell hubbub.

"Soon. Talk to Mom," I heard him tell her.

Now everyone's gone. *Oh, God, this can't be happening. Not us. Not mine. Not me.*

Charlie, do you remember when Stephen was in confirmation class and they studied Lent, its meaning and symbolism? And then we were on the way to the pancake supper on Shrove Tuesday, and he pipes up from the back seat, "So, is everybody excited about Lent?" Even his big sister had to laugh—as she slugged him, probably.

I went to the service tonight even though a big part of me wants to boycott church. You know how I feel—like you did after Stewart Larsen died—like you might now, if you were here. But you couldn't stay away, and neither can I, thank God, for I do not want to walk this valley alone. The service was comforting. Virginia went, Barry, too, if you can believe it. We shared an odd moment of grace when poor old Sidney objected to the singing of The Lord's Prayer. He was truly distressed, and we heard him behind us mutter, "The damn thing is not meant to be sung!" Heavens. What could we do but silently laugh until the whole pew was shaking?

The Bryants—you'd love them—are preaching a series on "A Christian Tightrope—Living Towards God's Promises." Tonight they dialogued about how Jesus in his very being—divine and human at once—helps us walk that tightrope. Jesus was walking it in the wilderness, choosing to trust in God's promises rather than take the old human options Satan offered. In the same way, they said, we too are all the time balancing our fervent desire for control with trusting God. My mind shot straight to Penelope. In this hellish journey we're having to take, will she maybe recognize and confess her human limitations and relinquish control to God? Not just in words, but in living?

They'll be here tomorrow. Stephen said he had to be firm about his decision to come, that she resisted mightily. Oh, Charlie, I just want him to myself! I want that so badly. Just me and Virginia and Barry and Stephanie and Mack. We're his family, not this strange giraffe-like creature named Penelope! She looks nothing like a giraffe; I don't know why I said that. I just feel like she's tromped awkwardly into our life from some strange place at the worst possible time. And yet, Stephen loves her. I'm asking with every breath for God to help me get out of the way and let the Holy Spirit help all this happen.

These last few days have been very busy, getting ready for them. Stephen will be in his room, of course; Virginia and I moved a bedside table from our room to his so there will be one on each side of the bed. I also got dark shades and Jim put them up for me, so the room can be dark enough to sleep any time of the day. I hung the painting of the church in snow that I got in St. Petersburg and placed his favorite reading—short story collections—on the chest of drawers. Dylan Thomas, too: he loves Dylan Thomas, you know. I doubt he'll want a television, but we can always add that. Maybe they'll bring one, I don't know. I tried to leave plenty of room for how they want to arrange things. Then I moved my sewing operation out of Virginia's room—it's been years since I've sewn anyway—and moved in a day bed borrowed from Sarah; this can be Penelope's space. So now, I have the house ready for Stephen to come home and die. Oh, God, Charlie.

"Don't forget to keep living through this, Rose; you have to take care of yourself," Sarah said last Saturday, catching me before I'd gone out to Virginia's to be with Stephen. "Remember Angelica's with me for the weekend; she'd like to spend time with you. C'mon, go to the game with us tonight." I did, and yet felt guilty for going off to have fun—even though there was nothing else for me to be doing. Had a ball. We sat with the Brewster-Leppard clan, and did those kids ever adore Angelica and vice-versa. She and Johnny buddied up, going to the concession and doing all the cheering yelling motions together. Deedee was delighted to see this little crack in Johnny's brooding. He and Angelica went down to the crowded floor at the end to congratulate Jacob. He looked very surprised to see her—and quite delighted! She pulled the lanky star down so she could kiss him on the cheek. When Sarah and I saw that, we gave a little hoot, delighted that this girl with a promiscuous past who's even had an abortion could give a kiss that seemed so sweetly pure. *And Charlie, I wish you could have seen Johnny's face when Jacob high-fived him! But you don't even know Johnny, you were gone before he arrived. Oh, this cycle of life and death and life—keeps us on the tightrope.*

<u>Second Sunday of Lent</u>

Genesis 17:1-7, 15-16
Psalm 22:23-31
Romans 4:13-25
Mark 8:31-38

Dear God, please strengthen Stephen and help him find the words to get Penelope under control. Comfort her and help her to trust in you and rest in you. Help her to give up her determination to cure Stephen of cancer, dear God. Please inspire her, instead, to treasure these days we have left with him and to open the gift of farewell. And the sooner the better, God, because she's driving us all nuts. Jesus thought Martha had misplaced priorities— she was no contest for Penelope! I pray for myself, too, God, trusting that you will build up my patience as we move through this. Manage my pain, Lord. And I thank you again for this wonderful man it has been my privilege to mother for 58 years. Amen.

What an awful prayer to have to pray. I've surrendered without a fight, I guess. Surrendered to God, I mean. I <u>want</u> to be angry, shake my fist at heaven, forswear my faith. But I can't. Especially not with Stephen right next to me, all faithful and peaceful. *You know, Charlie, I remember being angrier over Florence's cancer and dying than Stephen's; that's weird, no? Oh, but my feelings are up and down and round and round like a yoyo trick. Fortunately, anguish cannot sustain itself for too long at a time. I hit bottom the other night and crept into our bedroom to weep and quiver until dawn, Stephen's moans coming through the wall. That spent me. The next day—yesterday, Saturday—I was calm and exhausted and able to cope.*

Sometime up in the morning, after Penelope had pestered Stephen for a couple hours to eat a little something, she took us to the big rock in the woods. Very thoughtful of her again; she'd done this after Christmas last year, when she found out what a special place the rock is for both of us. We shuffled through last year's leaves with icy snow fragments clinging to them here and there. Stephen leaned on her and I followed carefully, on my walking stick. She went back to the house to get on websites and listserves and make phone calls.

And, of all things, Charlie, Stephen and I got to talking about your roller skating and that trip to the National Roller Skating Museum in Lincoln, stopping at other "shrines" between here and there. He remembered the car breaking down outside of that town in Iowa where the Majestic Roller Rink was and how you put on your skates and skated into town to get help. We laughed our heads off, picturing you gliding down the highway. Thanks for the memories, Charlie! Life was so simple and easy then it seems now.

This afternoon, Stephen was stretched out on the davenport underneath Cute Baby—Barry and Virginia and Stephanie and Mack had just left—and Penelope asked me what had been preached at worship this morning. I had to concentrate to remember. Finally Charlene's introductory phrase came to me, that the gospel lesson was "a familiar but disturbing story." So that got us into Mark, where Jesus tells Peter to get behind him, Satan!

"Things are hitting me in weird ways lately," Stephen responded. "I get what was going on with Peter, I think. He was caught off guard by the idea of failure and suffering and death—just like I am. He wanted their ministry to succeed, in worldly terms, that is; suffering and death were not part of the plan he had in his head—just like me. And then I think that reminded Jesus of Satan taunting him in the desert, so that's why he yelled at Peter like that."

And then Penelope had this strange little outburst of vulnerability. "What about 'ask what ye will and it shall be given?' Is my desire to help you stay alive a rejection of God's will, my beloved?" she asked him in alarm. "Is keeping you alive a satanic temptation that I need to relinquish? I can't!" and she hurried from the room. Dear God. I shrugged my shoulders at Stephen. He raised his eyebrows in reply, then closed his eyes and was soon asleep. Oh, my, Charlie, we are caught in painful mystery. Here we are, people of faith, who are supposed to have all the answers to suffering and death, but when it's our turn to suffer, we only want it to stop.

I told Virginia this morning that I thought Penelope was doing her best, and was trying just as hard as I was to cope with the situation.

"Oh, stop gilding the lily," your sassy daughter shot back. "She's a self-righteous old maid with OCD who..."

"Unkind, Virginia," I put in.

She sighed. "I know it. This is just so hard, Mother, and I feel like Penelope makes it even harder. I don't see how you can stand having her in your house. You're a better person than I am, and that's a good thing."

Well, I'm certainly no better than Virginia, but I do have more patience, which is coming in handy. Minute by minute is how I'm making it, Charlie. Like when Penelope barged in on me in the bathroom, not even knocking. I just closed my eyes and in a minute, that was over. And now, I'll remember to lock the door. Zounds, I've *rambled on and on. Thanks for listening—or whatever it is you do while I yak—if you do anything at all.*

This moment right now seems almost normal. Penelope and Stephen must be asleep; usually I can hear when they're talking, which they do a lot, nestled into each other in his/their room, often leaving the door open. She's shut down "Control Central" for the day, I think. That's what we call the other bedroom now. Merciful heavens, in just a couple hours after they arrived Thursday afternoon, she had set up her laptop, printer/fax, phones, and files in there; filled a kitchen cabinet with teas, seeds, elixirs, and I don't know what all; transformed the bathroom with hanging shelves for toiletries and hung their own towels (entirely unnecessary); and covered the dresser in his/their room with vitamins, herbal remedies, lip balms, lotions, dried fruits and vegetables, toenail medicine, pain killers and other prescription drugs. Good heavens. Anyway, all is peaceful this minute and my overwhelmed brain is beginning to think of the "real world, out there."

I missed the groundbreaking for the expansion of Rutledge Home, but it was quite the festive event, I heard. Twenty-five independent living units going up. Louella's got the vision and the money and, within a few years, the place will offer a home through all the stages and needs of life's last years. Who knows? Maybe I'll wind up there someday.

Miguel is a free man! Events were fast and furious. The day after Hector died in the burned-out car and evidence was pointing to Erik Schmidt having masterminded that, Erik shot himself. Mindy's take is, "Cause of death: hatred." He left a suicide note saying that he didn't "want to live in a world ruled by," and then he used a string of racial epithets. Authorities also found information on his computer detailing a plot he apparently implemented on the night of Esteban's death to get Esteban drunk and have him pick a fight with Miguel. What a lost and demented soul, poor Erik Schmidt, and what a tangled web he wove. And <u>then</u>, according to Mindy, others from Miguel's house stepped forward at that point last week, saying that Hector had actually grabbed the butcher knife and stabbed Esteban while Miguel was in the middle of it, trying to break them up. The other guys had been afraid to tell the truth because of intimidation by Schmidt and worries over their immigration status. As soon as Miguel's innocence was firmly established, the prosecutor got him out of jail.

They were in church this morning, Mindy and Miguel (sounds like a TV show), a happy picture of gratitude and praise. I heard Miguel say a couple times while receiving handshakes and congratulations, "Señor, he hear my cries." In the prayers, Pr. Morris prayed, "We thank you, God of justice and mercy, for sustaining our friend Miguel through difficult times and for his

81

freedom; and we commend to you, Father, the souls of those whose lives were lost in this tragic chain of events." So John was right—Miguel was taking the rap for Hector. "He thinks he's Jesus," Mindy says in exasperation. I'll be catching up with them someday—when I have time—for other people...

Right now, I'll pop my corn and turn on Masterpiece Theater. Probably won't stay awake long. Mental, physical and spiritual energy are at low ebb—ha! the opposite of the youngsters at church this morning. Rhonda had quite a lively crowd for the children's sermon. She had them play Red Light, Green Light—staying seated herself (her baby, Lynette, is due any minute), and then had a discussion about rules and how impossible it is to follow them, like stopping on time when someone yells Red Light! "Kids, it's better and easier to live in God's grace than to try and follow the rules perfectly." By the looks on their faces, they weren't really getting it. That's a tricky concept for us humans.

I'm just going to jot down a few notes, to keep my sanity, what little I have left. First, some grace notes:

- Stephen finally talked to Penelope about helping him die. I knew something had happened when I met her in the hallway on her way from their room to the bathroom, her eyes red and swollen. I'd just gotten back from the food pantry (another sanity keeper). "It was rough, Mom," he recounted seriously. "I had to yell, I even had to shake her." But maybe he got through; maybe she's finally accepted the awful truth. She didn't protest when he decided to stop Gemzar. He said the side effects—mouth sores, nausea, fatigue, fever and chills—would do him in before the cancer does, and doctors agreed with his decision. Also, I'd mentioned hospice services to her last week, but she wouldn't hear of it. After a very rough night recently— pain we couldn't contain, a bathroom accident—I was ready to force the issue, but she made the call and we've been inundated with hospice staff getting things set up. There was yet another mountain of paperwork to get that in place, which Penelope handles quite ably. *You don't know Penelope, of course, Charlie. She had a broken engagement 30 years ago and was still a virgin when she and Stephen met. Sorry to be so frank, but you know how Stephen tells everything. They started dating last year but got in trouble with the Church for premarital sex and Stephen wasn't ready to get married so she broke up with him so she could stay a pastor. Then after about eight months, I guess, right after we got back from Russia—I've been to Russia, Charlie, imagine that!—Stephen was ready for marriage and they got back together. They were both so filled with joy—and then the next thing, almost immediately, was the cancer. Poor woman.*

- Virginia went on a shopping spree for Stephen—shower chair, sheepskin for bed, sweat suits. Helps her not to feel so helpless. And Penelope went to the midweek service with Virginia and me tonight while Barry stayed with Stephen. Penelope slept through much of it. On the way home—in regard to the sermon series, the "Christian Tightrope" thing, she said, "I feel more like a clown than a high wire performer. I feel like I'm doing dreadfully." After a second's silence, Virginia said, "You're doing just fine, Penelope."

- Angelica sent me an email: Rose, I'm thinking of you like every second. This must be super hard for you. I can't even begin to understand how hard it would be to lose a child, no matter how old they are. I'm like totally praying for you and Stephen and his wife that somehow God's peace will fly in at little moments. This life isn't the end, don't forget. Every time somebody I know dies, I get more sure of that. The basketball game was great; thanks for hooking me up with Johnny Brewster. He's a really neat kid, reminds me of myself when I was his age. And how about those Smithys! Jacob's a really neat kid, too. ☺ Do I sound like a love-struck adolescent? I am! Love you, Angelica" Made me cry, naturally. And is "totally praying" the same as "pray without ceasing?" I think probably so. Jacob gave me a big hug at the service tonight. No words. No words needed.

- Malcolm Stafford dropped in to see Stephen and offer legal assistance. In the rush of the last six weeks with doctor visits and all, they hadn't even thought about that aspect. I hadn't either, truthfully. Minds are addled. So, Malcolm is handling Power of Attorney for Penelope, updating Stephen's will, etc. Kind and thoughtful. I still feel awkward around Malcolm. He's going to early service, I hear, and Cynthia continuing at 11 o'clock. When he offered to help Stephen "get his affairs in order" my judgmental side wanted to say, "Too bad you couldn't get your own affairs in order." Shame on me.

And some not so graceful notes:

- Mercedes got out the other night (good heavens, sounds like she's a dog) and almost got hit by a car. She told Josephine that's what she was trying to do, that's what she wanted. Josephine said she "gave her what-for" and made her think about ruining the life of the driver. She doesn't think Mercedes will do it again, but can't be sure. They're not having it easy over there, but both of the old girls are stubborn enough to make it work better than other alternatives, I think.

- Stephen had a taste for oatmeal the other morning. I cooked it like I always have, and he ate about half of it. "But you didn't eat mine, love. How is your mother's different?" Penelope asked. "I don't know; it just is." She kept stewing over it in the kitchen, and I said something like, "Don't worry about it; just so he eats." Suddenly, her eyes were filling with tears and she said, "I want to make him better," and her face twisted. "I fix things, Mama Rose," she sobbed, then stamped her foot like a 2-year-old insisting, "I fix things." She leaned on the counter holding her head, heaving grievous moans. I didn't know how to comfort her. Then she walked down the hallway to the bathroom. *God, this is awful.*

Exodus 20:1-17
Psalm 19
1 Corinthians 1:18-25
John 2:13-22

Penelope surprised me this afternoon. "This could be worse," she said, gazing out the kitchen window at the gently falling rain. "It almost seems too easy. I hear from families everyday—Jill's back in the hospital with chemo-induced meningitis, Jerry has blood clots all over his body and is in constant pain, another guy was vomiting feces because a tumor was obstructing his bowel. Families are traveling all over the place for treatment and their hopes for survival go up and down everyday. And here's our Stephen—nagging back pain that's manageable, wasting away in relative comfort, nothing to do but die." She was talking with that strange detachment that we get once in awhile.

She seemed to be talking more to the rain then to me, but then got up from the table and came around and put her hands on my shoulders and said, "I'm sorry, Mama Rose; you're his mother; I shouldn't talk like that." I patted her hand for a minute, tongue-tied, and she trudged down the hallway to lie down with him. A mix of feelings washed over me: isolated and lonely, sad, exhausted, but oddly buoyed by what she'd said. There is much to be grateful for in this dastardly situation. Stroking Cute Baby was consoling, but the weather was seeping deeper into my psyche—seems like it's been gray ever since they got here—so I went for this trusty journal.

Penelope and I had been having a cup of tea after the crowd left. Really, a very good Sunday afternoon for Stephen. He's taking Ritalin for energy and the side effects from the Gemzar are waning. He sat through the whole meal with us, even getting up to stand behind Mack in his high chair and help him eat with a spoon. Got messy but the two of them were pretty proud of themselves. Stephanie and Barry and Virginia had brought over a delicious lunch of pasta and salad, and then we played cards for a while. I get hopeful in spite of myself whenever Stephen does anything anymore. His 6' medium-with-a-paunch frame is only a memory and slim-sized sweatpants hang on him. It's as though we're seeing a different person each day. Helplessness overwhelms us.

"I don't know how people got through pancreatic cancer before the Internet," Penelope says. Honestly, she's on her laptop 6-8 hours/day—discussion boards, blogs, websites, Facebook. Thank heaven for it. She not only finds important information, but also has a support system and stays busy—and gives us time alone with Stephen. He brags on her developing expertise re. pancreatic cancer. "Honey, say that ERCP thing," he'll say, showing her off, and endoscopic retrograde cholangiopancreatography rolls smoothly off her tongue. (I just looked it up on the I-net myself to put it in here. Sad but true.)

We're coexisting fairly well, my daughter-in-law and I. There are often others here, usually Virginia, and now Matthew, CNA from hospice, a very special guy. That helps. Penelope and I are fighting the good fight not to fight. Something I did vexed her the other morning. Can't remember now what it was, but I was at the kitchen sink and she said, "Mama Rose, how about I take you out to the big rock…?" As she went through the door into the hallway, I heard her say under her breath, "…and leave you there." Fortunately, it struck me funny and I laughed and called out, "I heard that." She said, "Uh-oh," in a cheery tone. Little moment of grace.

Oh, Charlie, speaking of daughter-in-law, Denise came to see Stephen. He had called her himself to tell her. "How could I leave this world without talking to the woman I spent twenty-five years of my life with?" I imagine he and Penelope had discussed this, but I wasn't privy to that. Anyway, Denise took a day off from her work and drove up from Indy on Friday, I think it was.

"I'm so sorry, Rose," she greeted me at the front door. We both choked up and there was just too much to say to say anything. I led her down the hallway. She looked great—trim, well-dressed, well-coiffed. Denise always has taken care of herself and now made a dramatic contrast to the plump, frumpy Penelope in her well-worn denim jumper, dark circles under her eyes and in need of a haircut. Such an awkward meeting, a moment of time hanging there in their 3-second perusal of each other with Stephen on the bed behind them.

Denise extended her hand and said, "I'm glad to meet you Penelope. I'm happy that you and Stephen found each other."

"Thank you. I'll let you two visit," Penelope returned and went across the hall to Control Central. Denise sat down on the edge of Stephen's bed and took his hand. I went to the den. She didn't stay long, but from what we heard after she left, that which was necessary was spoken.

"Complete forgiveness and reconciliation," Stephen reported.

"That's good, love," Penelope replied half-heartedly.

Stephen added with a smile, "She calls me her 'wasband.'" Funny. More little grace notes, Charlie. But, My St. Lord, what a way for an ex-wife and the new bride to meet each other.

Worshiping this morning was a joy—a relief, frankly—to think about something besides Stephen. My powers of concentration have been pretty much kaput lately, and I reveled in the rich scripture lessons: The Ten Commandments from Exodus, the majestic grace of both the creation and divine law displayed in Psalm 19, Paul's profound juxtaposition with wisdom and foolishness, and Jesus' wrath in the temple. "He went where the wild things are," Maddie observed during Charlene's children's sermon.

And Lynette Bartholomew was baptized. Five days old. Rhonda and Frank and Jimmy, Joey, Lisa, Lauren, and Jackie stood like a spiral staircase around the font. The pastors invited all the kids to sit on the front pews so they could see everything, then welcome the baby with a touch on her toe. A little crowd management required but really nice.

Theodore and the children's choir sang "Do No Sinful Action," one of hundreds of hymns and poems written in the 19th century "for the instruction of the young" by that amazing Cecil Alexander. I would love to have been friends with her, I think. Theodore's perfect tenor overlay the children's pure melody as they sang, "Christ is your own master, He is good and true, And his little children must be holy, too."

The simple song was a nice complement to Charlene's insights about the Ten Commandments, how they often make us either unhappy because we can't keep them or self-righteous because we think we do—and that both of those understandings miss the point. The law is God's great gift to revive our souls and rejoice our hearts. The law tells us how to live happily and faithfully <u>together</u>, not how we must behave to win personal salvation.

Theodore and Lloyd made a point of telling me that they're leaving tomorrow with Louella to visit family in Florida for ten days and will be thinking of us and praying for us and so forth. Unspoken between us was the knowledge that Stephen might be gone before they return. *Oh, God, this realization breaks upon me like I've never really thought of it before and I startle and shake and cry out again. Why, God? My useless question is nothing but raw pain and it springs out of my heart before I can stop it. And you do not answer.*

I slept only fitfully last night, maybe an hour or two altogether, dream after strange dream flitting in and out, instantly forgotten. Grief is hardest at night. I had taken a bubble bath and sprayed myself with a body mist Zzztherapy someone gave me long ago, to no avail. I could hear sounds from next door—Stephen's labored breathing, soft murmurings between him and P., the sound of their muffled weeping, like a pair of mourning doves. I tried the ear plugs I got for the trip but could still hear.

Charlie, these writings barely reflect all that is going on in our house. Visitors come and go, bringing food and telling Stephen goodbye in different ways. Matthew from hospice comes every other day now to bathe and shave him and change sheets. A nurse comes, too, to oversee pain meds and reassure us about what's normal and what needs attention. His urine is dark brown like strong tea. That's normal.

Horrible decisions have to be made each day. Stephen started talking with Penelope and me about burial of the body or cremation one night. He got all philosophical, musing at how little difference it made, and then started getting silly, cracking jokes. I had to leave. I called Sarah and she came and picked me up and we went and found ourselves a glass of wine and talked of other matters. Stephen apologized the next day, says his sense of absurdity kicks in without warning—maybe a coping mechanism—and he forgets that other people are not seeing the humor. Sometimes I'm not sure how much more of this roller coaster I can take, Charlie. Now it's looking like his body will be an anatomical gift to IU's med school. Cornea donation, too, probably.

Miracle! I've never experienced quite such a rush of life and grace and joy. It started Wednesday night when Stephen went to the service. "I'm really liking this Ritalin," he's joked a few times, and apparently, it had kicked in. His general pain is increasing and he needs major help walking, but he wanted to go and we—Barry on one side and Penelope on the other— got him in there. Mindy and Miguel sat with us and so did Danny and Sherry.

As soon as Danny saw him, he had him in a bear hug. "St-St-Stephen! Oh, Stephen, you're so sk-skinny, but you're not d-d-dead." Oh, Danny. He wanted to sit next to Stephen—and did, despite Eugene and Karen's efforts to keep him from imposing. He took Sherry's hand and pulled her into the pew, and they plunked down between Stephen and Penelope—who were both delighted—with Danny smiling up at Stephen all through the service and playfully punching him in the arm.

Charlie, I tell you, that was the happiest Lenten service I've ever seen! Naturally, the hymns referenced death a good bit, but we were feeling "the glory of these forty days." I'm not saying there weren't any tears as we sang, but oh, my God, was there faith! And I felt your presence so strongly, Charlie. Afterward, dozens of people—practically everyone—hugged Stephen; Penelope, too. How—what's the word?— nourishing for both of them.

None of us wanted it to end and Barry and Virginia came home with us and I made chocolate sauce and had butter pecan ice cream on hand and it had never tasted so delicious. Stephen ate a couple bites. And THEN—

"Let's go to Chicago tomorrow," he said. We were puzzled, stunned. "Barry and Gin, can you go? I want us all to go to my apartment. There are some things there I want to give you, and I just want to be there one last time."

"We can go, Steverino," Barry said while Virginia sat there trying to comprehend.

"Let's call Stephanie and see if she and Mack can go," he said.

And we were all on the late train yesterday morning! A scene that will last in my memory is Uncle Stephen holding Mack at the window pointing out the sights. "Those are steel mills… Look at the water… See the big buildings, little guy…" and Mack would respond each time with his bright little, "Uh-huh," as though understanding everything. *Oh, God, how can joy and pain can be so vivid at the same time?*

We made our way slowly to the street and piled into taxis and were at 1600 Clark Street in just a few minutes, then up to the 14th floor. We'd all been to Stephen's place before, but under happier circumstances—although this occasion was pretty darn happy! The day was leisurely with lively conversation as well as moments of reflective silence as we looked down on the busy, spectacular view. So much life to see, including, on this particular day, demonstrators at the Chinese Embassy positioned on mats, praying and chanting for freedom for Tibet. Stephanie and her dad went down to the jungle hamburger place across the street and brought back lunch, including tasty milkshakes. Mack's first ice cream. We had to cut him off.

And Stephen had an agenda. He went through his apartment, parceling out... *This part was hard, Charlie, even amidst funny little presentation comments from Stephen and jibes back at "Steverino," of course. All I can say right now is that we each have some very precious mementoes. We got home late and Stephen's been asleep since, going on eleven hours. We can't help but hope that the expedition was a good sign, that there will be more good times with Stephen.* Can't help but hope.

<u>Fourth Sunday in Lent</u>

Numbers 21:4-9
Psalm 107:1-3, 17-22
Ephesians 2:1-10
John 3:14-21

Oh, God help us. Come quickly, redeem us from trouble, redeem these moments of excruciating pain, redeem us, God.

Sometimes I wish Stephen weren't here. Other times I'm so glad he is here, and this whole damned process is blessed. What a jumbled, jangled mess of emotions. Just now, he and Penelope really got into the mess.

I didn't go to worship this morning. The rain is pouring down, and I just didn't have the strength to get out in it. I'd had breakfast and gotten my journal and my Bible and had been sitting at the kitchen table still in my bathrobe staring at an icon of mother and child for I don't know how long when voices down the hallway started getting louder.

"Please, just leave me alone, would you? Just go away for awhile."

"Okay, love. We'll just do your toenail and you can rest."

"No, Penelope, no! Don't do my toenail, don't do anything. Get out!"

Stunned silence and then, "Stephen, how can you be angry at me?"

"You're angry at me, too!" he snapped.

"No. I may be angry at the situation, but..."

"You're angry at me, for taking so long to die, for interrupting your life..."

"No! Don't say such a thing..."

"It's true; admit it. And I'm tired of trying to be cheerful and console everybody..."

"Stop this, Stephen! You're making it harder."

"It is harder, it's the hardest of anything, and trying to always put on a better face makes it harder yet!" If Stephen could have, I think he would've jumped out of bed at this point and swept all the bottles and jars off the dresser in a grand gesture of frustration. But instead, I heard the door close. I waited a minute and went down the hall to see if Penelope was standing there, in need of comfort, but she was still in the room with him. I picture them caressing and crying this moment away, moving to a closer place of honesty and understanding in their budding relationship—which is almost over.

Lord God, I'm going to bed, too, pulling the sheets over my head. Give me some peace, please, give me enough energy to walk from here to there and lie me down.

Later

Merciful heavens, I slept until 3 o'clock. The weird thing is, nobody has come by or called all day, as though the whole world is resting from Stephen's illness this Sunday, leaving it to God, I guess. I'm refreshed now, by sleep and shower. Their door was open, and they were propped up against each other in the bed watching an old movie. I went to the kitchen and got the chocolate-covered strawberries that Marvin sent—"I hope the household will enjoy these. May they taste as sweet as you are, Rose. Stay strong, my friend." I took them in and perched on the edge of the bed. Stephen passed, but Penelope and I each snarfed one down. I asked how they were doing, could I bring them anything.

"We're okay, Mama Rose," Penelope smiled. (That "Mama Rose" title grates on my nerves. She started calling me that when she first visited last year, and I told her then just to call me Rose. I'll say something, at the right opportunity.)

Stephen nodded. "We're okay, Mom. Nothing like a few drops of morphine under the tongue to make you feel okay," he smiled with slurry speech. "All I really need from you right now is a big old hug," and boy, did he get one. Felt so good, even though he can't squeeze back anymore.

Just using the porta-toilet next to his bed takes all the strength he has— but he can still talk! He and I were having a few quiet moments yesterday, and tears sprung to my eyes when he said, "Mom, I'm sorry for all the trouble I caused in my younger years." *Charlie, he started recounting that awful night at the police station his senior year. When he got teary-eyed, too, I cut him off. What was the point of sinking down into long ago?*

"Apology accepted, son—and I have to add, kicking you out of the house was one of the most satisfying parental actions your dad and I ever took." That brought laughter, like I had hoped. But the seed was planted, and I've been thinking more about those hard times, especially the incident that summer he was home from college that finally forced us toward change. Heavens, Charlie, that's 35 years ago or more, but so vivid in my memory that it could have happened yesterday...

I smelled a sickening sweet-and-sour smell of vomit coming from his bedroom early one hot, humid morning after he'd left for a week-end trip

with friends. He had come in drunk the night before, gotten sick, made a feeble attempt to clean up his mess, and left. I marched like an automaton to the kitchen and mixed vinegar water and found rags. I got down on my knees to scrub and was suddenly sobbing, realizing that I was cleaning up my adult son's vomit because he was sick unto death.

Before this, I'd been rationalizing his drunken, irresponsible behavior—"boys will be boys," "rite of passage." How foolish, and at this moment I knew only too well, thinking of Dad's alcoholism, that Stephen had it, too.

"Where is this coming from?" I shouted. "Surely a good upbringing and spiritual grounding and faith in God can stand up against <u>beer</u>."

But it was not to be. As soon as he got back, we gave him a week to move out...

Oh! how valiantly that man has fought the demons, hasn't he, Charlie?

Last conversations, that's what we're having. Mostly mundane, sometimes painful, and even funny, especially when he's all doped up. "Who are you again?" he asked Penelope drowsily. "I'm your wife, love." "Really? Wow." And then he was asleep again.

Penelope and I overheard him talking theology with Jim the other day. I thought maybe we should interrupt, but Penelope shook her head, and we sat across the hall in Control Central and listened in.

"Either you believe it or you don't," was the first thing we heard Stephen say.

"And if I don't believe it, I'm going to hell?" Jim asked, in a challenging tone.

"I'd never say that. But, wait a minute, man; do you believe in hell?"

"No."

"Then what are you worried about?"

"Good point," Jim responded, and I could hear that he was smiling. "I guess I'm worried about you Christians saying that whoever doesn't believe in Jesus is condemned."

"The Christians I hang out with aren't so focused on condemnation. Jesus wasn't, either. He came into the world not to condemn it but to save it, not to punish but to love."

"So you go along with that salvation stuff, Stephen?"

"Oh, yeah, big time."

"So you think you're saved?"

"I've always felt like I was saved. My whole life—I mean overall, not every second—I've been in a safe place: the presence of Christ. And it's not just about me; the whole creation is saved. That's why I don't feel alone in this deal."

After a silence, Jim said, "I'm glad for you, Stephen, and I'm glad I got to know you, man, and…" Silence again, and some rustling, a hug, I think, and then we heard Jim make his way out the front door. Funny, when we first met, he introduced himself as a "hard core atheist." I really think, at the core, he's pretty soft. *Thank you, God, for Jim.*

Stephanie Rose spent a whole afternoon with him, leaving the little one with Grandma Gin. Lots of laughter exploding from the room, lots of murmuring, lots of silence, probably when he was dozing. She came out once, crying, to tell me that he brought up gifts in memory. He wants to designate her church as the recipient. St. Timothy doesn't really need money, he said, but he thinks Transfiguration is "out there" with risky ministries, so that's where he wants any donations to go. That just undid the child and she let out all her grief in my arms—fortunately, I was in a stalwart mood—and then went back in to laugh and talk some more, favorite niece with favorite uncle.

His birthday is Tuesday. He says he doesn't want a celebration, giving us permission not to have to come up with something, which would have been so hard and sad. This is one of many thoughtful gifts he's given us throughout this ordeal. *Oh God, there are no words to express the depth of feelings overwhelming me at this moment, a cast iron weight on my chest.*

I have just enough energy to call Virginia and Stephanie and see what's going on in their worlds; they always help me feel better. Sure would help if this rain would stop for awhile, too. Good for the water table but hard on our souls.

Lenten Mid-week 4

Yesterday the Bryants came by and gave us all communion—Stephen, Penelope, Virginia, and me. Stephen wanted to talk about his memorial service, so we did. Not too many decisions. Standard liturgy with Eucharist. Romans 8—neither death nor life, etc., will ever separate us from God's love shown forth in Jesus. Theodore to sing "I Know that My Redeemer Liveth." Strong, joyful hymns. Stephen spoke of how complete his life felt. Peace and calm prevailed as though we were in a holy bubble, protected from grief. We were still in the bubble when Malcolm came later in the afternoon with papers to sign. All seemed so right, truly a gift, bright and pretty and tied up with a bow.

A little while later, I heard Stephen trying to smother his sobs with a pillow. Penelope was absorbed at her computer and Virginia was working in the kitchen. I told her I was going to pay my water bill, drove out of town and parked behind that abandoned country church and cried and keened until I was empty. *It scares me how much I hate you right now, God.*

<u>Fifth Sunday in Lent</u>

Jeremiah 31:31-34
Psalm 51:1-12
Hebrews 5:5-10
John 12:20-33

    He is gone. This morning. 5am. Penelope knocked on my door and told me. I kissed his forehead, and we sat by him for awhile, each holding a hand. We said some prayers and wept. At seven, I called Virginia and Stephanie Rose, and they came right away. At eight, Penelope called Matthew. He and Penelope bathed him and dressed him. I called the church so they could tell everybody. At ten, Penelope called for them to come and take him away. The Bryants, Mindy, Sarah, Madge, and Josephine have come this afternoon. It is finished. He is gone.

I'm sorry I said I hate you, God. You know what I meant. Love, Rose

Lenten Mid-week 5

Penelope is still sleeping. I don't believe the girl has slept much at all since Friday night. I've heard her lumbering around the house in the darkness at all hours. The memorial service (yesterday, Wed.) maybe gave her a closing point of some kind. I slept soundly last night, too, until waking at 4:30 this morning with an aching dread at having to live the rest of my days without Stephen. I can't write anymore now. Can't sleep. Can't eat. Can't cry. Can't think. It's as though I'm anesthetized by my own pain.

Noon

Penelope is still sleeping. I remember when Poochie died when Virginia was about three. All day long, she wandered the house saying, "Poochie is so-o-o dead." Now, Stephen is so dead. The whole world seems dead.

9pm

The gloom lightened a little when Virginia and Barry and Stephanie and Mac came out this afternoon. Penelope got up around 4 o'clock and she and Virginia and Stephanie heated and presented a very fine meal from all the food that's been brought in. Meanwhile, Barry and I played with Mack, variations on peek-a-boo, initiated by him. Wonderful to have this little fourth generationer around, sweet and clueless. By the end of his game, he was just closing his eyes and then saying peep-boo when opening—and laughing harder each time, the crazy little thing.

Over dinner, we talked more about how good the service had been and all the different people who showed up from different eras of Stephen's life. We mentioned again how gratifying it was to receive memorial gifts for Transfig. which we handed over to Pastor Gail, Stephanie's pastor, who was present with us. Yesterday's conversation was more lively, though. I remember Barry saying, "That funeral really brought things to life!" Tonight was subdued; we're all worn out. And now, it's dark again and everybody's gone.

Charlie, I keep wondering if he's with you. I mean in a way that we can understand. I walked in the backyard earlier today and noticed tender green lily of the valley shoots springing up in the old bed. I thought of Jesus' image when he talked about his own death, of seeds dropping in the earth and dying. If the seeds die, he said, then they will bear fruit. But the fruit doesn't look anything like the seed, does it? I know Stephen is alive in eternity, but what does that look like? In my limited human imagination, I see the two of you embracing, but I don't know…

And Charlie, Penelope asked me a little while ago if she could stay a while longer.

"Mama Rose," she said, "would it be okay if I stay with you through Easter Sunday?"

"Of course, Penelope," I told her. "On one condition—that you stop calling me Mama Rose. Just call me Rose."

She squinted in thought. "Have I been calling you Mama Rose?"

Isn't that funny? How could she not know? I think she wants to stay because she'll feel closer to Stephen. And that's why I want her to stay. I will, too.

<u>Passion Sunday</u>

Isaiah 50:4-9a
Psalm 31:9-16
Philippians 2:5-11
Mark 14:1—15:47

Staying home this morning would have been easier—though the only thing worse than the sorrow stabbing me all through the service would have been sitting at home alone. Our umbrella blew inside out as we made our way through the parking lot. Penelope grabbed my arm, yelling, "C'mon, Mama Rose; hell hath no fury like two church ladies trying to get to worship!" and helped me through the back door. There's widespread flooding in the county, so the crowd was small. The singing of "All Glory, Laud and Honor" was anemic and disjointed from the organ in front to the voices in the narthex, and water squished in our shoes as we entered the nave holding palm branches. I felt like turning around and going home, but then Maddie Bowers slipped her hand into mine, her serious little expression saying, "I have known your sorrow." She escorted me to my pew, then went on to her place up front, making my soul sing for an instant.

As always, Jesus' entire passion was read, from Mark this year, from the anointing with precious oil at Bethany to being laid in the tomb. Different folks read, section by section, with verses of "Tree of Life and Awesome Mystery" sung in between. I couldn't sing at all, just rested in the voices of my friends. Verse 5 clobbered me with comfort and hot tears, the words like an echo, real but distant.

> God of all our fear and sorrow,
> God who lives beyond our death;
> hold us close through each tomorrow,
> love as near as ev'ry breath,
> love as near as ev'ry breath.

God, I'm glad your Holy Spirit breathes in me because sometimes, I hardly can do it on my own. My body seems too heavy to carry around, so I sit and sit, staring into space. My bed has become a cocoon; I pull the covers over my head and try to feel like a caterpillar, passively changing from one form to another, not doing anything but letting life have its way. For I feel helpless, I know not what to do to endure Stephen's death, this sudden, huge void, this chasm that separates us from him.

Danny sat with us, Sherry, too, clinging to us, literally, in their grief over Stephen. His mom Karen said she had to threaten not to bring him to the memorial service to keep him from trying to sit with the family there. "It would have been fine," Penelope said, and she and I had to smile at a little exchange these child-like adults had when the cries of "Crucify him!" were shouted out.

"They're mean; they want to kill Jesus," Sherry fretted.

"It's okay, Sh-Sherry; Jesus is gonna come b-b-back to l-life," Danny informed, patting her shoulder. This is progress in understanding for Danny. In past years, he has gotten greatly distressed at "Crucify him!" and yelled back, right in church, "No! D-d-don't! Leave him alone!" Which certainly added to the drama.

Mindy slipped in beside me during the reading. When Simon of Cyrene took Jesus' cross, she whispered, "That's what you're doing, carrying a heavy cross and following Jesus; remember, I'll help." This friend made my soul sing, too; I will be depending on her. And now, it strikes me that she and I didn't have our annual March 18th dinner to commemorate my Charlie and her Darien, who both died on that date. We were too busy—helping Stephen die.

Oh, God. I am still in shock. Even after seeing him waste away day by day in my own home and his lifeless body wrapped in white being rolled out the front door, slid into the hearse and driven away, I can't believe this has happened. At any moment, I still expect to hear his voice, see him in his bed, fix him a bowl of oatmeal—and get shocked all over again. God, help.

I barely tasted the bitter Lenten wine of Eucharist, just letting it touch my lips and putting the tiny cup back. "Let this cup pass from me," I couldn't help but think. But, ah, it's too late for all that. Stephen is dead, and my soul yearns for the sweet wine of Easter.

Penelope has mostly slept since the funeral, and this is good. She can't seem to stop calling me Mama Rose, despite apologizing and trying, so I'm letting that go. Doesn't bother me anymore. One thing about all that we've been through: she is becoming a more real person to me. The ladies' night out we had was a breakthrough. When was that, last week? No, the week before. Heavens, I've lost track of time totally. It was the Thursday night before Stephen died on Saturday. Virginia initiated the idea and Stephen talked Penelope into going. Barry and Mack kept Stephen company so Stephanie could go. Virginia drove the four of us into the city to Leapart's, her favorite restaurant. It's third generation-owned and seemed just right for our purpose, with its comfortable furniture and elegant carpets and drapes. Not too busy and Virginia had them seat us in a quiet corner.

"Let's relax with a drink," Virginia invited.

"None for me," Penelope quickly put in, her eyes on the menu. "I used to like a gin and tonic, but quit because of Stephen. Besides, I get too silly."

"Bring her a gin and tonic, just in case," Virginia quietly instructed the server. And Penelope did drink—and did get a little silly.

"Tell us about the first time you ever laid eyes on Uncle Stephen," Stephanie coaxed.

"Oh, honey," she smiled dreamily, "it was in worship, you know. There he was, halfway back on the aisle in the middle, a good-looking man about my age and no wedding ring. 'Mm-mm-mmm, what have we here?' I thought."

"In church?" Stephanie giggled.

"Honey, I'm a woman, even under my robe. And then when he showed up for a potluck dinner that week—and brought a dish—my heart was enflamed. His was, too, I soon discovered—to my everlasting astonishment..." she trailed off.

"Tell us about your family, Penelope," Virginia asked, trying to veer us away from the blues.

"My father died at his own hand when I was 9. Mother's never recovered—which I understand, to an extent—but she's always seemed determined not to recover. I have a younger brother who still lives with her in St. Paul; not a good situation. But all is not lost; I have Aunt Margaret, my mother's sister, who is a great lady, and her husband, Uncle Julie— Julius—and three cousins there; that's my main family." We got to know her a lot better in that pleasant, long evening which was a welcome respite for us all.

And Aunt Margaret came to Stephen's service, a lovely person, indeed. People came from the congregation Penelope is currently serving as well as from the church where she and Stephen met. That was telling, to see them comforting her and vice-versa, the bonds appearing strong and warm. Several of his high school buddies were there and identified a woman, a classmate who I didn't remember—who sobbed on my breast about how much she'd always loved him. Brad, boss and friend, was there, of course, along with the crew from the Shippensforge office where he worked for 30 years. Three people from the Chicago office came. Larry and Joe and Paula and a few others from AA were there. Most of the congregation attended. Jacob, fresh back from winning the state basketball championship, was crucifer. I loved that; he really lifts the cross high. Denise and her mother and father came. Dr. Majmundar as well, very sweet for our family doctor to do. Carolyn and Marcus Sauer came. I'd thought of asking Pastor Sauer to be involved in the service but figured he would prefer not to set that precedent. The Bryants did a wonderful job of everything, as expected. There were quite a few people I didn't know. Their presence was comforting.

John flew in from California. We included him in the family dinner at the church and I was comfortable chatting, but I didn't feel moved to invite him back to the house. Marvin sent a basket of flowers (which I've broken down into five lovely arrangements) with regrets that he was unable to attend and a promise to visit as soon as he could.

Ah, but back to the present. After we got home from church this morning, Penelope and I changed into dry clothes and had a little lunch together, then sat in the den for awhile. My soul sang again when she asked me about Stephen's childhood, details like first words and favorite foods and his school life. I got out school pictures and baby books and so forth. That was fun. Then I asked Penelope if there had been moments of grace for her in these difficult days. I got quite an answer.

"One night a few weeks ago—the week before we moved over here—Stephen told me to put on my best dress and took me out for dinner and dancing and I don't know where the energy came from but we went home and loved each other all night long, Mama Rose." She stared into her lap. "Passionately, desperately…" and she cried softly for a long time, and I did, too, right when I didn't think I had any more tears, rocking in my chair with my eyes closed and letting it flow. Then she blew out a huge sigh and looked at me. "I am so grateful for every moment I had with him. They don't add up to much, a tiny fraction of my life, but treasures of eternity, each one."

"I'm grateful for that too, Penelope," I said, utterly sincere. She nodded and hugged me and went weeping down the hallway to their room.

"Be gracious to us, O Lord, for we are in distress; our eyes waste away from grief, our souls and bodies also. For our lives are spent with sorrow, and our years with sighing; our strength fails because of our misery, and our bones waste away."

Maundy Thursday

Exodus 12:1-14
Psalm 116:1-2, 12-19
1 Corinthians 11:23-26
John 13:1-17, 31b-35

The three days of Jesus' death and resurrection have begun, and Penelope and I never got to church tonight. We'd arranged to pick up Mercedes and Josephine and got there about twenty minutes ahead of time. Her house, just a block off the square, is one of Shippensforge's "haunted houses." It's not got Victorian turrets or towers or anything, just a typical two-story. In fact, if it had ever been painted, it would go unnoticed. I don't know why they never painted it, but the weathered brown boards do give a deserted appearance. Mercedes hasn't done any home decorating for decades; if there are any curtains at the windows, they're raggedy lace and some are just covered with newspaper, long-yellowed. Josephine is gradually upgrading things inside.

We pulled into the rocky, grassy drive leading to the ramshackle garage and waited for a couple minutes, but they didn't come out the back door like Josephine said they would, so Penelope went and knocked. After a minute, Josephine opened it and talked to her and she came back and opened my car door and said, "Complications; we'd better go in."

Mercedes sat on a high-back wooden kitchen chair vacantly looking down at brown water in an old aluminum dishpan, Josephine hovered over her, washing her feet. Sidney was at the kitchen table.

"I looked in the back yard first, but she must have been stooping down right under the window. Were you, Mercedes?" Josephine asked.

"Maybe; I guess so."

"So I was scared half-to-death that you might be out in the street again and I ran out the…"

"No, I was just working in the flowers."

"Well, bless your heart, Mercedes, but I'm afraid it's been a long kinda' time since there have been any flowers out there. Right now, it looks like our Grandpa's pig yard, Rose, 'member that? Nothin' but mud out there right now. Anyhow," she continued as she gently washed, "I walked the streets a little piece that way, a little piece this way, and couldn't see a sign of you. So I called Sidney here…"

"According to our plan," Sidney put in.

"…and we drove around for pretty near an hour, I guess…"

103

"and drove back by the house a few minutes ago on our way to the police station," Sidney picked up the story, "and the headlights caught her, and by golly, there she was, in the backyard, knee deep…"

"…in flowers," Mercedes said softly.

"Sidney, please hold her feet in that towel while I change out this nasty water," Josephine instructed. He knelt down and Mercedes swung her feet over, and he held them until Josephine got back with fresh water. She put her feet in the warm suds and closed her eyes as Josephine began to rub.

"Oh, that feels so good. I think you people must be my—the kind of people who like me and are kind and good."

"You're trying to say friends, aren't 'cha, Mercedes?" Sidney said.

"Yes, that's it."

Penelope and I smiled at each other. We had sat down at the table by this time.

"Well, I hope someday I can help you back as much as you help me."

"That's fine, Mercedes," Sidney said. "We're all in this together."

Josephine patted her feet with a fresh, fluffy towel and put socks and slippers on her.

"C'mon now, Mercedes. Let's get you some clean clothes on, then we'll have some tea and toast."

They shuffled away and when they came back—Mercedes all cozy in her pajamas and robe—I was brewing the tea, Sidney toasting the bread, and Penelope buttering it. Mercedes settled at the table, and Josephine started getting out dishes.

"What's that red mark all across your face there, Jo?" Sidney asked, moving in for a closer look. "Is that from Mercedes hittin' you when we were trying to get her in the house?"

"Well, I reckon it is; it doesn't hurt at all, though."

Mercedes was looking at them, trying to make sense. Now everything was ready, and we all sat down and started eating and drinking together.

"I've forgotten your name," Mercedes said, looking at Josephine, "but did I hit you?"

"You did, honey, but you didn't mean to."

Mercedes got tears in her eyes.

"I'm serious; you didn't mean to do it, and it doesn't matter a-tall," Josephine insisted. "Please pass Mercedes the sugar; that's the way she likes her tea."

We quietly sipped, and after a minute Mercedes said, "I think we need that apple butter Granny made; it's in the refrigerator." Sidney scraped back his chair and hunted for a minute and set a jar of apple butter with a store label on the table. "I'm doubtin' that your Granny made this, but it looks mighty good." And it was. Sweet, spicy, smooth. "The icing on the cake," John would say. Oh, and goodness, I saw him today. He had said he was staying in town for a week or so, to tend to business. I was parked on the square and made no move when he walked by, just watched, my heart beating a little faster.

"God bless you; you're good people," Mercedes said to each of us with a hug as we got ready to leave.

"Maybe I'll just stay and watch Jeopardy! with you two," Sidney offered and was gladly received.

"Cousin Josephine, we're as close as the telephone," Penelope said.

Driving home, we saw church people on the road and pulled up behind Virginia at the light at Washington and Main. She let us drive by her to go into the garage and then pulled in the driveway.

"Where in the world have you been?" she said, getting out of her car

"We went to church at Mercedes's house," I joked.

"We really did," Penelope picked up. "Had footwashing and communion, more or less."

"Come in, honey," I said to Virginia, "and we'll tell you about it." Which we did.

There was a pause in the conversation, and Penelope said, "This thought came to me that we gave up Stephen for Lent."

"Penelope!" Virginia objected. I was shocked, too.

Penelope jumped up. "I'm sorry! These thoughts just come..." and she started down the hall.

"Oh, shoot," Virginia muttered, and went after her. They had a little tussle, Virginia trying to guide her back to the den, Penelope shaking her off, starting to weep and insisting she needed to be alone. Virginia prevailed, and sat her down on the davenport, and we waited in silence to see what would come next.

"Ten months; that's all the time we had together. My life was full and happy before I met Stephen, but he was my missing piece—and now he's missing again."

Virginia patted her knee sympathetically and said, "It's awful, we know, but now I'm thinking about that idea of giving Stephen up for Lent."

"I'm so sorry I said that," Penelope apologized again. "I don't know what it means or why..."

"No, it's okay—I was just so startled at first—but actually, Pastor Morris preached tonight about how giving things up for Lent can become little more than an exercise in self-improvement instead of a true offering to God."

"Are you finding a connection to Stephen?" I wanted to know.

"I think I am," she said tentatively, and paused in concentration. "Pastor said something like, 'We have to give up so much involuntarily—maybe our job, our health, our loved ones to death, and then ultimately, our own lives.' And he went on about how Jesus voluntarily gave up his life. He conquered death, he was not victim to it. And that is the promise for us; we, too, 'are more than conquerors through him who loved us.' I sat in the pew thinking, 'Stephen is not a <u>victim</u> of cancer. He died too early, yes, but he is more than a conqueror, he is part of…'—how did Pastor put it?—it rhymed—he is part of 'God's glorious and victorious plan.' I like that!" Then she added, "although it's already lost some of its power and meaning, just in this little while."

"I know. I like it, too, and believe it completely, but I know just what you mean about losing power," I said.

"Yeah," Penelope said. "Normally, that belief fills me with joy and energy, but right now," she sighed, "it's just words to keep hope and trust from dying altogether."

We were drifting into the deep waters of our grief, when Penelope said, "Let's drink us some alcohol, in memory of Stephen!" and we burst out laughing.

Charlie, the joke was that Stephen, your strong, courageous, on-the-wagon, recovering alcoholic of a son, decided right before he died that he wanted a beer. I think it was Monday, maybe Tuesday of the last week. Virginia, Penelope, and I were idly chatting around the bed, at his service, as he dozed in and out.

"You know what I have a taste for?" he said to Penelope.

"What?" she said with great excitement.

"Beer."

Beer?

"Good grief," he said, amused. "By the looks on your faces, you'd think I just asked you to light a stick of dynamite under my bed."

"But Stephen, why on earth now, after…" I started.

"For good behavior," he joked.

"It's only 1 o'clock in the afternoon," Virginia lamely observed.

"Gin, I'm about a millimeter away from eternity; 1 o'clock doesn't mean much to me."

"Your medications, love. They don't mix with alcohol."

"C'mon; this is the plea of a dying man, here. How about calling a doctor and seeing if it would be okay."

So she did, and the doctor said it would be fine, eat something from the grain group with it, if he could. So, Stephen had a few pretzels and about a half a beer a day for the rest of his life, savoring each swallow and saying too bad he hadn't thought of it sooner.

And on this night we, his women, opened a bottle of wine "to gladden the human heart" and toasted him for being free of the demonic force of alcohol and told stories about what a great guy he was and how we can't believe he's gone and hugged each other and cried some more, and now it's past midnight, but what do I care, Charlie? If I let go of time, I feel closer to you and Stephen.

Yes, moments like those with Penelope and Virginia are precious and healing, but eventually, we have to go to our separate chambers and bear this cross alone. Nights are the hardest. At least I have Cute Baby to hang on to.

<u>Good Friday</u>

Isaiah 52:13-53:12
Psalm 22
Hebrews 10:16-25
John 18:1—19:42

Grief is so strange; it's disconcerting and confusing. Today I've gotten into the craziest mental game of comparing Stephen's death to other deaths, and I just couldn't stop myself. And then my emotions whip me around as I admonish myself for grieving so deeply when, after all, he wasn't murdered when he was 21 like Chelsea Stutgren, didn't die of leukemia at the age of 6 like Millicent Avery's child, wasn't blown apart in war like Chad Brewster.

He way outlived Jesus and had a much easier death. Most victims of crucifixion wasted away on their crosses for days or even weeks. They were positioned on the main road at eye level to serve as a deterrent for insurrectionist activity, prey to birds and insects and the ravages of weather—and yet, Jesus died in just a few hours. Merciful God, is there a point to this horrendous contemplation?

Sarah and I were together today and, eventually, I told her about these incessant, perturbing thoughts. She had called first thing this morning and said she just wanted to drive, she didn't know where, just off into this glorious, sunny day, and did I want to go along? I surely did. Penelope didn't need me. She pretty much slept last week away—a good and healthy thing to do—and now she is grieving with her typical modus operandi, efficient and organized. She spent today creating a website about Stephen where people can leave messages and virtual candles and flowers, read the funeral sermon, etc.

Sarah and I drove west, into Amish country. We saw a buggy, then another, a bike, then another, and soon there were more buggies and bikes than cars, enroute to Good Friday observances. That amazing scene in itself was rejuvenating, a blend of "going back in time" and religious ritual that seemed pure. The sky was cloudless and brilliantly blue and my soul sang— and then wept—and then sang—and then wept...

Sarah and I talked of how immediately the Amish people in Pennsylvania forgave the man who invaded their peaceful country school house and killed their children and teachers, what a miracle that was, how they went to his family to comfort and assure them that they had nothing to fear in the way of vengeance. All of this was assaulting my brain, the beauty of the day and the bleakness within, the power of forgiveness and the anger I was feeling at—at what? Cancer, I guess. For a few minutes there, I felt like I was looking into a kaleidoscope of beautiful and disturbing images. I got a little nauseous.

And then Sarah reached over and patted my hand and said, "So how are you doing, Rose? How are you doing today?" And she waited in silence with sweet kindness while I looked out my side window, crying softly, wiping my eyes and nose...

Later

And I was appalled to realize that anger was building within me at Sarah for invading my privacy! Suddenly, I wanted to be home, mourning in my backyard instead of trapped in this car; but I knew as well that there was salvation in being here with someone I trusted who cared about my suffering. When I was finally able to speak, I forced myself to tell her about the comparison game. She didn't try to talk sense to me about each situation being its own and there's no wrong way to grieve, etc. I both appreciated and resented that, wanting opposite things at the same time. Good gracious, there was no way Sarah, or anyone else, could come out on top with me today. So, I stated the obvious—that comparisons are odious, or "oduious," as Will preferred—and we moved on.

"You know, Stephen and I went through our divorces at the same time," she said. "I think I told you about a conversation we had one day when we ran into each other at the post office, didn't I?"

"I'm not sure; tell me again," I said hungrily.

She started focusing and let out a chuckle. "You and Stephen are so religious, and Stephanie Rose, too, I realize as I get to know her. Not afraid to name the name. Okay, so we were both in the settlement process getting ready for court dates, and we, uh, vented a little. I said more about Bob than I meant to, and he about Denise, I suspect; fellow travelers, you know. And then he asked me something very surprising; he asked me if I felt safe." She glanced over at me. "Have I told you this before?"

I shook my head.

"Well, I wasn't sure what he meant, but then he went on to sort of list how he felt safe through the whole ordeal—safe that his pain would heal, safe from humiliation and guilt, safe from all the legal procedures and financial concerns. And then he said, 'It's pretty comforting to me to know that when I have to go through hell, God is there. Jesus knows. Jesus loves me.' He gave me a squeeze around the shoulders and wished me safety. And you know, that made an impact on me, Rose. Worries and fears didn't have so much power after that, even to this day."

"Now you've got me crying again."

"He's well worth every tear, my dear."

Thank you, God, for Sarah. And for all my family and friends. They comfort and understand, making your love very real. Your peace, however, I'm having trouble finding, but your love is everywhere in this sadness. Again, I pray in gratitude for Morris and Charlene Bryant, your dedicated servants. You have gifted them with hearts and talents that nurture our spirits well. In the name of your beloved son, who died so that we would know the wonder of your love, Amen.

The service tonight was like none other for me because it was about not only Jesus' death but about my son's as well. We sang the solemn reproaches, something new to St. Timothy but ancient in church tradition. Solemn, indeed; high drama. The choir sang Jesus/God's part: "O my people, O my church, what have I done to you? In what have I offended you? Answer me." And then followed a statement of how God had been faithful, statements like, "I led you through the desert forty years and fed you with manna. I brought you through tribulation and gave you my body, the bread of heaven, but…" and always the ending, "…you have prepared a cross for your Savior." Twelve times these verses were sung, each time with a power that came from another world. And twelve times, we believers responded in solid, bold chords, "Holy God, holy and mighty, holy and immortal, have mercy on us." At the end—silence, darkness, and, for me, exhaustion.

Penelope and I maintained the silence on the ride home and into the house, and she went straight to her room. I meditated on the icon of the crucifixion for a few minutes but decided nuts with that and replaced it with what I needed—the icon of the resurrection. Ah, yes.

And in a little while, I will crawl into my cocoon, sad yet safe. Like Stephen is safe.

Easter Vigil

Selected readings from:
Genesis 1:1—2:4a
Genesis 7:1-5, 11-18; 8:6-18; 9:8-13
Genesis 22:1-18
Exodus 14:10-31; 15:20-21
Isaiah 55:1-11
Proverbs 8:1-8, 19-21; 9:4b-6
Ezekiel 36:24-28
Ezekiel 37:1-14
Zephaniah 3:14-20
Jonah 1:1-2:1
Isaiah 61:1-4, 9-11
Daniel 3:1-29
Romans 6:3-11
Luke 24:1-12

I saw the dawn today, pink and glorious, ever more so after a dark and chaotic night filled with tiny, hideous nightmares that, thankfully, I can't remember. As soon as the day was fully bright, I slipped into my muddy boots that had been sitting on the deck since that day Penelope took Stephen and me—eons ago, it seems—to the big rock. Risky, I know, to walk by myself, but I was busting to go and the whole idea was to be alone, so I grabbed my trusty walking stick and followed that path again. In this sacred spot with its strong sense of the primordial, the creation was fresh, new life popping out all over. I saw it in the branches fuzzy with buds and heard it in the bird twittering. I smelled it in the wet, fertile earth and felt it in the warm wind sweeping through. And I felt <u>joy</u> again, for the first time since Stephen's diagnosis.

The brook was frightening, even from a safe and sunny distance, wider and faster than I ever remember. *God, receive the souls of those five people in our county washed away by these waters and comfort their loved ones in their grief as you comfort me in mine this very moment,* I prayed, utterly confident in God's promises to do so.

Part of my joy on this Saturday morning, Charlie, was in knowing how pleased Stephen would be. He said to me not so long ago, "I know you'll have to mourn, Mom, but whenever you can laugh and feel happiness, go for it, okay? Will you promise me that?" Even in that hard moment, the promise was easy to make, since that way of living is our shared faith. I keep thinking of "giving up Stephen for Lent" and seeing it more and more as a positive action on our parts, a lifting him up to God in complete trust that the promise of eternal life is surely fulfilled. And you know, Charlie, this is all so far beyond us; it's the blessing for all God's people, "as numerous as the stars of heaven and as the sand that is on the seashore."

When I got back from the big rock, Penelope was in her gown at the kitchen table in a very different mood from my own. She had in fact, closed the blinds against the glories of the day. But she was fighting the good fight with plans for breaking down and packing up in preparation for leaving Monday morning. I poured a cup of tea from the pot she'd brewed and sat down with her.

"Stephen was right to come here. Thank you for your home, Mama Rose, for letting us stay and for letting me stay this extra time. That's felt secure— but the hardest memories live here, too, you know, and I'm going to be glad to get away from them." And then with a deep sigh, she confessed, "I do feel like I'm heading out into the wilderness, though."

"The future without Stephen must seem bleak to you," I acknowledged.

She nodded and pulled a used tissue out of her pocket, weeping and wiping as she spoke. "I'd imagined the rest of my earthly journey with him at my side, especially my ministry. The folks in the congregation had met him—really liked him—we would have all done well together, I'm sure, serving the Lord in deed and word…"

"I know," I soothed, shedding a sympathetic tear.

"Now, without him—I just don't know… Oh, there will be miracles and manna along the way, God will be present, but, oh! such a desert…"

"I know, Penelope; I'm so sorry."

She found another tissue and cleaned her face, and we drank our tea in silence until she heaved herself out of the chair and carried her cup to the sink. I got up, too, and we embraced, then released each other, and she sighed, "I'd better get to the task. I'll make sure I get all our stuff out of the room so you don't have to deal with it," and padded down the hallway.

While she was organizing and packing I made chicken soup, which we enjoyed for a late lunch. She took a break after that and walked off into the woods. I carried a stack of sympathy cards that had accumulated over the last few days and thank you cards to fill out and settled on the deck. I had it on my mind to call next door and see what was going on. I had noticed a car parked out front early this morning and figured it was the midwife's. And then I heard Jim calling my name and yelled to guide him back.

He took the steps in one bound, his grin stretched wide.

I jumped up. "The baby's here?"

"She sure is, all 9 pounds, 3 ounces of her!" he beamed, grabbing me for a little whirl. "Anita's a regular Mother Earth over there, a hundred percent natural childbirth," he bragged.

"Was it tough on her?"

"Oh, yeah, 18-hour labor, and, yeah—tough with that big baby. But she's got this perverse thing going with her own suffering—better her than the world, you know—so she's feeling pretty proud and satisfied right now. And wants to see you and introduce you and the new girl to each other whenever you feel like coming over."

I was about to ask the baby's name when a strange noise came from the woods. We looked at each other in puzzlement and the sound came again, louder.

"Sounds like an injured animal," Jim said, and I realized what it was.

"It's Penelope." Her anguished bellows rang across the yard, and I grabbed Jim's arm and steered him toward their house—to get away and to give her privacy. *Hear the cries of your servant, O God.*

Next door was new life, in its most precious, miraculous form—a brand new baby. Jim placed her in my arms, Anita looking on with a tired smile. She's as brown as her mama, but looks like Jim, too. I stayed for a long time, rocking her and basking in the love of this sweet family. They haven't named her yet.

"We need at least 24 hours," Anita maintained, "to get to know her."

"Yeah. Wouldn't want to name her Larissa Mae if she's a Tamika Kay," Jim wisecracked. So, more joy in my world, and I left them with eager anticipation of times ahead with this little one.

The sun was dropping below the trees when I went back around to the deck and gathered my cards and came inside to take up my pen again. The house is dusky and still. I can hear Penelope's light snore and pray that she will rest peacefully for a while. And I, too, shall retire now. The whole family has agreed to meet tonight at St. Timothy at 11 o'clock for Easter Vigil. The Bryants have moved the service back to the middle of the night. None of us are sleeping too well anyway, not even Stephanie Rose, so we're all up for this spiritual adventure.

I'll <u>try</u> to get some rest, but I get more excited than a kid on Christmas Eve about this service, even in this year of our great sadness. Especially this year, maybe. This is the night! I'm already hearing the ancient hymn chanted out into the still darkness, as though we are huddled in a first century cave, proclaiming a radical new faith upon which we live and move and have our being:

Rejoice, heavenly powers! Sing, choirs of angels! Exult, all creation, around God's throne! Jesus Christ, our King, is risen! Sound the trumpet of salvation! Rejoice, O Earth, in shining splendor, radiant in the brightness of your King! Christ has conquered! Glory fills you! Darkness vanishes forever! Rejoice, O Mother Church...

and on and on the hymn goes, into the farthest reaches of the cosmos and the human soul.

Easter Sunday

Isaiah 25:6-9 and Acts 10:34-43
Psalm 118:1-2, 14-24
1 Corinthians 15:1-11
John 20:1-18

What an unusual Easter Sunday! Instead of having Easter dinner at mine or Virginia's house, we went into the city and gathered at Stephanie Rose's condo this afternoon, enjoying a feast carried in by one and all. Afterwards, we strolled over to the park a couple blocks from her place, lazily sunning ourselves on the benches and taking turns (except for great-grandmother) climbing with Mack on the playground fort, savoring the sweetness of resurrection while tasting the bitterness of loss. When Stephanie said, "It seems like Uncle Stephen is everywhere and nowhere," we all nodded. And we all slept in this morning rather than worship because we worshiped last night—and this morning, actually. Penelope and I got to bed around 3am. What a night it was!

As we held symbolic vigil to celebrate the resurrection of Jesus, I was thinking of our vigil with Stephen two weeks ago, and I suspect my people were, too. On that Saturday, Barry and Virginia and Stephanie and Mack had come mid-morning. The last time Stephen had spoken was around 3 o'clock in the afternoon. Stephanie had been sitting with him, and he told her he wanted to see everybody. This was the fourth time he had summoned us for a lengthy and meandering farewell. It was getting a little anticlimactic and nerve-wracking, frankly—even comical. But, of course, we filed in and circled the bed again. Jim had dropped in to see if we needed anything and we swept him in with us.

So, Stephen said one more final goodbye, doped-up and peaceful. He strung names together with phrases in the same slurred, disjointed speech, smiling at times. "Love one another—Mack truck—Steverino—Jesus—communion of the saints, resurrection of the body—Mom—Gin—thanks for the beer—come and see me—Denise—Stephanie Rose—the Cubs, the pennant—I see you, Jesus—through the valley—saved by grace…" and on it went, and we couldn't help but laugh, by this time, which surprised Jim, I think, since he hadn't been through it three times before. Just like Stephen, to make us laugh at such a moment. Oh, and it pained me so that he said Denise and not Penelope. How that must have hurt her, but what can you do? It wasn't really significant, but still…

And then the hospice nurse came, to make sure we had everything we needed. "Very soon," she said, and we called the Bryants and stood around the bed again and they administered the Commendation for the Dying as the sun waned outside. By this time, Mack was fussy, and they left with Virginia and Barry to spend the night at their house. I stayed up until midnight with Penelope, listening to his labored breathing, and then realized that she should/could/would be in bed holding him but for my presence. So, I said good night, kissing him, my tears dropping on his face. And then 5am and he was—gone. Still. *Oh, God, take my boy into your arms,* my heart sobbed.

Later

You know I'm envious, don't you, Charlie, that you and Stephen are now together somehow? Maybe wondrous is a better description than envious, for along with the jealousy, there's delight—with a strong curious edge. And I'm doing amazingly well, at this point, I think. Last night's service was splendid and glorious; those are high falutin' words, but the exact right ones. What went on there is about why I believe in God, the Father Almighty; Jesus Christ, his only Son, our Lord; and the Holy Spirit. Hearing the stories of God's mighty acts throughout history delighted me, protected me, and filled me with gratitude. I found myself thanking God over and over again for Stephen's beautiful life and, now, for his eternal rest. And how fervently I wish, Charlie, that everyone could know the peace and joy of God's great love.

Sometimes when we search for God, I think maybe our expectation is too large. I find the divine most readily in the details of life. God is present and powerful because I am able to keep putting one foot in front of the other through this heartache. And I don't mean just trudge grudgingly on. No, I am empowered to move ahead without bitterness and fear, with love and hope.

Maybe there are God's mighty acts and God's gentle acts. Mighty are the epic stories of faith we recall during Easter Vigil—the Creation, parting of the seas, dead bones knitting together and living again, and the zenith event, the resurrection. Then there are more modest, everyday circumstances that unfold by divine power. Such as the baptism of a teenager last night. His name is Tariq, he's fifteen years old. He is Louie and Rita's foster child, all of a sudden. It's a wild story; he burglarized their house a while back. I found out about the break-in from one of Louella's zealous letters to the paper:

Robbery Unjust, Indecent

Where is justice and decency in our world? This is a message for the fiends who broke into the Smith home on Maple Street, built by them and Habitat for Humanity: Have you thieves no self-respect? Why would you victimize innocent people struggling to make an honest living? Why not come and break into my home, 237 W. Washington Street, where there are plenty of valuables just molding and rusting? Please come and help yourselves, so my dogs can tear you to shreds and justice will prevail.

Louella S. Rutledge

Oh, Louella. We just shake our heads sometimes. Anyway, Louie and Rita introduced me to Tariq (tie-reek) when we were standing around the fire last night outside the church, and then Louie took me aside and told me the story.

"It ain't no fun gettin' robbed, Rose. You feel like they're still in the house, you know, so don't nothin' feel safe for awhile. The house was all tore up and church folk come and helped us put things back together. Crazy thing is, we're gonna' come out pretty good on the deal. Louella, she give us a thousand bucks, wouldn't take no for an answer. Most of the stuff we've done got back and insurance is payin' on what's busted or gone.

"Thing is, Rita and me got to talkin' 'bout how good God is and how we know right up front how forgiveness works, after what we been through with losing the baby and all. And see, they caught 'em, Tariq and this other feller, a grown-up man. So we prayed over it and then we went down to the station and asked the law what was gonna' happen to the kid and they said he'd be goin' back to juvenile. Said he didn't have no parents around, only grandparents and they wouldn't have him back. We asked if we could have him for a foster child. Everybody said, 'Oh, you don't wanna' do that,' but we just kept prayin' and just knowed that God had done for us and we wanted to do for him. So we kept goin' everyplace we had to go, juvenile court and whatnot, and by golly we got him."

By golly. And now what? How in the world is this going to go for the three of them? Hard to imagine that it will go smoothly. And what does Tariq's baptism mean to him, I wonder. He appeared very ill at ease. Being the only person of color in the crowd—well, except for Miguel and a couple little mixed-race grandchildren we see occasionally—is undoubtedly a stretch for the boy. Louie and Rita's place ought to be a better situation for him than the juvenile detention center—but then there's the cultural gulf between them. One thing for sure—God's gracious love is proclaimed in their deeds.

When Louie and I stepped back into the circle and I took my place next to Penelope, the rest of our party—Barry, Gin, Stephanie, Angelica and the baby—were just walking up through the darkness into the light of the fire. Steph greeted us with, "Where's Uncle Stephen?" We stared dumbly at her for a nano-second, and her head snapped back, recoiling at her own question. "How weird; I can't believe I said that."

"You can't believe he's gone, that's the problem," Penelope responded. "I have thoughts like that all day and all night."

Then Bruce Leppard intoned, "The light of Christ." All present sang back, "Thanks be to God," and we fell in behind the Christ candle carried by little Maddie's big brother, Bryan. It seems Maddie had insisted that she wanted to go to church at midnight, and when they showed up, Bryan got drafted to be acolyte.

And after the splendid, glorious service, we were invited across the street to the home of our pastors for breakfast at 1 o'clock in the morning. What a lovely gift that was for them to give to the congregation. We were quite small in the church, maybe 30 people, but in the house it was a festive crowd. They'd prepared scrumptious smoked salmon and a tasty vegetable quiche and yummy side dishes. We milled around, eating and chatting. Here are a few scenes: Louella lecturing Tariq about straightening up and flying right. Jacob and Angelica flirting with shy smiles and hanging out with Bryan Bowers and Tariq. Mack, between pillows on the guest bed, with Maddie's arms around him, both sound asleep. Theodore exclaiming to Lloyd, "Oh, and when you slipped that Neapolitan in, it was just too perfect!" and kissing him on the cheek right at the moment I entered the little hallway where they were alone. "What in the world is a Neapolitan?" I had to ask. It's a chord; that's all I could comprehend from their technical definition. And then Louella entered saying it was past her bedtime and she needed them to take her home. I seized the moment, though, to tell them how much the service had meant to me—beauty and strength for the morrow.

I know what lies ahead. There are moments when I dread the rest of my life. I fear the depths of grief. Even more, I fear the zombie existence that can move in and take over and I can hardly "lift a finger." Faith is my answer; God will wipe away my tears, now and in the hereafter—but not in the form of easy panacea. My prayer and resolution between now and my own passing over is from today's psalm—"I shall not die, but live, and recount the deeds of the Lord." That's what Stephen would want. That's what I can do. *Come, Lord Jesus, live in me.*

Acts 4:32-35
Psalm 133
1 John 1:1—2:2
John 20:19-31

Now. Now. Now. This moment. *Let me be in this moment, God. Let me feel what I'm feeling.* I sit alone on my deck, a pleasant wind blowing the clouds so that it's sunny, gray, sunny, gray, second by second. Trying to feel what I'm feeling. Trying to write my soul down. This is my way of moving through life, to feel-think-write-reflect-know-live. But there's so much today, almost too much feeling, too much life to express in words. So, I watch the clouds, feel the wind, listen to my heart, listen for God...

I think I'll go to Rutledge Home in a bit, get back on that track with visiting, see how the building project is coming along. Sam Benshaw is the person there I most want to see, rest in the wise peacefulness of his many years. He was at Stephen's funeral, transported by the very thoughtful Pam Turner. I just saw old Sam from a distance, a funny, fuzzy sight, his white hair completely out of control—eyebrows, ears, nose, thick thatch with colorful African cap perched on top. Reminded me of one of those folk craft "apple-faced" dolls with stuffed nylon stockings for heads.

Ah, but I'm not going to go today, I just decided. I need to be still, alone, listening, resting. I expected that I would have plenty of solitude and quietness after Penelope left last Monday morning. Funny, I didn't want her to come, and then I didn't want her to leave. When it was time for her to get in her car and drive away, we clung to each other at the front door, unable to speak. I felt like we were breaking a thread that connected us both to Stephen—a thread which had to be broken, of course, life has to move ahead—and away she went.

I waved goodbye, shut the door, and sank down on the settee in the living room, an uncommon place to settle unless visiting with company. I vividly remember an overwhelming sensation at that moment of how different the world was now, never to be the same as when Stephen was in it. He would never park in the driveway again or walk through that front door or call me on Sunday night. No more birthday parties, I thought, staring into space but seeing his little parties around the dining room table when he turned 1, 5, 13. This little house where we grew up together will never be the same. There's no point in calling that bedroom "Stephen's room" anymore.

I expected everything to be still and lonely for a while, but the phone soon rang, Virginia saying she'd come around noon to take me out to lunch. I dutifully went, for her sake as well as my own. She invited me to come and stay with them for awhile, but I didn't even consider it. I have to step into this new reality, this new world without Stephen, where death seems so powerful.

Gracious, loving God, thank you for being with me, strong in my heart, in my thoughts, in my emotions. Thank you for that dream about Stephen, where he came into the kitchen when I was working at the sink and put his hands on my shoulders and kissed the back of my head. Comfort washed over me in that quick flash and continues to do so whenever I recall it. I praise you, Almighty One, for your resurrecting power. Love is strong as death. We are never apart from your love. Even so, this is hard, as you well know, Jesus. Amen.

Stephanie and I have stayed close, too. The poor girl is all stressed out because, as a faculty member, she is being required to text and Twitter and be on Facebook. "Grandma," she moaned the other night, "I really think, in the final analysis, that technology is going to be the ruin of our civilization." Her earnestness made me laugh. She's a 21st century woman, on the cutting edge of gender studies and healthy eco-living and many other matters, but no techno-baby, that one. Fortunately, she has Angelica and Ethan for her IT support. And she has good support as she grieves. "I've always felt like I had two dads," she described, talking about missing her Uncle Stephen. "He was the dad I could tell everything without getting in trouble."

The week continued busy. St. Timothy is attentive. "How very good and pleasant it is when kindred live together in unity!" Charlene preached this morning and presented an idea I'll remember, basically that God's resurrecting power gives us two miracles. The first is the resurrection of our Lord. The second is the gathering of believers around that decisive happening. The creation of the Body of Christ is a treasured miracle to this old church lady. I really resonated, too, when Charlene went a step further, acknowledging the sad truth of how often the Church is perceived as a set of rules and beliefs rather than a way of living together that brings joy and provides "bread for the journey." *Please, Great God who has joined us together, help us live out, however clumsily, the miracle of being Christ's body in and for the world.*

As far as everyday life, my world is disheveled, unsettled, routines breaking down. Merciful heavens, I can't even hang up my clothes anymore, wash the dishes. This is how it was when Charlie died. I remember late fees and overdrafts; I couldn't even do simple business. Tuesday was especially restless and unproductive. I wandered around the house, trying to lock on to some project or other—finish my so-called e-Book, "Great-grandma Enjoys Mack's First Year," finish reading my novel, finish something—but no go. I took a drive around town, saw the realtor's For Sale sign in Florence's yard, thought of John gone back to California. He's in a serious relationship, according to Angelica. So much of my life is over.

The thought of going to circle in the evening helped me fight dreaded ennui. Madge had kindly said she would pick me up (I probably would have stayed home at the last minute otherwise), and it was good to be with sisters. When I heard reports of gifts given on behalf of those in need all over the globe—together with a sign-up sheet for weekly visits with Pauline Shuster at Rutledge Home to bring a little cheer into her troubled days—I was warmed with a feeling of walking together in the light of God and rejoiced once again that love is not a limited commodity but overflows and binds us together.

Deedee and mother Faye Leppard and mother-in-law Helen Brewster—women who know grief all too well—carried in lunch and spent Wednesday afternoon with me. We did our talking and crying about Chad and Stephen until Faye decided we'd had enough and got on the I-net to show us this remarkable and hilarious video of a 3-year-old conducting Beethoven's Ninth. Of course, that led to a couple hours of dancing hippos and old movie clips and a stirring rendition of "African Rainstorm." We also guffawed at a list of thought-provoking lines like, "Okay, so what's the speed of dark?" and "How many of you believe in psycho-kinesis? Raise my hand." Laughing is such a relief! Then Helen took us to a website about a group that plans trips to Iraq for Gold Star mothers. She's going in a couple weeks. Wow.

On Thursday, I had mixed feelings about working at the food pantry and opted to stay home—it had only been eleven days since Stephen's passing, after all. I worked in the yard instead, a good move. But that yucky sadness and restlessness took over the afternoon. Once again, I was saved by friends—dinner with Theodore and Lloyd. They'd invited me last Sunday. I'd said yes and asked what I could bring.

"Nothing, Rose; absolutely nothing," Lloyd said.

"I'll bring a bottle of wine; red or white?"

"No, absolutely not, Rose. I don't even know what the entrée will be. I must be in total control, you see, or I'll be on pins and needles between now and then" Lloyd fluttered, and I had to laugh. "Just bring your broken heart," he said, hugging me, and I had to cry.

They were their usual scintillating selves, witty and up-to-date with culture and politics and Aunt Louella's latest antics. She's about to get kicked out of the garden club for her harangues about how they need to take action against invasive plants or something. "She is my beloved aunt," Theodore said firmly before uttering the 'but' we all knew was coming. "But the woman accepts no compromise between good and evil—<u>her</u> definition of good and evil, naturally."

"For all the good she does," Lloyd quietly observed, "her actions are sometimes a form of playing God." Yes. We'll just keep loving and tolerating—and giving thanks for her ornery witness.

We talked a lot about Stephen. Theodore didn't know him very well as Stephen had moved to Chicago by the time Theodore came to town, so Lloyd and I told stories. I found out that there had been a showdown when Stephen was on church council years ago over Lloyd's homosexuality; some members thought he should leave. Stephen, according to Lloyd, had helped resolve the matter in Lloyd's favor, with "firmness and love for all." That's my son. These dear men gave me a CD of Brahms's "Let Not Grief Burden Your Soul," which I've played several times already, its straightforward words and music helping each time.

> Let not grief overwhelm you, consume you. Be quiet; trust God's intent and be content, my spirit. Why dwell today on sorrow tomorrow? Your Savior stands by your side, and you abide in favor. Then go about your serving unswerving, confessing: God holds the key to what shall be your blessing. Amen.

That phrase "…trust God's intent…" bothers me a little. I don't believe that God intends for Stephen or anyone else to die of cancer. God's intent is always loving, always about life; that is the true nature of the Divine. So when cancer—or anything tragic or cruel—happens (mysteriously), God's intent and purpose is redemption. I don't know how Brahms understood those words, but that's how I do.

I'm spending time with the new girl on the block, of course. Zahra Camille is her name. Zahra is Swahili for 'flower.' "So we kind of named her after you," Jim grinned, but then got serious when Anita went to change diapers. "Predictably, we're dealing with post partum depression. Even as proactive as we're trying to be, she's on the edge. Just wanted to give you a heads up." Fie. *Help us all, dear Lord.*

And an unsettling development for Mindy, too. I was telling Stephanie Rose how out of touch I've been with Mindy and Miguel and how I'm eagerly anticipating getting back on track with them, especially now that he's free and they're together again.

"Miguel's gone," Steph said.

"What?"

"He's gone, Grandma."

"For good?"

"Seems like it."

"Where?"

"Mexico, Mindy thinks. Gone back home. It's weird but not quite as sudden as it appears. She's got a pretty good handle on things and really does want to get together with you. It just happened last week, and she didn't want to lay it on you while you're in mourning, she said. Give her a call whenever you feel like it. She's probably going to wait on you."

Sigh. I wonder when I will feel like I have the extra strength to call her. I'm depleted right now. And as I look ahead to next week, I don't really want so much activity and relationship. I just want to mourn. We'll see.

Dear Lord, help Jim and Anita to be aware of your presence, whether they name you or not. Give them strength. Redeem their situation. Guide Anita to the help she needs for her joy in the baby to win out over the dark forces of depression. Redeem Mindy's situation, too. Help her with her confusion and loss. It's so good that she is in the community for this hard time. I know you will see her through, and she will walk this valley with Jesus as her shepherd, his rod and his staff comforting her. Amen.

My St. Lord, what a ramble this has been, Charlie! And you know what I'm going to do now? Keep sitting here, playing this game with the sun and clouds and wind. When the sun shines, it's the warm brightness of God's love. When the clouds cover the sun, Jesus is sitting beside me in the grayness. And when the wind blows, it's the Holy Spirit blowing away my blues.

Third Sunday of Easter

Acts 3:12-19
Psalm 4
1 John 3:1-7
Luke 24:36b-48

It is so weird, Charlie. I missed worship this morning, and my faith seems all tentative, just like that! Apart from the community, I become a different person. The thing is, my caring, intelligent sisters and brothers stimulate my thoughts and confirm my beliefs as we share doubts and certainties and live them out together. Separate from that, especially given present circumstances, the resurrection story seems dull, perhaps even meaningless, perhaps even preposterous. Oh dear Lord, perhaps even irrelevant. I'm wondering about it all, dabbling in disbelief. Oh, enough of this! God is love. I'm stopping right there. I'm going to eat a hearty lunch and go to Rutledge Home before I bog down.

Later

I checked out the new addition at Rutledge—wow, looks like a building already—and then headed straight for Sam's room. He had both hands on his cane, leaning forward, sound asleep.

"Sam," I said softly, then louder. He peered up at me through his thick lenses. I was about to identify myself when he smiled and said, "Why it's Rose, isn't it? Sit down here, girl, and tell me how you're getting along."

"I guess pretty well. How are things around here?"

"You mean at Rutledge Heritage Estate?" he said, an amused twinkle in his eye.

"Oh, yes, I saw the new signs. A name change to go with the expansion, eh?"

"I guess. Still the same place, though, and no complaints from me. Life is good."

"Are you looking forward to your hundredth?"

"Birthday? Surely, if the good Lord blesses me with that, and it's fine if he doesn't. I'm grateful for each day, but they're getting more and more redundant."

I understand. "You've seen a lot of living, haven't you?"

"More than enough," he somberly reflected. "And how fare the good people at St. Timothy this morning?"

"I didn't make it to worship. Not sure why. My daughter and her family are downstate visiting her husband's folks. And I didn't sleep at all last night, finally dropping off around 6am and sleeping until 10, so—I don't know—I think I was also a little wary of more joy than I could handle in this Easter season—when I'm…"

He nodded. "How long has it been since your son died?"

"Three weeks today."

"What a fine home-going you had for him."

I nodded and thanked him for being there. "You've lost a child, haven't you, Sam?"

"Two. Hazel when she was twelve and Wesley five years ago. I'd like to go home to Jesus before I lose another one. It's like no other pain, isn't it, Rose?"

His sympathy was making me cloud up. "Yes," I managed, and had the urge to share more. "I'm finding today especially difficult. The resurrection holds no power for me this minute," I confessed.

"That can even happen when we're right there in the pew, can't it?" he said knowingly. "Trusting God's promises and staying close with Jesus is hard in this world. That's why I'm not afraid of dying, because we don't have to keep trying; no more struggling against the devil; the battle's won. We're with Jesus forever, awash in God's grace."

We sat in silence for a time. Sam was thinking hard, I could feel it, something powerful coming up in him from way down deep. He went to another time and place—and took me with him…

"The Great Flood of 1927 devastated my world, wiped my family out. Some drowned right then, some took years to die from it. I went into a government camp, 22 years old, hoping for work, but I couldn't take that hell hole for long. I headed for Chicago like most poor colored people from Mississippi. I was well-educated for a Negro and got a job right away at the brand new Stevens Hotel looking over Lake Michigan, biggest hotel in the world. I made good money and I was ready to live it up. Conked my hair, got some Oxford bags and gold fobs down to my ankles. I learned the latest dances and found the Negro speak-easys and had some fine times."

I smiled at the thought of this venerable poet kicking it up in his younger days.

"One night, through the smoke and music, I looked across the room and there was the prettiest little gal I'd ever seen. 'Ain't she sweet, see her comin' down the street.' Yessiree, she was sweet. 'Ain't she nice, look her over once or twice.' I just looked once and knew I had to have her."

He looked down and paused, contemplating whether to continue, I think.

"I knew she was forbidden fruit; she told me the first time we danced that she was married. I did the wrong thing and our passion kept exploding. She warned me that it was getting dangerous, I should stay away, but I was young and foolish—and selfish. Her man came storming into the apartment when we were together one day. She pushed me out of the bed and told me to hide. I was behind the bedroom door when he threw it open and started shooting. She went down right away. I wrestled the gun from him and shot him in the stomach and again in the chest. I'd never touched a gun before. In seconds, they were both dead."

Impossible, I thought, my eyes glued to this old, old man, this friend, this kind and gentle person.

"I fumbled to put my clothes on and fled, sick and trembling, not stopping until I reached Mississippi. I worked on the federal levee project, but I was dead inside, guilty, terrified I'd be hunted down. Only by the grace of God did I keep going at all. I went to church not because I believed but because I wanted to believe—and I found Irene."

Yes, on "That Wonderful Cloudy Day," I thought, remembering his sweet poem about meeting his wife at a church picnic. I'll have to go back and read it again, in light of all this.

"I told her everything. 'Sweet Jesus,' she whispered and stared into my eyes like she was looking for a monster. And then she said, 'Samuel Benshaw, I cannot become your wife until you make this right.' I couldn't speak, but I nodded and broke down, and she held me, calm and strong, holiness surging through her. I knew at that moment that I could find healing and new life."

He sat there marvelling at Irene and God, I think, until I prompted, "Then what, Sam?"

"Irene's family was well-to-do. Her father was a professor at Tuskegee Institute. He entered into an arrangement on my behalf with an attorney. The four of us—her distinguished father, a highly educated lawyer, and Irene and I—marched into a precinct headquarters in Chicago on April 11, 1930, two years after the shooting. 'What do you boys want?' an officer asked, after making us wait a few minutes. I still remember the sneer in his voice and how it made me shiver. But there was a man of God there, Captain Levitt. 'Gentlemen,' he pronounced, coming out of his office, everyone turning to look at him. 'What do you gentlemen want? How can we help you?' God's healing power was at work again.

"There was a trial; I was found innocent by reason of self-defense but had to serve time for fleeing the scene..."

He stopped abruptly and looked at me. "You and I are the only two people on this earth who know about that time." I nodded my confidentiality.

"Are you shocked?"

I took a deep breath. "Oh, my, yes. I'm shocked by your past and—and—equally amazed at God's power in your life."

"Before the flood and my sinfulness in Chicago, I was pretty pleased with how God and I were doing. When all that misery hit, I lost God and lived each day in despair. Not until I turned my life over to Jesus—all the way—did I see in the blessed Saviour both my misery and God's love. He opened my mind, and I saw he was the bridge I needed, the bridge back to God, back into life.

"I didn't tell you her name, the woman who got shot. It was Grace."

My St. Lord.

As we were re-entering the present, I said, "Your story—my goodness, Sam—it's a precious gift I will carry with me; it speaks of resurrection; it helps me. Thank you, dear friend, dear brother."

We mortals have so many struggles in this life. Driving home, I thought about Jim and Anita. When I was over there the other day, I looked down at Zahra, cradled in my arms, and thought how new babies encompass the universe. *Charlie, I remembered holding Stephen on that spring morning so many years ago, and you came into my hospital room and we caressed his little fingers and toes and marveled at the love of the Creator. And hope—that's the only thing to call it—surged through my sadness as I beheld little Zahra's innocent and fresh beginning.*

But poor Anita is not doing well. As soon as we sat down in the living room it was evident that her cheerfulness was forced; it was painful to watch her, really. Then the baby started fussing and was soon bleating frantically. Anita tried to soothe her, patting and whispering, singing and rocking, but I saw her own tears coming, and after a minute, she put the baby in my arms and left the room. I walked around, jiggling the warm bundle of life against my chest until she quieted. When Anita came back, we talked about "new baby blues." I told her how surprised I was at my own feelings of depression right after Stephen was born, worried that I wouldn't ever be able to love him as much as I did Virginia.

"How long did it last?" she asked.

"Not long. Just a few months, maybe even weeks."

"But you're not mentally ill!" she said, sounding resentful and forlorn. "I probably shouldn't have even had this baby."

"That's crazy talk, Anita," I unfortunately said, and she started weeping again.

"Oh, Rose, I feel terrible acting like this when you're in grief. I just feel so helpless, so—so—out of control..."

I went and sat by her on the davenport and put Zahra back in her arms and squeezed her shoulders and bent my head to hers. We didn't talk much—exhaustion was in the air—but I didn't want to leave her alone; I wanted to mother her. After all, there would be no grandmother coming to help out; both of their mothers are gone. This was Jim's first day back to work, and I wound up staying until he got home, helping her fix supper and starting a load of wash. Of course, they're using cloth diapers, being such huge environmentalists. Jim read the situation as soon as he walked in.

"Rough afternoon, Nita?" he asked, hugging her to him. She nodded into him. "Did you take your new medication, babe?" She shook her head. "Oh, Anita, baby, you've _got_ to."

"And contaminate my breast milk?" she lashed out. "Do you want a junkie for a baby?" Oh, dear.

"I'm going to go now," I interjected, and Jim nodded glumly, his attention focused on his wife, the mother of his child.

And these children won't turn to you, O God. I guess they won't. But your spirit is within them nonetheless, so evident in their gentleness with each other and with your creation. Your love draws them together. Help me be a good neighbor. Guide me with your wisdom, strengthen me with the knowledge that in Jesus, our miseries and your powerful love come together in victory over this world's woes. Amen.

<u>Fourth Sunday of Easter</u>

Acts 4:5-12
Psalm 23
1 John 3:16-24
John 10:11-18

I can't get it through my head that I will never see Stephen again. Never share jokes, never enjoy that special way we had of sensing each other's moods and exulting in life as mother and son. It's all over. Dear God, it's over, gone. Friday night, I was bushwhacked with grief when I innocently watched a BBC production of "Romeo and Juliet" on television. I pretty much have that play memorized and yet I didn't anticipate the power that Act IV, Scene iv would have on me, when Capulet finds the lifeless Juliet. "O child! O child! My soul, and not my child! Dead art thou! Alack! My child is dead; And with my child my joys are buried." I grabbed the remote and switched off.

And now, Cute Baby's gone, too. I found her on the deck around noon on Thursday, lying there as though she was padding toward the door to scratch to come in and just gave out and sank down. Her body was still warm. I gathered her up and sat with her in my lap for awhile, stroking her soft fur and mulling over the miracle of life and the scandal of death, letting tears of gratitude and grief stream on out for her, for Stephen, for Florence Lawrence, for the world and all sadness everywhere. Then I wrapped her in that pretty piece of fabric I got when I went to Africa, and Jim helped me bury her in the woods when he got home. *Thank you, God, for that cute baby!*

Bob Thurgood died this week, too, a seemingly healthy man leaving behind poor old Mary, in her dementia, at Rutledge. Where's the sense in that? When I read his obituary—sudden heart attack—I automatically planned to go to his funeral out at Community Fellowship, but when it was time to get ready, I sank down on the couch, sad and weary beyond words. My life is just all messed up. I can't perceive anything rationally, normally.

This morning at church, for example, I was doing pretty well, composed and sitting contentedly with Virginia and Mindy and Danny and Sherry. But then things got a little wild at St. Timothy, Shippensforge.

For starters, the sermon was quite provocative. Well, let's begin at the beginning; the Bible was quite provocative. And when Pastor was hitting the point of us being commanded to lay down <u>our</u> lives for <u>our</u> friends, Deedee started crying—and I did, too. She was sitting in her usual place, way up ahead of us, but I could see her shoulders heaving and hear her quiet sobs, the pain stabbing so suddenly. Maddie, the picture of 6-year-old compassion, was staring at her from across the aisle. Pastor noticed, too, with a look of sympathetic concern, but carried on. What else would a preacher do? This is the gospel, and Chad is Exhibit A.

Goodness, Helen is in Iraq right now, with that group of grieving mothers. I imagine that was feeding into Deedee's distress. Helen had told us she wanted to be where Chad died and meet the people whose freedom he died for. Deedee and her in-laws have disagreed over the war from day one, she strongly opposed to American involvement, Helen and Jack proud that their son helped depose a ruthless dictator. They're pretty open and honest, thank heaven, tolerating each others' viewpoints (the elders more tolerant than the fiery young Deedee, I think). I suspect Helen's trip has torn open Deedee's wounds but pray that God will work it all for the good.

Okay, and next, Morris stated from the pulpit, "Jesus offers a stunning alternative to the way we cling to life, desperately afraid to lose it or even to lose its trappings. A crucial implication of our Lord and Savior's commandment and example—largely ignored by wealthy Christians throughout history—is for us to live more simply so that others may simply live."

"Amen!" Louella shouted! That was startling enough, but then she jumped up, Bible open, and started challenging us with First John. "How does God's love abide in anyone who has the world's goods and sees a brother or sister in need and yet refuses help?" Where was our compassion for the poor and needy, she demanded, and bemoaned our paltry contribution to the world hunger fund. Even for the zealous Louella, this was extreme. I noticed Theodore closing his eyes and slowly shaking his head. Morris stared at her for a minute after she plunked down in the stunned silence. Then he gathered himself, cleared his throat and said, "Exactly, Louella. And, um, thank you for your witness," and wrapped things up. Mercy, how awkward. But just think if we all had Louella's passion...

And, I must say, Eucharist seemed especially lively after all that, as though a trumpet had sounded. People still seemed fired up at coffee hour. An impromptu meeting set up when Jacob was talking to Louella about the trip he's been organizing to Mexico. It's coming up on a year since the accident that eventually led to Rosa's death. Jacob's stayed in touch with her mother and is organizing a mission trip to their village which he had told us about during announcements. Virginia and I joined their conversation in the fellowship hall to pledge our support. The three of them—elderly activist, upper crust baby boomer, and impassioned teenager—formed a ring of holy energy, me on the outside.

They set a goal to increase our world hunger offering five-fold and talked about starting a prison ministry. Normally, I think I would have been right in there with them, but in my present state, I looked upon their plans as impossible, futile. Was I thinking that nothing matters since my son is dead? I don't know. Whatever I was feeling was bad. I didn't feel like myself.

"What would you think about St. Timothy having a Covenant of Caring and asking all members to pledge that no one in this congregation will ever be in need?" Virginia said to Louella and Jacob.

I had to turn straight around and walk off so I didn't laugh sarcastically right in her face. I mean, it's a wonderful thought, and we already come pretty close to doing that for each other, I think. I'd sign it, I'm for it, but I can already feel the resistance and imagine the discussion about people's worthiness and not "pouring money down a rat's hole." I wish I could tell Stephen about it. He'd know exactly why I was amused. Oh, merciful heavens, I don't think I'm even making any sense.

And then there's the situation next door. Jim is scared "shitless" (he may very well be constipated with worry) that Anita is going to "do something." A girlfriend of Anita's has come to visit and then he has an aunt from Indy lined up to come and stay, as in 24-hour surveillance, it seems. "Check in on her once in awhile, will you, Rose?" he requested. Yikes.

And now, I wait for Penelope's call. Two weeks ago she called from St. Paul where she went from here to spend time with her Aunt Margaret. "Mama Rose, I did the craziest thing; I didn't even let my mother know I was in town," she'd reported. She's emptied Stephen's apartment. That had to be a huge and wrenching job, but she had it done in two days. Strange to think that his worldy goods have pretty much been disposed of. Last week was her first Sunday back in her parish, leading worship and all. "Hard but good, salvific." Salvific? Good grief, what a word.

Am I glad she's calling, like Stephen used to do on Sunday evenings? Yes. No. Comforting, but she's such a chatterbox, with words like salvific— and her acute sadness sharpens my own—yet she's a link to Stephen—and sharing the burden with her helps.

Oh, Charlie, dear and distant husband, "what a revoltin' development this is," like William Bendix used to say on "Life of Riley." I'm quite tempted to moan and groan for awhile, cry into my popcorn, but I don't think that will get me anywhere. But think about it, Charlie. This is what's going on in my life:

- *my neighbor is under a suicide watch*

132

- *my newly widowed daughter-in-law saps my strength*
- *my daughter has transformed from complacent cynic to Christian activist, in cahoots with my pastors (who demand more than I can possibly give), our congregational gadfly for the gospel, and a wild-eyed teenager with life-long psychic wounds*
- *a grieving widow brought me down, right in front of God and everybody, and her fallen husband's mother is on a trip that seems guaranteed to compound pain and prolong grief*

Oh, Charlie, even Will Shakespeare himself, plunged me back into my deep sorrow of losing a child. And all the while I long for that child, four weeks gone. This is too much, God! Too hard! What do you want from me? Whatever it is, I don't think I have it.

Oh, my gracious God, I am desperate for your presence. Shake me alive with the good news that this life is not all about me, that I am your beloved child amongst all your other beloved children. Make me know that Stephen lives with you, safe and peaceful. I praise you for the "stunning alternative" of life that you offer through your beloved son. Steady me with the protection of your rod and your staff, great God. Surely, your goodness and mercy are following me all the days of my life, including right now. Restore my frazzled soul, so I can be still and know that you are God and all is well. Amen.

<u>Fifth Sunday of Easter</u>

Acts 8:26-40
Psalm 22:25-31
1 John 4:7-21
John 15:1-8

Mother's Day. *Thank you, gracious God, for Virginia.* Not only did she—and Barry—host us for a lovely dinner and afternoon, but she also alerted me to myself this morning when I put my hands over my ears during Charlene's sermon. "Mother!" she whispered. "What are you doing?" and I realized I had my hands over my ears. Merciful heavens. I snatched them down, embarrassed. Here's what happened:

She preached, "Maybe the vine and branches image is comforting to us, pastoral and passive, like we just hang there hooked up to Jesus the Vine. Hardly. If we don't bear fruit, we're lopped off. If we do bear fruit, we're pruned. And, even though growth and beauty follow, pruning hurts."

I felt like putting my hands over my ears—well, I guess I actually did. Honestly, I just want to hang on the vine, but everyone seems to be harping at me lately. Could it seem that way because I feel like I have nothing to give right now? I feel empty and utterly discombobulated. Merciful heavens, I hope Charlene didn't see me.

Stephen danced around in my thoughts a lot today, naturally. I looked up a journal entry I wrote 52 years ago: "Mother's Day – Charlie's away at his skating jamboree in Canada. All day, the children were awful—smart-alecky, selfish, whiney. They threw the cards they made in Sunday School at me this morning, and that was it—until I got back from some quiet time at the big rock about 5 o'clock, and they had made a cake. Virginia helped Stephen write with icing on the cake: 'Best mom alive!' The kitchen was a mess, but the day ended nicely."

This day also ended nicely, despite my inner dullness which affects everything now. *God, you hear my cries, you show your face in the faces of my beloveds. I stand in awe and praise you for your sustaining presence.* Mindy was included in the family dinner today and told me about Miguel as we drove out to Virginia's in her spiffy little car.

"I thought he was the one, Rose, my soul partner. But, there was always this mystique about him, you know. And his messiah complex was a problem for me. I do think he's for real—his faith and passion for justice and living for others and all that. And messiahs do better without families, don't they? Plus—or on the other hand—I wouldn't be surprised if he has a family in Mexico."

Heavens, what a thought. "Did he disappear suddenly, no warning or note or anything?"

"Oh, there were signs. He was weirder than ever after he got out of jail. If he wasn't working at the restaurant, he was at Our Lady, lighting candles, on his knees praying. And he wouldn't talk to me. Our closeness was gone, like a fire in the fireplace gone out, just cold wood and ashes. I tried once, just to sit down and talk, and he said, 'Meendy, I leesten to God now, I hear nobody but my Father een heaven.' After that, I didn't see him for a few days, so I went by the house and they told me he had gone home—to Mexico."

She didn't get emotional until she said, "I thought we'd have a baby and finally I'd get beyond losing Darien."

And then we were at Virginia's, and Mack was running down the sidewalk, cheering our arrival with outstretched arms. There is no other welcome in the world like that of a child excited to see you.

"Hey, girl," Stephanie Rose said to Mindy, embracing us both and kissing me on the cheek. "How come you're not with the queen?" That's how they sometimes refer to Mindy's mother, Regina.

"Oh, she and Cindy are mad at me, I can't even remember what about this time, so how very cool that I have this other family," she said, bending over to pick up Mack and giving Angelica a squeeze. Barry and Virginia came out, too, and we chatted under the tulip tree, its flowers magnificent against the deep blue sky. All was cheerful until I said, "Poor Barry, just you against all us women," and suddenly Stephen was painfully missing. But the host handled the moment easily as he ushered us into the house, saying, "That's okay; Steverino is here in spirit, and I've got the little Mack truck to keep me company," and Mack gunned his engines, making us all laugh. I didn't know he could do that!

And then instead of our eyes watering in sadness, our mouths watered from the amazing aromas of yet another gourmet meal, Barry's special gift in honor of the mothers: Beef Wellington for us and a mushroom blend with the same seasonings baked in the puff pastry for Stephanie and Angelica, who has joined Steph in her vegetarianism,.

For her gift, Virginia made a contribution to Jacob's mission trip in mine and Stephanie's names. Barry's going! That's quite a sacrifice for him, giving up golf for ten days. And, it looks like Angelica will join the party, too. She said she was saving for it but wasn't sure she had enough time to accumulate the airfare, and Barry put in, "Oh, Gin and I will make up the difference—with the stipulation that you'll help drag my poor old body out of the sun if I give out."

And Stephanie put in, "Not too bad of a deal, spending all that time with Jacob, huh?"

"Yeah," Ang beamed, then sobered. "And this is going to be like really hard for him, so he needs good friends around." How true. And how satisfying to watch their developing friendship/romance.

We were too full for dessert right after the meal. "Not a problem," the chef said. "We'll have it later, after Mack and I take our nap while you all have your hen party." Which we gladly had. Stephanie complained at length about one of her students.

"He's a big old chauvinist, a real estate agent, probably a slimeball one, not like you, Mom. He's changing careers and just taking this class as an elective and treating it like a joke, constantly wise-cracking at my expense and…"

"Like what?" Mindy asked.

"Like calling the class "A Woman's Place Is Not in the Kitchen.""

"What's the real name of it?"

"Gender Implications of Spatial Relationships in Society, 1900 to the Present."

We snickered and she retorted, "Not so funny when I'm trying to maintain my authority with 25 students, half of them cocky and spoiled."

"Oh, lighten up, Steph," her mother advised. "Frankly, I think the name change is an improvement."

"Mom, he's ridiculing the class and me along with it! This course is a serious consideration of…"

Mindy patted her mouth in a mock yawn, and Stephanie gave her a little kick. I was enjoying every minute of this. "What's this man's name?" I asked.

"Bull," Stephanie snorted. "Well, it's Lawrence, but he goes by Bull. And I refuse to address him as Bull, so that's a bone of…"

We hooted. "Good grief, you sound like Super Fudge's kindergarten teacher," Mindy chided her. "Call him Bull." Stephanie's lower lip protruded slightly.

"You're afraid of him," Angelica said.

"I most certainly am not! Why would I be afraid of a boorish idiot like him?"

"I don't know, but the reason I think that is that I used to be afraid of William and Sarah because of the way they parented me. I like never knew how they were going to be, you know? And I thought I hated them, but one of my shrinks helped me realize that it was fear, not hatred. And I started praying for them after that, each night, after I said the Lord's Prayer, I'd pray for them. And now, after years of that—I think I actually love them, maybe."

"You've come a long way, baby," Virginia pronounced, and we basked for a moment in her transformation from a cynical, lost child to this sensitive young woman of faith.

Then Mindy wrapped up the conversation with, "So, yeah, Steph, face your fears and pray for him—by name—Bull." Too funny, but Stephanie Rose wasn't laughing.

<u>Wednesday</u>
Charlene came to call this afternoon. *The house was a mess, Charlie, a disordered tribute to the dysfunction of my grief. Bed unmade, outfit after outfit thrown on bedroom chairs or bathroom floor, sink full of dirty dishes, unopened mail piling up. I've got to get a hold of myself. I will, eventually.*

Anyway, Charlene inquired after Penelope.

"She's surviving through busy-ness," I reported, and told about the fundraiser she's organizing for pancreatic research and the book she's putting together chronicling the experiences several families have had with the wretched disease—in addition to the dynamic ministry with the congregation she's serving.

"Redemptive action. Sounds like Jacob and his mission trip," Charlene observed. "And how about you, Rose?"

For a minute, I could only nod, kindness making me teary-eyed as usual.

"You seem to be doing as well as anyone could expect. You know, Morris and I are so thankful that we got to know Stephen. Sharing his last days with you all was truly a privilege," she said, eye to eye, squeezing my hands across the kitchen table. "And, please tell me, Rose, did my sermon on Sunday upset you?"

"Uh-oh. I hope you didn't see me put my hands over my ears."

She laughed out loud. "I did, and I have to say, that may not be the last time, but it certainly was the first time I've had that happen!"

She waved away my attempts to apologize. "What was happening with you?"

"It was just my grief, I'm sure; I'm not myself," and I explained how I felt "under assault" and wasn't handling normal situations very well.

She thought for a moment and said, "Sometimes I wonder if Morris and I hit too hard on the challenges of Christian living—and the good news part doesn't come through strongly enough. Rose, did you hear the grace—that Jesus saying, 'Abide in me' is an invitation to life at its best?" she asked urgently, then quickly added, "Oh, never mind; you already know that."

And then Charlie, this kind woman of God asked me if she could load my dishwasher! "It just does my soul good to clean sometimes," she said. I gave tacit approval as she started doing it and she told me to "just go ahead and do whatever you wish..." and I changed the bed linens and straightened up the bedroom and bath, which felt great. I was going to clean my muddy snow boots still on the deck and put them away (before next winter!) and then sort through the mail when she left, but—I didn't; I caved right back in instead. Maybe I'll do it now. Nope. I'm going to put this pen down and sit and stare into space. I'm stymied again. Bloody stymied.

Acts 10:44-48
Psalm 98
1 John 5:1-6
John 15:9-17

"Help! Woman down!" I feel like shouting—but I don't have the energy. I can't live this way much longer. Virginia was here Thursday, I think it was, and walked into the kitchen and said, "What's that smell? Egad, Mother, it's your dirty dishes!" and cleaned up my kitchen again. She's been picking me up for church lately and this morning on the way home she asked if they need to worry about me yet. I'd had a hard time passing the peace, sabotaged by weeping which carried over into a silent melt-down at the communion rail—that I hope no one but she noticed.

"Mother, I know it's only been seven weeks—and we're all still mourning Stephen—and now Cute Baby, that's another blow—but you seem so..."

"I know it. I'm either restless or—or lifeless. Dysfunctional either way. Do you think I'm worse than when your dad died?"

She considered that. "You're older."

"Boy, that's the truth. I've never felt so old in my life..."

"Of course, I've/you've never been so old before," we said together and smiled.

I'm afraid I'm despondent. Even the creative, meaningful worship service this morning was like nothing to me. The Acts passage was expanded and dramatized to tell the astounding story of breaking down the long-standing racial barrier in the first church, how "...God has given even to the Gentiles the repentance that leads to life." "Of epic proportions," Morris commented, "on the scale of electing our first black president."

The singing of "Earth and All Stars" soared, praising God for everything from "loud clashing cymbals" to "loud boiling test tubes." All around me they were belting out from deep in their souls, "Sing to the Lo-or-or-ord a new song! ... God has done ma-a-a-ar-ve-lous things, I too sing praises with a new song!" And I stood there, numb with sorrow.

A new song. "The Church needs to sing a new song," Morris urged, "a better song than the alluring music of the culture that mesmerizes us and deadens our souls."

Heaven knows I need to sing a new song. This afternoon has been quietly excruciating again. I've listened a few times to a comforting phone message from Marvin saying that he's coming to Shippensforge sometime soon, hopes to see me, I'm in his thoughts. I try to read, sitting in one chair, then another, going over a paragraph three and four times and still not comprehending. I go out on the deck for a minute, sit down at the piano and play a line or two, eat half of something, turn the TV on and off before the picture even appears. I keep trying to finish this entry, just now starting again for about the eighth time.

Okay, this is it. I'm going to make a schedule for the week ahead, filling it full with good and important activities—time next door with poor Anita, food bank, visit Mercedes and Josephine, Lydia Circle. Maybe I'll even join the choir. I'll put in devotional reading time each day, piano practice, meal preparation and clean-up, spring cleaning of the whole house, family get togethers. There'll be no time for sinking down. I won't neglect grieving though; I'll schedule it. Time to read Stephen's old letters, remember and smile, weep a little, if necessary.

What do you think, Charlie? Okay, okay. If you were here, you would say, "C'mon, Rosie; that's not you." You're right, of course. That's Penelope's way, and she's great at it. I'm more of a bumbler. A creative bumbler, I'm going to say. One who bumbles along, trusting that God's grace is always present and that I will always—eventually—see it, despite myself.

Something's coming to mind, Charlie, hang on...I'm going to go wander around the yard and let the idea that's nagging me come to the surface...

....

Eloise Franklin! That's what was coming into my brain. She came to Stephen's funeral with Ethan and his parents—so kind of them—and she invited me to visit her. "Anytime, Rose," she said. "This is going to be a rough road. Whenever you've had as much as you can take and need to get away, drop everything and come for a visit. Please." So I'm going there, Charlie! Eloise is Mack's other great-grandmother, Ethan's grandma. We first met at Mack's baptism and had a ball. She's a cross between Florence—wicked wit, sarcastic nature—and Sarah—literary-minded, cultured. At Stephanie Rose and Ethan's wedding reception, we danced together down the middle of the dance lines. I'm going to go call her right now.

<u>Later</u>
We're all set.
Rose: Eloise?
Eloise: Rose! When are you coming to see me?

140

R: How about soon?

E: Mah-vlous, dahling. I'm so excited. We're going to have fun, Rose. Are you ready for some fun?

R: (Choked up. Silent.)

E: Oh, my dear girl. Tough times? Well, of course; he was your beloved son.

R: (Struggling) My cat died.

E: Oh, no; not that too. Come right away, Rose. How about tomorrow?

R: Um, well, I need to attend to a few things. For starters, I have a sink full of dirty dishes and my house is a mess. I need to...

E: Call someone to come in and clean while you're gone. You can afford it; you deserve it.

R: I guess I could. Then there are my neighbors—a young couple with a new baby and the mother has post partum depression.

E: What's your part in it?

R: Sympathetic ear, stand by...

E: Stand by for what?

R: (Thinking it through) To call the husband if she goes off the deep end and the ambulance comes, I guess.

E: Say your prayers for them, Rose, and get up here. What time can you leave in the morning?

R: (Slightly breathless) Oh, I guess around 10 or 11.

E: Perfect. Stop at a decent restaurant for a leisurely lunch, no fast food. You'll be here in time for happy hour. And when I say happy, I mean joyful, the kind of joy sadness can't destroy, Rose. God is with you, sweet friend; travel safely. We'll all be glad to see you.

Ascension of Our Lord/Seventh Sunday of Easter

Acts 11:1-11
Psalm 1
1 John 5:9-13
John 17:6-19

"Sweet are the uses of adversity," Shakespeare said, and the week I just had with Eloise in the thick of my mourning for Stephen was sweet indeed. Ethan had said something about his grandmother working at Dairy Queen, so I was quite unprepared for the neo-classical mansion rising into the sky with its huge, round columns. But since it bore her address in her small, northern Michigan town, I rang the bell. The heavy wooden door was swept open by a small, trim woman of indeterminate age who appeared to have lived a hard life so far. "Welcome in the name of Our Father Which Art in Heaven, Rose Harris. I'm Sylvania," and she hugged me into the foyer, as big as my house, I think, with a wide spiral staircase to the second story.

And then Eloise was there, looking the part of a wealthy matron, tanned and fit, with her chic silvery hair style and casual, expensive-looking slacks and blouse. She ushered me into the elegant library and mixed us some drinks, and we toasted Mack, our great-grandson, for bringing us together. I'm sure I was gawking, utterly disconcerted, and she told me a short version of her family's history. House built in 1878 by her grandfather, his fortune made in timber. She had a career as a classical pianist but arthritis ended that when she was in her forties. (I had not noticed the knots and twists of her fingers before.) Years later, after Randolph—Ethan's father, her only child—left home and her husband had died, she bought the Dairy Queen franchise when the place was about to go under and sold it back to the owner, interest free. She helped bring it back to profitability and even now, takes a shift occasionally, just for the fun of it. Eloise lives in a way that fills life with surprises—and we certainly had our share during my visit.

After her family history, she said, "Now, Rose, let us talk of Stephen. I'm so glad I met him at the baptism and the aborted wedding. If I'd known what lay ahead, I would have hung on his every word, 'experienced' him. But we don't know what lies ahead, do we?" Our eyes mirrored the wisdom of long years with their attendant sorrows and joys. "Tell me about him, my friend; tell me about your son."

Well. When have I had such fun? I'll credit the lovely buzz of the liquor and the lush ambience and Eloise's eagerness to know of Stephen—but mostly, it was Stephen himself, his humble, well-lived years, graced with humor and kindness and determination through struggle.

Tension left my insides and I felt at home in this lap of luxury, this affluent mansion, this—halfway house. Footsteps and voices had made it obvious that this was a busy place and when a door slammed, I asked if others lived in the house.

"Oh, yes. I've never lived here alone; couldn't stand that. Yes, there are always a few friends or relatives or brave, beaten down souls who need temporary refuge."

And Sylvania beckoned us to the formal dining room for a feast of grilled trout and morels, the delicate, delicious mushroom in season. Eloise's current guests introduced themselves during dinner conversation.

Sylvania began. "I was raised in Detroit. After not making it with Motown," she said with a self-deprecating smile, "I had a great career as a sous chef until I sliced up my fingers one time too many. That was before I knew Our Father Which Art in Heaven. I took step after step down wicked paths until I had no one and nothing except the beat-up car that was my bléssed home. Our Father Which Art in Heaven had found me by that time and told me to drive my car until it ran out of gas and there I would find salvation. My little Colt stopped next door, but no one answered my knock, so I came to Eloise's. That was eight years ago."

Jeff described himself as, "the snob of the group, for obvious reasons." Not everyone was amused, but I found him appealing, boyishly handsome in his mid-30s, tall and lanky with dark blond, tousled hair. "Eloise's mansion is well-known in my circle as a good place to crash after—well, after you've crashed; a good place to recuperate. And, Rose, all guests are entitled to beauty treatments from me. I'd love to give you a whole new look before you leave. I'm still trying to get Pete into my place for a pedicure."

"When monkeys fly," Pete, a wiry little guy close to retirement age, snorted. "Not much point in a house painter getting his nails worked on. Me and Eloise go back a ways," he said to me. "Rough business, house painting; hard to make a go of it. I check in here every couple years or so to dry up and get my bearings."

"I just came on Saturday," Lisa put in, then went on after a moment's hesitation. "I had to leave my husband Brian last week. He was showing violent tendencies. I'm on leave from my job as a social worker due to problems associated with obesity. I know Eloise from Dairy Queen.

"Brian's a big teddy bear—he really is—but life's doing its stuff on him. He's a realtor and was doing just fine until the economy did _its_ stuff. Then his mother died and left everything to his loser sister and, well, he's just not himself anymore. We'll get back together, I know we will; we've always had so much fun, until life started doing all these numbers on us. You can tell we love to eat and, with all the stress and stuff, we've eaten ourselves into oblivion."

Quite the little society we were. I looked forward each night to gathering round the table for Sylvania's artistically crafted, scrumptious suppers. We had lively chats on the patio surrounded by lush, green, early summer growth and brilliantly colored forget-me-nots. I went on a morel hunt with Pete and Jeff, unlikely comrades, and I also had those soothing, sensuous beauty treatments in the salon where Jeff works. Lisa and Eloise and I took a driving tour one afternoon to behold the splendor of the trillium, fading as it was. We were the motliest of crews, and I stand amazed at how we were bonded by the end of the week to handle the crisis that came Saturday night. Good heavens, that was just last night!

Eloise and I were settled in the library again for a cocktail before dinner. We laughed when we heard Sylvania rail at Lisa, "In the name of Our Father Which Art In Heaven, child, leave this kitchen before you burn the house down! Go set the table." Mouth-watering aromas were wafting in. I was at the window, taking in the colorful beauty of the gardens when a man came around the corner of the house, heading for the patio. We made eye contact; he did not look okay.

"There's a man in your backyard, Eloise."

"Probably David, Jeff's friend; he often joins us for Saturday night dinner."

"I don't think so."

She jumped up, exclaiming, "Uh-oh. It's her husband," and dashed toward the kitchen, yelling to Sylvania to lock the back door. Too late. We ran past a bewildered Lisa setting the table, and by the time we got to the kitchen doorway Sylvania was on the floor and the husband was rushing toward us demanding, "Where's Lisa?" He pushed through us, into the dining room.

"What's wrong with you, woman, leaving me and not even telling me where you're going?" he spewed, grabbing her by the arm and causing a crystal stemware to shatter on the table.

Sylvania started through the door yelping, "Unhand her, son of perdition, or your soul will…" and Eloise pushed her back to me—"Calm her, please, Rose,"—then approached the couple.

"Brian and Lisa, please have a seat in the drawing room for this conversation."

At which point Pete scuttled in from upstairs, hair still wet from the shower. "What in the hell's going on here?"

"This is nobody's business but mine and Lisa's. I'm losing everything in my life, and I'm not about to lose my wife. Lisa, you're coming with me," Brian said through clenched teeth, breathing heavily. Lisa winced from him squeezing her arm.

"Lisa, I advise you not to leave, and Brian, I remind you that there are witnesses to whatever you do," Eloise said, looking him steadily in the eye.

Brian's eyes narrowed into a scowl, and then he turned back to Lisa. "You must have a room in this swanky place. We can talk there," and Lisa said okay with a resigned nod.

"We shall accompany you there, and the door shall stay open," and Eloise beckoned us to follow them up the staircase. But right when they got to the doorway, Brian pushed Lisa in and slammed and locked the door. Lisa was yelling help and Brian was yelling at her to shut up and Eloise was yelling for him to unlock the door and Pete was trying to break it down and Sylvania was shouting to Her Father Which Art in Heaven, and then Jeff came running up the stairs, yelling to know what was happening. We filled him in, at which point I asked if we shouldn't call 911.

Pete and Sylvania shook their heads, and Jeff said, "They're worse than Barney Fife around here."

"He's right, Rose. We'll have a SWAT team of buffoons around this house within ten minutes. No, we're better off dealing with it ourselves, I'm quite certain."

Brian yelled through the door, "You people don't do anything crazy out there, you hear me? Nobody'll get hurt if you just leave this to me. No police, no drama. I just need to work this out with my wife."

Jeff quietly asked, "He doesn't have a weapon, does he?" and just like that, Pete yells out, "Brian, do you have a gun?"

There was a moment's hesitation, and Brian yelled back, "Maybe."

Lisa yelled, "He does..." but he muffled her.

"I think she was going to say 'doesn't'," Sylvania put in. I thought that, too.

"Oh, great; now we know," Jeff said, rolling his eyes. "The lunatic either does or does not have a gun."

"Everyone come to the drawing room to discuss this situation," Eloise directed.

"How about over dinner?" Jeff asked, to no avail.

Sylvania stretched her arms over us, closed her eyes, and pronounced, "Our Father Which Art in Heaven guideth, he sendeth his Son and his Holy Spirit with wisdom from on high for this moment."

"How about some daily bread?" Jeff muttered, as we started down the stairs.

It was so crazy. I was simultaneously alarmed and amused—and reassured by Eloise's composure. We were just finding a seat in the drawing room when Brian yelled down that one person was to come and negotiate.

We ran to the stairs to see him retreating, and Eloise called up, "Negotiate for what, Brian?"

"I'm not sure; maybe money. One person and one person only," Brian called back, and then shut and locked the door again.

"Our Father Which Art in Heaven says to cast lots," Sylvania declared as we regrouped in the drawing room.

"Okay, Sylvania, you need to cool it," Jeff said in exasperation. "Our father—or mother—which may—or may not be—in whatever in the hell heaven is, needs to give us some space here." He took in a breath, puffed his chest out a little and said, "I'll go. I'm the man of the house."

Pete flinched but was silent.

"I shall go. This is my house and my responsibility," Eloise stated.

While they were arguing, Sylvania broke off four straws from the hearth broom. She handed them to me and said, "Truly the Lord is in this place and will guideth the anointed one to draw the shorter straw. Rose, you are a holy visitor and excluded. Mix the straws and hold them for us."

Eloise shrugged in permission, so I turned my back to them, arranged the straws, turned back and held them out.

Sylvania drew the short one. "Here I am, Lord," she said, heading for the stairway.

"I really don't think he has a gun, Sylvania. I didn't see one on him," Pete encouraged.

A few minutes later came the terrifying boom. Jeff bolted for the foyer, Eloise right behind him yelling, "Oh, my God." I was glued to my chair in shock for an instant, listening to the commotion, hearing Lisa yell, "Brian, come back!" and Pete yelling that Brian had run out the back door with the gun. We thought surely Sylvania had been shot.

Eloise and Jeff were dashing up the staircase when I reached the bottom of it, where Pete was standing. But suddenly, there was Sylvania at the top. We all froze and didn't move until she said, "Why stand ye gazing up into heaven? A son of perdition awaits salvation."

We stared at her, then Pete said, "Now just wait a doggone minute. You're not saying that we need to go get that son-of-a-bitch, are you?"

"Surely it's time to call the police," I urged, "with the gun…"

"That's not Brian's," Lisa said. "He was rummaging around—I apologize, Eloise; he's not himself—and found it in the wardrobe and was checking it for bullets, I think, and it went off."

"Good heavens, it must have been Papa's, in there for twenty-five years…"

"Our Father Which Art in Heaven says we have nothing to fear," Sylvania said, descending.

"Eloise, there's an irrational man with a loaded gun!" I appealed again.

"I think we're okay, Rose. You stay in here," and she fell in behind Sylvania and Lisa, who were moving swiftly toward the patio where Brian sat, holding his head with both hands, the gun in his lap. Through the dining room window I could see Jeff sneaking up on him from behind, but before he could make his jump, the women got there. Sylvania stretched out her arm to Brian and said, "Thou shalt not follow wicked ways when it is the will of the Lord that you delighteth in his law. Give me the gun," and he placed it in her hand. Whew.

Lisa and Brian were left to huddle on the patio while the rest of us helped Sylvania get dinner on the table. About 20 minutes later than planned, we all broke bread together. Normal cheery conversation prevailed, Brian quietly wolfing down the delectable meal with the rest of us. Everything seemed so ordinary that I couldn't help but ask when an appropriate moment occurred, "Is this evening's incident a normal kind of occurrence?"

"Heavens no; we've never had a loaded gun in this house before," Eloise answered.

"Eloise, you're forgetting that daughter of perdition and her sidekick who attempted burglary in the middle of the night," Sylvania put in. "But we were never in danger, Rose. Know ye that this is a safe place under the protection of Our Father Which Art in Heaven and return as often as you can." Hm.

We stayed at the table for a couple hours, extremely relaxed after the extreme stress. Tall tales were told, and poignant reminiscences, and stories of "surviving life," as Jeff put it, which encouraged Brian, it seemed. His mood calmed and brightened.

At the front door as he left, Sylvania pronounced a benediction of sorts. "Thou art in need of the Son of God, Brian, for the Son of Our Father Which Art in Heaven giveth true life. Your sin and shame and all fears will be rendered powerless before everlasting love, child of God." He nodded, got in his car, and drove off, having agreed to return today for further conversation. I wonder if he did. I plan to return another day—I guess.

Wow, I didn't know I was going to tell that whole story, but it was just so darn unique and remarkable. It was—what's the right word? Christlike, I think. Christ was present so fear did not immobilize and grace and peace prevailed. Yes, I believe that crazy cast of characters did what Jesus would do.

Pentecost

Acts 2: 1-21
Psalm 104:24-34, 35b
Romans 8:22-27
John 15:26-27; 16:4b-15

Did that incident at Eloise's last Saturday night really occur? Seems like a wacky dream now. I've read my account of it a few times, though, and yes, it was as real as real gets—and the saga continues. Eloise reports that Brian has now taken up residence with them. "Praise Our Father Which Art in Heaven, for thy soul will surely flourish in this place," Sylvania welcomed him. A nephew of Eloise's has joined the group, too. Harry, whom she describes as, "Nocturnal and neurotic—and oh, yes, trangender—born Harriet—a good and kind soul, amazingly intact for what he's been through." What a place, that halfway mansion of hers.

I keep thinking of Sylvania saying, "Why stand ye gazing into heaven?" For these last weeks since Stephen died, I feel like I've been symbolically standing still, looking up into heaven for comfort and answers. And I've decided that the time has come for me, like those apostles in disarray after losing Jesus, to tune into the presence of the Holy Spirit and throw myself into life again. I am more than ready to renew my trust in God's promises and obey Jesus' commandments with energy and confidence—I think, I hope. Stephen would want me to.

The clean, fresh-smelling house I walked into last Sunday night was energizing. (Virginia's cleaning crew came in while I was gone. I stubbornly had them skip Stephen's room, like it's a shrine or something.) I'm getting back into the whirl at St. Timothy after being on the fringes for so long. Mindy and I chatted in the pew after worship this morning.

"They got that right," she commented about the Romans passage. "The whole creation groans and longs, not just me, solo. And the point is not that 'misery loves company.' The point is what Pastor Morris said. What did he say?" she asked, cocking her head earnestly. "That the groaning isn't 'sad and hopeless,' that's what he said. It's that as we groan, we hope. We somehow know that everything's okay, even if we can't see it and can't know the details. Yeah, it's the Paraclete that helps us know."

I find it hilarious, Mindy using 'Paraclete' in daily conversation. She loved the word immediately upon hearing Marcus Sauer explain how it's another name for the Holy Spirit, the Comforter, our Advocate. Now, she slumped against me and quietly said, "My main groan is that I want to have

149

a baby. Rose, I want a child so much," she broke off, biting her lip to keep her tears from spilling. I took her hand and nodded. "And I don't even know how to pray about it, so I'm glad the Paraclete is praying for me. But my sadness," she added, "doesn't keep me from being glad that Charlene's pregnant."

"She is? Mercy, I really am out of it around here. That's very happy news. I've thought she was looking awfully tired lately; that's probably why."

She nodded, sat up straight, stretched, yawned, then said, "Let's go do something fun. Can you?"

"Sure, let's! Great idea. What shall we do?"

A lazy afternoon in Avery Park, that's what. Mindy and I went home to change into picnic clothes, and she was fine with me calling Sarah to join us. We three picked up subs and chips on the way. Sarah had poured a bottle of chilled Riesling into a thermos, and we settled at an out of the way table, partly in the sun and partly shaded, and munched and sipped. "Heaven is today," I thought, another of Sylvania's sayings. There were lots of people on this Memorial Day weekend. Between the three of us, we knew most of them.

"There's my former husband's former business partner," Sarah noticed, and re-hashed her divorce for a few minutes until cutting herself off. "Backwards is not a good direction for me to take."

"There's Paco and Jesus and the other Jesus," Mindy pointed out when a group of several Mexican people moved by at a distance. That got us re-hashing all the events with Miguel. "I'll always cherish our time together. I'll always love him—I guess—if I knew who he was," she ended with a sad little half-laugh.

"There go Louie and Rita and Tariq," I said. "Wonder how they're getting along. He was with them at worship this morning. How's he doing at school, Sarah?"

"Predictably, I would say. It's a tough go for an African American at SCHS."

"I thought maybe there would be several black kids by now."

"Tariq makes three, still 0%. And the three don't seem to have much in common; why should they? Jacob Turner's nice to him, but Tariq's a loner at this point. I've seen his name down for In School Suspension a couple times. He generally looks sullen."

"Just like now; he's about to trip on his lower lip," Mindy said, nodding her head towards them trudging onto the ball field. "I mean, 'What's wrong with this picture?' A black adolescent male from the city plunked down in a house with a white couple from rural Kentuckiana—how's that ever going to work? Louie and Rita have hearts of gold, but... Last Sunday before church I heard them talking to Malcolm about adopting. He was telling them not to rush it." She stopped to think for a minute. "You know what? That Malcolm is a regular Paraclete."

"Excuse me?" Sarah said.

"Advocate, helper. He was really encouraging to Miguel and hooked him up with a good defense lawyer."

I totally agreed with her and talked about the wonderful family attorney he's been for us. I can't begin to number all the other people he's helped get through bad times, and he's helped the church a lot, too. Sometimes for pay, many times not. Malcolm was at our side when Charlie had to deal with the aftermath of his accident that killed Stewart Larsen. And again, competent and comforting for Stephen at the end—and still working with Penelope to settle the estate. I hate feeling estranged from him because his marriage has broken up. I really want reconciliation—and, yes, we'll find it. *God of love, help me, guide me. Intercede for me, Holy Spirit.* I'll act on this soon. Whew, I hadn't realized until this moment how much of a burr in my soul this situation is.

Back to the picnic. Mindy said, "Hey! Maybe I should adopt a kid, maybe an older one. Wow, Tariq would be about Darien's age. Oh, but I don't mean ..."

"Darien?" Sarah asked.

"He was my 5-year-old son who was killed in a car accident with me at the wheel. It's been a long time, but I still miss him—although that's getting a little weird, trying to remember him the way he was and then imagining him as a teenager; messes with my head. But, the most important part is that I've forgiven myself, mostly, thank God—and St. Timothy—and good friends," she said, giving me a special look.

"Alright, I'm going over and join the ballgame for a little while—but don't worry, I'm not adopting Tariq," she called back over her shoulder.

Sarah and I walked around, chattering like mad to catch up with each other. She'll be cooking out with her kids and grandkids tomorrow and then four more days of school, "intense and anti-climactic all at once." I remember that well. She was fascinated by the scene in Eloise's mansion, visualizing it as a stage play—"There would have to be a full stairway in the set." Intriguing idea. I'll play myself, standing around looking alarmed.

I told her about burying Cute Baby. Jim and I took her out in the woods and dug her grave and marked it with a special rock. We gazed down in silence for a minute and then he said something like, "She was a great little cat. I know you'll miss her," and squeezed me around the shoulders, and I said my favorite lines from Christopher Smart's "Jubilate Agno." "For I am possessed of a cat, surpassing in beauty, from whom I take occasion to bless Almighty God." I miss that sweet, warm furry creature everyday; probably won't get another.

Sarah asked about Anita. Goodness, what to say? On a tightrope, in the jaws of the dragon… "Struggling," I said.

"So, are you worried?"

"Oh, yes. Very." There was a crib death in town that everyone's talking about, and Anita's been obsessing on it. She wanted to go to the funeral, to be there for these people she didn't even know. Jim talked her out of it ("She might as well watch <u>Roots</u> in one sitting…"), and then caught her looking at websites about crib death. What in the world is it that drives her to immerse herself in suffering and take herself down like that? Poor Jim. His face is drawn and sober all the time now. Marilyn, his aunt, very nice person, goes back to Indianapolis tomorrow, I think. And then will Anita take her medications properly? Stay calm when Zahra fusses? Be able to fend off her constant fears and sorrows? Yes, we're worried.

"I'll be thinking positive thoughts for them," Sarah offered. Me too. Praying without ceasing.

As we were leaving the park around 5 o'clock, who should be coming in but Josephine and Mercedes, each hanging on one of Sidney's arms and him looking mighty contented. I think the old curmudgeon is being softened up by his faithful caretaking of Mercedes. Why, he's gotten her house painted! I gave him accolades for that; it looks like somebody lives there now, and between him and Josephine, the inside is seeing great improvements, too. Happily, Mercedes seems happy about the improvements rather than confused. Josephine is making a trip to Mississippi pretty soon to check on her house and take care of some business, but she's definitely coming back. How fabulous that this arrangement is working out so well for both her and Mercedes.

Charlie, this delightful afternoon has completely banished the blues that hit yesterday when I was polishing the bathroom fixtures with one of your old socks from the rag bag and broke into sobs with deep longing for the way it used to be on Saturday afternoons when you were here. Missing Stephen, feeling alone and lonely, Virginia and Barry away, Stephanie and Mack and Angelica taking a holiday at the dunes. But I finished my little cleaning job and then sat on the deck surrounded by spring's glories and let—ha!—the Paraclete breathe into me. Jesus was very present, with his love that knows no bounds and victory over death. Memories transformed from painful to delightful. The Spirit and Julian of Norwich prayed with me, "Teach us to believe that by your grace all shall be well, and all shall be well, and all manner of things shall be well. Amen." Yes, all is well—though I wouldn't mind a cuddly ball of gray fur purring in my lap...

Trinity Sunday/First Sunday after Pentecost

Isaiah 6:1-8
Psalm 29
Romans 8:12-17
John 3:1-17

Zahra was baptized this morning.

Anita pushed things to crisis quite dramatically yesterday, startling me awake near dawn, about 6 o'clock, but storm clouds keeping it dark. I heard banging on the glass doors to the deck and jumped out of bed still mostly asleep, racing through the house, my heart pounding. There she was, in a long, dark velour robe that zipped down to the waist, still unzipped. I slid the door open and stepped out, and she said calmly, looking past me, "I just tried to kill myself. I nursed Zahra and put her back in her crib. I went to the kitchen and got my pills out of the cupboard and poured them into a bowl. I filled a glass with water..."

"Anita!" I yelled hoarsely into her face, shocking us both.

Her eyes opened wide, then went wild. "Help me!" she yelled back. "Help me, help me, help me," she begged, shaking my shoulders until my teeth hurt. "I want to live. I don't want to die. I don't want my baby to die."

"Did you take them? The pills?"

She shook her head no, and my chest loosened up. I tried to open the door behind me and go in the house, but I had pulled it shut and it was locked. So I zipped up her gown and guided her to a chair and sat down at the table next to her. Sheet lightning behind the woods silhouetted the huge trees, and there was thunder in the distance, and Great God in the morning, what to do? Take her home, of course, but something inside urged me to talk, just the two of us, before taking her back to Jim.

"It's the second time since Aunt Marilyn left that I've done that," she confessed in anguish. "Oh, Rose, I don't want Zahra growing up in this awful world—I should have never had her—she probably has the same crazy genes my mother and I have—and she could die of SIDS, I just couldn't bear that—and I'm ruining Jim's life, he used to be happy and funny, I'm taking him down. Rose, help me!" she repeated miserably.

She paused to take a ragged breath and then raved on. "What's to become of me? I'm so lost. I'm wicked in a wicked world." She stared in horror, and then cried, completely undone, her voice alarming, "I've thought of killing Zahra, smothering her with a pillow. I don't deserve to live!"

I put my fingers on her lips. "Hush, child! That's over, let that go. You are forgiven, Anita. God knows you love your child. God loves you, don't you know that?" I pleaded, my arm around her shoulder and head to head, as we have been before.

The lightning and thunder were escalating and the wind picking up, and I prayed, *Come, Holy Spirit! Come now! Release this woman from her agonies! Release my anxious thoughts from the possibility that she might one day succumb and...*

"I used to know, when I was little, when I knew all the stories and songs. I thought I knew God loved me then," she said softly, in short gasps. "But then I grew up and saw all the evil in the world—and the mystery of it—of God—of trying to believe in love when everything is such a mess—it was too hard..."

I had to raise my voice to be heard. "You can start over. Think of yourself like Zahra, God's brand new creature, beloved and safe. And this great God sent us a child, the only son, to live among us and to save us Anita, from our worst fears..."

Then everything shook with a deafening crack of thunder and the heavens lit up with flashing. Our heads tilted back in awe. She hunched down trembling and was so quiet, I began to worry. I was trying to decide what to do next when something told me to close my eyes and wait. The storm moved away as we sat there, her head bowed, me gazing at her and praying without words. After a few minutes, she stood up and said simply, "I give up. I want God. I mean it! I'm going to tell Jim," and she turned and marched toward their house.

I followed her to make sure she went in, then got my outside key from its hiding spot in the flower pot on the front step. A gentle rain began to fall and I went inside and made a lumberjack's breakfast, enjoying every bite and wondering what was going on next door. I found out when Jim came over later in the morning to ask me to be their congregational sponsor for the baptism. They had already called the Bryants and set up an afternoon meeting with them to prepare, and he asked me to be there.

"This is a life and death matter," he said. "Shoot, Rose, you know how I feel. I'd be more likely to get de-baptized myself than to baptize my kid, but—we've got to do something radical or..." he couldn't say the words, "or we could lose both of them."

He was subdued and Anita serene when we all got together in their living room. There was no pretense, everyone knew this was a charged situation. I admire Jim for deferring to Anita and what is needed at this time—and yet, maintaining his integrity.

There was major discussion as they went over the service. In fact, the pastors remarked that the conversation was far more theological than most; usually they just went over the procedure and didn't talk much about beliefs.

At one point Jim said, "I don't <u>want</u> anyone dying for me." No one responded. What could we say? It's a done deal.

Whether or not he would make the promises along with Anita was a question. "I'm against evil but that's about as far as I can go with all this."

"How about this?" Charlene proposed. "'Will you be an example of love and righteousness for your child?' Could you promise that, Jim?"

That was okay.

So, this morning, he stood staunchly by while I presented Zahra Camille Ferguson for Holy Baptism. First Anita joined St. Timothy, affirming her own baptism. Then she promised to fulfill the responsibilities entrusted to her regarding Zahra's "growth in the Christian faith and life." Jim made his promise. As sponsor, I promised "to nurture this person in the Christian faith as I am empowered by God's spirit, and to help her live in the covenant of baptism and in communion with the church." And the people of God there assembled made their promise "to support Zahra and pray for her in her new life in Christ."

Anita was radiant. During the passing of the peace, Jim thanked me and said, "This is a good thing, even if I don't personally buy the party line." I sensed great relief in his soul. I noticed at the top of the page of the baptism service in our new hymnbook it says, "God brings those who are baptized out of death and into life." So may it be.

He and Anita have made another big decision. She's going into residential treatment in Indianapolis. They've been making inquiries and in a few days should have everything set. Therapy, rest, medications adjusted, supervision. Jim and the baby will stay with Aunt Marilyn, and be able to see Anita everyday. He can do some of his job remotely and then take family leave as needed. They expect to be back in 2-4 weeks. What courage, what love.

Also—this was sweet—during the passing of the peace right after the baptism, Maddie Bowers, along with the other children who were upfront as witnesses, shook Zahra's foot in welcome, and Maddie said to Anita, "I really love your baby. Can I come to your house sometime and play with her?" With a soft, surprised laugh, Anita said yes, they would like that and then asked me about Maddie later. We wondered at her seriousness. What is going on in her life, out on that farm, her mother gone (cancer) for eight months now, we never see her dad, Randy, he didn't even come to Bryan's confirmation, and Bryan's 17 now, I think, and seems a sad and serious kid, too. *God, be with them. We are blessed by their presence. Help us to love.*

And with all Jim's unbelief and impatience with religious trappings, didn't it just have to be Trinity Sunday? I jokingly apologized to him. "Sorry for the triple-dose of theology that nobody can quite explain."

He smiled. "That's okay. When Morris started out, 'What's up, doctrine?' I figured the sermon wouldn't be too dry and ridiculous—and it wasn't."

I liked the sermon, too. God is <u>beyond</u> us as the Creator/Father, <u>among</u> us as Jesus/Son, and <u>within</u> us as Holy Spirit. God is community and relationship, by nature. And so, we live in community—now richer by having Zahra and Anita—and Jim, sort of.

And I am moving back into the routine of St. Timothy after the fragmenting, marginalizing effects of grief. There are several families I don't recognize, one in the form of, I think, grandparents and a little girl, a flashback to Stephanie Rose with Charlie and me in the days when Virginia was adamantly unchurched.

When we heard about adoption (as children of God) in the Romans passage, I looked over at Rita and Louie and Tariq, his face stoic as usual, and said a prayer for each of them and them together.

Deedee told me this morning that Claudia and Michael are divorcing. We knew they'd had some trouble spots but thought they'd come through to a better place. Drat. Horrible, sad news—I guess. I don't know anymore. Maybe it's the best thing that ever happened. But it seems horrible and sad to me. All of the above, perhaps. I'll have to give her a call when the time seems right.

Ha! In an ironic turn on the "here I am" theme, Madge was overcome with enthusiasm at Lydia Circle the other night, volunteering to deliver comfort kits to the jail and then lamenting it as she drove me home. "What was I thinking? I'm just going to call Helen tomorrow and back out." Her commitment waned quickly, like a puffy soufflé deflating. I can relate. I've been know to personify a fallen soufflé.

Another routine I'm going to try to get back into is visiting at Rutledge Home. Pastor Ruskin lives there now, and Pauline Shuster continues to stir things up. Pam says she needs a private room—she's on her fourth roommate in less than a year—but can't afford it. She may have low cognitive skills, but she's smart enough to hide the pills for her bi-polar condition and spit them out later, Pam says, and then sneak around finding sweets to eat until her blood sugar level elevates dangerously. Poor, unhappy person.

But despite activities and routines, my mourning goes on, Charlie; the loss stabs like a knife sometimes, though I'm able to wash the dishes and hang up my clothes now, most days. In fact, sometimes I get this little urge to sort and organize and do deep cleaning; I believe that would be therapeutic—starting with Stephen's room. That's a bridge I need to cross—but not yet.

He visits in different ways. In dreams, like one where he was little—and was taking a bath—at your mother's house—and—and— oh yes, and called out to me, "I'm okay, Mom." Doesn't the psyche work in such strange ways? But, again, that goofy dream brought such peace!

He visits through others' remembrances, too, like Jacob Turner telling me about the ski trip Stephen chaperoned several years back and stayed with Jacob on the bunny slopes all day until he was ready to go on his own.

I still can't believe he's gone. I catch myself picturing him in his Chicago apartment and wonder if he'll drive over for the Fourth of July. Penelope is in the Holy Land on her supposed-to-be honeymoon. So, I might have to cry a little tonight, in longing for him and, cry out my love and sorrow and gratitude. But I'm okay, Charlie; don't worry. I guess you don't know what worry is anymore. What a blessing, you lucky bum!

Ezekiel 17:22-24
Psalm 92:1-4, 12-15
2 Corinthians 5:6-17
Mark 4:26-34

Charlene looked awfully tired this morning, but she challenged us nevertheless. "People of God, let us see ourselves as part of a new creation! Could we do that, brothers and sisters, looking at each other through the eyes of Christ for the sake of God?" During the silence that followed, I thought about how much conflict and pettiness and judgmentalism would be eliminated if we did that. And I thought, too, about how I've been blessed to see people differently lately. The most dramatic case is Malcolm. I've been praying for and "leaning toward" reconciliation with him, so I was happy when he called last week and asked if he could come by. I was apprehensive, too, knowing that his marital difficulties would probably come up—and they did—and the conversation wasn't easy—but it was good.

To my surprise, Malcolm told me that our family had influenced them to join St. Timothy long years ago. He described quite vividly, in fact, sitting in the pew behind us on one of their first visits. Stephen was teasing Virginia, making faces at her, and she was fighting back, refusing to ignore him. *Charlie, he said, you put Stephen in a gentle headlock and I "cuddled" Virginia firmly to me and continued worshiping. Sounds like a typical Sunday morning with the young Harris family! He and Cynthia liked our "relaxed propriety." How about that?*

I was also surprised when he said, "Rose, I consider you to be one of my mentors in the faith—and that's why it's important to me to..." and he faltered a little and cleared his throat and made confession. 'Twas a sad story of a mutually loveless marriage that I had never suspected. Like most people, I suppose, I was taken in by their dashing good looks and polished social presence and assumed that they had a wonderful marriage.

"Cynthia and I did not do well," he began. "Outward appearances were far too important to us. We sacrificed our integrity and our happiness in favor of our reputations and our lifestyle. But that came to a screeching halt for me when we had a grandchild stillborn back in the fall." I remembered them being on the prayer list. He said that in his grief over the baby's death and his guilt over his adultery, he was drawn to the Scriptures, delving into the story of David and Bathsheba.

"Now don't get me wrong, Rose; I don't believe that God killed the child to punish me for my sin, I certainly don't think that. What happened is that the event made me look at the horrible farce of my life: my unfaithfulness— to Cynthia, to myself, to God. I finally faced up to it, and my spirit was broken." His furrowed brow showed the darkness of the road he's traveled. "'…a broken and contrite heart, O God, you will not despise,' David sang in one of his psalms. I had never really known contrition before, never felt broken like I was. But David's words gave me hope that I could be forgiven—and I have been.

"John Milton helped me a great deal, too. Have you ever read his 'Doctrine and Discipline of Divorce'?" Yes I had, long ago, and appreciated Malcolm emailing me the pithy passage:

> Marriage is a cov'nant the very being whereof consists, not in a forc't cohabitation, and counterfeit performance of duties, but in unfained love and peace. […] It is a lesse breach of wedlock to part with wise and quiet consent betimes, then still to soile and profane that mystery of joy and union with a polluting sadness and perpetuall distemper; for it is not the outward continuing of marriage that keeps whole that cov'nant but whosoever does most according to peace and love, whether in marriage or in divorce, he it is that breaks marriage least; it being so often written, that Love only is the fulfilling of every Commandment.   ~John Milton

Seems pretty radical for over 350 years ago. I think Milton's thoughts would have meant a lot to Stephen; I wish he could have heard them, Denise, too, when they were struggling through their divorce with feelings of failure and even questioning their status as people of faith. Sarah would appreciate it; I'll make sure she knows of it. And Claudia, as well. I have no doubt she and Michael are doing whatsoever they can "according to peace and love" as they part. Sometimes I sense that we're moving toward a time when divorce will simply be a life passage, not so heavy with sadness and regret. That in itself seems sad to me—and yet, people ought not to live plagued by guilt or bitterness afterwards either.

According to Malcolm, Cynthia is on the road of bitterness. "But, Rose, as odd as it may sound, I love and care about her more than ever. Small comfort to her, I know, after years of neglect and deceit, but I see her more clearly for the beautiful person she is, no longer an opponent or—or—

problem. And I truly believe, Rose, that she is better off, free to be herself. I pray everyday that she will see that. I honestly wish the best for her."

He didn't say anything about the proceedings. The word around town is that Cynthia is "taking him to the cleaners" quite handily, and that he is acquiescing at every point; not much choice for him, I suppose, since he's the transgressor. He also said that he would like his future wife and me to meet someday, "when conditions are more favorable. Her name is June; she is being changed as much as I am." He plans to move to Chicago soon; hard to imagine not having Malcolm Stafford, Esq. around Shippensforge; he's an institution. And a clay jar, like all of us, but nonetheless God's vessel. *How I thank you, God, for reconciliation with him. And may he and Cynthia receive this great gift, too. Amen.*

Another person who is coming more into focus for me is Maddie Bowers. Mindy and Virginia and I were seated at coffee hour this morning, and she brought her cake and sat down with us.

"Sometimes you're not in church," she said, looking from one of us to the other, clearly expecting a response as she took another bite of cake.

We exchanged amused glances, rendered speechless for a moment by this sober child.

"Well, I visited a friend a couple weeks ago," I said.

"Do you stay home sometimes because you're sad about Stephen dying?"

Goodness. "Yes, sometimes, but mostly coming to church helps me feel better."

Mindy said, "Sometimes I stay home because I'm sad. And, to tell the truth, Maddie, sometimes I don't come just because I feel lazy or tired."

"Virginia?" Maddie said, calling for her response.

My heavens, it was hilarious, this kid putting us on the spot! Virginia mentioned holiday traveling and not feeling well once, but not the 10-4 real estate open house she hosted last Sunday.

"I like it when everybody's here every Sunday," Maddie said. Oh, my heart. I wanted never to miss worship again, to be there for her every single time.

"Bryan won't come anymore. I make him get up and bring me, but he gets mad, but I don't care."

"You call me if you ever need a ride, Maddie. I'm serious," Mindy said, scribbling her phone number on a napkin and shoving it across the table. Maddie nodded.

"How's your father?" I asked.

"He's pretty sick, I think." I wondered what was wrong—and I also wondered if I had ever seen Maddie smile.

Then Bryan came up to the table and said, "C'mon! I'm out there waiting for you," and strode off. She stood up as she took her last bite and picked up her plate and the napkin with Mindy's number, holding it up to Mindy with a little nod, and headed for the door.

"I want her," Mindy sighed, watching her cross the room. "Did you see the look on her face when the cherub choir sang, 'Oh, who can make a flower? No one but God, it's true.'? Honestly, she seems like she already gets everything. And then when Rhonda gave out the seeds during the children's sermon—it was like she'd been given a diamond ring."

"I wonder what's wrong with her father. Should we check?" Virginia put in, and we decided to tell the pastors.

Yes, several of the munchkins seemed excited about getting seeds to take home and plant in reference to the parable of "The Seed Growing Secretly." Reminds me of Stephanie Rose when she was oh so little, peering into the Styrofoam cup from nursery school with the bright green grass growing up out of the black soil and looking up at me and asking, "How, Gwama?" No one but God, child. Life and growth are automatic in God.

For all of the above, gracious God, I give you thanks. You fill my life with good things, my cup overflows. Saturday night with Marvin was a delightful surprise. I am trying not to judge on externals but to know him as part of your new creation, even though he isn't particularly interested in you. He does have a mystique, God, but I hope he is not up to trickery in his wealth and dealings. He certainly is flourishing, by earthly standards. If he is righteous, he will flourish in you; if not, he is doomed. For now, I am just trying to have the eyes of Christ toward all people, including him. Guide me, give me insight, may his heart be open to that which is good and loving. Amen.

I still can't quite believe last night with Marvin. The rest of my "rich, full life" seems quite mundane in comparison. When he called in the morning to say he was in town and wanted to "engage" me for the evening, he said to dress for dancing. Didn't think I had any such outfit—don't dance much—but there was the gold dress I wore for Stephanie's wedding, just the right frock.

We went to the downtown Hilton, and the evening was special in every way—food, drink, and conversation. By the time we took the floor, my apprehension about dancing was wined and dined away. Marvin took me in his arms and we moved easily into the soft rhythms of the band. I felt decades younger than my four score and two as he led me in slow, graceful steps. We talked and laughed a little, but when I fell silent and leaned into him, my chin on his shoulder and eyes closed, I know he knew that I was thinking about Stephen. He held me closer and soothed me with his hand on my back, his cheek against mine. This was the sweetest, most healing grief I have felt through the whole ordeal. I prayed as we danced, *Thank you, God, for this tender, caring man.* No tingles. He just seemed like the best kid brother in the world.

The plan was for him to worship with Mindy and me this morning, but he had to fly to Seattle on urgent business instead. What an unusual life. Why is there so much urgency? More to come, I guess. Marvin and I do seem to have a real friendship developing. *Please, God, don't let him be up to any mischief.*

<u>Third Sunday after Pentecost</u>

Job 38:1-11
Psalm 107:1-3, 23-32
2 Corinthians 6:1-13
Mark 4:35-41

That's a Jim question, I thought, when Charlene started her sermon on the Bible story of the day, Jesus calming the sea. "Who then is this, that even the wind and the sea obey him?" In other words, "Who then is Jesus?" I went a little crazy imagining Jim sitting in the pew responding to the story and what Charlene had to say about it. Bits of knowledge that I've picked up over the years started knocking around in my head, and I fantasized a theological discussion between Jim and me.

"First of all," he would say, "the so-called <u>sea</u> of Galilee is actually a shallow lake…" and he would probably point out that, quite naturally, storms on the lake could get quickly violent as wind blows through a pass and then stop as quickly when the wind dies down.

And I would parry, "True—and the Gospel writer knew that but deliberately constructed the story to hook up with familiar scriptural images. Those who first heard it would have been put in mind of the parting of the Red Sea, and God's power over the storms sung of in Psalm 107, and the taming of the chaotic water 'in the beginning.'"

"Fine, Rose, the Bible is literature and image and symbol. But if Jesus supernaturally stopping a storm is questionable, what's left? Who then is Jesus?" he would push back, with that sly twinkle in his eye.

"Jesus is at one with a God who has power over all that is dangerous and frightening, that's who. And those disciples right beside him were just as scared and unsure as we sometimes are; we're all in the same boat. They experienced his power firsthand and believed and testified with their lives so that we can, too. "

As he shook his skeptical head, Anita might put in, "I like Rose's ideas better than yours, Jim. In fact, yours is more of an un-idea."

Okay, that's enough. She probably wouldn't say that.

He called the other day and said things are going "reasonably well," sounding tired and tentative.

Gracious loving God, I pray for little Zahra and her mother and father in their life and death battle. May they each in their own way be hearing you say, "Peace! Be still!" and know deep down that all is well. Thank you for your son, Jesus our Lord, and his buddies. I'm so jealous of them! What joy it would be to walk with him and talk with him. Anyway, thank you for inspiring the ones who recorded the events for us, so that we, too, may believe. Amen.

Carolyn Sauer called yesterday to talk about Claudia's divorce. In the course of the conversation, I read her Milton's insights on the subject. I think she was weeping and asked how she and Marcus are doing.

"Like a ping-pong ball. Some days we hum along smoothly, but others, it's as though gray clouds hang over the sun and communication lines are down. Boy, is that enough mixed metaphor?"

"I don't know, Rose; we're hanging in there, especially for Brittany's sake, but that's about all I can say. It's hard; I don't know if it should be this hard." Fie. Sigh. *Thank you for being with them, dear God.*

Sometimes crisis seems the order of the day with so many of the people I know, but, thankfully, some are "struggle free" at the moment. Like Josephine and Sidney. Their names are fitting together more and more, or, I could say, they are fitting together more and more. He's driven her to Mississippi; they're there now! She calls him Sid and he calls her Jo, and they seem to be having a good old time. Not like lovebirds. More like a couple of odd ducks, paddling along side by side. Josephine's demeanor continues as unemotional, somehow detached, and yet caring—but something's different. She seems more alive, I guess I'd say. They're very pleasant to be around and make a nice threesome with Mercedes. I'll take a turn staying overnight with her this Wed. and Thurs.

My precious family, too, diminished as we are, is in pretty good shape right now, within the context of missing Stephen terribly. Barry and Virginia brought in Chinese the other night.

"God, I miss Steverino," Barry exclaimed after his fortune said, "The connections of a close associate will benefit you."

"Cubs tickets?" Virginia guessed. He nodded and we all laughed and then talked about our Cubbies for about an hour. This could be the year! The fact that I often forget to tune in and watch them is an indication of continuing grief that seems to climax midday and dog me through the evening. I can hear Stephen saying, "C'mon, Mom. You can do better than that. Don't let the Cubs down!"

And what fun we had in at Steph's recently. Mindy went with us and Ethan/Dada was there, too, as well as Angelica. We played this game that combines charades and drawing pictures and word guessing and trivia; what a blast! A little too demonstrative for Ethan; he played on the floor with Mack, who fearlessly threw himself on to his dad's body time and time again. 'Twas a beautiful sight to behold, the characteristically unexpressive

Ethan giggling breathlessly as they wrestled. I'll have to call Great-grandma Eloise and report.

Stephanie was comical complaining again about her student, Bull. They had an unpleasant encounter when they randomly parked next to each other in the university parking lot. He was waiting by his shiny sports car when she went out to go home.

"He points to this little tiny scratch where my door had bumped his. He about went into apoplexy when I tried to brush off dust to see it better. Talk about putting negative energy out into the universe! Honestly, that guy is one of the most obnoxious people I've ever met."

By the smiles that passed between us over her head, I'm pretty sure we were all thinking the same thing: that he feels the same way about her. But none of us were moved to say it out loud. What a trip, my dear granddaughter.

Now, off to Rutledge Estate.

<u>Later</u>

Pam Turner, my favorite nurse, was on duty. She could be added to the "struggle free" list. On second thought, though, it's not that she isn't dealing with weighty matters, but that she is dealing well with them. We talked of the mission trip coming up in a couple weeks. For an 18-year-old, Jacob has done a remarkable job of organizing—with her and Greg's help. Fourteen people are going, including Barry and Angelica.

"This will be good for Jacob, but so hard, too. We'll see Rosa's grave, just think about that," and she shook her head anxiously. "I'm glad Angelica's going along; she's good for him. And Greg and I will be right there, too, of course."

"Greg," I said, thinking of something that I'd seen about him lately and then realizing it was his divorce notice in the paper.

"Yes. Divorced again."

"How long were they married?" I asked.

"Seven years. The biggest mistake he's ever made, he says. I say good for him. He's been miserable; what's the point in that?"

I thought of asking if there was any chance of them getting back together but checked myself. My children accuse me of not knowing the difference between caring and nosiness, but I do (she insists).

Other than Pam, my most significant conversation at Rutledge was with Steve Hagendorf's wife. I talked to her a bit about when he was principal of SCHS, but she was understandably not too interested in those times. Today is his 64th birthday, and they don't expect him to live much longer. He doesn't swallow on his own, is skinny like a skeleton, has respiratory ailments constantly.

"There will be no sadness, I assure you of that," she said, gazing upon his empty stare. "He's been dead for a long time. Thirteen years of Alzheimer's. I wouldn't wish it on anyone." My former boss, twenty years younger than I, wearing diapers. Heavens.

Most of my people were sleeping, including Sam, and I wasn't in a mood to wake them. I had planned to spend the most time with Pauline Schuster, but frankly, I was relieved when she was away visiting her sister. The construction process has been a godsend, Pam reported. Pauline sits in the garden all day long watching—and eating candy bars she's hidden in her wheelchair. She's tickled when the workers wave to her. And she's in a private room now, thanks to Louella's generosity. Like Theodore says, "Aunt Louella is a gruff little woman who does a lot of good. You have to take the whole package."

Now I think of one more little piece of this day I want to include, a memory brought on by the epistle reading about, once again, reconciliation. I was reflecting on Paul's remarkable graciousness and—ouch!—Kenneth Johnson came into my mind's eye. I'd like to forget the incident that floated up, but, alas, I remember it like it was yesterday, even though it happened during my college years, ever so long ago...

"This campaign has been very difficult for me," Kenneth began, addressing the student body. A guilty heat crept up my face. **"My trials and afflictions are of little consequence in comparison to what our boys in uniform are enduring and the hardships and challenges in which our nation is embroiled. And yet, for the sake of continuing to work together on this campus for the common good, I am moved to speak my mind. The stress of having to defend myself against unfair charges has taken its toll in sleepless nights and the aggravation of certain afflictions. By God's grace, I have endured with, I hope, honorable behavior and a gracious spirit.**

"I've spoken frankly and want you to know that I have no hard feelings about the campaign. I pledge my support to the president-elect and my utmost respect to each of you. Though you may not desire my friendship, I assure you that I desire yours."

Kenneth had gotten 6% of the vote, I had gotten 32%, and Ethel Kutzel, our new student body president, the rest. Both Ethel and I had clearly benefited from Kenneth's 4F status. 4Fs on campus, regardless of the reason they were rejected for military service, were automatically looked down on. Blatantly unfair, yes; one of several injustices in the fearful and frenzied patriotism following Pearl Harbor. Just running for office was quite an act of courage on Kenneth's part, and his opposition to having an officer training school on campus worked against him, too. He had changed his

position on that as soon as the U.S. declared war, but, no matter how many times he clarified that, Ethel and I kept using it against him.

I felt like a child sitting there in that auditorium, a naughty one. I had let ego rule and become unconscious to what was good and right and true. Over the next few days, I swallowed my chagrin and planted myself outside Kenneth's classroom one afternoon. When he came out, I thanked him for his message and apologized for my behavior and the fallout that had affected him. He extended his hand, and I took it...

What power in his gentle handshake, what peace in being reconciled. Like God does with us, Kenneth initiated reconciliation even though he was the one who had been wronged.

God of grace, thank you for the example and the experience of Kenneth Johnson and for Paul the apostle and for the love of Christ, fully and freely given for us. Help us to behold your wondrous works, to follow you out of any distress, and to allow you to calm our storm and find delight in quietness. Trusting you to provide, I ask all this for myself and my family, for the Turners and the Sauers and the Fergusons next door and Sid and Jo, for St. Timothy and the whole Church, for the world. That pretty well covers it. Good night, God.

Fourth Sunday after Pentecost

2 Samuel 1:1, 17-27
Psalm 30
2 Corinthians 8:7-15
Mark 5:21-43

> ...it is a question of a fair balance between
> your present abundance and their need...
> As it is written,
> "The one who had much did not have too much,
> and the one who had little did not have too little.

So said Paul to the Corinthians when their church was doing well and others were in desperate need. And the beat goes on, Morris picking it up this morning.

"Giving money is a powerful way of getting in on God's love. Going way back to the ordering of the manna distributed in the wilderness, God gave us the model for sharing our excess with others in their need."

And then Tariq stole the offering! I wonder if he interpreted the message to say that he was the one in need? I got a little bit involved because Madge grabbed me in wide-eyed distress as I was coming out of the bathroom and heading for coffee hour.

"Rose! Something awful's just happened," she gasped. "That boy of Louie and Rita's just took the offering! I was about to put it in the safe for the count tomorrow when one of the youth needed help with the copy machine and I went back there and then out of the corner of my ear I heard this slight little sound and rushed back to the desk and he was going down the hall with the bag and went into the Men's Room." Yikes.

We hurried to the fellowship hall and got the pastors and Louie and Rita. Louie and Morris went straight into the bathroom and found him with the cash in his pocket; he had slid the zipper bag with the checks still in it behind the trash can.

Yuck. What a thing to have to deal with on a Sunday morning after hearing the good news and singing the wonderful songs and enjoying the love of one another. Yuck. The pastors moved us into their office.

"Tariq, son, why'd you do this?" Louie shot at him. "You know we'd get you whatever..."

"I ain't your son. Don't ever call me son again," he glared.

"Okay, let's take some breaths and sit down here," Charlene suggested, and I said, "Madge and I aren't needed, I don't think, are we?" and they dismissed us with nods and we left the sad little family to deal with the sad situation.

Help these, your children, to know your compassion and your steadfast love, O God, as they handle this incident. You do not willingly afflict or grieve anyone, and there is always redemption in you. May your grace prevail and relationships be restored. Amen. Oh, dear. Right there in the church.

Money—and generosity—have been front and center in my life lately, with the settling of Stephen's estate. Over 2 million dollars! We are all astonished. *And listen to the irony of this, Charlie—the same day Virginia and I met with Malcolm and Penelope about Stephen's will, I got his $79 AAA membership renewal in the mail. Ha! We've been buying an auto club membership for a millionaire! Just kept it going as his birthday present all these years since he turned 18 and got his first car.*

These business matters have brought me down a little, Charlie. Penelope came to town to get everything squared away with Malcolm. Stephen left nothing to us, faithful to the abundance—need dictum. Most definitely, none of us are in need, financially. Six charities, including an organization to assist families dealing with pancreatic cancer, will soon be surprised with very handsome checks. Plus, he had set up an endowment some years ago with churchwide offices that we didn't even know about. Our boy lived modestly, worked hard, managed well, and knew deeply the joy of partnering with God—in life and death. How proud we can be. Oh, and say, proud of Virginia, too. The giving to the world hunger fund is on a steep upward tangent, in large part because of her determined coordination and cheerleading. I know giving is not all about money, but money sure can change people's lives for the better. I believe she is doing a very good thing in the sight of God.

This was our first time to see Penelope since she left the day after Easter. My last image of her was with puffy eyes with dark circles under them and stooped shoulders, so it was good to see her looking more rested and fit. She was just back from her "pilgrimage" and had supper with Virginia and Barry and me and rattled on about those Holy Land adventures, which, I'm glad to say, were most interesting. She stayed overnight with Barry and Gin. "Hope you don't mind, Mama Rose; I just can't sleep in that room again, at least not yet." I assured her that I understand totally—I can't even go in it—and said a cheerful goodbye at the restaurant, but gloom closed in on me when I walked into the house.

I played my CD of Clara Schumann's music, lovely and comforting, and had a glass of wine before retiring but didn't sleep well. "Weeping lingered for the night, but joy came in the morning," with the first pink light of dawn when I took a piece of chocolate cake to the deck, savoring each bite and thinking about our fine son. The chocolate cake was because of Eloise. She eats a dessert first thing each day to celebrate how sweet life is; we did it every day I was there. She and I talked Friday night.

"How are Brian and Lisa doing?"

"Quite well. Sylvania has them on a strict and delicious diet and they're working out with Jeff at the gym several times a week. I think they're starting to lose a few pounds. They're in counseling. Brian thinks he'll close a house deal soon. So just think if we'd called the authorities that night; he'd be in jail, and what a waste that would be."

"Are you sure you feel safe?"

"Absolutely. That crazy night was simply a rough patch of sea that's been calmed, thanks to 'Our Father Which Art in Heaven.'"

"Very faithful of you indeed, Eloise. Why, I would no more take unstable people into my…"

"What about that Garfield person you were telling me about, that transient person you befriended? And that other family from years ago with all the children and the prison record? And young Angelica smoking pot in your house?"

Hm. I guess maybe we are similar in our approaches to people at risk—and in our faith that God smooths rough waters, that Jesus is mysteriously present in danger.

There's more to write—

- about Theodore and Lloyd's marvelous "silver notes" this morning—they'd gotten the girls ensemble from the high school to sing and their pure voices were simply perfect for Corfe's "I Will Magnify the Lord"—everyone was transfixed but none more than Mindy and Maddie—I could see both of their faces with the same rapt expression
- about two uneventful nights spent with Mercedes—although living with dementia is anything but uneventful—she went missing in the middle of the night but I found her sitting on the toilet seat in her night clothes in the dark in the tiny downstairs bathroom and we had to change clothes
- about Helen's account of her time in Iraq—she found it comforting to see where Chad was killed—and here I am, avoiding the room in my own house where Stephen died

- about fun with Sarah, who is on her way to Katerineburg at this moment
- about rear-ending Matthew—from hospice who worked with Stephen—not much damage—need to hang up my car keys, I guess—very nice to see Matthew despite circumstances
- and on and on…

but I'm done. Writing energy expended. Doubleheader, that's the rest of my day. Then peanut butter popcorn, maybe check my email, play a little piano, read my novel, get to bed with hopes for peaceful slumber.

Oh! but I must mention the cat, a pretty yellow thing, gold striped, young, affectionate, hanging around for the last several days. I guess I'll take her to the vet.

Thank you, God, for all of the above. All of it.

Fifth Sunday after Pentecost

Ezekiel 2:1-5
Psalm 123
2 Corinthians 12:2-10
Mark 6:1-13

"Who does he think he is?" they said to each other. "Who do you think you are?" they demanded of him. And somehow, in the midst of all that, right there in his home church, scripture says that Jesus had a power failure.

Which makes me think of yesterday when I went next door with a taco salad sans meat and fresh rhubarb strawberry pie to welcome my Ferguson neighbors back from Indy. As I was leaving, Jim cracked, "When you see Jesus tomorrow, tell him we need the day to ourselves to regroup before I go back to work Monday, but we'll see him next Sunday." A lite comment, and yet an indication of how little power Jesus holds for him. In contrast, Jesus is the power in my life.

Wait a minute here. What am I saying? If you believe in Jesus as Christ, he has power; and if you don't, he doesn't? No, that's not right; Jesus' power is constant, uninfluenced by our perceptions—because it is God the Creator's power, fully revealed—human and divine—coming to us through the Paraclete—sacred spiritual being—and yet, he is portrayed in the Bible as briefly losing that power...

Oh dear, this is getting way too heady. Let me bring it back to earth, back to Jim and me. Although I'm not wanting to compare (that's odious), but to understand.

Understand what?

The ineffable; give it up, Rose.

No, but wait... Jesus' identity, that's what this is about.

Right—the ineffable. Stop trying to eff. 'Tis futile.

Yes, I guess so. That's basically what Charlene concluded in her message this morning.

"We don't have to understand Jesus to love him, revel in him, cling to him," she said earnestly, on her tiptoes. "We don't have to articulate an impressive theology to see God at work and name the sacred in our lives and in our life together. Here, in the Body of Christ, we help each other expect to see kindness and love and perseverance and say, 'Thank you, God!'"

Ironically (or not), the fragile, troubled Anita seems to have more of a feel for divine power in her life than the more confident, carefree Jim.

"I am exhausted, Rose," she said, after we hugged and I asked how she was doing. "I feel empty and—and—powerless. I feel like I am nothing, nobody—in a good way, I mean," her eyes shining. "Strong, peaceful. The therapy was the hardest I've ever done, excruciating about my mother and her suicide and my father—where was he? But God was all through it, ever-present."

Jim came down from upstairs with the baby, still waking up from her nap, and placed her in the cradle of Anita's arms. She smiled down at the bundle and said, "I am quietly confident about Zahra and me and the future. God's grace is sufficient, I keep trying to remember. I am in a new place."

She certainly is. What a transformation. Her strength radiated across the room, a strength I'd never sensed in her before. *Thank you God, for the workings of your Spirit in the life of this beautiful child of yours.*

They were a topic of conversation when I had the Bryants over for Sunday dinner today. The pastors were happy to hear my report of what Anita said yesterday. Morris had visited them in Indy about halfway through their time down there, and they'll be staying close—because that's the kind of pastors they are. In a word, excellent. (Not perfect, but no need for me to dwell on their gaffes and shortcomings; there always seem to be plenty of others tending to that!)

Our conversation was wide-ranging:

- Danny Bennett, Hero – All over the papers, on local TV, medal presented by the mayor for pushing a coworker to safety, turning off the gas, and grabbing the fire extinguisher to put out a grill fire at Burger King. Big old heart-warmer, for sure, and we're all proud, of him, naturally, but I understand Karen/mom's feelings: "Sure he did good, but all this fuss is like they think anyone with Down's Syndrome doesn't have any brains at all. I mean, really, using a fire extinguisher is not exactly rocket science. Plus, now we have to live with him!" she laughed. He's definitely enjoying the attention, eager to say to whomever, "I p-p-put out the fire at B-Burger K-K-King!" and thump his heart and point heavenward, like a star athlete. He's a star, all right.

- Preaching – I thanked them for their solid sermons, and they were eager to talk about preaching. They want sermons to be more conversational. What would I think of asking for verbal responses during sermons or having "turn to your neighbor and discuss" moments? My, I'm not sure about that; once in a while, maybe, I advised. And they talked of "walking the tightrope between ego and inspiration." Morris put it well. "If speaking for God doesn't make the

174

preacher quake in his boots, some self-examination is probably in order." Charlene's pure faith and insight hit the mark of why their sermons hit the mark: "Our only confidence is in Christ. That's what we're always trying to get across: the power of Christ present in each one of us." And this was funny—she confessed that she wasn't much looking forward to preaching on the beheading of John the Baptist next week, that she "couldn't find much gospel in that story." Morris exclaimed, "Are you kidding? It foreshadows Jesus speaking truth to power. He and John embody and embrace the most outrageous paradox of the gospel: that true belief can get you killed—but in that death is our salvation. In their actions, we see the freedom to be ourselves, boldly taking risks..." Charlene smiled and said, "Okay, okay! Thanks, honey. I've got something to go on now." I was glad to hear that sermonette because I won't be there next week; we'll be at Transfiguration with Stephanie Rose for a presentation of the gifts given in Stephen's memory.

- Stephen and how I'm doing – As much joy over him as sorrow, most days, I reported. Still hard. They're grateful that they "crossed paths, however briefly." People at church mention him a lot, so they're still getting to know him, they said. That was very nice, comforting.

- Maddie Bowers – Morris has stopped by the farm a couple times but not connected with Randy yet. One evening, he was pretty sure Randy went out the back door when he knocked on the front. "Doesn't seem like a healthy situation. Bryan and Maddie seem weighted down, like they're dealing with way more than kids their age should have to, especially Maddie." We all agreed she is a unique child and we want to be a church family to her, as needed. Heavens, how else would we feel since she chose St. Timothy at the age of 5 and is one of the more faithful members?

- My new cat, maybe – She's fixed and probably up-to-date on shots, according to the vet. Has a chip in her ear, so the vet put out the info and if the owner doesn't respond in 30 days, she's mine. I enjoy her but am preparing myself that she'll be claimed. I'm not naming her in the meantime; I just call her Kitty Cat.

- Mission trip – They leave tomorrow. Morris is wondering what he's gotten himself into—"I'm not really in shape to work long hours in hot sun..." But he's excited, too, and very impressed with Jacob's effort. They're going to work with the church in the village to renovate and perhaps expand its school. To help with that, Jacob recruited a friend of the family who is an architect to be on the team.

This is truly "a path unknown," as Morris put it. *Thank you, great God, for providing their every need.*

- Marsha, church secretary – I keep hearing disturbing tidbits about her. Virginia said she asked Marsha last week to leave a message for Morris and Marsha said, "Sure, I'll leave a message—for what it's worth." So I asked them if Marsha was behaving herself. They looked at each other hesitantly and acknowledged challenges but closed the discussion quickly. I smell trouble.
- Tariq – He's left Louie and Rita for a new foster home. Rita and Louie are disappointed, but their faith seems "as strong as a steel cable," Charlene said. They've gotten to know his grandparents and tried to part on good terms with the lad in hopes of staying in touch, but the boy's defenses are deep and strong.
- And, finally, we talked about their pregnancy. Quite something, after 12 years of marriage and longing for a child. Fertility counseling and drugs. "A little boy," Charlene smiled radiantly—and tiredly. Due in November. "And there's just one, not five or six," Morris exulted.

Thank you, God, for the gift of these, your servants, and for delightful time together.

Sixth Sunday after Pentecost

Amos 7:7-15
Psalm 85:8-13
Ephesians 1:3-14
Mark 6:14-29

We worshiped in darkness and devastation this morning. Tornadoes swept through sections of the city Friday night and Transfiguration "took it on the chin," as their stocky, southern drawling Pastor Gail put it. We started out in the nave, open to the heavens, the roof torn asunder. Whirling wind was evident in wrecked and scattered pews, and everything was soaking wet. Most of us had never seen anything quite like this before.

The paradox of our faith (some would say absurdity) lived and breathed through this scene and through the ancient psalm. "Folks just like us wrote this song, this beautiful poem, at a time like this moment, when all seemed lost and they were so overwhelmed they could hardly think—just like us," Pr. Gail introduced it, and a fast, clear beat on bongo drums started up, joined by guitar and flute and the bright melody, "Lord, Lord, Lord, let us see your kindness. Lord, Lord, Lord, grant us your salvation." We caught on to the tune and there was dancing, too, as we fell in behind the cross and made our way out of the rubble on to the sidewalk and around the corner into the gym, which was virtually untouched by the storm.

"People of God," Pr. Gail shouted, "shalom is so thick in this place you could cut it with a knife!" and "Amen, preacher!" went up from the usual congregation, interspersed with twice again as many worshipers, settled on folding chairs, still no lights except candles.

"You may not believe this, I can't quite believe it, but the Holy Spirit is working so hard right now that I kissed Mayor Bill on the cheek," she said to hoots and laughter. "Now that's a downright miracle after all our skirmishes over city codes and whatnot, trying to do our ministry, follow our God, and seemed like the establishment was against us—and he kissed me back!"

At the appointed time in the service, Barry, with Mack in his arms, and Virginia and I stood by while Steph presented the money contributed in Stephen's name—$10,000! Heavens, how the money poured in, ranging from Maddie's solemnly offered 50 cents to check after check in the hundreds given by business associates and well-to-do friends. Penelope's church sent a handsome sum. We all wished she could have been there. Gin's going to call her tonight and describe the whole amazing event, tornado and all.

Talk about bittersweet, Charlie! When Pr. Gail started the little ceremony, "In the name of our risen Savior, we are gathered here to remember before God our brother Stephen Michael Harris..." it was like being at the funeral again and utter sadness welled up in me. He would have been proud of us, though, standing strong and faithful, keeping our tears in our eyes—until later.

"This is all so wonderful," Stephanie exulted as we walked outside and had a private family moment before moving on to the picnic. "But I'd rather have him," she broke down, her father folding his arms around her, and all of us having a little cry. And I'll ask you again, for the hundredth time, dear husband and father—he's okay, right? He's there with you, right?

Oh, God, help me. LordLordLord, let me see your kindness, grant me your salvation, save me from the dark and heavy places.

The cookout that Transfig's group, "Home-cooked Food by the Homeless," put on was just what we needed. Amidst food, drink, and merriment, dozens of folks greeted us with gratitude for the gift. Just thinking of how many people's lives Stephen has touched is of great comfort. Oh, dear, but that's enough on the subject for now.

To change course, I'll recount the unlikely scene at Lydia Circle on Tuesday. Wine was central to the evening—which was fine with me, of course. We were at Faye Brewster's. She served a ritzy buffet, and several hearts were quite gladdened with the Pinot Grigio. Not so for Louella, unfortunately, who grew more zealous than ever about social justice, poo-pooing the baby layettes we assembled as tokenism. Good heavens.

But we got an amusing account from the carload of ladies who had driven down to the penitentiary to visit Genevieve Lachman, our sister serving time for embezzlement. A cell phone was inadvertently taken in and rang at a bad time. And they turned down a wrong road as they were leaving and were pursued by guards. Genevieve wrote a thank you note for the visit, teasing that she was afraid they might have jeopardized her early release!

Helen was program leader and was going to talk about her trip to Iraq, interweaving passages from Lamentations, but the wine made her too weepy to do it, which was probably just as well because it would have been hard on all of us, especially Deedee.

Deedee's circle leader now and tried to run the business meeting but it turned into a rambling, repetitive discussion of everything pertaining to St. Timothy, from the secretary getting fired (major brouhaha) to somebody sneezing seven times in a row during the sermon Sunday (that was hilarious), punctuated by people complimenting each other's shoes and ringing phones answered on the spot. Anna Louise brought up Claudia's divorce, so that naturally led to news of other divorces and autopsies of several of them. On another night, I might have been vexed by such disorder, but this night I contentedly sipped and gazed fondly upon the faces of my sisters in Christ, alive in the joy of being together, perceiving gossip as caring, laughter as grace. Faye counted the offering and gave a whistle. "You girls have gotten your tens mixed up with your ones tonight, I think; this is great!" We were a few inches off plumb—in a good way.

Off plumb in a good way makes me think of Mercedes and Josephine. While each day has its challenges, they continue as a good combination. And Josephine's selling her house in Mississippi and settling in Shippensforge permanently! I was taken by surprise on that one. We talked about it the other afternoon when I'd stopped by. She and Mercedes and I were sitting around the kitchen table drinking her southern style iced tea—which I can hardly drink; it's sweet enough to pour over pancakes, instant diabetes—but it was cold on a hot day and the ceiling fan stirred the air and lawn mowers buzzed outside.

"Well, it's kinda' odd, I reckon, but I don't feel that connected down there, even if it's always been my home. I've got no kin there and the house is too big for me by my lonesome. Mercedes needs me, no tellin' for how long," she reported in her simple, slow manner, and then said, seriously, "I think the good Lord wants me to move here. And Sid does, too." Aha.

He came in the back door as if on cue, sweating and puffing from trimming up the yard. "Hoo-wie! Hot out there. Got any of your sweet tea for this old fella' after I wash off?" and he went through to the bathroom.

Suddenly, it was so obvious, the two of them together, or three, I should say—a trio of people drawn together by need and purpose. Mercedes is able to stay in her house, Josephine seems more calm and content than I've ever known her, and Sidney is clearly enjoying himself as "the man of the house." God at work, people living in Christ day by day, in want, in need, through ups and downs. A beautiful sight, one of those little glimpses, little in-breakings of how life is supposed to be.

And now, I finally have the moment and the spurt of energy to clean off my snow boots and get them off the deck—in July, for crying out loud! My deck and back yard are low key this year, no planters or hummingbird feeders, no birdhouses cleaned out. Spring this year was not a time to maintain routines. I hate like anything to admit this, but the yard is too much for me. I need a yardman, I guess. But all is well. "This is the day the Lord has made. Let us rejoice and be glad in it."

<u>Seventh Sunday after Pentecost</u>

Jeremiah 23:1-6
Psalm 89:20-37
Ephesians 2:11-22
Mark 6:30-34, 53-56

Jacob and his group reported on their mission trip after worship this morning. We had a potluck brunch in their honor. Pam was telling me that this was the first time they'd been together since they stumbled off the plane, dazed and exhausted, and Jacob had planned for them to dish up their plates and go into the parlor to have some quiet time before their presentation. Didn't happen. People kept cornering them, so they finally gave up on that and sat down to eat with others and started telling about the trip and answering questions.

Healing was a main theme of their program, with photos and videos and personal accounts.

"As you all know..." Jacob started out, and I looked around at faces old and young, fixed on this young man and thought what courage he had to stand before us like this, because we all do know, we know the whole story of that terrible spring day last year when a teenaged girl's life was abruptly interrupted, eventually ended, as a result of his actions.

"As you all know, Rosa Mendez lost her life here in our town because of a freak accident that she and I had. What's happened can't be changed, however much we all wish it could. I've wondered many times how I could go on, but God has always been with me, inside and out, giving me strength. And you have, too, so I want to thank you," and he had to stop for a moment.

His divorced parents gazed steadily at him, chins up, eyes shining, Pam's lip trembling, Greg's hand on her back.

"I'll never get over this completely, I don't think," he continued, "but I went to Rosa's hometown for healing, and I found it."

Then he switched gears, bringing a gentle laugh from the crowd when he said, "Mexican Catholics can be a little crazy..." (I had to smile myself, at Mindy muttering, "Ain't that the truth.") "One day," Jacob continued, "Rosa's brother thought he saw the face of Jesus in the mortar mix." He smiled dubiously with a tilt of his head, and we laughed again. "A couple others saw it, too, and there was some high drama for a few minutes. They wanted to let the whole batch harden, but we couldn't afford to lose it, <u>and</u> we couldn't see Jesus, so we talked them out of it.

"But I didn't need a figure in the concrete to know that Jesus Christ was present. I felt his healing power the whole time, felt myself getting stronger and more peaceful. We did some good stuff with those people, we helped improve their school, but God's grace and healing meant the most to me."

Angelica spoke next, a little ill at ease, blurting, "There were miracles all over the place, and the one I want to tell about is Juan, Rosa's brother." At first, she said, he was very hostile. When they arrived, Rosa's mother invited them into her house, but Juan stood in the door, refusing to let "Rosa's killer" pass, and this terrible fight broke out between mother and son. "But gradually, he, like, thawed toward us, and the, like, demon of anger or whatever, left him. And like Jacob said, Juan helped out with the work, and on our last night, he asked us into their house and presented us with gifts. That was a miracle, totally. Also, the village fixed us a big dinner and Juan played his guitar and sang for us and we all danced together." And there, before our eyes, was an artsy picture of Juan playing his guitar in the foreground and a blurry whirl of dancers in colorful clothing behind him, followed by a video of same, obviously taken with a phone, jerky with crazy perspectives.

Morris told us that he was appalled at the corruption they encountered. They had to pay several bribes along the way, just to get the job done, and the people treated it as routine. "God is not mocked by such economic injustice," he insisted, and quoted Jeremiah, "Woe to the shepherds who destroy and scatter the sheep of my pasture!" On the other hand, he described the priest and sisters representing God well and said they "basked in the joy of oneness in Christ, conflicts resolved, divisions healed, mission accomplished."

Barry showed pictures of the building process. The first one showed the delivery of concrete blocks and the last one was of the dedication—including the processional cross and candles and clergy—of La Escuela de Rosa Mendez de Santo Jose´ de la Iglesia. They renovated two existing classrooms and built two more. He admitted that he didn't think they could complete the project in the eight days they had. "And I never met Rosa, but from the testimony of those who knew her, this was a most appropriate tribute to a young woman who wanted to be a teacher—maestra—and had the potential of being an excellent one." He paused for a moment. "And I just want to say one more thing." He stood there looking down in thought. Virginia edged forward on her chair, and Stephanie and I glanced at each other. Finally, he went on. "I stand before you as a skeptic, a bystander when it comes to God and the Church—but things unexplainable and indescribable happened in what seemed like a God-forsaken corner of the world—and I am very grateful for the privilege of having been there." Virginia and Steph raised their eyebrows at each other. That was a lot for Barry.

For her part, Pam said that at the beginning she thought they might need "to shake the dust off our sandals and abort the mission. There was the conflict with Juan and suspicion of us gringos and the bribes and confusion about the project and trouble getting materials..." And she gave a moving account of talking through the discouragement the second night they were there. She told how she and Jacob and Greg described for the rest of the team the strength of Rosa's spirit and her determination in the months between the accident and her death, living as a quadriplegic. "Keeping Rosa in mind kept us going until the problems smoothed out and the building really got underway. After that, each day of miserable heat and grueling labor was a joy," she concluded, laughing with us at the contradiction.

Greg was the last to speak and seemed to have the most difficulty but finally got out one sentence. "I came back healed, too, and hopeful that I, like Jacob, can find God's grace and forgiveness after inflicting injury on others." Boy, this was just about more candor than we could handle. After all, the injury he inflicted—an extramarital affair leading to the break-up of his family—was quite different from Jacob's innocent accident. But what better, more appropriate place to be painfully honest than in Christian community? The hug that followed between him and Jacob obviously meant a lot.

And then Jacob wrapped up by telling us that the next phase is to equip the classrooms with chalkboards and other equipment and supplies. He announced another Mexican fundraiser dinner and someone yelled out, "Si, si! Fiesta!"

Jim and Anita were there with wide-eyed little Zahra, thrilling us all with genuine smiles and curious eye contact and velvety vocalizations.

"Two Sundays in a row," he said to me, holding up two fingers for emphasis.

"Yes. How are you faring?"

"I like the extra curriculars best—cute kids singing, food, Powerpoints. When the religious stuff starts, I pretty well zone out—although I liked that line in the confession about 'the earth groaning under our demands;' that's true. By the way," he asked with his sly grin, "how exactly do you raise your Ebenezer?"

I didn't think he really wanted me to explain that biblical term in a hymn written in the 17th century, so I just laughed. Hearing Anita's robust soprano raising her Ebenezer in "Come Thou Fount of Every Blessing" was fun, though.

"You know I'm here for only one reason, Rose," he felt moved to say. "To save my family's life."

Nothing wrong with that reason.

You know, Charlie, a congregation on any given Lord's Day includes quite a variety of saints/sinners and a potpourri of reasons for being there. As I drove home, I kept thinking about Greg Turner. You knew him well from working together on various church tasks. This guy's been through the breakup of two families, and his relationship with St. Timothy has been severed by it all, too. And Charlie, as I sat there behind the wheel, this deep sadness engulfed my heart, and then came a torrent of sadnesses—Rosa's death, Jacob's burden, Louie and Rita and Tariq not working out, Stephen gone and...STOP! I don't know who said it, me or the Holy Spirit or both of us at once, but I actually slammed on the brakes, and do you know what? That flash flood of griefs and grievances ceased, just like that. All was well, and all was blessing, and I drove on in jubilation for not sinking unconsciously into pointless blues. Aren't you proud of me?

Stephanie, Angelica, and Mack followed me home from church—and fussed at me for erratic driving and told me that I'd run a red light, undoubtedly when I was lost in the blues. Aargh. I can't stop thinking of that little accident I had a couple weeks ago. Every time something like that happens—oh, I tripped and fell down taking the recycling out Tuesday morning—I feel like I'm losing ground. Well, what else is to be expected at this point in life, I guess. I repeat, aargh.

Steph drove us out to Virginia's for the rest of the day. Late in the afternoon, we were treated to Barry's famous barbecued ribs, eating on their patio surrounded by a rainbow hedge of plush peonies, except that it was just too hot, and we wound up carrying our plates into the dining room.

Barry and Ang gave us more details of the trip. "And you and Jacob are becoming much better friends?" I asked Angelica. Her cute smile and the nod of her head with its black, close curls showed such happiness. Jacob's going to IU in the fall and she's planning to go visit him. Hard to believe this is the sad and angry goth girl of a year ago, confused and nearly hopeless. I could raise an Ebenezer to God's help and grace coming through for her. And now it occurs to me that I could have told Jim that the big stone we placed on Cute Baby's grave is an Ebenezer, a sign left to mark a new beginning, always in God. Oh well, I can tell him that anytime.

Mack entertained us as only an 18-month-old can, prattling on unintelligibly with earnest expression and turning round and round until he staggered. My St. Lord, that kid is the cutest thing I've ever seen since his mother and grandmother were his age! Golden hair (about the color of Kitty Cat's; if I get to keep her, I think I'll name her Gold Baby), Steph's hazel eyes, Ethan's cute little nose. What joy! I'm going to call Eloise tonight and describe the antics of our little great-grandboy.

It had been dark for awhile when the Cubs game went into extra innings and they won AGAIN! They had to go 15 full innings and when Barry brought in roasted peanuts and beer, it almost seemed like we were sitting and cheering in Wrigley Field. Sweet life. *And here's what's kind of weird, Charlie. Stephen's name was mentioned only once today— about how he'd be loving the Cubs' season—and other than that, I didn't even think his name. This is good, I guess. Healing.*

Eighth Sunday after Pentecost

2 Kings 4:42-44
Psalm 145:10-18
Ephesians 3:14-21
John 6:1-21

"Man! Nobody who knew me in high school would believe I'm a Eucharistic minister," Mindy marveled after the service this morning. I bet she's right—but now we both are. She talked me into it.

"But I feel like I should be slowing down, Mindy, not taking on more You don't understand how tired I get."

"Oh," she said, considering me with her magnified eyes. "Okay—but it's only once a month—we could be a team—I'll pick you up every time, I promise—we'll just go do our people and I'll bring you right back home. Or how about this—I'll take you out to eat each time, too. That way we'll make sure we have at least one time a month to really catch up with each other."

I couldn't resist. So we met with the pastors and four others last Wednesday night and reflected on what communion means to us and what it means to take it to others. We went over the brief service we would use and checked out the individual communion sets with their tiny cups and little vials of wine and sterling silver case for wafers. We talked about possible situations, like people with dementia who might not remember how to eat and drink and what we should do with leftover wafers and wine. Next, this morning during worship, the communion sets were placed on the altar to be consecrated along with the other elements. Finally, after communion, we six Eucharistic ministers went forward and received a kit and were sent out with a prayer—"Gracious God, loving all your family with a mother's tender care: As you sent the angel to feed Elijah with heavenly bread, assist those who set forth to share your word and sacrament with those who are sick, homebound, and imprisoned..." Mindy and I are assigned to the folks at Rutledge Estate, so that works well for me, too. We set out straightaway after the service.

As promised, she drove, stopping for a nice meal on the way, insisting on paying because she still feels so rich, having a "real" paycheck coming in regularly, but then she was short on cash and couldn't find her credit card, so I paid. That's my friend Mindy—but not a problem; I was happy to pay. As we walked across the parking lot, equipped with our communion sets, Bibles, the service, and God's grace, she took my arm and squealed, "Am I excited or what?"

We had agreed that she would commune George Rizenhouer, Mary Thurgood and Pauline Shuster and I would have Sam Benshaw (if he wants it; he's not a member of St. Tim), Pastor Ruskin, and Mitch (if he wants it; he's not a member either. Of course, they all can decide whether or not they want it, members or not; it's not a forced thing.)

And then Mindy said, "But wait a minute; why don't we get them all together in a circle and do it? I mean, that's what Eucharist's about anyway, right? Togetherness?"

I certainly couldn't argue with that, and we made sure the activities room was available and agreed to round up our folks and meet there—but that didn't happen, no circle.

Pauline insisted on being by herself because she "doesn't like other people that much, especially today." Oboy, her heart was ready, huh? The poor thing has gained so much weight they're having to order an extra wide wheelchair for her. She's having more and more diabetic comas, too. *Help her to be aware of your presence and avail herself of your strength, O God.*

Mitch didn't have much idea of what communion even was, so I wound up spending some time in explanation, and he wound up passing on it.

Sam was out and about with a great-grandchild visiting from out of town.

Mary Thurgood could not be waked up. I mean, she was alive but in a deep sleep. Alive in body, anyway; not much left mentally. And Bob, perfectly sound of mind and living a full life, drops dead of a heart attack. *What's up with that, God?* we ask.

Pr. Ruskin understood the bread and wine but not the walk-down-the-hall part. Every time I would say, "We're going to meet in the activities room," he would smile pleasantly and say, "That's fine, dear lady. I'm ready," and stay planted in his chair, so I just went ahead and gave it to him. When I read the story of the feeding of the five thousand, however, he about said it word for word with me.

So George was the only one in the activities room and I stopped in the doorway just as Mindy was starting the service. "When our congregation gathers for the celebration of Holy Communion..." she began. And then "...I bring to you this same bread and wine..." They were face to face next to one of the big round tables, he in his wheelchair, she in a regular chair, the elements beside them on the table. Bent over severely with his curved spine, George held his head up to look at her as long as he could, lowering it as needed. He peered into her eyes when she addressed him, gazed upon her lips as she read the lesson, jerkily moved his head to focus on her hand when she picked up the wafer between her thumb and forefinger and raised it between them, saying Jesus' words, "Take and eat..." then the little glass of wine held high, "Take and drink…" They said the Lord's Prayer together, he haltingly for lack of breath with eyes fervently closed, and then the body and blood given, received.

After she gave the benediction, George asked her to say a prayer for Lois, his wife, and in the slightest sound or movement, I realized that Lois was standing right beside me, but they were oblivious to us.

"Okay. Is she dead or alive?" Mindy asked.

George chuckled, and Lois did too, with a quiet sniff. "Oh, she's very much alive. She has terrible arthritis, though, and our daughter has cancer, and I just want to thank God for her and pray that she will stay strong."

Mindy said a sweet prayer and George said thank you and how much it meant to him to receive communion from her and she thanked him, too, and asked, "Could you tell it was only my second time? Pauline a little bit ago and you."

Lois and I entered the scene at that point. She kissed George and then introduced herself to Mindy. They had seen each other at church but not ever met. Lois became hostess and served us coffee and a sweet in the dining room. Daughter Susan's chemo is going well, they told us, and the prognosis is good. And they talked about what a great guy Stephen was and asked how I was getting along. Lois had been at the funeral, of course. She's working with Virginia on the World Hunger Appeal and expressed what I so often think: "I am just mystified that we don't feed all the hungry, abolish this problem from the globe. God's provided the resources; all we have to do is distribute them properly."

"My pure-hearted, naïve wife," George commented fondly.

"I'm serious," Lois said, though none of us doubted that. "Why it wouldn't even require sacrifice, just all believers giving a modest amount. And you know what? We could accomplish more than we can even imagine if we would let the power of the Spirit work in us."

"The eyes of all look to you, and you give them their food in due season. You open your hand, satisfying the desire of every living thing." God's work; our hands. And I can see Mother saying that prayer before every meal, I can hear her voice.

So, today was full of communion. Mercedes, Josephine and Sidney—the three musketeers, I've started calling them—were at late service, and I noticed that Mercedes is so shaky with palsy that they dip her bread in the wine and put it right in her mouth. The Bryants have brought back real bread instead of wafers, I'm so glad. It doesn't really matter, of course, but the bread sure is tastier and good symbolism, the one loaf, broken. Plus, just like Eucharistic ministry, it gives people another way to serve. This morning's bread was baked by Mercedes and Josephine. On the other hand, you might get a piece "big enough to choke a cow," like somebody said.

Anita was at the altar railing, too, holding Zahra to receive a blessing. I'm finally starting to breathe easier about Anita. She doesn't like how her medication dulls her, she says, but it's working and she seems committed to taking it. "People suffering still makes me sad, bothers me a lot, but with the pills it's like they're far away and there's nothing I can do about it, so..." Okay, so the drugs give her a more normal perspective.

Theodore and Lloyd are on vacation and Mary Jane Evans filled in, as usual, on the piano. I wish they'd hire someone who could really carry the service, but nobody wants to hurt Mary Jane's feelings, which is a good thing—I guess. She and Jerry really need the money, too; he still hasn't found work. But, sadly, Mary Jane screeches as she plays. "Let Us Break Bread Together" was a disaster. Way too slow, thought we'd never finish, and then all three times on the chorus, she reversed 'knees' and 'face,' singing, "When I fall on my face, with my knees to the rising sun..." Well, who hasn't done that, but—all three times at screech level? Please.

The musical setting for the liturgy that we're using in the summer is upbeat and "very dance worthy," as Mindy says—and does. Charlene moves with it, even Morris, in his stilted way, and lots of the kids. The kyrie eleison/Lord have mercy is pretty peppy, which seems a little contradictory, but I like singing and swinging, "Kyr-i-e e-lei-son, on our world and on our way. Kyr-ie e-lei-son, ev-ry-day." One of the teenagers livened things up with his electric guitar, playing along with Mary Jane, ending with the perfect twang.

We were sitting on the front pew because Maddie and Mindy have started sitting together and Maddie likes sitting upfront. I want to sit by Mindy, too, but it's quite a transition, after sitting in the middle on the left side facing the altar for five decades. I was also concerned that Virginia might not want to move, but she didn't care. So here we are on the front row on the right. Bird's eye view. And we were engulfed in giggles by Mary Jane screeching and falling on her face. Except Maddie., who just regarded her seriously.

During the prayer when we pray for people "in our hearts or on our lips," I whispered 'Stephanie," who is in South Africa for a world forum on women and children in poverty, for her safety and awareness of the Holy Spirit's presence. Can't wait to hear about it all.

2 am Monday—Venting session

Oh, how I wish I could confounded sleep! Five or six solid hours would be heaven. It's about aging and arthritis and the unsettling haunts of grief. I am making good progress with Bach's Well-Tempered Clavier piano exercises; I play half the night away sometimes. The door to Stephen's room stays closed, otherwise I'm liable to walk by and visualize him lying on the bed, wasting away. Things that go bump in the night make me just about jump out of my skin, and here's what just happened: a rubber band holding a set of markers broke and they scattered off my desk onto the wood floor, for crying out loud. The universe is against me sleeping, rubber bands conspire to keep me awake! I lay in bed unnerved for a minute and then crept out with 911 entered on my cell phone and my thumb on the call button. But I guess I won't press charges against the markers. I wish I weren't so jumpy about such things, though; I never used to be.

Well, I can tell I'm not going to be slumbering anytime soon. Oh, well; let me try and not brood. I'll just live it up with some wine and cheese and a few episodes of MASH, and when I get sleepy, try again. A purring, furry creature in the lap would be nice, but I am bereft of cat again. Kitty Cat's loving family showed up yesterday, day 28 of the 30-day waiting period. And that was fine, a happy reunion sweet to see. Her name is Hermione.

Exodus 16:2-4, 9-15
Psalm 51:1-12
Ephesians 4:1-16
John 6:24-35

Morris most certainly had in mind the current complications over Marsha's firing when he started his sermon this morning with one of those statements that goes without saying: "Unity is much easier as a concept than as a lived-out reality." No kidding. We're in the muck here. Marsha has not gone gently, unfortunately, which was quite predictable. She's been around long enough and manipulated the system long enough to have a loyal following, which she is keeping agitated.

Anna Louise is waving Marsha's banner. Honestly, I try to love A. L., but… Why is it so hard? Okay, let me count the ways: first of all, she has very little emotional intelligence, doesn't seem to understand cause and effect when it comes to her actions. Like that time when she and her nephew confiscated the icons from the chapel and hid them because they thought they were idols. Arrogance, that's her second obnoxious trait. Why, she had the audacity to print this in her "Around Town…" column: "Marsha Watson, former secretary at St. Timothy, has the misfortune of battling cancer and having to look for a new job at the same time. She's a darn good secretary. Contact aroundtown@gmail.com if you can help." She probably views this as an act of compassion, and I guess that would be the best construction to put on it, but, in my viewpoint, she is hardly "making every effort to maintain the unity of the Spirit in the bond of peace" at St. Timothy.

And darn the luck that Marsha has cancer. That sounds callous, and I do wish the best for her, but she was a most unsatisfactory secretary long before the cancer came, encouraging drama and conflict however she could. The congregation has suffered from this low grade "staff infection" long enough, and most of us are glad that the Bryants have had the gumption to solve the problem. They've done it right, working with the Mutual Ministry people and the Parish Council, postponing the firing until she completed and recovered from the latest round of chemotherapy. Her severance package was more than generous and she's on her husband's insurance, so there's no economic hardship.

Heavens, I wonder how Charlene and Morris are doing with A.L.'s outrageous behavior. To me, she directly and publicly challenged their authority, and the church's, too. She partook of the body and blood this morning at their hand, as usual. In fact, she prepared everything; it's her month for altar guild. And I have to say, nobody does that better than she does; she really has a gift for attending to every detail so that Eucharist is enhanced. Ironic, yet let us value these strengths in each other—and speak the truth in love. Maybe someone's done that with A.L., holding her accountable for divisive behavior.

"The giving of the manna in the wilderness is a story about trusting God to provide what is needed," Morris continued in his sermon. "God will provide both bread and unity. Meanwhile, we can trust or we can grumble."

Can't we do both? Actually, I think we are, rather effectively. We'll get through this little wilderness moment over Marsha fine, I predict. The grumbling will die away. Who knows? Maybe what I perceive as A.L. doing something terribly wrong will have a synergy that God blesses with redemptive power. So, relax Rose. Trust. All is well. Just do what the children said in their singing of the simple melody "Will You Let Me Be Your Servant, Let Me Be as Christ to You?" Sounding like little angels thanks to Theodore's guidance, they sang, "We are pilgrims on a journey, we are trav'lers on the road; we are here to help each other walk the mile and bear the load." We just need to do that.

Theodore was not pleased with the adult choir today, though. "They sounded so desperate," he lamented, shaking his head. "No breath support, some yell-singing. Very sad. We should have practiced this piece for at least another week."

"Oh, well, Theo," Lloyd comforted. "It's just one song, one day; let it go."

"Right," I added. "Your music is such a gift and builds us up in wonderful ways, Sunday by Sunday. Seriously, Theodore and Lloyd, your ministry inspires us for the ministries that we try to carry out. I don't tell you often enough how much your work means to me. And maybe the anthem was a little off, but that's quite the exception."

"You're absolutely right, dear friends," Theodore bounced back. "You can't win 'em all—unless you're the Chicago Cubs!" and he clapped me on the back. "You must be so pleased, Rose!" Oh, yes. One's favorite team winning spices up life considerably. Each game is a highlight of my day.

Another highlight in my week was a visit from Liz Metcalf, class of 1980-something. What a delightful surprise after all these years, and gratifying that she wanted to see her old English teacher. I recognized her easily, the biggest change being straight teeth instead of the very crooked smile and protruding front teeth I remember. Her boyish figure has filled out somewhat, and gray streaks her honey blonde hair, still short and wispy around her small face. Same big, pale blue eyes, full of fun and mischief. Same high-pitched laugh with a nervous edge. Liz was the best Puck ever; she could have gone straight from SCHS on to the stage of the Globe Theatre. She updated me on her life after graduation: moved to Chicago for college, a social worker, lives on the near north side with her partner and their two kids.

"I guess you knew I was gay, Mrs. Harris, back then? Because I talked to your husband about it."

I nodded. "He did tell me about a few Friday night conversations you two had at the roller rink. But Liz, you know the consciousness was very different then, and I never talked to you about it. Sexual identity was still a forbidden subject, mostly, and mysterious and complicated."

"Yeah, tell me about it. I was lucky to figure out who I was pretty early and accept it. Mom went insane at first, but she's grandma in high gear now. Do you ever see my mother?"

"Once in a while, out and about, but not often since she left St. Timothy some years ago. Isn't she out at Community Fellowship now?"

"Yeah. The Fellowship has a pretty much don't ask, don't tell attitude, and that suits Mom," she said pensively, and then gave a little laugh. "Oh, my God, I'm just remembering this craziness in our living room not too long after I first told Mom I was lesbian. I'm this 16-year-old kid trying to hold my life together and she's this moralistic widow completely distraught over having a gay child and she's reading me all the prohibitive verses from the Bible, about how I should be killed and whatnot. Her voice is getting louder with each one and I start yelling back at her. We're both losing it, screaming at each other, and all of a sudden the Bible goes flying through the air. I don't know if she threw it at me or if I grabbed it and threw it or what.

"It seems hilarious now, but right then we were both horrified. We stood there staring at each other for the longest time—and Mom turned to leave the room—and I said, 'Mom, don't go—don't leave me.' And she stayed, Mrs. Harris, and that's the last time we ever talked about it, but everything was pretty okay between us after that."

That was powerful, Charlie. And guess what. Remember that mustard seed bracelet you gave her for graduation? She told me that she wore it constantly for years, and now her daughter wears it. Isn't that neat? She talked of you so fondly and was sorry about Stephen dying. I cherish the time we had together. She promised to visit each summer when she comes back to Shippensforge.

Okay, I'm beat, by the heat and by busy times. Like the fun time a bunch of us had last night at Mercedes's house. There's a new activity/ministry at

St. Tim called Carry-In. People fix a meal once a month and take it to the home of someone who needs a little extra attention and then spend the evening for a game night or visiting or whatever suits. So, Sidney and I were there; I'd made a devil's food cake that I have to admit was out of this world delicious. Millicent and Jay Avery came with chicken baked with cranberry sauce and orange juice and curry (yum!). Sherry and Danny brought salad. This was a date for them; Karen and Eugene are trying to get them out on their own more. They were a hoot playing canasta against each other after supper. "D-d-don't do it, Sh-Sh-Sherry, don't k-k-kill my heart, baby!" Danny said the first time she melded before he did. We gave him a good laugh, so he got a little more dramatic every time she laid down cards. She giggled and gloated. How delightful it was to have young people amongst us oldsters. Millicent and Jay took them home.

Sidney dropped me off and I found a note in the front door from Marvin. "In town only briefly. Hoped to catch you. Next time. Please give Mindy warm greetings from Uncle Marvin. Take care, Rose. You're always in my thoughts." Darn. I would have stayed home if I'd known, just to have another moment in his comforting presence.

But back to the fun dinner. I can't get over the changes in Josephine. Instead of that weird, nearly hysterical laugh of hers, she's laughing normally and appropriately. Sidney said to me, "Don't ya' think Jo's doin' better? We're gettin' her off some of those damn feel good pills. She doesn't need that many." Excellent. *Thank you, God, for this relationship, this Sid and Jo friendship. Life is filled with so many surprises—and many of them are good! And all are redeemable, through your gracious love. Amen!*

I wish I could talk with Stephen like we used to on Sunday nights. This is an idle exercise, but I've been wondering how his life would have gone. He and Penelope would be married 5½ months. Would he have found a new job? Or would he have taken retirement and helped her in her ministry? Would he visit often, or... Oboy, this is not a good direction.

Virginia called. She and Barry and Stephanie Rose (36 hours after returning from Africa!) are going over to Penelope's next weekend to participate in that walk-a-thon P. has organized to benefit pancreatic cancer research. I was invited, of course, but opted not to go. Too old, too tired, too sad, too not wanting to deal with Penelope's energy. I'm glad they're going, though. I'll sponsor them and then enjoy hearing all about it.

Tenth Sunday after Pentecost

1 Kings 19:4-8
Psalm 34:1-8
Ephesians 4:25—5:2
John 6:35, 41-51

For the third week of our readings from John's Gospel, the same folks that were miraculously fed are still following Jesus around trying to figure him out. Charlene summarized it this way:

"First they said, 'Cool trick with the loaves and fishes, sir. You must be a prophet, a king,' and our Lord responded, 'I am the bread of life.'

Next, they said, 'Let's talk about manna. Are you like Moses?' and he said, 'No, I am the true bread from heaven.'

Finally, in today's reading, they say, 'But aren't you just Jesus bar-Joseph?' and he claimed, 'I am more than that. I am the living bread. I will die for you.'"

The people could not swallow the truth that Jesus is the true and full revelation of God, that he and the Father are one. They had no idea that the "bread" he offered would meet their deepest needs. And Jesus didn't try to make things easy for them to understand either. Some commentators, Morris mentioned (another dialogue sermon), have dubbed it the "obnoxious discourse," due to the puzzling, challenging tone of Jesus in this string of conversations. That's amusing, but why did the writer depict him as so difficult? Charlene suggested this: "Following Jesus is not easy, and if we're serious about doing so, we might as well get used to the idea that eating his body and blood lead to the cross." Right. Not easy to swallow.

Maddie made us laugh with her take on Jesus saying that whoever comes to him will never be hungry and whoever believes in him will never be thirsty. "I don't want to never be hungry or thirsty ever again!" she insisted, quite alarmed. Mindy and I looked at each other, trying to come up with a response, but just left it; how do you explain metaphor to a 6-year-old? Besides, we always feel like she's teaching us. Plus, she makes a point. Hungering and thirsting are important—after God, after righteousness, after food and drink. No appetite is not good, doesn't nurture.

Maddie and Mindy are becoming close chums. They went to VBS every night last week, Mindy driving out to the farm to get her.

"She has this—what can I say?—this purity or something. She's so clued in to others, so kind and caring for a little kid," Mindy said to me.

"She imitates God?" I suggested, thinking of Ephesians 5:1.

"Yeah—except God's not so serious and worried. Honestly, Rose, it's become my life's desire to see that little girl smile. Have you ever seen her smile?"

"Yes!"

"When?"

"When you were honored this morning," I realized. "Well, 'smile' may be stretching things a little, but her face was happy and proud and just plain radiant when you received your orchid."

"Really? That's awesome. And, man, what about that orchid? Am I a renewer of society? Even to be mentioned in the same breath as Florence Nightingale and that other nurse, the one who died of yellow fever—wow."

She and Pam and half a dozen other members who are health care professionals were called forward and prayed over and presented beautiful orchids on this day of commemoration for Florence Nightingale and Clara Maass, "renewers of society." Wow, indeed, and how very empowering, to line up today's saints with those of days gone by. Oh, and health care reminds me that Pauline Shuster didn't come out of her last diabetic coma. Forty-three years old. Sad. Several of us from Lydia Circle attended her funeral at a Methodist church outside of town and burial in the church cemetery. She often attended circle meetings when she still lived in the group home. Other than us, there were only a few relatives to honor her. Rest in peace, dear Pauline.

This morning's service was a lovely island of coolness and calm in the vast ocean of hot, dry summer mornings. After the floods of spring, we've had little rain, only teasing thunder storms, except for those few days of tornado weather with deluges that brought us back from the brink of drought. The climate of my soul seems tied into all of it— flooded/drowning one day, dry and cracking another, refreshed by rains the next, tossed about by storms. Grief can still engulf me at any moment, deep despair that Stephen is gone, never to be seen, heard, touched again. Sometimes a bitter regret fills my mouth, almost chokes me with a mix of how hard life is and disgust at my succumbing to its woes. I should be better, I should try harder, I am not enough, is the wretched refrain. "This poor soul cried..." the psalm says. That's me. "...and was heard by the Lord, and was saved from every trouble." *May it be so, gracious, loving God.*

However would I bear up if I existed in a refugee camp or just had my town and people wiped out by tsunami or tornado? Or had MS, like George Rizenhouer? My life is easy, comfortable, privileged, deeply blessed. Which takes me back to the cool, calm sanctuary of worship and community this morning.

Charlene and I had a nice moment, greeting each other after the service. She seems to be back to her perky self after the deep fatigue of the early months, and I said, "You're looking well. How are you feeling?"

"Great, thanks, although yesterday I was so tired I could hardly go. Morris was an angel. I slept in, he fixed a fabulous brunch, then I laid down on the couch and slept until his touch woke me for supper, ate, and went to bed. I got up this morning ready to journey on!" A few more months and they'll have a precious bundle to cuddle.

Virginia and Barry got back from Penelope's a little while ago and stopped by. "Here you go, Mama Rose," Barry said, hugging me. "That's from Penelope." The fundraiser was a huge success. Mack frequently stole the show, preferring to push his stroller around the track to riding in it, until he was just so exhausted he had to give in.

When I asked how Penelope is doing, Virginia responded on the different levels of public and private. P. told them that she still has dark nights of the soul over Stephen, but that, also, their short time together seems like a dream that's almost hard to remember already. "Simultaneously hard, weird, and blessed," she described.

Publicly/professionally, she's packing in even more projects and events, she admitted, so there's not enough energy to mourn at the end of the day. They took her out to lunch after worshiping at her church—sans air conditioning. "Like the olden days—hot as hell, sweat pouring off everyone," Barry described.

"It was awful," Virginia agreed. "Last week's storms had shut off the electricity until yesterday afternoon, so they didn't realize until this morning that there was damage. But, my goodness, there was one woman there who was unreasonably angry at…"

"Holy Toledo, she was mad!" Barry put in. "We sat behind her and when she turned around, Gin nodded and said how are you…"

"And she said, 'Don't ask,' and turned her back on me! She groused to several people, blasting Penelope and others for not checking the HVAC system, yada yada yada. Penelope says she's always mad about something."

"The irony was rich," Barry laughed. "Here's Penelope preaching about being tenderhearted and forgiving and then here's this banshee…"

"Good thing she started early, so she can blow it all out before the sun goes down," Virginia quipped. "Maybe she thought she was speaking the truth in love."

More likely she didn't think at all—which is exactly what Paul is telling us to do. Think about how our actions and words affect each other. Ha! like Josephine is trying to get Sidney to do. The three musketeers are on a late

196

service schedule now, since Mercedes is sleeping better at night. Josephine and I walked out to the parking lot together after the service and found Mercedes and Sidney at an impasse. He had the car door open and was saying, threateningly, "Get in the car <u>now</u>, Mercedes." M. was looking up at him in—confusion? defiance? amusement?

"She won't get in the damn car," he whined to Josephine.

"Get in the car now, Mercedes," Josephine cooed, and in she slid.

Sidney slammed the door and huffed his way to the driver's side.

Josephine smiled at me. "It's his tone of voice, but he's makin' good headway on that—and on his cussin, too. Rose, dontcha' know, he's just makin' room for the devil with that language, bless his heart."

"He's a good soul," I offered, and she nodded.

"I think he's startin' to see the light that he makes things a lot harder for everybody when he's grouchy as a hibernatin' bear roused up. It's a lot easier to be nice, dontcha' know?"

Exactly. Paul is urging us to take the easy way of building each other up, of not grieving the Holy Spirit, of forgiving as we are forgiven. It's easy—just imitate God, that's all. Easy—just give ourselves up to each other as Christ gave himself up for us.

Proverbs 9:1-6
Psalm 34:9-14
Ephesians 5:15-20
John 6:51-58

Lady Wisdom took the stage this morning. "She invites us to dwell in her house, a place of life, rather than in the house of her opposite, Folly, whose house is a place of death. Lady Wisdom instructs us that to live wisely is to live well, to delight in God's will," Charlene preached.

After the service, when Maddie went to visit with Zahra, Mindy said to me in her thoughtful way, "Maddie's like Lady Wisdom Jr. Do you know what she said to me the other day? She said, 'I don't know why Bryan likes to do bad things.' 'Like what?' I said, because I'm always nosing around for information because there's something bad wrong there, Rose."

"Do you think she's being abused?"

"No. I think it's more neglect, that's my sense; she doesn't give out the signs of abuse—but you never know, that little girl way out there in the country with a big brother and father who are socially withdrawn and no mother around."

"So what bad things did she say Bryan's doing?"

"Smoking, mostly. You can smell weed all over the place."

"Have you encountered the dad?"

"Randy? Nope. He's always out in the field or up in the barn or in his bedroom, and the kids won't even knock. I went out to the barn looking for him last week—I wanted to ask if Maddie could stay overnight sometime—and I'm pretty sure he was in there, I heard rustling up in the hay loft, but I wasn't about to climb up there after him. I mean, he deserves privacy, I guess, and...gosh, I just don't know what to do..."

I nodded. It's a dilemma. "Just doing what you're doing is a lot—being an adult friend," I encouraged her.

"I want to be more than a friend. I want her," she said with a look of determination as she watched the little girl playing with the littler girl.

Thank you, God, for your presence in, above, below and around this situation and within and beyond these, your children—Maddie, Bryan, Randy, and Mindy. May they be guided by your ways of wisdom and your love that we see so clearly in the Christ. Amen.

We filled our front pew on this Lord's Day. The typically late Mindy Lucas was first in place because she's getting Maddie to Sunday School these days. Virginia and I slipped in next to them, and then Danny and Sherry honored us with their presence.

Lady Wisdom and Jesus set the table for our meal. "Come and eat and drink," they say in the continuing saga of his "obnoxious discourse." Why did he have to be so graphic? Charlene emphasized the offensiveness of our Lord's words simply by repeating them. She leaned forward in the pulpit and spoke right into our faces—"Those who eat my flesh and drink my blood…" And Danny totally caught the spirit of the Jews who were actually standing there listening to Jesus a couple millennia ago. He and Sherry let out a pronounced, "Ewww," and Danny said, "I'm n-not drinking b-b-blood, un-uh!"

To laughter, Charlene said, "My point exactly, Danny and Sherry."

And Maddie leaned across Virginia and me to say, "It's not real blood, Danny; it's just wine pretending to be blood." He considered this for a moment. I'm sure he would have argued with any adult, but to her he said, "Oh. Okay, M-M-Maddie." Problem solved, for him. And look there—Maddie does have a sense of metaphor after all.

Well, and the rest of us had to deal with the raw words, too. I felt that Charlene's sermon helped draw us deeper into Jesus' revelation about himself. Risking another outburst from Danny and Sherry, she talked about people in survival situations staying alive by eating the flesh of those who didn't survive. Literally, physically, that flesh eaten sustained life, became a part of the other, abided within the person who ate it. Christ has taken the initiative to do that for us, willingly saying, "Here is my body. Eat it. Live." Kind of like Stephen's cornea, now abiding in another, giving new life.

"Abide in me" was Charlene's basis for any kind of sense-making. "When we kneel and eat the bread and drink the wine, we are physically connected to it, right? It goes into us, it becomes part of us, it changes us. When we take Jesus into our spirits by believing that he is who he says he is—very God of very God, given for the life of the world—he abides in us and changes us."

She hit us again about life as a community, too. "When we take communion, we're not taking it by ourselves, are we?" she said, looking straight at Danny. Conversational.

"No, Pastor Charlene," he called out.

"No, we're not alone. We're kneeling shoulder to shoulder with each other, believing together, helping each other to live wisely, sticking together against the collective insanity that all too often characterizes this world that we love…"

Yes, I thought, as I kneeled shoulder to shoulder—with my compassionate daughter, activated by the Christ abiding in her; with a trembling Danny and giggling Sherry, anticipating the bread and wine; with Anna Louise, whose shenanigans regarding the firing of the secretary have ceased after a visit from Paul Wakefield and the pastors; with Penelope, in communion with us from a distance; *with you and Stephen, Charlie, from an even greater distance; with all the saints in all times and all places. Together, we draw life from Jesus to keep the Church, his "Body," alive. Sometimes this earthly body of merely human beings limps along, sometimes it makes great, courageous strides for the sake of the world and in the name of the Father, Son, and Holy Spirit.*

Big news from Jim and Anita—they're getting married! "I knew this would happen once we started down the God path," he teased her, "but I'm glad; it's all good," and he pulled Anita to him and kissed her on the cheek as she playfully scolded him with a "Jim!" shake of the head. September 12 is the appointed date.

Thank you, God, for the love which joins this family together and for sustaining them through painful difficulties and helping them find their way. Double Amen! Hubba hubba!

Stephanie and I talked the other night because we were sad about Stephen. I honestly can't remember which one of us called, but we were in the same mood and helped pull each other up and out. On other matters, Angelica's upset with her. She graduated from the online high school after just turning 17 and has gone from wanting to spend a weekend visiting Jacob at IU to wanting to enroll there fulltime. Steph thinks she's too young and should stay with her for another year and take classes at her university. Well, Ang had talked to her dad and he was willing to foot the bill, but then Stephanie called William and he agreed with her concerns about maturity and changed his mind. Naturally, Stephanie is taking the full fury of the child's disappointment. I hope Angelica doesn't fall into former habits and run away.

So much more to write but no more time. Sarah's picking me up in ten minutes and I probably won't be home till late. She wants me to help her plan for her fall production of "The Merchant of Venice." We're going to watch the movie with Al Pacino as Shylock and Lynn Collins as Portia. Sarah's wanting to take a break from the fall comedy the kids usually do and follow the portrayal in the movie—the dark side of Venice, anti-semitism, Shylock more a victim than a villain. Should be interesting. She wants me to help, but I don't think so. Those days are gone. Way gone.

200

She's fixing us a fresh vegetable feast with quinoa, "the supergrain of the future." Steph's big on quinoa, too. We'll have plenty of time for musing and meandering—see the pictures and hear the stories from her Russian trip and get caught up on each other's families. *Thank you, God for this fabulous friend. And there she is, beeping in the driveway. Amen!*

Cubs, I'll be with you in spirit; let's get back on the track now, don't you dare blow your lead.

<u>Twelfth Sunday after Pentecost</u>

Joshua 24:1-2a, 14-18
Psalm 34:15-22
Ephesians 6:10-20
John 6:56-69

Poor Rose. Poor, poor me. I've had a bad fall. Anita and the baby and I have gotten into a morning walk routine, right at dawn in the fresh coolness. But Wednesday, my toe caught on uneven sidewalk and I pitched forward on my face. (Ha! I "fell on my face with my knees to the rising sun…") Glasses broken, front teeth broken, wrist broken, a cracked rib. What a mess. The ambulance ride was kind of fun, but other than that, fie and drat, for life is so much more strenuous now. Thank heaven it's my left arm.

Hitting the ground like that is a harsh and horrible insult to an old body. Part of me wants to stop walking altogether rather than risk it ever happening again. Such a contrast with little people like Mack, of supple bone and short memory, who fall twenty times a day, maybe cry for a second, then start tearing around again.

I haven't cried. I've wanted to, but I've refused, indulging instead in talk therapy. Long, enjoyable phone conversations with my people. Stephanie says Angelica's still mad at her about the college situation, but Jacob told her that he thought she should wait a year before enrolling at IU—and then he really wanted her to come there. She accepted it from him. So, she's going local for her freshman year. In fact, she's taking one of Steph's classes.

I've also gotten caught up with Sarah and Claudia, single again—with two kids, and the Sauers, and Eloise while I sit here and recuperate. That's kept my spirits up, along with overeating. Oh, so much food! What are the kind people thinking, to bring rich desserts and creamy casseroles laced with cheese and topped with crispy carbohydrates? I'm loving every mouthful, but undoubtedly gaining weight. So that's my sad story.

The health care system has worked efficiently for me, and for that I am grateful. I'll get my teeth capped this week, after the swelling goes down, and new glasses this week, too. I saw Dr. Majmundar on Thursday for a general check following emergency room treatment. He says my wrist should heal fine and be as strong as ever in six weeks. I thanked him again for coming to Stephen's funeral as well as for the beautiful card and note he sent just a couple weeks ago, sensitive to how grief goes on. What a fine man, Ajit Majmundar. I told him I consider him a soul brother. "Yes," he laughed. "A Hindu soul brother, a Christian soul sister." Yes.

Virginia came over this morning and we watched the Presbyterian service on TV. I'd read in the Evening Gazette about their new pastor. She, too, was preaching about Jesus' offensive, annoying verbal assaults and how his unadulterated message drove some of his disciples away. I had never noticed John 6:66 before—after probably reading or hearing it 50 times!

I asked Virginia to fix me something healthful, and we lunched on salad and wheat toast and watermelon out on the deck. A little hot but not so humid, praise the gods of weather. We got to talking about Stephen, as usual. Stephanie Rose told her that Transfiguration has decided to use his money for college scholarships for inner city students. They're endowing half of it and adding to that fund so it will perpetuate itself. The Stephen M. Harris scholarship fund.

Still so hard, Charlie. Gin and I sat there in silence for the longest time after she told me that, gazing into the trees, and then she laughed softly and told me a story I'd never heard before. Remember how you and Stephen loved John Coltrane, listening to his albums many a Saturday night? Well, a couple weeks after Stephen had gotten his saxophone in the fifth grade, Virginia was passing by his room and there he was in his Sunday pants and dress shirt with the sleeves rolled up, swinging that sax around with his eyes closed like he was Trane himself, but nothing but squeaking and squawking coming out. "I don't know why I didn't make fun of him, but I'm glad I didn't," she said, and as quickly as she'd laughed, she choked up. "Oh, Mother," she whispered and picked up plates and hurried into the house. If Trane/Stephen is nearby, tell him I said hi—and tell him that he'll soon be supporting young scholars. Oh, Charlie, I'm taking big breaths to keep my heart from cracking open again.

Mindy and Maddie stopped by after Virginia left. They had done Eucharist ministry at Rutledge ~~Home~~ Heritage Estate. I need to start using the new name, especially with that beautiful building going up. Already, it has a homey look to it; I can visualize people having a pleasant life there.

"Gosh, I wish you could have been there, Rose. We had our circle in the big room, herded them in there like sheep, didn't we Maddie?"

Maddie nodded. "I pushed a wheelchair, and I helped with the bread and wine, too. I helped set it out on the table and poured wine in the little tiny glasses."

"They loved having a kid around. Mrs. Thurgood didn't know what to do with the wafer, just held it in her fingers looking at it and looking at me until I popped it in her mouth, but her face lit up when she saw Maddie."

Yes. Children and animals in nursing homes work wonders.

"Who partook?" I asked.

"Her and Sam and Mr. Rizenhouer and Pastor Ruskin and—seems like there was one more… oh, I think I'm thinking of Pauline. She was there in spirit, maybe." Then, "I've been thinking of Garfield a lot," she said. "It was two years yesterday."

"You're right. I hadn't realized."

"The amazing Garfield Temple. I'm so glad he wandered through our lives, aren't you? Remember…" she laughed, and we reminisced happily for a few minutes about our unique friend, person of faith, whose demons won for a terrible moment two years ago, and he took his own life. The awful sadness of that day has faded. I wonder if sadness over Stephen ever will.

Maddie was staring at me through all this and finally asked me, "Do you hurt? You look really bad."

She made me laugh and the observation was certainly accurate to describe my black eyes, neglected hair, and all the rest. But I knew she was serious and told her of my soreness and headaches and how hard getting comfortable to sleep is.

"But don't worry, Rose; you're going to get better."

"Thank you, Maddie; that's very encouraging." Yes, I'm going to get better, I thought, unlike your mother.

Under my direction, Mindy made us a batch of peanut butter popcorn and we ate it with a spoon, like cereal, with tall glasses of cold milk. They liked it as much as I do. Then, I was content to let them go their way.

Mindy had called the other day to tell me she'd finally caught Randy on his way in from the field. Depressed, she kept saying. The whole family's depressed, the farm's depressed, the dog and cats are depressed, depression hangs in the air. Randy said it would be fine for Maddie to stay overnight with her.

"Shoot, he acted like I could just have her. I had my phone number written down for him and he said 'Okay' when I gave it to him. 'Okay.' That's all he said, and he doesn't know anything about me! I'm telling you, the man's not well. His clothes are filthy, there's no life in his eyes; it's spooky. I wanted to say—well, I didn't know what to say. There's this invisible wall around him."

I can't remember Randy from high school; I guess he was one of those kids you just don't notice. His mother came to church once in awhile. She seemed very shy, or "backwards" as Josephine says. Maddie told Mindy that her Aunt Barbara comes once in a while, Randy's sister from over around Elkhart. Some other aunts and uncles live far away, she said. Again, I marvel at that little Maddie, insisting that her brother bring her to St. Timothy and inserting herself into the community the way she has. Why, that is clearly an act of survival—and a huge blessing for us. And what a blessing for her to have Mindy. After our visit, they went next door to Jim and Anita and Zahra's. Surely that adorable doll baby with her smiles and coos will bring a smile to Maddie's face.

Another therapeutic measure I've taken is continuing to sort, organize, and eliminate. I had Jim bring down the half dozen boxes from the attic and set them by the davenport in the den. I've only gotten through one—working with one arm and having to read and look at everything slows me down and plays with my emotions. Eighty plus years of photos, diplomas, programs, newspaper clippings, letters. I found this one yesterday, from The Editor, Dad, written when I set out for college. I remember it.

Sept. 1, 1939

Dear Rose,

At this juncture in your life, I want you to know how proud I am of you, and confident that you will continue to excel as a student and as a person. These times are not easy, and while I don't want to cast a shadow on your young life, I am afraid the shadow has been cast despite my wishes. Evil forces are on the march and the future seems not only unpredictable but uncontrollable as the scourge of fascism that's taken root round the globe now manifests its hideous blooms.

Stay diligent in your studies and strong and safe through whatever is to come. That would be my prayer for you, daughter, if I were a praying man. When I make the effort, unhappily, it seems as though I am just talking to myself. Nevertheless, I urge you to follow your mother's example if you find prayer an authentic exercise. And, if so, pray for me, that my editorials provide wisdom and encouragement. Pray for your good mother and your gentle brother. Stay firm in faith that there is a Higher Power stronger than these present troubles.

With love and esteem,
Your father

Clarence Brinkley, Dad, aka "The Editor" to Dewayne and me. A good man who lived well despite his struggles, his demons. I thank God for AA, more spiritual for him than organized religion. That was an amazingly faithful fellowship; he made peace with the Higher Power there, I believe.

The TV minister this morning suggested that we try to see ourselves as one of the characters in the gospel lesson. Might we be Jesus, having a hard time explaining truth, getting impatient, resorting to drastic means? Or the disciples who turned back, put off by the challenges that lay ahead, unable to buy his story? Or the twelve who stuck with him, Simon Peter at the head? That's who I want to be, Simon Peter. Do I believe that Jesus is the son of God, fully revealing divine love? What else can I believe? Where else would I go? Whom else would I worship? He has the words of eternal life and eternity is now, heaven is today. As for me and my house, we will serve the Lord—the Higher Power—who unfailingly sustains with grace and comfort and joy. Amen.

Thirteenth Sunday after Pentecost

Deuteronomy 4:1-2, 6-9
Psalm 15
James 1:17-27
Mark 7:1-8, 14-15, 21-23

Thank you, God of compassion, for your healing power. This week has been so much better than last. The soreness is almost gone, but I wonder if I'll ever fully regain my strength—or confidence. "You're aging, you're declining," my body drones. Oh, and I might as well say it out loud: "You're dying," I sometimes hear.

Virginia's wanted me to convalesce at her place, but I've resisted that, finding ways to manage daily tasks. That's tiring and tricky, but I want to be in my own house. Sometime I will likely have to leave this place where I have dwelt for so long, through joys and sorrows of all shapes and sizes. After the fall, nothing seems assured.

Once I got over the initial trauma, it seemed very important to get right back in the saddle—of walking, that is, especially since driving is not an option for the next several weeks, which is probably just as well, given the little traffic incidents of late. So, I'm out and about, my sling holding my broken wrist against me. Walking the six blocks to the square has always been pleasant, and I had Jim pull out the fold-up grocery cart from behind some stuff in the garage; it steadies me as well as hauling my stuff.

Yesterday, I was running (walking) a couple errands when John came into my mind as I passed by the odds-and-ends shop across from the courthouse. In fact, I chuckled out loud recalling an exchange between him and the owner one afternoon last year when we were browsing. The owner—can't remember his name—invited us to sign his petition to have a concrete tablet bearing the Ten Commandments installed on the courthouse lawn. We declined; that wasn't a cause that appealed to us.

"You humanists?" he challenged through narrowing eyes.

"We are Christians, sir, and you?" John said, squaring off.

"You don't believe in following the Ten Commandments?"

"Isn't your store open on Sundays?"

"What's that got to do with it?"

"Seems to me you're honoring the Sabbath with your lips but not your heart."

"I've got to make a living."

"Fine, but that's a human way to live; you've abandoned God's commandment."

The guy's face was getting red. "If you don't like the way I run my business, maybe you better vacate the premises."

"You throwing me out?"

"If I have to."

Now the stare-down. Good grief. But the Holy Spirit swooped in and took John over, as I saw it.

He took a step back and lowered his shoulders. "Look, mister, I'm no better than you; I break the commandments, too. But what I'm trying to say is that living by the rules is not what's most important. Having a hunk of concrete with words etched on it isn't going to change what's inside people."

"Whatever."

We left amidst that uneasy truce. John, the Banty rooster. Man of substance. Ah, memories. We had a good adventure. According to Angelica, Florence's house has sold. John put part of the proceeds in a trust fund for Ang and the rest of it he gave to the Mennonites for peace with justice programs. Well done. Florence would be pleased. And, he's gotten married. Wow, for the first time at 87 years old. I wish him well, with a relieved smile that I'm not the bride!

Being back at worship this morning was invigorating, with an excellent sermon from Charlene. She made this striking statement: "The gospel is only one generation away from extinction." As if to underscore that message, Rhonda taught our children well, quite a crowd up front for an end-of-summer Sunday. (By the way, Mindy and Maddie are firmly established on the front right pew, but I've reverted back to my long-standing location. This old dog just can't learn that new trick.) Rhonda threw out this question to the kids: "Does anyone know what a child of God looks like?"

"A angel," a munchkin guessed, and then Rhonda passed out small mirrors to each one with the title "Child of God" written across the bottom. "Everyone of us is a child of God. See how beautiful God has made you," she urged as they gazed at themselves. "Remember who you are and how children of God live. We love God and Jesus and we love ourselves and we love each other. Sometimes we might forget who we are, and then we might live in crazy ways, like thinking that getting is better than giving or that we're not good enough."

Maddie carried her mirror back and solemnly held it up to Mindy's face. Virginia and I heard Mindy give a happy little yip which made us laugh. She nodded, then and pulled the child to her, and they nestled against each other through the sermon. "What a pair, those two," Virginia mused with the same satisfaction I was feeling. *Thank you, God who loves as a perfect parent, for bringing them together. Protect them from harm and guide them in your ways through the uncertainties in the maze of life they are walking.*

Baby Zahra had come into possession of one of the Child of God mirrors, and mommy and daddy were still sitting in the pew having fun with her and her reflection when I was making my way out after the service. I slid onto the bench in front of them to visit. Jim asked me if I was ready for more garden goods and brought them over a little while ago—all washed, cut up, and ready to eat.

We fell into one of our theological discussions. It started with Jim exclaiming, "Oh, Jesus! It's pouring out there!" He was settled in the recliner and I on the davenport. I looked over my shoulder through the double glass doors out to the deck. Sure enough, a summer shower was raining down out of nowhere, the sun still shining. Should be a good rainbow somewhere out there, I thought.

"Sorry," Jim said.

I looked back at him, raising my eyebrows in question.

"About Jesus."

I was totally confused.

"About saying Jesus' name in vain."

Oh. I shrugged my shoulders. I've come to the point that the taking of the Lord's name in vain is far too ubiquitous in the culture to worry over.

"He was a heckuva guy, that Jesus. I have to admit I identify with his obnoxious side, busting religious people for their hypocrisy," he grinned.

"Yeah, that would work for you," I grinned back.

"You know I'm not against you Christians, Rose, at least not the tolerant ones. I'm not against the idea of God, either, really; I just find the concept—silly."

Was he looking for argument, intellectual conversation, or meaningful dialogue?

"C'mon, Jim. You've read Joseph Campbell—and others—on the power of myth. I had the impression that you accepted religion and ritual as important to human existence."

"You're right, I do—for other people." He thought for a moment, gazing past me into the mist rising after the brief shower. "To be perfectly candid, though, I never cease to find it odd that intelligent people need something bigger than themselves to believe in. At the same time, the stubbornness of people like you, clinging to primitive beliefs and practices in this rational, science-enlightened age, intrigues me."

Intellectual conversation. Okay, I can do that.

"You make me feel like Great-grandmother Neanderthal on the verge of extinction." I gave a hollow laugh because that really is how I feel much of the time. "And you've brought us to a topic we've discussed before: transcendence. You reject it; I can't live without it."

"The futility bothers me, the wasted motion and thought and effort—chanting chants and lighting candles and praying prayers seems so needy. How can you kid yourselves like that when you look around at the shape of the world? The same problems and suffering caused by both human and natural disasters—I mean it just goes on and on throughout history while you all stand there singing 'In the Sweet By and By.'"

I tried to think fast. "That's not even in our hymnbook. This morning we sang 'Great Is Thy Faithfulness,' about an unchanging God with no variation or shadow, always present to cheer and guide with strength for today and bright hope for tomorrow…"

"Yeah, and that's another thing; religion is easier for people like you—English majors getting high on imagery and music and all that. Oh, I know there are scientist types who believe in God—but they probably write poetry on the side. Anyway, God and church—they're just not for me."

"So are you miserable sitting through worship every week?"

"Not so much. I entertain myself and keep it in a sociological experience slot. I listen up and form arguments for discussions such as these," he teased, then went sober. "I'm there for only one reason."

Aha. He's said that before. Now we were moving into meaningful dialogue. I kept my mouth shut so he could direct it.

"She's doing pretty well. I'm not sure she magically believes in God again since we've started going to church. It's more like she's caught in the undertow of nostalgia brought on by singing and nice words and kind people. But that's better than being caught in an undertow of depression."

"Well, yes, I should think so. I'm so glad Anita's holding steady at this point. And your baby is precious and smart and fascinating—and your garden is growing beautifully—and you have a good job that you like. Life is good, eh, Jim?"

"Yeah, pretty darn good. And thanks for not saying 'blessed.' This is not about God," he felt moved to stipulate once more, "even though you think so."

Argument, now, he seemed to be wanting.

"Yes, that's what I think."

"Oh, Rose, Rose," he shook his head. "God does whatever you say, don't you see that? You all make God up, so if you say God is love, well, yeah—God is love, not because there is a loving God but because you're looking through God-Is-Love glasses. If you say God is your strength, you're stronger, but it's your own strength summoned up, don't you get it?"

I didn't feel like taking his bait. What was the point? And then he walloped me.

"What about cancer in a world that your God is supposed to be running? What about Stephen?"

"That's not fair," I said evenly, my eyes stinging.

"Not fair? Your son dies in the prime of his life and you can't speak up for your God?"

"Sticking the knife in and twisting," I accused, and he shook his head in earnest denial. And then I heard Stephen's voice urging, "Talk to him, Mom," and I immediately went calm. But I was also growing weary.

"At this point, I only have two more things to say, Jim: # 1—faith is not primarily about making sense, and # 2—you, sir, are a wonderful example of a person who lives according to God's love."

"You saying that about me doesn't make God exist."

"That's for sure; God's existence is not dependent upon human opinion."

"Good one," he smiled, making a "psss!" sound like a drop of water on a hot griddle.

Oh, this dear, wonderful man. I don't know if the belief gap between us can be bridged. I don't think so. I sense a divine presence in the world at all times and in all places. He doesn't. If I didn't, I would be living in despair, of all people most pitiful. He's moving through life quite well his way.

At the front door upon parting, he said, "So then you're not concerned about my salvation?"

"Heavens no!"

"Well-put," he smiled. "But why do you scoff at the question?"

"Because I'm not in charge of salvation. Now don't get me wrong; I want you to live well and fully, now and forevermore; to feel saved, safe, hopeful, happy..."

"You're not a typical Christian, Rose; most of them think I'm headed straight for hell."

"I hate to think that's typical," I protested. "Those are just the people who get the most press."

"Maybe," he said with a goodbye squeeze, careful of my wrist.

We were both talked out. If I'd said one more thing, it would have been, "Find Zahra's little mirror when you get home and look into it for a while." Jim, child of God. *It's probably good I was talked out, wasn't it, dear God? I leave it all to you and to your Son, love incarnate, and your Spirit, dancing around the world. Amen—and I mean it. So be it.*

<u>Fourteenth Sunday after Pentecost</u>

Isaiah 35:4-7a
Psalm 146
James 2: 1-10 [11-13] 14-17
Mark 7:24-37

Sarah and I had our traditional Labor Day Weekend get-together: worship at her Unitarian church and then out to lunch. Lunch held surprises, but I'll start with the service. As usual, the members of the congregation mingled waters from their travels and adventures in a sparkling, splashing celebration of creation. Into a beautiful ceramic dish, Sarah poured her water from Ekaterineburg. Many states and countries were represented, in fact every continent! Stuck in my memory are a family who traveled to Guatemala to adopt their child and a soldier recently returned from Afghanistan.

The folks had also been invited to dress in their work clothes. Noticeable were a fire fighter, a chef, a musician couple in long black gown and tuxedo, a few with names embroidered on their shirts or nametags from car dealerships, restaurants, etc., and several medical workers in scrubs or office uniforms. Oh! and a cow, a woman who works on the sidewalk in front of the downtown Chick-fil-A at lunchtime. She told about going into the bank across the street to cash a check and security wouldn't let her in because no mascots are allowed. She was one mad cow and kept trying to sneak in through other entrances. So funny.

The readings of the day were from Walt Whitman, Harriet Beecher Stowe, Carl Sandburg and Maya Angelou and the message was entitled "Proper Patriotism." A string quartet played Aaron Copland, and there was a time in the service for those who were unemployed to share what kind of work they were seeking and for those who knew of jobs available to describe the positions. Very thoughtful, very kind, those Unitarians.

Now, the lunch surprises. Sarah and I headed with watering mouths for the Lion and Lamb restaurant and cultural center. Closed, out of business, engulfed by weeds. What a shame and disappointment. But we moved on, heading downtown to a place she knew with several vegetarian entrees. There, we met Patricia.

Loaded with backpack and bundles, she approached us on the sidewalk as soon as we got out of Sarah's car, asking for money to buy a hamburger across the street. Yikes! The poor! We automatically shook our heads no and continued walking, but she walked backwards in front of us (right under a

"Panhandling Prohibited" sign) saying, "Please ladies, even the homeless need to eat." She has straight brown hair pulled into a long ponytail and is slender and tanned and freckled with bad teeth, probably in her mid-forties. She wore a tank top and those shorts with all the pockets, cargo I think they're called, and army boots.

Sarah and I were caught in that sticky web of have vs. have not, compassion vying with judgmentalness. I was sure my thoughts were bombarding her brain, too: this woman could be conning us, she might use the money for drugs, she could/should just go to a food kitchen, we can't feed the whole world... But Sarah—and I love her for this— pushed through the awkward moment and invited her to be our guest in the restaurant.

"Deal," Patricia accepted with a business-like nod. Sarah and I sealed the deal with the same nod, exchanging surprised smiles, and we made our entrance.

A perky hostess greeted us with, "Two for dinner?"

"No, three," Sarah said as Patricia maneuvered her stuff in behind us.

"Oh," the hostess said with a look of dismay, probably identical to my expression on the sidewalk a couple minutes prior.

Sarah commented later, "Patricia's had a fascinating life, hasn't she? How much of it would you guess actually happened, maybe 50%?" Maybe. There was the carnival life, then the army hitch with injury in the line of duty and ELS (Entry Level Separation), then part ownership of a car wash, then a goodly inheritance from an uncle, who turned out to be her father, which was stolen by her cousin/brother, then work as a rodeo hand, then reuniting with a daughter born of a teenage romance and put up for adoption who is now a famous singer ...and then...and then... She's talking to someone about a book deal, a memoir entitled God's Not Done with Me Yet. She showed us the cover photo, a fuzzy picture of her on a horse. We were just about to order dessert when she got a call and had to go meet someone. She thanked us and gave us each a hug and her business card, "Patricia Latimore, Highly Skilled in Many Areas," with phone number and email address. We definitely got our money's worth. She was most entertaining. And who knows? We may see her memoir on a bookstore shelf someday.

"You know, I'm glad Patricia had enough faith in our compassion to persist with us until we responded," Sarah reflected as we drove back to Shippensforge. "But no matter how many times I encounter poor people face to face, I'm never prepared."

"Same here," I said. "I get all uptight and start judging them, irritated that they've intruded upon my life. And all the while Bible verses are running through my head, Jesus commanding, clearly and often, to love and help..."

"He even tells us to think of them as him…"

I nodded, and we rode on in silence. I thought of the ever-widening gap between the rich and poor. What a scandal it is, and yet so many people are indifferent. If it weren't for the Church—and other nonprofits—I'd hate to think of the massive suffering in the world. St. Timothy's fundraising to alleviate world hunger is bringing phenomenal results thanks to Virginia and Louella and Lois putting on the heat. Faith enlivened by good works and good works a direct outcome of faith. We love because God first loves us.

Sarah and I had a mishmash of conversation, my mind flitting from one bizarre thought to another, as it is wont to do, contemplating big and little situations. I confessed to her that I hadn't yet given Stephen's room a thorough cleaning.

"Rose, why don't you move into the new apartments at Rutledge?"

"What? Merciful heavens, Sarah, I'm not ready for that."

"Are you sure?"

"Yes."

That's all that was said on the subject, but—thank you very much, Sarah—I can't get the notion off my mind now. Oh, I've thought of independent living at Rutledge in the future—the distant future. But there's no good reason for me to leave this home sweet home yet.

As soon as she dropped me off, I changed my clothes and then went into his room, as though on a dare. Five months ago, Penelope had stripped the bed of linens and made it up with the spread, so everything looks normal, but there's still a smell. I can't really describe it; it's not strong or unpleasant but needs to be banished with furniture polish and window cleaner and a thorough vacuuming. I opened the drapes and looked out into the neglected backyard, rubbing my aching, healing wrist and wondering when I'll ever be able to resume caring for this little corner of the world entrusted to me. I pulled a few weeds one-handed the other day, but quit when I almost lost my balance. If my cast comes off October 5 as scheduled, maybe I can separate some bulbs before frost.

Then I looked in all the drawers—empty, and slid the closet door open, discovering something Penelope, despite her thoroughness, had missed. Way back in the corner of the closet were the pajamas he was wearing when he died. *Oh dear God.* I picked them up and smelled them, smelled Stephen. And I hugged them to me and lay down on the bed and wept and wept and slept a fitful sleep until dark. And then, I closed the door, not knowing when I will open it again, and put the pajamas in the washing machine. *And something else has happened, Charlie. You're the only one I'm going to tell.*

I was sorting through a couple boxes from the attic that Stephen left here when he and Denise separated. I found a note tucked into his 1984 pocket calendar: "Thanks, Stephen. I find you attractive, too, but I don't get involved with married men. If you're ever single again, look me up. Barbara"

Are you as shocked as I was? I keep trying to read him innocent. Maybe he just wanted to have a woman's perspective on something and she misunderstood or maybe it happened during one of those times he fell off the wagon and he... I just want to put it out of my mind, but that note has thrown me for a loop because of so many reasons—because I thought he was almost perfect (except for alcoholism); because I thought I knew him inside and out; because I'm always wanting to think that my people and I are better or different from the average, sinful person and we're not; because it complicates my grief. Darn you, Stephen, for complicating my grief!

I know you agree, Charlie, that the note from Barbara doesn't matter. I'm going to do my best to let it go.

After crying and sleeping and talking with Charlie, I feel like demons are leaving me. If it weren't for my wrist, I'd sit down at the piano and play some Mozart and lively hymns for awhile. Like a miracle, God has come again to save. To open my eyes to the truth that all is well. To unstop my ears so I can hear the good news of gracious love for everyone, everywhere, all the time. To make my heart leap in joy for the manifold blessings that are mine. My fearful heart is strong again. God is here.

Jim thinks it's just us when this happens, but this power is far more than human resilience and astounds me beyond measure. Praise the Lord, O my soul! I will praise the Lord as long as I live; I will sing praises to my God all my life long.

Remind me, dear God, to start each day with a Hallelujah!

And I almost forgot—I came across something good from the attic, too; that photograph of mother and her family taken in 1908 in Detroit when the Cubs won the World Series. Mother/Helen was 11 and was there with her parents and her sister, Beatrice, Aunt Bea. This is a good sign. I think it's going to be the year for our lovable losers. Oh, and another thing—Pam and Greg Turner were at the restaurant. Sarah and I saw them back in a corner, but they didn't see us. They look good back together.

Isaiah 50:4-9a
Psalm 116:1-9
James 3:1-12
Mark 8:27-38

I honestly didn't think we were going to make it to worship this morning. Mack put Stephanie's car keys in the trash, and we didn't find them until about five minutes to 11. Her car was parked in the driveway so I couldn't get mine out either. After 10 minutes of intense searching, she finally thought of asking Mack if he knew where Mommy's keys were. "Yush!" he solemnly announced with a firm nod, gazing up at her with his beautiful hazel eyes. "Go get them," she said, and he raced to the kitchen on his chubby legs and pulled them out of the trash can. He is a cute little doll, but that was nerve-wracking.

All is quiet now. They left after lunch and I had a restful nap. I expect a call from Virginia soon, back in town after she and Barry went to an away football game with their gameday trailer. Penelope may call, too—she calls about once a month now. Until the phone rings, I'll relax into my journaling.

Stephanie Rose and I saw more than usual of each other this week. Monday I went into her place to stay with Mack. That was the first day of classes at the university, and she had called at 7am because her usual childcare person was sick. "I'm so desperate I'll take a one-armed great-grandma," she pleaded, and Virginia drove me in right away. Mack and I did pretty well, diaper changes being the trickiest task, but, with Velcro instead of safety pins, we made it. He played by himself more than I expected, while I watched in fascination. His name for me is something like "Dah-moze" (Grandma Rose). He fed his doll, then brought it to me. "Dah-moze burp baby." Too cute. Book after book he brought and climbed into my lap to listen, pointing and naming some of the pictures. When he napped, I did, too, because I'd left in such haste I didn't take my novel. Couldn't turn the television on to watch the ballgame either. Three remotes and a tower of black electronic appliances stymied me. On—Off just isn't what it used to be. The Cubs are still leading their division, that's the important thing.

Then she and Mack came back out on Friday night and stayed for the weekend so we could have good catch-up time. We put clean sheets on Stephen's bed for her, and while I was at Jim and Anita's wedding yesterday morning, she did the deep cleaning of the room. When I got back, her eyes were puffy from crying, but she said it was a sacrament for her and very healing. *Thank you God, for how much we love Stephen and for these healing moments when you are so very present.* I'm keeping the door open now.

Mack's loving my piano and we love sitting him on our knees and having him point his little fingers and playing chopsticks together. He and his mom probably did that about 20 times. Leisurely conversations with Steph were a treat. We spent a couple hours on the deck Sat. afternoon, autumn evident in the air and in the gentle sun and in the subtly changing color of grass and leaf. Being with Stephanie always feeds my soul. She honors me with her openness about what's going on in her life. She talked about this Bull character taking another of her classes, she thinks for the purpose of harassing her.

"He's still mad about me scratching his car, I'm sure of it, and I wouldn't be surprised if he tries to get back at me by acting up in class. I'm actually afraid of what might come out of my mouth, that he might take some little thing I say and misrepresent it out of context and report me for something," she worried.

"That seems unlikely unless he's some kind of malcontent. Do you get that impression?"

"No, not really. Angelica's in the class, too, and she thinks I'm way off base."

I tend to think so, too. Stephanie sometimes gets worked up over nothing, and let's hope that's what it is, vis à vis Bull. Heavens, there are enough real alarms going off without conjuring up more. We got on to the topics of climate change and the growing gap between the rich and the poor and the dire implications of all of that.

"Have you started hearing that it's really too late to reverse global warming? That we need to shift our focus to surviving the catastrophic results?" she asked me anxiously.

Yes I have, but I'm not ready to accept it. I'll probably die before experiencing any of the serious consequences, but I worry about what Mack's generation might face. And then I told her how the food pantry's been shut down twice recently because the shelves are empty. Too much demand, not enough donation. Troublesome. And then there's drought and famine in Africa. And, My Saint Lord, we barely touched on all the scientific and technological developments happening at break-neck speed. Stephanie's horrified by computers with their "artificial intelligence" being smarter than human intelligence. "And Grandma! Immortality by 2045! What are we going to do?" she groaned. Definitely unsettling.

Nonetheless, she said scary scenarios don't weaken her faith. "God is still my refuge and strength and all that. I'll call on him as long as I live, I know I will, and I know in my bones that even if this planet ceases to exist, the One who made it will somehow redeem it."

But she fretted about how hard it is to share her faith with others. "I'm not much of a disciple these days, I'm afraid. I want to tell the story of Jesus and how I live in his love everyday, but I think I have the same problem Peter had in the lesson this morning. I want Jesus to be powerful in a different way, in a shazam way. I want God to solve the problems, conquer evil now and decisively, you know? If that's how it worked, I'd probably be more enthusiastic about sharing."

When I nodded in complete understanding, she demanded, "How do we live with that disconnect between how we want God to be and how God really is?"

"By asking the questions, by voicing the doubts and fears, by sticking together in community. You're doing it, Stephanie, we're doing it, just like Peter did, clumsily, uncomfortably, discipleship in fits and starts," I tried to reassure—and take heart from my own words. "By rejecting the worldly definition of power and giving ourselves over to the power of crucifixion and resurrection, the power of love." Sounds simple but isn't. Nonetheless, a person made a good stab at testifying to that kind of faith during worship this morning—Anna Louise Burnside, of all people.

About a month ago, the Bryants presented the idea of celebrating in Sunday morning worship not only God's mighty acts in history but also divine activity in our own lives. They invited people who felt drawn to share in this way to meet with them. Together, they would find the language to frame the experiences as testimonials.

So, Anna Louise was one of the volunteers, and this morning she testified about how God had helped her cope with the death of her nephew, Albert Shea. He was killed in a car accident about a year ago. He was still on our official roll at the time, though he had left St. Timothy just a week or too before the wreck. Albert fundamentally disagreed with some of our denomination's beliefs and practices and, unfortunately, he was devious and divisive. His sudden death was hard for many of us because the chance for reconciliation after all that had gotten stirred up seemed to be gone. And the thing is, Anna Louise participated with Albert in his judgmental words and arrogant actions that injured the Body—the same kind of behavior she exhibited when Marsha was let go. So, most of us were pretty surprised, and quite moved, really, when she talked about the problems and the estrangement, and, with genuine emotion, actually said the words, "I'm sorry…" She apologized for Albert, too. "I know he would want me to," she said, and closed with something like, "I still miss Albert every day, but I know he lives on in God's grace. And brothers and sisters in Christ, when I turned to God for help, he heard me—and finally, I heard him, too, and called on him to change my life. I love the Lord, for he has—has saved my life."

Obviously, doing this meant a lot to Anna Louise in her loss, and it meant a lot to all of us, really, this deep sharing in community. This moment of reconciliation was a real gift to me because I had spoken to Albert quite harshly not long before he left the church. Through Christ, with Christ, in Christ, in the unity of the Holy Spirit. That's how we live together.

Despite our best efforts, examples of imperfection abound. I held my breath when a strong-willed child and his father were the gift bearers, approaching the altar, his little hands cradling the glass decanter of wine. The nervous father was trying to hold on to the top of the vessel when the boy wrested it away, wanting to do it his ownself. The stopper flew out and drops of wine splashed, but total catastrophe was averted, and the eucharistic gifts arrived intact and were blessed and given. Whew.

The altar flowers "were given to the glory of God and in celebration of the marriage of Jim and Anita Ferguson." There were just ten of us at the 10am wedding yesterday—the bride and groom, the Bryants, Anita's uncle (a U.S. District Court of Appeals Judge) and his wife, Anita's girlfriend Janey and Janey's man, Jim's Aunt Marilyn, and me. Oh, and Zahra, of course. Jim held her the whole time because she began to fuss whenever they tried to hand her over to one of us. The service didn't take five minutes and there were no tears, not even happy ones, only smiles. Afterwards, they threw themselves a nice brunch reception at their house for the little group. Zahra went down for a much-needed nap, and we had a pleasant time to visit and celebrate and enjoy wonderful organic vegetarian dishes. All seems well with the household. May it ever be.

Mindy is growing more and more concerned about Maddie. She pretty much stays with Mindy on weekends now. Apparently, she does any cooking and housework that gets done at the farm—at six years old. Randy doesn't seem to be around much, doesn't seem to be working the farm. Sarah says Bryan's already missed several days at the high school just three weeks into the new year. Mindy's consulted with Malcolm about the situation; he's mostly in Chicago now, but he's hooked her up with Adam Farmer, his junior partner. Adam is exploring what would be involved in approaching Randy about getting some custody rights. Obviously, Randy could put a stop to Mindy's contact with Maddie at anytime. That doesn't seem likely right now, with him so debilitated and indifferent, but the future is unpredictable.

Oh, and just what I don't want to hear. Mindy tells me Marvin is in some kind of trouble. It's about business, something about taxes or customs. Nothing major, I hope.

<u>4:30am Monday</u>

I just had to write this down. I'd been sitting on the deck sleepless for a while, enjoying the full moon, and a coyote came into view, slinking across the yard and into the woods with a rabbit in its mouth. Doesn't have anything to do with anything. Just an amazing sight.

Jeremiah 11:18-20
Psalm 54
James 3:13—4:3, 7-8a
Mark 9:30-37

Paul Wakefield was supposed to be honored as this year's Steward of Distinction during the service this morning, but he wasn't there because he stopped to help people who were having car trouble. But we didn't know that, and he never misses worship, so we were concerned. Paul didn't know about the award and the son, Murray, and his family had been called and were on hand for the occasion. He tried to reach his dad, to no avail, but finally, Paul showed up at coffee hour and cleared things up.

The overheated car had stopped just a couple blocks from the church. I know, because I had driven by the vehicle with smoke billowing out from under the hood. I felt very sheepish for not stopping, probably along with some others who had driven by, but I didn't want to be late for church (drips with irony). Paul didn't give details, just said he helped them "get squared away." The family, parents and three children, looked pretty raggedy to me. I once heard a preacher put words in Jesus' mouth at such a time: "Those are the ones who look most like me."

God, I'm sorry I'm not a better person. Help me take your son's commandments more seriously and be more responsive to "the least of these." Thank you for your servant, Paul. In the name of the greatest servant, Jesus, your son, our Lord. Amen.

Mindy, Maddie, and I went straight to Rutledge Estate to give Eucharist between their noon meal and Sam's birthday party. Mindy's very tense lately, worried about Maddie—and Uncle Marvin. She's stopping by the farm every day but only found Randy there once last week, surprising him in the barn where he was sitting on a bale of hay staring into space, smoking and drinking, beer bottles all around. In the shape he's in, he could have burned the whole place down, according to her. She told him she was concerned about Maddie and Bryan. "Maddie and Bryan's fine," he said, and got up and went back where the stalls are. She wasn't inclined to follow. She and Adam, the lawyer, are considering various options: contacting Randy's sister, who seems to be his next of kin; getting Child Protective Services involved; approaching Randy directly about Mindy getting more involved.

As for Uncle Marvin—I did a search on Marvin Whittaker and sure enough, there he was in the NY Times. Oh, my word! I couldn't believe what I was seeing. Indicted for tax evasion alright—30 million dollars worth. Ye gods!

His attorney described him as "an upstanding citizen of the highest order and generous philanthropist, a successful international businessman operating entirely within the law." The U. S. attorney described him as "a crook, flagrantly devising schemes to hide and launder money and participating in complex investment instruments for deceptive purposes."

I floated down the Neva River on a yacht with this man! Now I remember Stephen warning me after that excursion to be careful. "Careful of what?" I'd asked him. "Just don't let wealth and charm make you lose your head." An apt comment, it now seems.

"OMG, Rose!" Mindy said when I told her about the article.

"Could it be true?" we asked each other incredulously.

He's extremely bitter about his poor childhood, Mindy says, and described himself to her as a modern day Robin Hood who has angered the authorities because they want the money he's giving to people who really need it. I'm afraid that my intuition is more along the lines that Marvin has succumbed to selfish ambition and then rationalized his behavior, lying even to himself. Shakespeare had him pegged, methinks: "The fool doth think he is wise, but the wise man knows himself to be a fool." This is terribly disturbing. I want him to be the wise, gentle, cultured, caring person I danced cheek to cheek with, not the crook. But—I don't think innocent people usually get indicted by the federal government.

"And listen to this," Mindy worried on. "Uncle Marvin's put money in a trust fund so I could go to medical school. It's set up so I can only use it for that purpose and I don't have to pay any taxes on it. He called me last week and told me not to worry, that the money was safe and everything was 'perfectly proper,' but—man, I don't know."

Calm our souls about these situations, please, dear God. Guide Mindy and the lawyer to do what is best for Maddie and help all concerned, including Randy, to be aware of your gracious presence and the peace and possibility you provide. And what of Marvin, God? His wisdom is not from you, I fear. Despite the good he does, he seems to be motivated by envy and selfishness and caught in a web of wicked actions contrary to your ways. May he somehow come to know you and draw near to you. Guide me with your mercy in my reactions, lest I forget that he is your precious, beloved child and that Jesus gave his life for Marvin as much as for any of us. Amen.

In the midst of our anxieties, distributing bread and wine in the name of the Father, and the Son, and the Holy Spirit this afternoon had a joyful, liberating edge to it. The activities room was active, indeed, people bustling around hanging streamers and balloons and setting up the cake table for Sam's hundredth birthday celebration. So, we gathered in the small space by the aviary. A crowd of Sam's family were on hand for his party, and he invited them to commune and a few followed him to our makeshift church. Pastor Ruskin, in his Alzheimer's cloud, actually asked Mindy if there was a meeting of the NAACP going on! He was in good form, greeting everyone like pastors do and happy to read the gospel lesson in his sonorous tone. Lois Rizenhouer was there with George, their affection for each other radiating out into the circle. Mary Thurgood stayed in bed, oblivious to the world for lo these several years. I pray she will just sleep away soon, especially now that Bill's gone. Mitch has not communed before, but stayed put on the loveseat when we came and received when approached, patting Maddie on the head when he handed his empty cup back to her. "Whoever welcomes one such child in my name welcomes me…" Since I'm impaired (how glad I'll be to get rid of this cast; the itching is awful), I spoke the words while Mindy did the physical labor of love.

And then a marvelous party for Sam. He recited a poem he'd written for himself. Of course, I loved it.

Sonnet for a Centenarian
With gratitude to William Shakespeare, and apologies

I've strutted and fretted my hour onstage,
But alas, my brief candle burneth on.
Like royal fruit, I'm mellowed by my age,
Yet to the one true vine I e'er cling on.
With a hey, a ho, a hey nonino
A century of tomorrows ever creep.
Life is but a springtime flower, and so,
Will I wilt when I lay me down to sleep?
The web of life is of a mingled yarn,
Crimes despair if not cherisht by grace.
No grain nor goods now fill my empty barn,
As I prepare to meet God face to face.
    Aye, soon I'll pass from this terrestrial ball,
    My tale told by God, signifying all.

If my mind is that sharp when I'm 100, maybe I would want to live until then. On the other hand, there seems to be a lot developing in the world that I really don't want to witness. A butterfly died in my hand yesterday. It was in the grass, a faded, yellow monarch. Its wings, jagged and torn on the edges, opened and closed very slowly. I slipped my hand underneath it, and the exquisite creature made no motion to fly away. One more open and close and it was still. I rested it on the table on the deck where it remains. Isn't that how we would all like to die, peacefully, gracefully and still beautiful at the end of our natural span of years? Not like Stephen. Not like Mary Thurgood.

And not like Mercedes. She's declining so rapidly now. The other two musketeers and our team take good care of her, but she went missing again when Jo was taking a shower and Sid fell asleep during Jeopardy! Someone a few blocks away saw her on the sidewalk in her bathrobe and took her into their house. She couldn't tell them her name, and they were about to call the police when she remembered it. They looked up her number in the phonebook, but Jo and Sid were out looking for her at that point. Eventually they connected, but a scary time was had by all by the time they got her home. And yet, on occasion, she can still make sense, like when Sid and Jo were having a discussion about mixed race children. Next door to them is a child with a Vietnamese father and Mexican mother.

"Just don't seem right," was Sidney's position, and Mercedes says, "Well, Jesus was mixed race—half God and half man." Ha, Sidney. "'Tain't the same," he muttered, but she got him thinking.

Whew, I'm suddenly exhausted, ready for peanut butter popcorn and whatever the Brits have to offer on PBS tonight. *Remember those shows, Charlie? Didn't matter what it was, we just loved their accents and great acting. But before that, you know what I think I'll do? Relax into some prayer and meditation. Probably a euphemism for a nap, but Mindy's inspired me. She was saying when she brought me home after Sam's party and dinner that she needs to start carving out that kind of time for herself again. She'll get into pretty good routines with time in the morning and at night for several weeks, and then gets lax with it. "And then all hell breaks loose," she said. She's a funny girl, Charlie. "When I forget to pray," she said, "my mind gets very weird. I start making bad decisions and worry myself sick." Understood. So, I will give myself over to listening to God now. If I fall asleep, that's okay. God's voice speaks in our slumber, right?*

Numbers 11:4-6, 10-16, 24-29
Psalm 19:7-14
James 5:13-20
Mark 9:38-50

Charlene got us "involved" in the sermon this morning like she likes to do by asking us each to confess a wrongdoing to another person. I wanted to blow a whistle and call a foul on her for "Inappropriate Something-or-other" at first, but then I was surprised how well her little ploy actually worked. Our confession didn't have to be some deep, dark secret, she said, and might just be a small blooper that was amusing. There was discomfort and hesitation, but in a few minutes we had paired off and the nave was buzzing with laughter and earnest engagement. After a couple minutes, she had us switch speakers. Then the final step was for us to place a hand on each other's shoulder and, using our partner's name, pray this prayer: "Gracious and forgiving God, we pray that (Virginia) may know your healing mercy and forgiveness of all sins. In the name of the Father and the Son and the Holy Spirit, Amen."

Virginia's confession was not lightweight. She admitted stealing a house sale from a colleague (Eunice) several years ago. She had talked about it before but always in a self-protective way, justifying her actions. She was too emotional to say amen after the prayer, but accepted the spirit of it with a rare hug for her old mother. Quite a moment for Virginia—and me, too.

I noticed Madge in the row behind us pair up with a visitor at the other end of the pew, a middle-aged man who looked like he wished he'd stayed home. I wonder what in the world they shared. They seemed to come out okay, though; they were pals at the Ministry Fair afterward.

People were really talking about the confessions. Deedee laughed to Virginia and me that she was glad to get a teenaged hit-and-run fender-bender off her chest. More seriously, her little Johnny confessed to his Grandpa Bruce that he hated God for letting his father die. Strong stuff for a 7-year-old who's been mourning his father's loss for over two years now. Yet another breakthrough on his lifelong journey, we pray.

Predictably, Sid groused about the activity—we could hear him from clear across the aisle—but wound up confessing to Jo that he loves her and wants to marry her! Mercedes confessed to the two of them that she didn't know what was going on.

Karen, Danny's mom, told me that he confessed to her that he likes sex with Sherry. "I told him, 'That's good, son; you don't have to confess that,' and he said, 'O-k-k-kay. Yippee!"

Charlene based all this on the appointed reading from the book of James: "Therefore confess your sins to one another, and pray for one another, so that you may be healed. The prayer of the righteous is powerful and effective." She preached, "Jesus and his brother James urge us to trust each other and to trust God's promises. Children of God, let us dare to live lives that take God's amazing grace seriously."

Morris and I had a nice visit as we strolled through the Ministry Fair. He, too, was surprised at how well the confession exercise turned out. I applauded Charlene for her creativity and the courage to implement it.

"Yeah, she's great," he said, "but Charlene gets lots of plates twirling and then—this is confidential, Rose—she starts sounding like Moses, overwhelmed in the desert: 'This is too much, God; I can't do it!' I'm used to it, it's just her way, but with the pregnancy ...well, just pray for us, would you? Pray for her to remember that she can't do it all—and doesn't need to try." I assured him I would.

The Ministry Fair was Charlene's baby, too. Lots of folks were involved, about 20 booths, I think, with all manner of projects and causes. "Worship the Lord your God and love one another," said the banner over an archway as we entered the transformed fellowship hall. The choirs from cherubs to seniors with drums and guitars and all manner of instruments brought everything alive with peppy global music. "God is uplifting the people. God is the power within us. Hope is our music and freedom our song and together our voices will ring."

Virginia and Lois Rizenhouer raffled off a gorgeous appliquéd quilt at the World Hunger Appeal booth, another $1000 to get food where it's needed. The Sewing Circle donated the quilt and also had on display a clothesline of the colorful "Little Dresses for Africa" they're now making out of pillowcases. I'd not heard of this project, but apparently it's capturing the imagination of groups all over the country, outfitting hundreds of thousands of girls in Africa in simple dresses. Louie and Rita are trying to start a chapter of Overeaters' Anonymous, Louie jovially telling any interested persons, "The body is God's temple, right? and I've put a few additions on my temple that need to come on down." There was "a just cup of coffee" and fair trade chocolate as well as sub sandwiches sold by the kids for their latest trip and grocery carts for donations to the community pantry. Let's fill those shelves up! The housing ministry's booth was a cleverly decorated tool shed with pictures of many happy families—

including Louie and Rita—receiving keys to their brand new homes and, of course, sign-up sheets for the current construction. Disaster Relief was on hand with details about the elaborate system in place to respond immediately to earthquake, fire, and storm, etc.

"Isn't this great, Rose?" Anita exulted. Zahra was wide-eyed in the carrier on Jim's back taking it all in. Anita gave me a big hug and said how happy she was to be part of St. Timothy. "Here's what I'm seeing: Disaster—boom! the Church is there. Hunger—boom! the Church is there. This room is alive with hope—and with help. I'm loving it!"

She wandered on, and Jim said, "Are you thinking what I'm thinking?"

"That a while back she would have found this depressing?" I guessed, and he nodded.

"And, I'm loving it, too, church lady. This really is cool."

"How's married life?" I joked, and laughed when he gave the obvious answer.

"After being together for seven years and married for two weeks, I'm not seeing much difference."

Very fun church day, but boy, was I exhausted. When Virginia dropped me off, I headed straight for my bed, undressing and crawling between the sheets and sleeping until the phone rang. It was Penelope. She was very blue.

"Mama Rose, please don't think I'm complaining, but honestly, I think I'm going to spend more time on Stephen dying than I had with him alive." Blunt. "I'm still getting bills and the insurance company is disputing some charges. Sometimes it seems like a huge mess that won't ever be over." Right. I asked if we could help in any way. After all, if it weren't for her, Virginia and I would be taking care of all this, I reminded her.

"No, it's okay. I shouldn't even have gone into all that. The first thing I should have said was 'How are you?' I apologize. This is a tired time of the day for me. So, how are you, Mama Rose?"

I told her about the Ministry Fair and other goings-on. We talked of Stephen for awhile, sharing never told stories. I have a lot more of those than she does, of course. She enjoyed hearing about him having a loose tooth knocked out when he caught a football from his dad in the front yard and me making them re-enact it so we could get it on film. She thanked me for lifting her spirits.

Stephen hadn't been a topic of my conversation in a while, Charlie; it felt good talking about him. Ha, husband, do you want to know what I confessed this morning? I told Virginia about breaking your Uncle Earl's leg that summer he stayed with us to recuperate

227

from hernia surgery. She and Stephen had left home by then and she said she'd never heard how it happened; I suspect I was too ashamed to tell her. But that's the kind of thing you never forget.

Good heavens, your Uncle Earl was an unhappy old fellow, and so patronizing, calling me "little lady" and ranting about "education these days" and lazy, ignorant teachers. And then came that hot, fateful day of the incident when unpleasant arguing between us was in the air. Virginia was aghast when I told her how I'd swung the car door as hard as I could, not realizing that Uncle Earl hadn't pulled his leg inside. Fie, that was a horrible moment. I'd been very careful helping him transfer from his wheelchair to the front seat, but we'd been fussing and he'd pushed me roughly away, causing me to stumble backwards and hit my ankle bone sharply on the wheelchair footrest—and I'd swung back, so to speak. I'll never forget those long, miserable hours in the emergency room. And yet, redemption came. I couldn't believe my ears when I heard Uncle Earl say to you as soon as you walked in the house that night, "Charlie, the first thing you need to know is that this was an accident, clear and simple..." That was really something, wasn't it? And Uncle Earl and I were far more companionable the rest of the summer. And yes, confession is good for the soul, because God's grace abounds. Excuse me, there's the phone.

That was Mindy, coming back through town after taking Maddie home. She saw an ambulance in front of the Bryants' house. Morris came racing out of the driveway in his car and they took off, lights flashing and siren screaming. *God! Please let everything be okay.*

Eighteenth Sunday after Pentecost

Genesis 2:18-24
Psalm 8
Hebrews 1:1-4, 2:5-12
Mark 10:2-16

Worship is a whole different ballgame without Charlene. A bounce, a sparkle is missing. Oh, Morris is a wonderful worship leader, too, the word was faithfully spoken and the sacrament duly administered. But there will definitely be a Charlene-shaped space until she returns, and nobody knows when that will be. The baby seems to be okay now, everything stabilized after some bleeding and labor pains last Sunday night. The goal is a full-term pregnancy, and that means another six weeks. She's in bed for the time being, with all of us pitching in. Her mother, here since last Monday, worshiped with us this morning but has to get back to her work. Morris's mother may be coming for a spell.

I add my prayers for this family to all the others, Creator God. May this child have a safe and healthy birth. Thank you for holding his mother and father in your forgiving love and please provide a double serving of patience for Charlene as she is forced to rest. And patience for Morris, as well, who will surely need plenty of it, too. Jesus loves them, this we know without a doubt. Amen.

Jesus' love for us and desire for us to live richly and fully according to the Creator's plan was the main message of the gospel, heard over and over in different ways. Morris repeated emphatically throughout his sermon, "We are children of God, not self-improvement projects." He urged us to "accept our destiny as Jesus' brothers and sisters, the same destiny as his—to live in the kingdom of God, here and now and yet to come."

Lloyd and Theodore and their singers and instrumentalists proclaimed the word, too. Why, we usually have to go to symphony hall to hear music like this. Theodore's perfect, pure tenor soared on an anthem by Haydn, from The Creation. "And in his eyes with brightness shines the soul, The breath and image of his God." Oh, and this was too precious—when Theodore gently, sweetly sang the words about Eve—"She lo—ves him, she lo—ves him," Sherry grabbed Danny by the head and kissed him. Eugene had to break them up! They are a lovey-dovey couple, but Karen says things can be pretty rough when Sherry gets her feelings hurt. That sounds normal.

I'll always feel like God created us for each other, Charlie, and then when we would reach our limits, the Creator was there with boundless love to shore us up. How blessed we were.

What a mystery, this love that draws couples together in radical commitment and then sometimes lasts and sometimes doesn't. Why are some able to have healthy relationships while others—who put forth just as much effort, maybe even more—and trusted in God for help, too—can't survive? Steven and Denise. Claudia and Michael. Pam and Greg (that break seems to be mending; he's coming to church with her now). Carolyn and Marcus, I fear. I hope I'm wrong about the Sauers, but I have this awful premonition that they're not going to make it together much longer. Boy, I hope I'm wrong. *Dear God, please let me be wrong.*

But no matter what, "Greater love hath no man than this, that a man layeth down his life for his friends." God's love knows no limits and never fails. And that love, fully present on earth in Jesus, always, always, always advocated for the vulnerable ones. They're the same in our day as back then—women, the poor, the sick, the children.

The children. Tragic news. Tariq was shot and killed. Just last night. Morris announced it. His grandfather called Louie and Rita this morning and they went to be with the family. He was vulnerable, yet another black youth cut down by a culture drowning in violence and misplaced priorities and prejudices and—heavens, it's so horribly complicated. The sinfulness and senselessness is as infuriating as it is tragic.

You have given us dominion over the work of your hands, O God, and look what we do with it. So now, as always, we cry to you for comfort in our agony. May the boy's family and Louie and Rita feel your presence and have at least some fleeting sensations of your peace right now and heal with time. Jesus said, "Let the little children come unto me," but he didn't mean like this. Now Tariq's troubles are over, at least. Tariq, child of God, is resting in Jesus' arms, forever blessed.

I can't write anymore. Too sad, too old, too tired of life. The Cubs are floundering. Sigh. I shall retreat, hoping for sleep.

Later

I had a blessedly restful nap; having the cast off my arm is the most wonderful feeling. Then a fun visit with my neighbors, beckoned over from my deck to theirs for bruschetta topped with their fresh tomatoes, basil, onion and garlic, and a glass of Jim's first batch of homemade wine. Most refreshing and a good thing, for I was fortified to receive Mindy when she rang the doorbell a little while ago, distraught. We seem to be taking turns, almost like a relay race, passing off the baton of comforter for the next one in distress.

And when I say distress, that's what I mean. Mindy was a mess. She was straight from taking Maddie home, where Randy met her when she drove in and told her not to come out to the farm anymore. I let her vent first; she went through those five stages of grief quite dramatically in about fifteen minutes. What's happened is that Child Protective Services (CPS) visited Randy, and, in response, he told Mindy to stay out of their business.

When she was mostly repeating herself, I interrupted her with an invitation to sit at the kitchen table with a candle and the icon of Jesus. She flinched, then wiped her tears and nodded. I don't know everything she was thinking as we sat in silence gazing at the image, the "exact imprint of God's very being," as the writer of Hebrews put it. But in time, she calmed and thanked me and asked for a glass of water. And then we got to the realities of the moment.

Basically, she poured out three miseries and I countered with three—um, what shall I call them?—blessings or assets to counteract the miseries.

- She's petrified of losing Maddie and concerned that Maddie is in danger. I reminded her that she has confidence in Adam, her attorney, and that he will help guide her through and that situations like this can go back and forth very quickly. I also reminded her that there is no evidence that Randy has ever shown violence toward his children, and she had to agree with that.
- She's all downhearted about Uncle Marvin (as am I), not only disillusioned, once again, with someone she had admired (like Miguel), but tied up in knots about what to do with the money he's put aside for her. Again, she seemed to feel better when I pointed out that Adam is quite capable of advising her on that matter. She herself concluded that she hadn't planned on the money before, so it's not like she's going to lose anything.
- She's lonely without Miguel, she whimpered, but when I asked her if she would want to resume the relationship if he came back to town, she quickly said no and admitted that she'd probably gotten "kicked to her glory" when he took off.

She seemed relatively peaceful when we walked to the front door, and so was I. We were centered on Christ, back to hope and trust, even in the thick of troubles. We marveled at the huge, full moon and were staring at it when Mindy thought of something. "It didn't even register with me until now, but get this, Rose: Randy was wearing a T-shirt that said, 'Farming is a harrowing experience.'" We laughed and hugged and she went on her way.

Mindy is an extraordinary person. The thing is we all are, because of Christ. Another irony, sort of—Jesus came as one of us, but instead of him being ordinary, he showed us that we're all like him, heirs to the kingdom of God.

I don't know when I've seen a full moon as bright as tonight. Reminds me of Christ's radiance, reflecting God's glory. Charles Wesley's great hymn comes to mind: "Made like him, like him we rise, A-a-a-a-a-lle-e-lu-u-ia! Ou-rs th-e cross, the grave, the ski-es, A-a-a-a-a-a-lle-e-lu-u-ia!"

Amos 5:6-7, 10-15
Psalm 90:12-17
Hebrews 4:12-16
Mark 10:17-31

Our service seemed exceptionally staid this morning compared to the "homegoing service" for Tariq on Wednesday afternoon. Even as I return contentedly to my tradition, I am grateful and glad to have been there, expressing the same truths in a different style. "...varieties of gifts, but the same Spirit..."

Tariq's grandparents' pastor, a dignified orator, began his message with prayer. "'Lord, you have been our dwelling place in all generations,' and you do not fail us now. 'You turn us back to dust,' and we are still yours. 'A thousand years in your sight are like yesterday,' and we trust eternity..." He pressed on in fervent testimony to a God with whom he has an intimate relationship, judging by the resonant confidence in his voice.

Earlier, upon arrival, we had filed by the open casket, seen the lad we barely knew dressed in a white suit with a red rose on his lapel. He was a handsome boy, I remember thinking as I stood there looking down at him, trying to understand the moment. I also remember thinking, "What is death?" and "Death, be not proud..." There were maybe 20 of us there from St. Timothy to support Louie and Rita and to mourn and to worship. And worship we did. The singing was boisterous with lots of swaying and outright dancing and hand-clapping at times. A large choir in white robes backed up the alto soloist who belted out an anthem, "God Is."

In his sermon, the preacher talked about Tariq, describing him as a precocious and spirited child who came to this church with his grandparents until a few years ago. Then things "ran way off the track," and he became something of a child of the street and joined a gang, breaking their hearts. "And you have no guilt in this, Harriet and Arthur," he assured them. "God knows—we all know—you did your best. And isn't it a comfort that Tariq always came back to the church on Mother's Day and Father's Day to honor you?" Yes, Louie and Rita had brought him here on those days, I recalled.

But mostly he preached about God's plan for creation and about us submitting our lives to that plan, both individually and corporately. In the classic manner of black preaching, he whispered to us and thundered at us, reminding us of the ways God's people have always resisted dependency. We are no different today than those "stiff-necked Israelites," he said, who worshiped their own religiosity and made an idol of prosperity. "In such an unfaithful mess of misplaced priorities, that evil which is contrary to God's gracious will flourishes. The wages of sin is death!" he thundered. "When will we learn the lesson?" He ended as he had begun, with prayer, in an emotional explosion that rocked us all. I'll try to capture the power of it...

"To heal we have to kneel," he said, coming down into the aisle among us and falling to his knees. "Kneel with me, sisters and brothers," he softly invited. "Kneel the best you can," and there was a loud motion of swishing and murmuring as we did.

"Get on your knees and pour out the grief in your hearts over the loss of this young man. Get on your knees in confession to God Almighty that we failed him!" his voice rose and trembled over sobs and moans.

"Get on your knees to our Saviour, yes—Jesus, yes—the Christ of the universe, God's anointed one," ringing to the rafters, then suddenly subdued, "and ask him for healing, children of God.

"We ask you Jesus, we ask you Lord, to look upon us with pity and heal us, Lord. Heal us from the affluenza infecting our souls. Heal us from bankrupt values! Heal us from prejudice against any man, any class, any race, any created thing!" he shouted.

"Amen, Yes, Lord, Save us, Jesus," the people murmured and shouted like a descant, and he prayed on in pounding cadence. "Heal us from being overwhelmed by the challenges of this age! Heal us from fear that leads to frustration that leads to apathy that leads to self-protection that leads to the decay of human community that leads to death for us all, oh Jesus!"

"Take this child into your arms, merciful God, this your beloved son, Tariq, and hold him for eternity as you always have, precious Lord. Hold him now in your kingdom of grace, hold him in peace, hold him in victory over the grave! Into your hands we commend his spirit. Amen, blessed Lord!"

We were all clinging to each other and rocking and crying. I even saw Morris swipe his eyes. And then suddenly all was hushed by soft music and pallbearers going forth to follow the casket out of the church. The family slowly followed, heads held high in suffering, and a soloist sang what has become an anthem for such occasions, to the sober tune of "Ah, Holy Jesus."

God, we have heard it, sounding in the silence:
News of the children lost to this world's violence.
Children of promise! Then without a warning,
Loved ones are mourning.

Heal us from giving weapons any glory;
Help us, O prince of Peace, to hear your story;
Help us resist the evil all around here;
May love abound here!

A profound mix of grief and hope it was—called faith. Our group gathered around Louie and Rita afterwards and heard that Tariq had called them on Thursday before his death on Saturday. In fact, they had a date set for him to come and spend a weekend. He had told them he was getting out of the gang and his goal was to change his ways so that his grandparents would take him in again and he could get his education and so forth. Evidence indicates that he was shot by gang members for trying to go straight. "Help us, O Prince of Peace, to hear your story…"

Mindy had met us at the funeral and updated Morris and me on the Maddie situation as we walked to our cars. Things are moving in a good direction since that amazing little girl insisted that her father take her to Mindy's last week. The doorbell rang and when Mindy answered, there stood Maddie in the beam of the headlights of her father's truck. She squinted into the light and waved her father away and said, "I need to stay with you. My daddy's too sick." She told Mindy he'd been asleep for a long time and she couldn't wake him up and when he finally did wake up, she had told him that she was too scared to stay with him and that he needed to go to the doctor. "If you don't take me to Mindy's, I'll call her to come and get me," she'd threatened. "He started hugging me with his scratchy beard and he smelled yucky and he started crying and then he said okay."

So Adam, her attorney, and CPS have met with Randy to talk about granting Mindy some custodial rights and getting treatment for himself. Because of Maddie's action, Bryan is back in school after several weeks of truancy, too. Hope is running pretty high that support pieces are in place for Randy to find the pathway out of his depression. "A little girl with a big soul," Mindy describes Maddie.

Then Mindy asked me if I had heard about Stephanie and Bull. Uh-oh; something bad has happened, I thought. But Mindy responded to my concerned expression with a bright smile and announced, "They're going out!"

"Oh, come now, Mindy; you can't mean it," I blurted, trying to take it all in. And then I remembered… "Wait a minute; there was a message for me on my answering machine that I found when I got home from food pantry yesterday. She said for me to call her tonight—and she sounded happy. Maybe that's what it's about."

"Yup," Mindy beamed and nodded. "They went out last night."

"What in the world?" I questioned.

Mindy gave a little hoot and said, "It's quite a story. You'll enjoy it."

And I did. Here's what happened: In class last Thursday, Bull had posed the question, "Is feminism still necessary in our post-feminist world?"

"That question irritates me to begin with," Stephanie established. "Only a fool can look around and think feminism is unnecessary. Plus, I thought he was being a smart-ass—oops, sorry Grandma, smart aleck—and trying to put me on the spot. Angelica told me later that I overreacted, and now I realize she was right. But at that moment, I gave a long answer meant to put him in his place, you know? I just spit out the list of evidence to the contrary: rape has already been reported on campus this year; childcare and eldercare continue unvalidated and undervalued; the wage gap, for crying out loud, with women and children in poverty all over the world.... Ang caught my eye and tapped her watch—I was so into it, I'd gone five minutes overtime. And the whole time he'd sat there with this patronizing grin on his face—at least that's what I thought.

"Well, you know me; I stewed about it and dreaded class on Tuesday, but then on Monday, I stopped to watch Buddhist monks who are on campus this week building a sand mandala. I was edging into the circle gathered around them and brushed the person next to me and looked up to whisper excuse me, and it was Bull! He whispered no problem and when he saw it was me, he smiled the nicest smile, like he was glad it was me. So, we stood there for a few minutes watching this beautiful, amazing process and brushing arms and, oh, Grandma, I was tingling, and I knew he was, too."

And when he stepped back to leave, she did, too, and they turned to walk in the same direction, and he immediately said, "Look, doc, I don't know why you have it in for me, but I'd like to figure it out so we can at least have a peaceful coexistence." And they met at the park near her house last night and went for a long walk and talked their heads off and then stopped for ice cream and she's in love!

And then Charlie, that beautiful, crazy granddaughter of ours confessed that she felt like a dope for getting all stressed and forgetting her faith. "It's like God is just standing there with everything I need—peace and wisdom and courage—and I forget to reach over and take it." Yes. It's called the human condition. Morris preached about that this morning, quoting Hebrews: We all so easily forget to "approach the throne of grace with boldness, so that we may receive mercy and find grace to help in time of need," he said, when that should be our modus operandi. And there you are, Charlie, right at the throne of grace all the time!

Morris talked, too, about the foolishness of not making a bold approach since we're naked before God, anyway. I've always liked that, I find it comforting, not threatening, that God knows me inside and out—and loves me more than my mind can imagine.

So, tonight God knows how frustrated I am; I just wanted to scream in the kitchen a little while ago when I couldn't open a new jar of popcorn. I tried that twister aid that Virginia got for me and I just simply didn't have the strength in my wrists and hands to get it open. This is ridiculous. I was playing tennis just a few years ago. Seven or eight or—wait a minute—how old am I? Okay, ten years ago. And it's not the biggest deal ever about the jar—I just ate something else, of course. And I know my wrist is still weak from the break. It's the insult of old age, that's what's maddening. This afternoon the sportscasters were talking about the pitcher being old—39. I understand the relativity of it, but humph! And who cares anyway? The Cubs didn't make the playoffs.

Job 38:1-7
Psalm 91:9-16
Hebrews 5:1-10
Mark 10:35-45

Another member gave a testimonial this morning, Madge Humphries. Morris edged forward on his seat. Everyone was expecting some silly, shallow, self-righteous piece of piety, I supposed, since that's what we're used to from Madge. I like what Jo said about her the other day in response to Sid calling Madge "...that floozy little holier-than-thou type..." Jo blessed her heart, of course, and then said that "anybody who has that powerful of a hankerin' to love Jesus and do what's right can't be all bad." And I have to say, Madge did a pretty good job of saying what the psalm of the day can mean for people of faith.

"At first I was simply going to say that those are God's promises and they're true, but then I realized that they're not, always. Oh! I mean in a way they're not—like sometimes we do dash our feet against stones—so to speak. And in our Bible study we talked about not letting parts of the Bible stand alone because there's a..." she fluttered her false eyelashes in thought, "...what did you call it, Pastor Morris?" and she turned toward him.

"Broader witness," he supplied.

"Yes, a broader witness putting the whole Bible together that says just because we're Christians doesn't protect us from everything. Why, my grandmother, who was a God-fearing woman if ever there was one, mixed bleach and Lysol together to clean, and she suffered horrible lung damage the rest of her life, so that just goes to show. But the broader witness is that we're supposed to keep our faith no matter what and be willing to take up crosses no matter where they may lead.

"And also important is that God is our refuge, and that's totally true. Believe me, folks, I've had my heartaches, but I've always taken refuge in the Lord. I've tried other refuges—like shopping and comfort food—but they don't work in the long run, even though they're blessings from God. Oh, now, I don't mean that..." Morris stood up at that point and graciously helped her stop so he could start his own testimony. He continued with the theme of discipleship.

I found myself applying everything he said to Marvin, who came by to see me the other day. I'm not sure why. I think he may have been looking to me for some kind of absolution. I wish I could give it, but I can't. When

Morris quipped that the only part of being with Jesus that James and John seemed to get was the glory part, I saw that same grasping, egocentric quality in Marvin.

The way he hangs around with the rich and powerful makes the Robin Hood persona he tries to assume quite absurd. Good heavens, he even appealed to me that, despite his unbelief, he tries to be Christ-like! That was offensive. He isn't being Christ-like, he's clearly doing business as usual with the world, even if he does give lots of money away. "The abuse of greatness is when it disjoins remorse from power," applies as well to Marvin as to Julius Caesar, I fear. And, in the classic sense of personal tragedy, the saddest part is how he is deceiving himself.

When he came, he sat down on the settee in the living room, carefully placing his expensive fedora beside him.

"You know, Rose," he said in his stately manner, "your God had a habit in the Bible of choosing unlikely candidates to do his work. I was born into poverty and never formally educated, but I am nonetheless being used to confront unbridled power, the Internal Revenue Service itself, a modern day tyrant every bit as oppressive as the Roman government was in Jesus' day. Predictably, they are trying to crucify me."

He wasn't looking at me but rather out the picture window and continued so, lost in his own thoughts as I tried to deal with the outrageousness of what he had just said. How could this be the same person who felt so close that night on the dance floor? At this moment in my living room, there was nothing but distance between us.

"Marvin, I don't think you know who Jesus is," I said quietly, "and I don't think I know who you are."

He stayed on the settee looking out the window for another moment. I wasn't sure he'd heard me. Then he stood, brushed a piece of lint off his jacket, picked up his hat, and made his way to the door. I fell in behind him. He turned, looked into my eyes with a smile, kissed my hand, and was gone.

I spent that evening at Mindy's, commiserating. She and Maddie were finishing up bedtime prayers. She said thank you for "little Mack truck and baby Zahra, my two favorite kids" and "God blessed" a long list, including Daisy the cow. She prayed for "Bryan and Daddy to get better," and asked God to help her remember her spelling words on the test tomorrow, then gave us each a hug around the neck and snuggled into her pillow, eyes closed, brow furrowed.

"Has she laughed yet?" I asked as we settled on the davenport, folding the pile of laundry between us.

"No, but she's cried. That's a breakthrough."

"What did she cry about?"

"Daisy the cow, who died the other day. Ostensibly about Daisy, but about her sad, young life, too, I'm sure. She totally lost it; it was good."

Mindy and Randy are to sign papers on Tuesday. He's agreed to shared custody with no stipulations.

"That's good, right?" I asked when her face wasn't happy.

"Yeah, for sure. There's just so much for her to overcome. I hope Randy makes it Tuesday; he's really in bad shape, totally a loose cannon. And..." she leaned back and closed her eyes, "it looks like I have breast cancer."

"No!" I said so loudly I was afraid Maddie might hear and come out.

"Maybe not, but I felt the lump last night and had a mammogram this afternoon and it sure looks like it to me, just like the images of all the malignant tumors we saw in class. My mom had a radical mastectomy when she was 37 and lost the other breast 10 years later, so..."

"Maybe it won't be anything, Mindy; usually it isn't. We'll hope for that."

She nodded and reached her hand across the laundry and said, "Pray." I did, as fervently as I know how, thinking of how I prayed for Stephen... And then she turned our attention to Uncle Marvin.

"Dang, he really is messed up," was her comment when I told her what he'd said at my house. "So let me get this straight: he thinks he's God's instrument but doesn't believe in God. That's convenient. He can do whatever he wants if there's no God to see him—and then take pride in it. Wow. Messed up."

"Heavens, I hate this. Do you think there's any way he could be innocent?"

She shook her head. "I asked Adam if that could be possible, like could he have been framed or something? We did some checking on the Internet and Adam says it's a classic case of tax evasion and probably a lot more. Probably paying cash for artwork on the black market, then selling it for cash or bonds. He said he'd bet that Uncle Marvin's had a few fires, too."

"Fires?"

"Yeah, over the years, so he could collect insurance, lose records. You wouldn't believe how many companies he owns, all over the world. But Adam said he might get off easy because it looks like he's got lots of people in high places who are indebted to him—or just plain like him, like we do. As for the med school money he says he has for me, Adam's advice is, 'Run, Mindy, run. Don't touch it.'

"And here's what Uncle Marvin said to me on the phone the other day, he said, 'Melinda, in regard to my present legal difficulties, I am laboring with integrity and intensity to preserve my reputation and your respect for me.'"

Hm. That's more than he said to me. I expect that I'll never see him again. That's distressing, but even more confusing. Will the real Marvin Whittaker please stand up? I had to laugh, though, when Mindy and Maddie came back to pass the peace with Virginia and me this morning, and Mindy said to me, "I just want to tell Uncle Marvin to gird up his loins like a man, like God told Job!" Yes, Marvin, gird them up, let your arrogance fall away, listen to God, and answer him: Where were you when God laid the foundation of the earth? Answer that. If you would, you'd have a fighting chance at true life.

With all these trials and tribulations nipping at our heels, Mindy, Maddie and I were pretty low energy holding Eucharist at Rutledge, but we did it, and I trust God's grace was truly shared. This afternoon the group was Lois and George, Sam, Pastor Ruskin (who says the words of institution each time we do, after having done it for so many years), Mitch, and Mary Thurgood. Mrs. Thurgood just happened to be in her chair so Maddie rolled her on down to the circle. She didn't protest, and yet from outward appearances, she doesn't get anything out of it. Why can't this poor woman die? Bill's been gone since Easter and here she is, her skin like cellophane, her poor hurting feet turned in on each other, fed through a stomach tube. *Awfully crazy, God.* "Apply Here for Independent Living Apartments," a prominent sign announces at the new building next door. Maybe somebody should fill out an application for Mary to live in heaven.

On the other end of the time-to-be-born-time-to-die spectrum, Charlene and the baby are doing well. Only three weeks to go. She's bored silly and eager for visitors. I stop in for a little while each week. She could stock a store with her knitting projects and has read a small library. Gotten into one soap opera, too, which embarrasses her. She made me promise not to tell. Poor her, she doesn't like baseball at all. Amazingly, according to Morris, she's been a model patient, so much so that the doctor has cleared her to attend worship. How good it will be to have her back with us. I miss her energetic, beaming praise. That woman "joys in the Lord" like nobody I've ever seen. *Thank you God, for your presence through all our comings and goings and inbetweenings.*

<u>Twenty-first Sunday after Pentecost</u>

Job 38:1-6, 10-17
Psalm 126
Hebrews 7:23-28
Mark 10:46-52

Blind Bartimaeus has always had a fond place in my heart. I love that he boldly yelled out to Jesus even when people were telling him to hush, and I especially love that "he sprang up" and went right over when Jesus bid him come. Would that all of us people of faith could be as persistent and confident. Bart <u>expected</u> Jesus to transform him, to make him see.

That's how it's been with me through my long years, God continually transforming me with gracious, healing love. I expect no less at this point. Also á la Bart, I yelled out to God the other day, stomping around the house demanding to see, to understand. I was thoroughly discouraged with aging and insecure about what might come next. And then God and I got things figured out—I'm moving into Rutledge Heritage Estate's new apartments. I really am. Rose Harris really is. Right away. As soon it's ready. Takes my breath away to think about it, but I'm 99% sure and I'm ready to sign on the dotted line. I hosted a family dinner last night to tell them. They were shocked, but so what? So am I.

"Mother, you can't mean it!" Virginia sort of shrieked. "This seems premature…You don't need that yet…"

"Back off, Gin; she's of age," Barry said, smiling at me like I'd "gotten one step ahead" of the efficient, decisive Virginia. I smiled back. We like to do that once in a while.

And then here came the next generation at me. "Grandma, this just seems so sudden. In a month? Can you even dissolve a household you've lived in for 60 years in a month?" Stephanie Rose sort of demanded.

Generation 4, Mack, had a much more reasoned approach. "Ice keam, pease, Dah-moze?" was his response.

Of course, these were not surprising reactions from daughter and granddaughter, Charlie. As we talked on, I realized that even though the decision is mine, it's only natural for Virginia and Stephanie to have strong feelings. After all, this is the only home Virginia ever knew until she left as an adult. And this is very much "Grandma and Grandpa's house" to Stephanie, who's been here through every imaginable circumstance over all of her 33 years. So they vented, and we reminisced, and by the end of the evening everyone was on board and excited.

Charlie, there is a reason I made the decision so fast—Rose says sheepishly, for it's a silly old reason, indeed, on the surface. Here's what happened: Thursday morning, my vision went blurry, and I panicked. I looked in the mirror and smiled to see if one side of my mouth was drooping, but—well, I wasn't sure because everything was blurry. I went next door to have Anita check me out, forgetting that she and Zahra have water baby classes on Thursdays. So I called Jo, who said my speech was not slurred. I could raise both arms without any trouble, too, so I decided I hadn't had a stroke. That's when I started yelling out to God.

"Why is this alarming me so, God? Why do I feel in danger? I believe in you and your promises! I trust you! What's going on here?"

And we talked. I reminded God (how hilarious is that, reminding God?) how everything has changed for me since Stephen died. How I can feel loosed from my moorings by the least little thing, and how sometimes I hardly feel at home in my own house and get all anxious when I can't open a silly jar.

And then it happened, Charlie, as usual. From beyond, clearly from God, peace flooded through, and I could see; the way was clear. I felt, and still feel, three days later, that this is the right time for me to make this change and that Rutledge is the right place; they go together perfectly, the time and the place. I sat on the davenport with my eyes closed. During quiet prayers of gratitude and asking for guidance after my little panic attack, I was happily determined to get over there as soon as I could to start the process. And (here comes the silly part) when I opened my eyes, I saw a glint on the rug and there was one of my lenses, fallen out of my frames. Oh husband, such a ridiculous, Rose-like tangled web I wove, left to my own devices! Blurry vision? More like blurry brain.

Maybe the idea of honoring Louella was part of my decision, too. Funny, she's one of those people you can't imagine dying, yet poof! She's gone. Theodore and Lloyd and I were saying this morning that we keep expecting to see a letter to the editor from her, objecting to her obituary.

"I can see it now," Theodore joked. "'Dear Editor: Perhaps the simpleton who wrote my obituary thinks that benevolent acts are performed to gain praise from one's peers. On the contrary, I was distressed by the emphasis upon human achievement without one mention of almighty God, who makes all things possible. Louella S. Rutledge.'" I could see it, too. Oh, Louella, you made your mark! And you're still making us laugh.

"Very few knew how far her congestive heart failure had progressed," he soberly reflected. "She just kept going until she dropped, never even missed a Sunday."

That's so true; she hosted Lydia Circle exactly a week before her death. "I think she would really have liked her funeral, Theodore, especially the angel song."

"Oh yes, 'For God Commanded Angels to Watch Over You.' Yes, Mendelssohn was Aunt Louella's favorite composer. And she especially liked Psalm 91 for the irony of Satan quoting it to tempt Jesus to throw himself off the pinnacle of the temple. 'What a fool, that Satan!' she would say."

"Oh, horrors, that reminds me of a true incident that is almost unbelievable. Rose, you'll appreciate this, and it's quite timely since we sang, 'A Mighty Fortress,' this morning," Lloyd put in. "I was at a hymn sing once—with a denomination that shall go unnamed—and they sang only the first verse of that great hymn, leaving 'the old satanic foe' quite handily 'to work us woe' with no equal on earth!" That was funny, and I think would have even brought forth a snort from dour old Louella, now with the saints who have gone before…

I went to another funeral last week, for Steve Hagendorf. Sarah and I went together. We had both been teacher to his principal, and it was good seeing several colleagues from days gone by. Nothing in the service in the funeral home gave away what his faith life might have been. He was eulogized in a mediocre way, basically that he did no harm, which was fitting to those of us who knew him. Saccharine tapes of "Sweet Hour of Prayer" and the like were the only music. Not that I have anything against that song; my soul has often found relief in sweet hours of prayer. But anyway, the message was only about Steve Hagendorf, just the opposite of Louella's service which witnessed to the cosmos and God revealed in Christ, even unto the ages, all of them.

There's a new little creature in the cosmos at St. Timothy: Auburn Hillary Howe. Great rejoicing in the land over this child, since Jimmy and Vickie have suffered the loss of a stillborn child and then a miscarriage. Pretty soon, we'll be celebrating the birth of Baby Boy Bryant, too. And a radiant Charlene was back at worship this morning, all of us rejoicing for the great things the Lord has done for us.

Mindy is very much in the parenting business now, legally signing Maddie's report card and carrying the child on her insurance policy since Randy has none. Randy also signed with his sister Barbara for shared custody of Bryan; in fact, Bryan's even gone to live with his aunt for the time being. Randy's kept some of his counseling appointments, which gives Mindy hope that he may be gaining ground, but she's also sorry that he isn't taking any initiative to see Maddie. "He's still sick," Maddie says knowingly and isn't too upset.

Mindy's having surgery on Wednesday, so she was on the prayer list this morning. After the service Jo asked her why she was on the list and when Mindy told her, she said, "Oh, honey, I'm powerful sorry, and I guess I better get on the list, too, 'cuz' my breast cancer's back. I was fixin' to tell you, Rose; I just found out." My St. Lord. Like Betty Ford and Happy Rockefeller. What are the odds? *God, help us all.*

Oh, and let me make a note right now to be in touch with Cynthia Stafford. She came in right before communion, looking awful. God seemed to guide us together to pass the peace, and she said she'd like to get together. She and Malcolm stay in my prayers.

I hear there's a World Series going on, ho hum. Not really interested because the Chicago Cubs already won it last week—in my dreams. Oh, it was beautiful! The dream clearly harkened back to that chilly, drizzly day Stephen and I went to Wrigley Field for the last time. Seems absolutely impossible that was only about a year ago. In the dream, the whole family was there, and I mean going back with the generations. Stephen was wearing his favorite Cubs hat just like he was that day, and Barry and Virginia and Stephanie Rose and Mack were there and we were cheering wildly. Didn't see any of the game—the dream began just after they'd won. We were jumping up and down screaming and hugging each other and turned around and there was Mother/the child Helen, and her sister Beatrice and parents, just like in the picture, right behind us, jumping up and down and screaming, too. My 11-year-old mother looked at me and waved! That was one of the happiest moments of my life—even if it wasn't real. Or was it? And whenever I share my dream, I preface it by warning that no one is allowed to say, "Well, that's probably the only way those Cubs'll ever win." Just hush, ye of little faith.

<u>All Saints Day</u>

Isaiah 25:6-9
Psalm 24
Revelation 21:1-6a
John 11:32-44

I am laser-focused on my move. I'll resume normal activities after the transition. Or will I? This is <u>big</u>; I don't know what lies ahead. But for now—no food pantry, no Lydia Circle, no out to lunch or visiting. If people want to see me, they can come by—and I'll put 'em to work! I'm not even going to see Sarah's production of <u>The</u> <u>Merchant</u> <u>of</u> <u>Venice</u>; just can't. Worship and move, that's my life for the next month. Well, it's already down to three weeks. This week, though, I had two occasions I couldn't miss: the dinner after the All Saints Day service this morning for the families of those St. Timothy members who have died over the year and an awards banquet where Stephanie Rose was honored.

First, All Saints Day. A rose on the altar for the birth of Micah Paul Bryant provided a circle of eternity as we read the names of our "dearly departed" since last November 1. A chime was sounded after each one:

Dorothy Crawford
Pearl Johnson
Stephen Harris
Robert "Bob" Thurgood
Pauline Shuster
Joyce Parker
Tariq Washington
Louella S. Rutledge
Randy Bowers

I wanted Stephen's chime to hang in the air forever, but it couldn't, of course, for we had to move on to the next saint. Wait a minute, though—in truth, that's exactly how it works, isn't it? No matter that our earthly chimes fade from our hearing; God's new heaven and new earth is moving toward us with great power, and in that place the ringing reverberates eternally, a glorious resounding. We've glimpsed this glory in Jesus coming to be with us and wipe away our tears. And Morris expanded on that most precious image of having our tears wiped away, pointing out that God will also wipe away the tears we have brought to others' eyes. I never thought of that before—the tears I've caused.

I was eager to share that with Mindy in regard to Randy—how all the pain he experienced as well as inflicted will be redeemed. Mindy's the one who had the first premonition of what he had done. Stephanie and Angelica and I were visiting her in the hospital the day after her surgery. So was Adam Farmer, the lawyer who's been helping her. We were talking about how Maddie was doing with Regina, Mindy's mother, who was keeping her until Mindy gets home.

"I stopped by the farm Monday and asked Randy to keep her for a couple nights," she was telling us. "I thought maybe he was doing a little better and it would be good for the two of them, but he couldn't. It's the first time he ever used my name. He looked right at me with tears in his eyes and said, 'I just can't do it, Mindy.'"

And suddenly, she sat straight up, jerking her IVs and gasping in pain and said, "Adam, go check on him! Get the police and go check on him. I'm afraid something's happened." As he went out the door, Mindy called, "Check the barn." And there they found him, hanging from a rafter. *Oh, dear God. Another horrible, unnatural death in our circle. Help us, God. Come to us, be with us.*

We bereaved families talked about all this death over dinner, lovingly prepared and served by the circles. Our table included Barry, Virginia and me, and Louie and Rita and their guests, Tariq's grandparents.

"I don't know how folks goes through these things on their own," Louie observed, Rita adding, "We used to try that, but it didn't work out so well, did it, honey?"

"No, sir. The good Lord planned for us to go through life and death hanging on to each other in Jesus' name," declared Arthur, Tariq's grandfather, in something of a paraphrase of the prayer in the bulletin: *Almighty God, you have knit together your elect in one communion and fellowship in the mystical body of your Son, Christ our Lord.*

And then Harriet, the grandma, more or less reiterated the sermon we'd heard. "But Lord, Lord, like the preacher said, if we truly live the way Jesus leads, it can be mighty hard." And she and Arthur told us what they were going through. A man who moved in next door to them is a convicted sex offender. Other neighbors found him on the public registry and are pressuring the landlord to kick him out.

"For the love of Christ, where's the man to lay his head?" Harriet asked, her elderly eyes squinching up as she turned her head in puzzlement. "I don't especially want to live next door to a sex offender, I'm not a fool. But where is mercy for this sinner? What would Jesus do? What has he told us to do, time and again?"

"Be not afraid. Love one another. Show mercy," Arthur answered. That's what they're trying to do, and their neighbors are furious and snubbing them for defending the man's right to stay there, "the same neighbors that came to the church a few weeks ago and helped us mourn our boy," Harriet worried. As Morris reminded us, serious discipleship is "costly, inconvenient, and uncomfortable—at best."

An innovation this year—Charlene's idea, I understand—was for us to bring photos of loved ones who have "entered the Church triumphant." (Sid wanted to know why in tarnation we would bring pictures of people who have transferred to another church. Bless his heart.) During worship, the pictures were placed on a table upfront with candles and icons. Harriet and Arthur brought one of Tariq in a band uniform with a trombone when he was 13. Virginia brought a great one of Stephen on their pontoon boat one summer, hair blowing, big smile. We set them in the middle of the table while we ate. And then Louie said what a crying shame it was about Maddie's daddy.

"The obituary didn't say much, but it made me think he took his own life," Rita more or less inquired.

I nodded. The obituary was sparse. Local farmer Randall James Bowers, 42. Died unexpectedly at his home. Veteran of the Gulf War. Preceded in death by parents and wife, Marilyn. Survived by children Bryan and Madeleine, and one sister, Barbara Bowers Andrews of Elkhart. Private graveside service Monday [tomorrow]. That was about it.

Adam took Mindy home from the hospital Friday morning. She wound up with just the malignant lump and a few lymph nodes removed with treatments to follow. I talked to her last night, and she said Maddie's clinging to her for dear life. She stayed with her in the hospital for two nights and is distraught that she couldn't help her father get better

"She understands that Randy was sick, that's a good thing, but this is going to be a long haul." And then there was the sound of a foot stamping or a fist pounding and she burst out, "Suicides make me so mad! I know people are in bad shape at that point, but if they could think of all the pain they're causing instead of just what they're feeling..." It's true, and I knew she was hurting for Maddie. "At least, Randy loved the kids enough to get them settled before he did it. That's something to be thankful for, I guess," she sighed.

We couldn't help but hearken back to Garfield, too, wishing that these men could have seen the one true light in their dreary darkness. *Unto you,*

248

God of our hope, we commit these brothers, now done with suffering, to your eternal care. Amen.

"So Adam's been very attentive," I felt like mentioning.

"We've really hit it off, but friendship only, for now. We don't want to ruin what we have by dating. Besides, his divorce isn't even final. He's not touching me until that's over. I made that mistake back in my dark period. Not going there again."

She signed off with fatigue after congratulating me on my decision to move, said I was giving my family a real gift by "taking charge of my own destiny." I guess I'm in charge. Virginia's drawn my two-room apartment to scale and arranged my furniture. That's fine. I don't have many opinions about such stuff anymore.

Okay, time to relax so I'll be rested to get busy again in the morning, but first, one more thing to write about—Stephanie's award dinner where I met Bull. His nickname is fitting, he's a big guy. I was surprised by his appearance, so opposite to Ethan. Not handsome in the traditional sense, not a sharp dresser, casual sloppy, I'd say, already balding with wispy, reddish hair and beard, and the loveliest eyes, blue and smiling. Stephanie seated him between us so we could get acquainted, and our Q and A session was satisfying.

Q: So you're changing careers?

A: Yeah, I was in real estate, flying high during the boom, but when the bust came, I was knocked on my keister—and that was the best thing that ever happened to me. I'm thinking of law enforcement..."

Q: Do you have a special interest in Women's Studies?

A: Not at first, just took it as an elective. But then I got this crush on the teacher... They both smiled.

Q: Have you forgiven Stephanie for scratching your car?

A: Oh, yeah, with a chuckle. And she's learning to appreciate the automobile a little more...

I was impressed that he was equally interested in me. "I hear you're going through some big changes yourself," he said, and we talked at length about my decision to move, with him putting in about his grandma in a similar situation. Very nice guy, this Bull. He has my Grandmother Seal of Approval. I didn't ask him what he thinks of my amazing great-grandson. We'll save that for later, should there be a later. I glanced at him several times during Stephanie's impassioned response to receiving the Jamison Award for Outstanding International Achievement on Behalf of Women and Children in Poverty. I liked what I saw on his face, a mixture of intrigue, fondness, amusement, pride.

Happy. I feel happy about Bull, Charlie. Everybody likes him. Stephanie's right, he's easy. You and Stephen would be happy, too, I feel sure. And, my, would you ever enjoy your great-grandson! Mack's learned the power of no, and I just love it. I suppose we might have gotten impatient at times when our kids were at that point, but mostly I remember us being delighted and fascinated when our 2-year-olds discovered their voices in the world. I pity the parents who take it personally and turn normal growth and development into power plays, you know? Okay, signing off for now, great husband, father, and grandfather.

Well. I feel worn out, emotionally, but All Saints Day wasn't grueling and grief-stricken in this year of my child's death. Rather filled to overflowing with the rich blessings of faith, crazy and ambiguous as they are, or at least seem in this world.

Oh, just one more thing: Stephanie handed me a small paper bag at the dinner with a book in it. She explained that it was a memoir that she'd bought from a woman who was selling it on the street. "It's just offbeat enough that I thought you would probably enjoy it," she said. Yup. <u>God's Not Done with Me Yet</u> by Patricia Latimore. Good for her!

Twenty-third Sunday after Pentecost

1 Kings 17:8-16
Psalm 146
Hebrews 9:24-28
Mark 12:38-44

"They devour the widows' houses and for the sake of appearance say long prayers." I gave a start when I heard Jesus say that in the gospel lesson this morning. He was talking about widows and clergy of his time, of course, but my mind shot straight back to a true life story of 40 years ago. Seems like just yesterday I was sitting at Jean Fowlkes's kitchen table not believing my ears...

"Really, Jean? Willard Wilson is your landlord?"

"My minister, too!" she snapped, "But not for much longer. He's got a heart of stone, that man. We have two weeks to find another place. Says he's taking me to court for three months back rent, too."

Neither could I believe how high the rent was for the modest 2-bedroom house. Both of her kids, John and Susan, were in my classes, and I had stopped by because their performance and grades were steadily edging down. Jean and I knew each other well. She was my favorite cafeteria lady, feisty and funny and always saving portions of my favorite foods if I was late to lunch.

"We've been having it rough since Harold died. I'll tell you, Rose, poverty and grief make a bitter mix, and now we're really up against it. We're all three working night shift at the pizzeria, and the ends still aren't meeting. Maybe Buddy'll let us sleep in the booths," she joked. "Anyway, we're all tired and stressed out—but they'll get those grades up, don't worry. They'll just have to work fewer shifts. The good news—and there's always good news, even if you need a shovel to find it—is that God will provide."

And then one Saturday night when she and the kids were closing Buddy's down, Rita Wilson, Willard's teenaged daughter, got in trouble out in the parking lot.

"She'd been flirting with that Jenkins boy; you know, the one from out on CR 40, he must be 25. Well, that little chick had no idea what she was getting into," Jean told me in the school kitchen on Monday morning. "At the end of the night, she told her friends to go on and she and Jenkins were the last ones out. Susan watched them climb in the driver's door of his truck—one of those crazy high-riding things with the huge tires—and then Rita changed her mind. She started screaming and trying to get out and he was trying to pull her back in. John and I went running out while Susan called the police. Jenkins took off and Rita came back in and called home."

She lowered her voice confidentially. "And Mr. Annual Prayer Breakfast of Shippensforge offered to forgive our back rent if we'd forget what we'd seen. Rose, I looked him right in the eye and said, 'You can do whatever you want to, Preacher; I don't care. God will provide.' I have to admit I liked the worried look on his face. Oh, we're not going to spread it around. That's not our style." Miraculously, it seemed at times, God just kept providing and providing for that family...

"Beware of the scribes," like Willard Wilson, who do not love the Lord with all their heart, soul, mind, and strength, even if they are professional holy men. He's retired from his church now but still holds property all over town and takes advantage of the disadvantaged. He both prays and preys. *Dear God, I pray for Willard Wilson. Amen.*

Speaking of landlords, Theodore will be mine now, sort of; that's a funny thought. He's been elected chair of the Heritage Estate's board and will undoubtedly continue Louella's benevolent, sound business practices. Whenever Mercedes needs nursing care, he's already assured us, she will have it at Rutledge, even if her financial resources give out. Louella's generosity without the grumpiness. Bless her heart, of course.

My progress in moving is steady. I punctuate work with playing the piano, for it's not going with me. Deedee's taking it; that makes me happy, a good home with all those kids to enjoy it. Occasionally, I have helpers. Sarah packed all my lamps the other night; that was a big thing. Anita has been over for a few hours, as helpful as baby Zahra will allow. Jim comes by at the end of each day to heft the boxes I've packed into the garage, stacked in categories: Taking with me. For Virginia. For Stephanie Rose. For Penelope. Habitat Thrift Store. Recycle. Trash. At my request, Virginia and Stephanie have planned a kitchen and bathroom packing marathon for the very last night so I can function smoothly until then. The physical process is amazingly orderly. *The emotional part of it less so, Charlie.*

Understandably, right? There's so much I hate to lose but space is very limited. One little example: the baby quilt stitched by your aunt that three generations have laid on. Now you see, Stephanie might have another child and I'd love to see that babe rolling around on that quilt when they come to visit me in my new place, and I was trying to decide whether to take it with me or give it to Steph when Virginia grabbed it out of my hands and threw into the giveaway box saying, "Good grief, Mother. Stephanie has more baby blankets than she knows what to do with. She can just bring one when she comes." Now multiply that decision (although I still might pull it back out) a hundredfold. Virginia's approach is sensible, Charlie, but... I'm just saying, this is hard. There's a time for every purpose under heaven, we know, and after lo these many years of building up this household, it's my time to break it down, and—it's about

252

loss—and change. But in the thick of the process, all is really very well. Whew! Thanks for letting me vent, Charlie. I feel better.

So, I hardly leave the house anymore, keeping up with people by phone, as needed. Carolyn Sauer called one evening. She doesn't call just to keep in touch, so when I heard her voice, I figured my fear about her and Marcus splitting up was coming true.

"Rose, you wouldn't believe what he's done now. He sent a letter to everyone in the congregation asking those who are serious about discipleship to come to a special meeting. He said, and I quote, 'my heart is grieved by lukewarm Christianity' and went on about how middle class Christians today are more like scribes than widows and..." her voice caught, "and, as usual, he did it without even talking it over with me beforehand. Well, you can imagine it's a mess here. People are mad and confused and—a lot like what happened at St. Tim's. I just think this is the end for me, Rose."

She rattled on with me inserting an occasional "I'm so sorry" or "Oh, dear." She thinks Marcus needs to be in Africa or the inner city where he can feel like he's saving a life a day, following Jesus to the –enth degree. Pastoring the well-to-do is killing him.

"He's such a good man, Rose, I know that," she wept in obvious anguish. "but our pain bodies are in constant conflict..."

What in the world are these "pain bodies" everyone's having? Claudia said the same thing when I called her a while back to see how she was doing since separating. "Our pain bodies are just too big, especially Michael's," she said. I assume "pain bodies" refers to the bad things that happened in childhood or whenever that we all bring to our adult relationships.

The sad sum of all the parts is that the crazy, wonderful Carolyn can't take any more of the serious man of faith Marcus. She loves him with all her heart and divorce is not what she wants, but they're only hurting each other... She's moving out, getting an apartment in the same town, keeping things as smooth as possible for Brittany... Another account of the transformation of the institution of marriage in our time.

And yet another example—Sidney proposed to Jo that they get "unofficially" married, and he move in with her and Mercedes. "C'mon, Jo, it'll be so much easier." Well, they might be broken up over that. Of course, Josephine's not going for it. She said one night when he was bellyaching about how hard it would be to get her insurance straightened out and they might have to pay more taxes she told him, "Sid, you listen here. I live by the Lord, and he doesn't approve of shacking up. I'm not about to let little old things like filling out forms put me off the straight and narrow..." She hasn't seen him since, except when he comes by to take Mercedes to appointments. When she asked him why he hadn't been coming around, he fired at her that he was trying to stay on the straight and narrow. She doesn't seem anxious. "I believe he'll come around to right thinking. It's all in the good Lord's hands."

And I leave everything there, too, with a warm tummy full of peanut butter popcorn, and a brain whirling with tomorrow's task list which I hope I'll be able to switch off, and a peaceful, grateful soul... *though you know, God, my sadness and perplexity over the Sauers' parting. Thank you for your closeness to each of them and their devotion to you. You will bring them through. And you know how I can still be sabotaged by grief over Stephen, like the last time Penelope called and got us both crying, much to our surprise, when she remarked that sometimes she couldn't bring his face up in her memory. And you know my distress over those of your children, my brothers and sisters, who suffer day to day without the necessities of life and how my soul longs for the day when all will be fed. You know, oh God. I will praise you as long as I live. Amen. Good night.*

Daniel 12:1-3
Psalm 16
Hebrews 10:11-14 [15-18] 19-25
Mark 13:1-8

From the first note of Lloyd's stirring prelude to a firm "Thanks be to God!" at the end of the service, I sensed a remarkable confidence in the air at St. Timothy this morning. There's no earthly reason for it. Our air conditioning unit was destroyed last night for the copper—vandalism, vulnerability, and more financial insecurity. And our prayer list is as long as anybody's arm over illness, divorce, death, natural disaster, war, famine, and so on, here and around the globe. Our confidence is not in what we see around us but in what God has done through Christ.

Testimonial Sunday again. Jimmy Howe testified, coming forward with a big grin and a visual—baby Auburn, in her baptismal gown. "God's promises are true," he beamed. "We had two other children, too, Nathan and Taylor. For whatever reason, they went straight back to God before they were even born. We've felt the presence of their spirits, though, especially Vickie has. Those kids have never been dead to her. I don't know how, but Vickie's never wavered in her faith, never doubted God's promises of redemption. And now, here we are with this little doll, this child of God, and our hearts are bursting with joy as we turn her over to God officially this morning, in baptism. And turn her over to all of you, too, to help us love and nurture what God has given." Such radically honest sharing of faith! We're getting more comfortable with these personal testimonials. I may give one myself someday.

Kneeling for communion, I watched Mercedes trudge up, Sid helping her kneel, Jo on her other side. Her mind grows cloudier, and the body fails, too. They have to remind her to swallow now. But she "approaches God with a true heart in full assurance of faith." And so does Jo, confidently and cheerfully starting a chemotherapy regimen that she'll probably be on for the rest of her life. She and Sid have reconciled, but the marriage question is unresolved. Ha! At coffee hour Sid was trying to get Jim to talk to Jo and convince her that it would be okay for them to live together.

"It's the dad-blamed government that's pushing us into these immoral behaviors. Why, we could lose a couple thousand dollars a year by being in a higher tax bracket," Sid fumed. "But if a nice guy like you, a family man and a believer and all [Jim flashed me a grin and roll of the eyes] would talk to her about times changing and how everybody's doing it..."

"Whoa, slow down there, Sid, I'm afraid you're on your own with that one, man," Jim responded, deftly changing the subject. "As a matter of fact, though, I'm looking for folks to help with a Rotary project getting clean water to people..." His pep talk was provocative and confident. Quick statistics, gap between rich and poor noted in the same breath with loving your neighbor, vivid description of the project. Sid soon signed on. Jim clapped him on the back, jubilantly signaling me that Sid was # 5 recruit of the day.

Good to see this confidence; it's crucial to community. Engenders frankness and bold action—which I was happy we took at the called congregational meeting after the service. Despite our precarious financial situation, we committed to an ambitious goal in the churchwide anti-malaria campaign "to help end the reality that a child dies of preventable malaria every 45 seconds." Heavens, we can easily do this, probably without much sacrifice, but such generosity is not so common in our I-me-mine culture obsessed with stuff and money. And the truth is, in addition to fully funding the anti-malaria commitment, there are probably half a dozen people in this congregation who could write a check for that new AC unit and not even feel it. Well, I guess I could. Maybe I will. Okay, I will. *"The boundaries have fallen for me in pleasant places." Thank you, God.*

Speaking of where boundaries fall, I just read an article in a newsletter from a church relief agency about a family of five in Somalia suffering the worst drought in 60 years. They were almost down to no food, having eaten their goat and chickens, and one hot morning, they gathered the dried up vegetables from their garden and began walking to a refugee camp. After ten days, with no food the last two, they arrived, finding four times as many people in the camp as it was built for. They stood in line for hours to receive the last of the measured food and water for that day. They shared what they had with the people who had been in line behind them. Before they ate, they all knelt in prayer. *Dear God, how little we know, how much we have.*

And then I think of Marvin and his ilk. That misguided soul sent flowers and a note again, still playing for sympathy and belief in his innocence. The flowers of the field did nothing wrong, so I'm enjoying them, but that man needs to have his mouth washed out with soap. He wrote, "The arc of the moral universe is long, Rose, but it bends toward justice, and I will be exonerated." Such maligning of those profound words of faith born out of suffering and injustice! What an empty life poor Marvin has, as I see it, skipping right over "innocent until proven guilty." I'll stay in touch with him, though, if he wants to, ever hopeful that his dark side will be redeemed while treasuring his light side of kindness and generosity.

I see it everywhere, redemption. Cynthia Stafford and I ran into each other at the cleaners recently—I was picking up my living room drapes that are going to work in my new place—and she asked me to have a cup of coffee with her. I didn't feel like this was going to be a restaurant conversation, and we wound up across the table from each other in my kitchen. "She walks in beauty," that Cynthia, even as she ages. I stared at her while I made coffee and she shrugged out of her jacket and settled her purse. Long, blonde bangs brushing her finely-formed brows, large and expressive hazel eyes, clear skin and dimpled cheeks. She caught me looking at her, I think, and took it as an invitation. After a moment's reflection and a deep breath, her nitty-gritty story of faith poured forth.

"The anger that rose up in me over Malcolm's infidelity felt like a separate being was living inside of me." She felt no need of counseling because she was fine; Malcolm was the transgressor. She spent money "with vengeance and glee..."

"When our grandchild was stillborn, I stuffed my grief deep down inside and just carried on with normal activities," she winced. "'The wronged woman' became my persona, and I glided self-righteously up to communion every Sunday."

We fixed our coffee and she took a long sip, then described driving to church not so long ago. A "huge, horrible ball of hurt inside" forced her to pull over. Miserable and desperate, she begged God's help. She said she "turned herself over to God in a way I've never done before, I mean it wasn't even me, I can't even describe what happened." Immediately, the message came to her to forgive Malcolm.

"And I did, somehow, grace and relief washing through me, flooding out all the anger and humiliation and the big ball of pain. It was amazing, Rose; I felt weak, but I felt cleansed. I went on to worship and arrived just in time for communion."

"That was the day we talked about getting together?"

She nodded and I laughed to myself at how I'd thought she was in bad shape. I took a satisfying swig of the hot, strong coffee and asked if she had told Malcolm that she'd forgiven him.

"Yes. Yesterday I finally mailed him the letter; it took me awhile to write it. I asked his forgiveness, too; no one's ever blameless in these things— though I'm learning, thank God, that it's not about blame. I don't know what kind of relationship lies ahead for us. At this point, I can't imagine having anything very meaningful, after all that we've said and done, but at least we can move forward forgiven."

And then she really surprised me with a heartfelt apology for neglecting me when Stephen died. She'd meant to bring food, send a card, stop by, but she was just too wrapped up in her own troubles. Forgiveness asked and given once again. "Grace sufficient to the day."

"What a relief, Rose," Cynthia said at the end of our visit, "finally to let loose of my need to be better than Malcolm. It takes my breath away sometimes to think how I almost settled for that instead of opening myself up to grow and change. Life is so exciting now!" And I'm excited for her, and Malcolm, too, for this is good news for both of them. *Thank you, God. "In your presence there is fullness of joy."*

Just a note about Johnny Brewster. Deedee told me that he asked Morris if Chad's name was written in "that book" they talked about in the Bible, the one that had the names of people "delivered from anguish."

"Absolutely, and yours, too, Johnny. Everybody who wants to be with God is written in there," Morris told him. And then Johnny asked Deedee if they could go to the library and check the book out. Precious. And how good to see faith forming in this child who's already known anguish.

Wow, Saturday is moving day. The weather forecast is clear and cold. Of course, we all know how reliable weather predictions are. *You always swore you'd never be a meteorologist, Charlie, because you couldn't deal with that much failure. I tell you, all predictions are subject to adjustment. I already knew that, but Stephen's passing has made it painfully clear. I make no predictions about my future upon leaving this homestead, either. I enter my new world nonetheless with confidence, Charlie, because of Jesus giving himself for the world to reveal the power and love of God. Now, wish me a good night's sleep in preparation for a vigorous week.*

<u>Reign of Christ Sunday</u>

Daniel 7:9-10, 13-14
Psalm 93
Revelation 1:4b-8
John 18:33-37

Leaving my house was not as hard as I expected. *Heavens, Charlie, you would have shaken your head over the impromptu farewell ritual your three generations of women had on Friday night. After we packed up the kitchen and bathroom, Stephanie wanted to sit on the deck. Virginia and I were game, so we went out there all bundled up, stared at the stars and drank some wine. Time slowed way down.*

Stephanie remembered Garfield's farewell party we had out there one happy, hopeful summer night. "And now he's shining like the stars forever and ever," she murmured to the heavens. I peered gratefully into the dark woods that you and I enjoyed so much and thought of the big rock and felt perfectly peaceful about not going there anymore. We talked and gazed and emptied the bottle and Steph went and got the last one I had and we drank on, feeling happier and happier.

Virginia told us about sitting on the deck with Stephen one afternoon back in April and him telling her a bunch of things he had planned to do if it weren't for dying. Silence met that startling announcement, and then, of course, Steph and I asked what was on his list. Charlie, can you believe Virginia couldn't remember one single thing? That hung sadly in the air, and then Stephanie Rose started to giggle at the absurdity of pondering what he'd said because what difference did it make? In our mellow state of mind, that seemed cheerful and sensible, and soon we were all three laughing our heads off. Everything was blessed, Stephen shining brightly in the stars, too.

We calmed down and after awhile Virginia said, "Hey, what happened to the stars?" We teased her that she was too tipsy to see them, but clouds actually had moved in and snow began sifting down. We listened to the soft glistening sounds until we were crowned with icy sparkles. I threw back my last drink of wine like it was a shot of whiskey and, finally, we held each other up and slipped and staggered back inside.

And then, oh dear, we realized that none of us was in any shape to drive, and the plan was to spend the night at Virginia's. So Charlie, at 2am we called Barry to come and get us! You can just imagine his disgust, but the three of us couldn't stop cracking jokes and giggling, so by the time we got to their place, he was part of the party. We all fell into bed and came back the next morning and vacated the premises. What a last hurrah for our house, huh? And thanks for the good life we lived there, dear husband.

And now, presto! I'm in my brand new home on Sunday afternoon. "Contentment overflows my soul and fills the air." That quotation describes me perfectly on this Lord's Day, though I can't remember who said it. The space is cozy, with its peculiar, fresh smell of newness, and the dark green cedars decorated with fresh snow right outside my window are a pretty sight.

Twelve of us took up residence on opening day yesterday, and Rutledge Heritage Estate provided lunch for us and our moving crews, a very nice touch. By 4 in the afternoon, I was sitting on my davenport with furniture in place, boxes emptied and gone, curtains and pictures hung, and bed made, thanks to my beloveds. Around six, Jim and Anita carried in supper, and Jim connected my computer and printer while Anita and I played with the baby.

Surely this is one of the smoothest moves ever. Uh-oh, except for Bull's visit to the emergency room for his broken toe from Steph dropping her end of my heavy dresser. Oh, and another break—my bedroom window when Barry swung the iron railing of the bed frame a little too wide. Oops. But maintenance has already repaired it. And then there was the false fire alarm with everyone having to go outside in the cold. Oh, and a loud argument between two residents in the lobby over where one had parked his scooter. Okay, there were a few glitches, but I am here and all is well. Lean back. Close eyes. Long, deep breath.

I sit here in my new life riveted on the future, wondering. For example, what will it be like to see Marcus Sauer? He called and is coming to visit next week. Not only are he and Carolyn separated, but he's suddenly resigned his pastorate. That seems drastic. My friend and spiritual mentor, but—unbalanced? Or rather, is he an unlikely prophet going against worldly ways to follow a higher calling? *Lord, help me be a good friend.*

And another meeting coming up, equally bittersweet. One of Stephen's cornea recipients has contacted Penelope and we're meeting him in Chicago sometime after the holidays. A man about Stephen's age, he wants to thank us in person for his sight—a direct result of Stephen's death. *Fortify me God, for that strange moment.*

And the other possible encounters in my future. Maybe Mindy and I will visit Marvin in the federal penitentiary someday! *Blessings upon him, gracious God.* I eagerly anticipate the February luncheon with Carolyn, Deedee, and Claudia; half of us will be divorced, I guess. *You hold ex-wives and wasbands everywhere in your forgiving love, dear Lord—and are present to sustain those couples living unhappily, too.* I hope for another visit to Eloise's mansion in trillium season. *God, whatever wild stories are waiting to be written there, I rest assured of your presence!* Next Sunday, the gatherings and events to plumb the rich depths of the Advent season begin again, and then the "holidaze." *Thank you for the holy <u>adventure</u> of Jesus breaking into our human lives as your Son and your Self.*

On a more mundane level, I wonder how I'll do in close and continual proximity to others. I know four of the other residents, and it's a 50/50 split between the ones I like and the ones I don't. Fun ahead! *Grant us all forbearance, God.* How much longer will I drive? Night vision's getting tricky and driving in unfamiliar territory is pretty uncomfortable, but I'm definitely not ready to give up that huge independence. *God, give me the grace to quit when I should—or maybe a little before.* And how will I do without a piano? There's the one in the commons but not for playing in the middle of sleepless nights. *Sustain me through the adjustments, faithful God. "All I have needed thy hand hath provided…"*

Weirdly, moving has changed the way I perceive the whole world. Virginia picked me up for worship this morning and the streets and buildings of Shippensforge looked different as we drove through town. And when we entered the nave, I had the craziest sensation of not having been to St. Timothy for a long time. The paint on the wall looked fresh and new, the lights brighter, the flowers especially colorful.

And the people—they seemed like long-lost relatives! As we entered, Charlene was carrying her screaming, squirming bundle back across the street to their house. "I guess I'm overly eager for him to meet everyone, but he's just too croupy—so I'll see you ladies another day," she shouted over the infant cries, keeping his face covered in the chilly breeze.

Danny and Sherry greeted me in the narthex. "M-M-Me and my b-baby want to come to your new house and play c-c-canasta, Rose," he said. "Sounds great!" I said, and watched them as they joined Mindy and Maddie on the front row, appearing more like a regular, married couple than newlyweds with developmental disabilities.

And the Ferguson family looked like a regular church family, too, shushing Zahra's jibber-jabber while hanging amused and amazed on every syllable. And why shouldn't they look regular? Because Jim doesn't think he believes in God? Ha, he's probably not the only one in the crowd.

Now the three musketeers; they looked strange, an unlikely family. Mercedes sat between Sid and Jo, and I had to concentrate them back into familiarity. Cousin Weirdifine no more; that person is gone, or, I'd rather say, born again, maybe—not so flighty and—weird. Meanwhile, the person of Mercedes continues to leave us. She said to them recently, with a sweet smile, "I'm getting—far, far away—but it's okay." The faithful Sid attends their every need, waiting grumpily for their Valentine's Day wedding.

Pam and Greg Turner and I waved at each other when they caught my eye, together on the back row. Pam says they're not sure they'll marry again but are getting acquainted on a different basis than ever before. (If I were writing the book, they will marry again—and have a good and healthy marriage. Ha, live happily ever after.) Jacob was with them, home from college for Thanksgiving. He and Angelica are "going steady," I think (though that's probably not the current term). The haunted look has left his young face. And there was a nice moment of meeting Cynthia in the narthex with a silent smile and tight hug, like a period at the end of our conversation last week. New beginnings everywhere.

Peace and joy pervaded my soul even as Morris lifted up fellow believers living in desperate situations. He reminded us that John's apocalyptic images in Revelation were written to seven actual congregations, like us in many ways, as a word of hope to people caught in life and death struggles which most of us will be spared.

As middle class Americans, we are not without struggle, Morris clarified. Everyone experiences personal chaos from time to time. (Mindy's and Jo's breast cancer, for example. I have a feeling they're both going to beat it. Again, if I were writing the book that's how it would be.) To celebrate the Reign of Christ means to stand with all those who suffer, Morris preached. So doing, we confess our belief that a loving God created the world and will not let it be destroyed, not ultimately. And we profess and proclaim that Jesus, the Son, is God-with-us, present and powerful precisely where the forces of evil seem strongest.

"That's crazy talk, what we believe, you know, Rose?" Mindy mused as she and Maddie took me back to Rutledge. "I mean, I know that's how we see the world, and we believe it's the truth, but—there's no way we can prove it. Each religion sees the world their way, and all of the -isms see it their way, communism, capitalism, nothing-ism or whatever you call it..."

"Yes?"

"I don't know what my point is. I'm just happy and thankful to belong to Christianity."

Ditto. Maddie, too. I could see her in the rearview mirror, perched on her kid's booster seat and strapped securely in. She was looking out the window, and when Mindy said she was happy to be Christian, Maddie nodded.

Mindy treated to Chinese and they were the very first Sunday dinner guests around my table. Afterward, we went over to the nursing care center for Eucharistic Ministry. With Mary Thurgood not up to coming, the circle in the activities room was Sam, Pastor Ruskin, the Rizenhouers, and Mitch, who saw us as he wandered by and came in just in time to receive the elements and left immediately, still chewing.

We ended up in Mary's room, forewarned by an attendant that "she's not in her right mind and is seeing people who aren't there." When we stepped in, I heard her say something about or to "Grandfather." Her cloudy eyes were bright and I don't know how to describe the expression on her face—beatific, I think—as she looked at the ceiling where the people were.

"Mrs. Thurgood, do you want to have communion?" Mindy said right into her face. She looked at Mindy and pointed to the ceiling. We decided to go ahead, and she seemed content to receive the morsel of wafer dipped in the wine.

"She's almost dead," Maddie observed as we walked down the hall. *Please, God, let it be so.* "I wonder if her name will be written in that book when she dies, that book Johnny was talking about in Sunday School. He says his dad's name is in it.

"Mindy, is my mom's name written in it?" Mindy gave me a quick, hesitant look and then nodded her head at Maddie.

"How about my dad?" Same hesitant look and another nod. "And the name Darien is written there, and Stephen, too," Maddie stated.

And then—she laughed. Maddie laughed!

"Johnny thought he could get the book out of the library. That's funny. It's not that kind of a book."

Mindy grabbed her up and whirled her around the hallway, her eyes squeezed tight, a huge smile on her face, and planted a hoarsely giggled kiss on her daughter's cheek.

Thankyouthankyourthankyou, God, for joining those two together, by pain and loss and trust that you will wipe away their tears. They are a treasure for me. And, now I lay me down to sleep in this new place and pray, dear God, that you will help me for the rest of my days to follow in your ways. You have taught me through every joy and my biggest sorrow that life in you is the truest, richest, most satisfying life. And I have tried to make your ways known to my children and tried to keep them ever in mind with the aid of my brothers and sisters in the Body of Christ. And when doubts assail, the laughter of a child will tell my heart once again that you are the Lord of the universe. Thine the amen.

ACKNOWLEDGMENTS

For this third time around with *Sunday by Sunday,* I express my deep appreciation to the following:

Judy Aebischer, Editor, whose professionalism, keen reading, and candid critique once again made the book immeasurably better and saved me from myself several times;

Mary Anderson, Theological Editor, also my pastor, who not only critiqued and improved the manuscript but graciously allowed me to use and even, on occasion, quote from her excellent, soul-feeding sermons;

Diane Smith and Robin Weber, two more sets of eyes, hearts, and minds whose responses led to good and important revisions;

several individuals who advised me so that I could do my best to write accurately: Rick Ring of DeKalb Memorial Hospital on EMS services in Indiana; Lisa Strahs-Lorenc on pancreatic cancer to whom I give special thanks for generous and open sharing and for the poignant book she put together, *Pancreatic Cancer: It's a Family Affair;* Christine Parham on hospice services; Priscilla Fossum, Chris Kendall and Charles Cook on legal situations; and my mother Bobbie Fossum again, along with dear friend Earl Olson, on life in the 1920s-30s-40s;

my fellow parishioners at Incarnation on Devine in Columbia, who have supported me in so many ways in these writing adventures and inspire me Sunday by Sunday. The contribution of the musicians, under the direction of pastor and cantor Jim Parham (whose exhilarating sermons have also influenced the writing) rocka' my soul; and while these stories are fictional, there are musical happenings that may well seem familiar to the congregation;

all the folks at workingpreacher.org, a rich resource I used heavily, for solid biblical interpretation and theological insight. My devotional life was enhanced along with my writing, and I hope I used the material in faithful and appropriate ways. I am indebted, as well, to textweek.com for its depth of relevant resources for liturgy and lectionary;

Wade Lowder at PrintSouth and graphics designer David Hedges, wonderful professional partners in book production; Jason Godfrey and Ray Sipe (pagination specialist!) for IT support;

Kickstarter, an online platform to support artistic, creative projects. Through this organization, I raised the funds to print *Sunday by Sunday III* and highly recommend Kickstarter to entrepreneurs needing start-up money. I am exceedingly grateful to everyone of my 56 backers and especially to these people for their most generous pledges: Andy and Vivian Fossum, dear friends desiring to remain anonymous, Candace Spasojevich, Elizabeth and Rob Roma, Marty and Kelly Fossum/Duffy, Betty Dodds, Georgia and Jason Godfrey, Susan Thornton, Pat Blackwell, Cheryl Behymer, Mary and Jim Nichols, Chris McCay, Diane Smith, Helen Doerpinghaus, Julia Prater, Bobbie Fossum, Eileen Parr, Lee Thornton, Larry and Diana Cristy. Thanks not only for your contributions but also for your encouragement and affirmation;

and my dear readers. I love hearing from you. Please stay in touch!

cfossum@sundaybysunday.com